UPCOMING
TALES OF THE FORGOTTEN GOD
BY DAN HAMILTON

THE CHAMELEON LADY
THE EVERLASTING CHILD

TALES OF THE FORGOTTEN GOD

THE BEGGAR KING

Dan Hamilton

Illustrated by
Jack Stockman

INTERVARSITY PRESS
DOWNERS GROVE, ILLINOIS 60515

InterVarsity Press® is the book-publishing division of InterVarsity Christian Fellowship®, a student movement active on campus at hundreds of universities, colleges and schools of nursing in the United States of America, and a member movement of the International Fellowship of Evangelical Students. For information about local and regional activities, write Public Relations Dept., InterVarsity Christian Fellowship, 6400 Schroeder Rd., P.O. Box 7895, Madison, WI 53707-7895.

Cover art: Jack Stockman

ISBN 0-8308-1671-2

Printed in the United States of America

Library of Congress Cataloging-in-Publication Data

Hamilton, Dan.
    The beggar king/Dan Hamilton.
        p.   cm.—(Tales of the forgotten God)
    ISBN 0-8308-1671-2
    I. Title.   II. Series.
    PS3558.A4248B4   1993
    813'.54—dc20   93-19200
                                                 CIP

16   15   14   13   12   11   10   9   8   7   6   5   4   3   2   1
05   04   03   02   01   00   99   98   97   96   95   94   93

—CONTENTS—

ONE

The Dead of Night

HERE IN THE HIGHLANDS THE WINTER GRAIN WAS RIPE FOR harvest. Spring had begun to bring warm days, but the nights were still cold and sometimes frosty. And this spring midnight clung to the village like an old woolen blanket, shutting out the world and muffling the sounds that might otherwise have drifted from house to house within the village walls.

An old woman huddled alone and sleepless by the smoldering fire in the village square, gazing long into the darkness, seeing nothing and noticing less. But she roused at the creak of iron gates and the sound of slow footfalls clear but soft in the silence. She waited, looking toward the western gate of the village. A man came walking there, his faint shadow leaning before him, away from the bright moon at his back. Drawing near into the dim light of the all-night fire, he slowly shifted from a black silhouette into a dusty beggar wrapped in a stained cloak and sheltered under the weary brim of an ancient, shapeless hat. His steps betrayed the knowledge that his feet had endured too many miles, and that perhaps his blisters had not yet turned to calluses.

The beggar stopped before the woman and peered at her, as though surprised to see her alone and awake in the depths of the night. She bade him welcome, and he asked where he might find food and a corner in which to sleep.

"There is no more food to be had," she said, "for it has all been bought and laid aside for the stranger who gives life to the dead. And no room either, for all places have been claimed in hope that the stranger will tarry here."

The beggar collapsed wearily on the stone paving. His voice held a note of interest that denied the hour and his fatigue. "Tell me of this stranger," he asked.

She was silent for a space, groping in the close darkness for words. Then she began in a low tone, curiously numb and flat. "We heard first the tales from another village—word of a tall man in white who raised the dead to life and gave away gold while voices sang in the sky. And that he left under the midday sun, mounted on a white charger with a harness of gold and bells of silver. Heading south, it was said, and perhaps on his way to this very village." She paused, shifted restlessly, and sighed before going on. "So the rumors said. All our people purchased fine food to store in hope, gathered gold to lay at the stranger's feet, and made ready rooms to house the healer. They prepared for him and lined the road beyond the north gate to await him. You see, death is no new visitor here. Red plagues and old age and wild beasts have all helped fill the graveyard within the walls of this village. I cannot blame the people for their dreams, though I did not join them. Their hope lies only in new things revealed.

"But no stranger came that day or the next. Some crept back to their houses. Some feared that he would never come and that they would never find their blessing. Those who wield power still sought the right to host the stranger and lay their dead at his feet.

"Then yesterday there was dust on the horizon, and a man came riding—a tall man in a white robe on a white stallion, with a harness trimmed in silver and gold. The crowds surged to meet him, cheering, pleading, and all but bore him under. He lifted his voice, but no one could have heard him. They brought him here to the square, where our richest man had placed the body of his eldest son, slain in a wine-sotted brawl over the affections of a woman. The stranger stood bewildered next to the body, and he asked the people what they wanted of him.

"They demanded that he raise the dead man, to do the wonders he had done in other towns. He replied that his name was Candolel, that he was not a god but a merchant, and that the power of life rested not in his hands." She paused for a long moment, and the heaviness of her heart was betrayed by the words she did not say.

She drew a long shuddering breath and continued. "He denied that he was their desire, so they killed him. They pulled him down in their rage, and beat him, and left him dead in the square.

"At least, so these things were told to me, for I came only in time to find two dead men here. And now the people have returned to their houses to wait until the true healer comes. Perhaps some of them are afraid of what they have done, but they bear their guilt lightly."

The beggar was silent while the woman gazed at his faded cloak and sore feet and weary limbs. "This town, like others," she added, "is not overkind to beggars. But I, too, have wandered and sought the favor of those unknown to me, and so I will not despise you. Yet, I am only an old woman, and I have nothing that anyone—even you—would covet. My hut is not far from here. I can offer you little but stale bread, well water,

11

and a place to bathe your feet. I have an old stable where my donkey sleeps, and you may put his straw under your head for a pillow. It is little enough, but I offer it to you freely."

He thanked her quietly. And then they rose, and she led him slowly through the town.

"I am Abra," she said over her shoulder. "I am the outcast."

"Call me Covenant," he responded. "I am the king of beggars."

Their voices barely bruised the hush of the empty streets. They passed under the stone arch with its squeaking gates.

"There is no watchman here," she told him. "These gates are here to keep the wild animals out." She brandished her walking stick at the shadows, adding, "But if you travel alone, you clearly are not afraid of them."

"No, I am not."

"Then what are you afraid of?"

"I am afraid of nothing, but I believe that the greatest dangers are the beasts that live within the walls."

She nodded grimly, and they passed out along a lonely pathway. She pointed to a grove of trees near at hand. "Candolel is buried there."

"Who buried him?"

"I did."

"I see two fresh graves there. Is there not a graveyard within the walls of the village?"

She did not answer him, though fresh tears came to her eyes. They walked on, and he let her silence stand unchallenged. In that same silence, they reached her dwelling. There, she tended his torn feet while he sat in a pile of soft rushes. Later, she divided her portion of bread with him.

"Woman," the beggar said softly, "your eyes betray their sadness. You may weep before me without fear, for I speak the language of those who grieve." Then her hidden river of tears spilled over its banks, and she wept, and spoke to him of her daughter, dead a fortnight, taken by the red sickness that had clawed the village.

"Your only child?"

She nodded.

"And she sleeps in that second grave, does she not?"

She nodded again.

"Why is she not buried within the walls? And why is not Candolel, for that matter?"

"Because I am still a stranger here, even after many years; my fathers did not live here before me. The village is only for those who have been here forever. So it is I who must dwell out here and Kali who must sleep in unhallowed ground. As for Candolel, the village is not worthy to hold his grave."

He stared into the decrepit hearth at the tiny fire that held back the sting of the night. "Forgive me if I renew your grief. This stranger—Candolel—why did you give your care to him? Not even kind women bury strangers in hallowed places, places where old, deep love lies sleeping."

"Twelvemonth ago . . . twelvemonth ago Candolel was found near this village, a traveler wounded and stripped by thieves. The people ignored him, and he recovered here in this cottage. Kali tended him. In time, he chose her for himself, and she him, with my blessing. Then he left for the great town called Glory to deal there and regain his fortune. He came once again with a pledge for Kali, and then promised to return for us both when wealth was again fully his, when he could ride proudly through the village and let the people gawk as he came to us and brought favor to a house of outcasts. That would have ended our sorrow here, and we would have returned with him to Glory."

"Why does Glory draw you so?" the beggar asked. "What lies there?"

"Where else but Glory? Where else might one find kings and palaces, fountains and magic stones? All *this*," she said, sweeping her arms wide, "is a vacant land with but a single jewel in it: Glory! It is a place of many great secrets."

"And at least one great secret it has forgotten it has," smiled the beggar.

"A new life—an end to hardship," she continued, unhearing, as though lost in a dream. "I have never been there—but Candolel has . . . had been. It is truly great, and a place of dreams fulfilled. All who live there have riches and a name.

"But does it matter now what is there?" she continued, not expecting an answer as she stoked the fire and wiped strands of hair from her tear-soaked face. "Without Candolel and without Kali, I have no hope of Glory."

"There are other ways to enter Glory than in splendor, and other ways to live than to be served."

The woman turned from the fire and looked at her guest, but did not answer. He waved a hand back along the path toward the willow grove. "Twofold is your right to sorrow, and yet you do not seek the gifts of the coming stranger?"

"No! I fear him! If he holds power over the grave, he is not a man but a god come among us. And if a god, then terrible is the price he may demand in exchange for healing, and more terrible yet his wrath if we presume upon him. No," she said, shaking her head, "I pray only that he will pass us by."

"Yet all your hope lies buried in the dark embrace of the earth," said the beggar. "Even if the lifegiver walked here tonight, you would not seek his favor?"

"No," she replied, sinking onto a low stool by the hearth. "I will not, nor could I even draw near because of the people who claim higher rights—and back their claims with hammered gold. And what could I sacrifice to him? My donkey?" She laughed, but there was little humor in it. "Even the most miserable god would reject that offering. And I have neither gold nor silver. Yet, I do wish that I might dare to brave the power of the gods. But better is the death that comes to all people than the destruction that comes upon fools."

"If this stranger throws coins to the needy, why should he be tempted by gold and silver? And if he is drawn to you by

praise and fame, why does no one know his name?"

She had no ready answer.

"Why do you even believe that this stranger will come?" he persisted. "Or that he holds power from on high? Perhaps he is only a rumor."

"If the old stories are true," she replied, "then he is a *promise* and not merely a *rumor.*"

"The old stories?" the beggar prompted, relaxing in his pile of rushes as though he were settling to hear a long tale.

"The old stories," she repeated, "of the Elder God and the Lost City."

"I have not heard some of those tales for many years. Please tell me again, that I may have them afresh."

"I have not heard the words since I was a little girl," she replied, "but I have forgotten none of them." She paused, remembering. "In my village, an old man would sit late before the fire, and I would come to sit beside him and listen to his words in the darkness." She recited the words shyly but readily, as if she had often said them silently in her heart. "Once, there was the City," she began, using the ancient pattern, "where dwelt the Elder God and all the men and women and children he had made. All shone, all had joy, and all were loved. The City was full of life and wonders and trees with fruit good to eat, and the Elder God walked among them and dwelt in their midst.

"A great wall surrounded the City, and in the walls were many gates. But beyond the gates lay the wilderness—forbidden to all, though left open to their feet—and at each gate was a path that led winding into the wilderness. Although the gates had been fashioned by the Elder God and marked with his warnings, the avenues beyond were made by his ancient enemy, who hated all good things everywhere. And that same one sang a haunting song in the distance, beckoning the curious on.

"All that the City dwellers needed was given them freely by

the Elder God, but they were not content as long as the un-trodden paths to the unexplored wilderness shimmered in the sun. One by one, boldly, or sharing their indecision in groups, they ventured out onto the narrow paths to see what lay beyond. The Elder God called after them and pleaded with them, but their curiosity deafened their ears to his voice. And from there they vanished. None ever returned. And even though none of those who left ever returned to the City, the people there still wondered about the wilderness. They said to themselves that it must be wondrous indeed if the adventur-ers chose it over the City. So they too went into the face of the silence, and vanished. Soon they were all gone, and the City stood empty."

"What happened to those who left?" the beggar asked soft-ly, as if continuing an old ritual.

"First, the wilderness lay before them, then beside them on either hand, and then it surrounded them. And the wilderness terrified them, for there were lions there, and wolves, and fierce things that lived in the sea. Darkness fell upon them, and rain and thunder, and the world was changed in a great shaking and windstorm; the people turned, but could not find their way back to the City." She hesitated, and her pause covered long measures of unspoken time. "After many years of wandering, Glory was built as a reminder and a memorial, hoping that the Elder God would return to them there. But he has not. Even today the City is still lost, and the Elder God has forgotten us."

Her voice trailed off into the night, as exhausted as her thin frame.

TWO

A Night for Names

THE BEGGAR TURNED TO HIS HOST AND REPLIED, "WHAT YOU have heard is true, but you have not heard all the truth. The City itself was never lost; it was *abandoned*. The Elder God removed it to a safe place, until the time comes for its streets to be walked again. It is humanity that is lost, and the path back to the City that is forfeited. The City is still the center of all the universe, and there the Elder God still reigns in unapproachable holiness. The City has a heart, and that heart has a name, and that name beats at the core of the earth, and clocks the candling of the stars.

"And the Elder God is not forgetting, but forgotten; not the forsaker, but the forsaken; not the abandoner, but the abandoned—not the one who is sought, but the one who seeks.

"Those who departed did not come back, for they could not:

the path betrayed them. It was not like other roads, for it was not made, but only suffered, by the Elder God. He himself had promised them that he would make them roads and highways through the wilderness, so that all the treasures yet to be discovered would be theirs as well as the City. Had they trusted him, his roads would soon have been under their feet to wander, and the roads would have been theirs to explore, and the wonders beyond theirs to conquer. But they did not wait until they had been tested, approved and empowered. Instead, they went in their own strength, and it was the wilderness that conquered them. It is still called the Lost City," he noted, "though it is not the City which is lost, but people who are still lost in the wilderness."

The flames crackled. She was silent, and he continued. "Glory was built as an echo, where they believed the City had been, yet Glory is only a well-meant but wicked and hopeless shadow of the City that was lost. They made themselves a king, to remind them of the Elder God. Since that time, we have lost count of the years, yet Glory has endured. And although kings still are crowned, the memory of the Elder God has faded from the land. Still, in no place is he altogether without a witness."

"I do not know if the Elder God is real or not. I hope that he is."

"You know more than you think, and you think more than you say. Why do you think the people walked away from the City?" the beggar asked. His voice was still soft, but it no longer carried the tones of the ritual.

"I don't know. I know only my own heart. I know that we are hopelessly human."

"You are human, but not as hopeless as you think. One may have hope, and never know it."

She stirred the fire with one hand before she responded. "Some say there is still a secret door, and behind it a dark and dangerous path to the City, winding its way back if only one could plumb its mysteries. But if there is a door leading to such a path, it is hidden, and no one knows where it is. So I was told by my forebears, who were told by theirs, whose own fathers had lived in the City."

"Only the Elder God can make such a thing—and all will remain lost in the wilderness until he comes to find them or sends one from the City to open the road of return."

"Such a one has been promised. He has not come."

"Perhaps he has—and you have not yet learned to recognize him." After a moment of thoughtful silence, the beggar stood. "We have talked much," he said. "You think you know who I am, but despair clouds your certainty. You have believed without seeing. Now there is something that you must see, for I do not think you can see without increasing your belief."

He took her arm and guided her outdoors through quiet fields, letting the moonlight embrace her sorrow. Bats joined them overhead, then flicked away into the blue-black bowl of the universe. Stars glimmered everywhere above, granting light but no warmth.

The beggar led her at last to the graves beneath the weeping trees. "You fear the dark gods," he said, "but there is One who is not dark. I know you have not forgotten the Elder God. But are you willing to trust the One who savors love and not the smell of smoke or sacrifice, who treasures the spread of mercy above the cold clink of coins? One who would not despise the gift of a donkey? One who knows that cold water may restore what fine wine cannot, that stale bread may give life where silver bars fail? He has long known your longings and your hopes. And for your faithful hopes and your kindness he has already ransomed your dead."

He turned to her. "What does this earth hold? Candolel? Kali? Perhaps not." She stared at him as he spread his arms above the double mounds. "Come, children!" he commanded, and there came a shudder in the darkness, a ripple of reluctant earth, twin convulsions beneath the grass. From the cold wombs of the graves, the reborn burst forth in an explosion of disregarded dirt. Abra, first silent with fright, then weeping with wild joy, embraced her daughter, then Candolel, then the beggar, and then all three. Love renewed by love renewed the chill air.

At last, the beggar urged them all toward the hut and the waiting fire.

"Go to your home," the beggar said, "and I shall return to you there. I have one last task to perform before we all leave this village behind. No longer will you forget the Elder God, for you shall indeed enter Glory—but in his name and not in your own. Return to your home now, all of you, and tell no one."

"Who is there to tell?" asked Abra. "This is everyone I know and love and trust!" But the beggar was already a lost shadow in the vast cover of the night.

They walked home together, hand in hand, beginning to tremble now with the awe that follows sudden joy. Kali and Candolel, reluctant to be enclosed again by walls, stood before the hut. Not knowing what else to do, they waited. Holding Kali's head against her shoulder, Abra whispered to her, "Do you remember anything? About being . . . ?"

Kali shook her head, trying to clear it of confusion. "I cannot remember," she said at last. "It was not painful, but it was extremely dark and sad. There were others, and we were all waiting."

"Waiting for what?"

"I'm not sure. I think we were waiting for someone with power."

"Perhaps it was the beggar."

"If it was, where are the rest who were with us? I do not know who they were, but I could feel them and hear them. I think I would know them again if they drew near."

The three waited then in warm silence and wonder until the beggar appeared again, trailing a magnificent white horse behind him. "He has been cared for," explained the beggar, "but

21

his harness and trappings are gone."

"A small loss," said Candolel quietly, caressing his horse's nose. "They can be replaced."

"He is a fast horse, and strong," noted the beggar.

"He is. That is why I named him Roadreeler."

"That name will serve. You will one day have need of his swiftness—but that will be many months from now. Tomorrow is your immediate concern. What is your dream in Glory? Wealth and fame?"

No longer sure of the value of his dreams, Candolel nodded mutely.

"You shall have not fame but success," continued Covenant, "and not wealth but resources. Blessings and property will come to you, but not to be hoarded. They shall be used for others. Glory is indeed a chosen place; your hope is there, as is your destiny. You shall all go. I will follow after you, and then you will follow me." Nodding at Candolel, he said, "You have a house, and a place for business." It was not a question.

"I have a shop for dealing," said Candolel, "and rooms above it. It is small, but it is enough for the three of us."

"It will seem smaller," Covenant smiled. "You will not be three alone for long. I will send others after you, and you must house them until I arrive. They will know your house by this." He handed Candolel a carved slab of wood, weathered well by the wind. "This is my mark. You shall fasten it beside your door."

Candolel took it and turned it over in his hands. "Are you not coming with us?"

"No," Covenant replied. "I have other places to visit—other towns."

"Are you needed there?"

"I am, though they do not yet know it. But I am not finished here. I have new names for you all—and new tasks as well." He pointed to Candolel and Kali. "The villagers think the two of you are dead and lying beneath the trees. Let them believe

22

it as long as they will; let your names die here as well. You should carry new names into your new life.

"Instead of Candolel, let us bring forth a new Candle—a great candle to shine for the Elder God—and Moonflower, the maiden, to bloom beside him and help fuel his fire."

He turned to Abra. "And you they will not miss, though your life is not yet ended. The tales you have been told so faithfully will not stop with you; I promise you many children to sit at your feet and listen to you. Now your name shall be Trueteller."

Candle looked uncomfortably at Covenant, not understanding his need for a new name.

"It is a small thing I ask of you," said Covenant gently. "Were it not for me, and for the faith of this woman in the stories of old, you would be sleeping tonight—and every night forever—in the embrace of the earth."

He turned to Abra—Trueteller—again. "Some other wanderer will come and sleep in this place and call it home, even as you did."

"How did you know that? I have not told you that tale."

"Perhaps it is time you did. You have not yet told me all your griefs."

"Please," she asked of him, "please, before you send us away—I have a pilgrimage to make."

"I know," he answered, drawing her aside from the others. "There is one whom you have not spoken of, one who is neither here nor buried here."

"My husband."

"Where is he?"

"Gone. Perhaps dead . . . if not dead, then long vanished. He left me here many years ago. We lived alone in the forests to the south of here. I was already with child"—she gestured to her daughter—"when he left to sell the good things he gathered from the floor of the forest. He did not return that day, that week, the next, or even after the next moon."

"And you came here?"

"I had to. My time was drawing near, and I had no one. There were wolves in the deep woods and lions in the hills, even as there are now. Kali and I have stayed on the edge of this unfriendly village, but each year I have returned to the house in the wilderness and made my mark again beside the door, trusting that if he ever returns he will know that I am still alive. The arrow I have carved there points north; if he returns, he will know where to look for me."

"My path leads south from here, through those very forests. I will make this year's mark for you," offered Covenant. "I will carve the sign of Glory beneath it, and I will make my mark under that as well. Should he ever come that way again, perhaps he will know that I have been here as well."

Then the beggar spoke to them all, and they listened, and when they were done they began to pack their few possessions into a crude saddlebag.

Moonflower stopped suddenly and turned to Candle. "I cannot find your pledge necklace," she said nervously. "My mother kept it when I died, but now it is no longer on the mantle."

"Nor can I find yours," he answered sadly. "It may have been taken from me after . . . after the fight in the square." Disappointment betrayed itself in their eyes.

"What have you lost, children?" asked the beggar. Moonflower thought he sounded more patient than curious, as though he already knew the answer and were playing a child's game.

"Candle gave me a pledge on a chain for my neck," she answered, "half a medallion that had our names intertwined. His half—the part he kept—completes my half, makes it whole. Now both pieces are gone."

"Your pledge to each other is more than hammered metal," said Covenant. "Your promises may endure even when silver ornaments are lost, though a word is easily broken and the metal cannot be rendered without tools." He smiled. "You will find this to be true for many things: that which is the most fragile is also the most durable. And those things you think most durable will be the first to perish. I say to you that the sea will burn up and the mountains fall before your pledges fail."

They contented themselves with that promise. And as the morning brought them sufficient light, the three rode away bareback on Roadreeler. They traveled east and then north in a long curve that would bring them at last to Glory.

The beggar, with a sack of food for himself, started off toward the south on Trueteller's donkey, the forests far ahead and the great hills rolling in their midst. He stroked the donkey's flank as they paced along. "You should bear a better name as well, my friend. Let us call you Kingsburro, for someday you shall carry on your shoulders the King of Glory."

The people of the village, still watching the northern road for a sign of the healer, took no notice of any of them.

THREE

The Lion
of the
Hills

T HE FINAL TINGES OF THE DAY HAD JUST FADED FROM THE forest. Unseen in the underbrush, a thin young man watched as his sister placed her newborn infant on the rock slab in the wilderness. A lion roared somewhere—not very far away— and the girl vanished quickly along the narrow path through the trees. The lad waited only a heartbeat, and then he bounded to the rock across the clearing and snatched the baby girl, still sleeping from the drugged milk.

And then the moonshadow of the lion fell over them, and its roar ruled the darkness.

Screaming defiance, Damon lashed out with his dagger while shielding the baby between his back and the stone. Still cloaked in darkness, the lion roared in his face and slapped his blade spinning into the curtained reaches of the forest. Damon closed his eyes and waited for the end.

Lions smell like sudden death and savaged meat and terror, he thought, surprised, *but not this one.*

Then the roaring stopped, leaving only his heart thundering in his chest and his gasps rending the night. Damon opened his eyes—and blinked, for there was no lion, only a man outlined in the moonlight. It was a beggar, wrapped in a dusty cloak and brandishing a staff. The beggar lowered his stick and said, "You will not need your weapon. There is no harm for her here—or for you either, this night of all nights."

Damon could think of nothing to say or do. Clinging to the child, he slumped down and backward against the side of the rock.

The beggar smiled at his silence and sat down on a fallen tree trunk to wait. Though the day had been warm, the evening was already fierce with cold, and their breath left halos around their heads.

"Where did the lion go?" gasped Damon at last.

"There was no lion," the beggar said. "There is only me. I mean no harm to your sister's child, or to the man Damon who guards her."

"How do you know who we are?" Damon asked, suspicion scraping rough edges into his voice.

"I know many things that are not readily visible," replied the beggar. "I know not only your names, but why you are here."

"But this child has no name!" said Damon. "Her christening was to be called *unwanted*, and to be cast away for the lions to devour."

"You are wrong almost beyond measure," replied the beggar, gazing away into the forested darkness at some sound only he had heard. "She has a lovely name indeed, but no one has bothered to give it to her yet. That, in part, is why I came."

"Who are you?"

"My name is Covenant, and I am true to my name."

"What sort of riddles are you speaking?" Damon looked

around uneasily. "I should be gone by now. There are lions about."

"My name is Covenant, and I am true to my name. There is nothing for you to fear tonight. I am the lord of all lions, and I send them where I will. They will stay away until we have finished here."

"What do you mean? I have done what I came to do."

"And what will you do now?" the beggar asked, leaning toward Damon and his burden. "She has no one to turn to and nowhere to go. You have cast your lot with her, and now you also have no one to turn to and nowhere to go. You came to rescue her, and you did so at great risk."

"I had my knife."

"And you tried to use it. Had a true lion come against you instead of this old beggar, I know you would not have been less brave. You would not, however, still be alive."

The beggar settled back against the tree again as he spoke. "Even as you have saved her from perishing, so have I saved you both. And now I would deliver both of you into a different life.

"You must carry this child to Glory," continued Covenant, "and see how I deal with the unwanted of the world, for this child is not alone." He turned and faced the great rock, his arms spread in a mixture of appeal and agony. "There are many wretched rocks akin to this in lonely places, where the young and unwanted or the old and unneeded are left to perish—either from the teeth of the cold or the teeth of the lion."

"But where is the lion?" Damon asked, still nervously scanning the darkness.

The beggar growled low but surprisingly loud in the stillness, and there was no longer any doubt from whose throat the roar had issued. Damon scrambled backward, clutching the child and trying to cradle her at the same time.

"You need not be afraid," said the beggar calmly. "Although everything evil in the woods is terrible, not everything terrible in the woods is evil. And a fierce outcry is essential; if I did not come and split the night with the song of the mighty, the exposers would linger to make sure their outcasts died. This way they run, and believe, and are secure in their folly." He lowered his voice, and his eyes bored through the darkness. "But you must answer this question: Will you leave your family for me? And for her? I offer you both a home in Glory."

A donkey brayed twice in the near distance while Damon thought.

"I cannot go back," he said, "and I cannot go with you. My mother is dead, and my father is old and ill. I am sure that my sister will also bring him to this rock when he is too feeble to stop her. How can I rescue him from the lion as well? I cannot hide in these hills to wait for my father. But I cannot return home either."

"I know your father well enough, though he does not yet know me. I will know the season and the hour of his trial in the wilderness, and I will send you to aid him. That is my promise to you. But if you will receive my promises, you must obey my commands: Go to Glory, and take the girl with you."

"But what of my sister?" Damon asked. "She may turn and do this again."

"She will not," he said, and turned the question around. "But what of your sister? Why did she cast this one aside?"

"She would be happy only with a boy."

"Then she must wait in vain. I have spoken a word against her, and she shall bear no son, and never a child again. She will long for her boy forever and he will not come, because she has despised the child that was given her."

Damon had no reply, and he gazed past the beggar into the dark distance. The girl in his arms slept on.

"Except for my father, there is little to leave," Damon replied after a measured pause. "My sister does not honor me, and her husband has no respect for me. I have no children, for no woman would have me." He turned his face toward the silhouette of the beggar. Old swellings and wounds beneath scars showed plainly in the moonlight. "I know that no one wants me, and I can think of none who need me—save for this one who scarcely knows that I am here, and does not understand anything at all."

"She needed you, and you came. You needed me, and I came as well."

"I do not understand," he said, puzzled.

"You have no more need to understand than she does. You can only reach out and take what is given to you."

"But why did you come tonight?" asked Damon. "Surely you cannot come here every night!"

"I do not need to journey here every night, for most nights there is nothing here that a lion would want. It is my business to be wherever and whenever I am needed. I knew she would be here. And it pleased me that you would be here as well."

The unseen donkey brayed again. The baby roused and began to cry. Damon could not comfort her, but she ceased her howling when the beggar eased her onto his shoulder and murmured to her.

"Come," said the beggar, "there is a house nearby. Let us go in from the frost of the night." He turned and walked away with the baby.

"A house? There is nothing in this wilderness but the dens of animals!"

"Now, perhaps, but once there was a family here. Their dwelling still stands."

He led Damon into the underbrush, pausing once to point wordlessly to the ground at their feet. Damon scrabbled in the soft loam and recovered his knife. He slipped it back into his belt without comment, and they moved deeper into the forest. Soon they came to a stand of trees where a donkey browsed the remains of a scattered sack of grain. Beyond those trees was an abandoned cottage, its walls hidden by years of vines, the wooden door long since rotted and fallen in.

Damon could hardly see at all, but the beggar seemed to know the way. Once through the arch of the doorway, Damon could see the tiny fire glowing in the heap of stones that had once been the fireplace. For the first time, there was enough light for him to see the beggar's face clearly.

He was not handsome, but his visage inspired trust. He was neither ancient nor fresh-faced, and both warm and worn at the same time. The beggar returned the baby to Damon and stepped outside again to throw down more grain for the donkey. The child remained content and fell asleep in Damon's arms.

Damon looked about him carefully, though there was little enough left in the cottage. On the post that had once held the door, he found the mark of a heart carved large upon the wood. There was an arrow emblazoned beneath it, and many marks below that. All these marks were gray with time, and he could not quite number them in the ruddy, shifting light. Sixteen? Seventeen? It was hard to tell. There were three new chiseled signs at the bottom and a handful of fresh wood shavings on the floor.

The beggar joined him at the doorway and asked, "Do you see this mark?" His fingers lingered on the weathered heart.

"Yes."

"It is the evidence of old love never abandoned, still proclaimed for all the world to see. Do you see these many notches below it?"

Damon nodded.

"These are the signs of hope long nurtured against fear in the face of the witness of time—one mark for each lonely year that has passed. Such a love is not easily defeated. Do you see this new notch?"

"I see it."

"I put it there with my own hands early this evening. It is the mark for this year. And do you know the symbol beneath that?"

"All know that sign. It is the mark of Glory."

The beggar nodded. "And beneath that?"

"I do not know that sign."

"It is my mark, and this same sign is emblazoned on a house in Glory. Find it, and tell the people there you have come in my name."

"But they will not know my name."

"They will welcome you anyway. And your name, from now on, shall be Lionheart. Old names are good, new ones better, and true ones best of all. It is a name you should bear for the moment, for you dared to face the lion for one who had no other champion. It is also a name you should bear for the future, for I call you to take my place in rescuing others from the rocks of exposure. You shall lose nothing and gain much. I promise you that if you leave your family here behind, you will have both children and parents of your own forever."

Damon gazed down at the baby. "I already have her, to begin with."

"You could not keep her for long, by yourself."

"Why not?" the boy bristled.

"You have cared for children before, but never for the new-born. She would die in the midst of all the love you would pour out upon her. But," the beggar continued, "her future is secure in me. It is your future that must be attended to."

"I do not know that I can trust you."

"You can trust no one else. You have no more choices, it seems. The child trusts me, though she chooses for reasons you have long forgotten. I tell you, go to Glory and see for yourself. The house of Candle will host you until another place is made ready. Ask after Trueteller there, to help you care for the child. Soon, I will be there as well." He leaned over and produced a small sack from the shadows behind him. "Here. You must find the way from here, for I have other business to see to. But I shall not send you alone to Glory. The road is long, and it wanders, and there are animals that threaten. Therefore, I will call to you two friends you need fear no longer."

He growled softly into the night, two separate calls, and was answered in kind. A great shadow appeared from the shadows, and another behind it. Two massive lions emerged from the doorway into the dim circle of the fire, and Damon knew there was no place to run.

"Do not be afraid, Lionheart," said the beggar. "You dared the lions for her, and for your bravery you shall have them to command. There are other wild beasts than lions, but none of them will bother you as long as you are escorted. Wolves will not come near you. Nor will bears disturb your passing, and snakes will slither away at the sound of your approach. These two will carry you to the edge of Glory."

"Carry?"

"You will ride." He beckoned to the larger lion—a male, Damon could see now. The lion came to Covenant and crouched at his feet. Covenant mounted and drew Damon up in front of him before the boy realized what was happening.

"My beast waits in the trees over there," the beggar continued. "Our road is long, and we have not yet come to the end of it." Then Covenant dismounted and left Damon on the lion's back. "The bag holds food and water for your journey. Sit lightly, and twist one fist into his mane, and you will go where he goes. As for her," he said, pointing to the infant cradled in Damon's free arm, "she will sleep much, and she has been provided for." Damon looked bewildered. "You will recognize the provision when her hunger comes." The second shadow, a lioness, nudged his leg, and he began to understand.

Damon's decision crystallized within him, and he knew that he need not give voice to it. The bulk of the great beast beneath him brought him peace now, surprisingly. He stretched and could almost hear the beggar smiling in the darkness. "I will go," he said. "But surely *she* cannot continue without a name."

"Then let us call her Woodswaif. I know her true name, her final name, but for now that shall be my secret alone. Do you know enough now to begin?"

"I think so," replied Lionheart, watching the lioness drift to nuzzle her mate. "But how can I return later and take your place? I am not a lion."

"Neither am I—as you can see," returned the beggar, spreading his arms again, his smile beaming brighter than the moonlight outside. "But one need not be a lion to be their king. And I can teach you how to roar."

— FOUR —

After
the
Rain

T HE BEGGAR ON THE DONKEY RODE SLOWLY BETWEEN THE vast fields of grain, past the open pit strewn with small stones, and through the waiting gate into the village. Storm clouds gathered like gray mountains in the distance, several hours' riding away. The village was quiet—far too quiet for midday. The beggar heard only one faint sound, a low rumbling from the far side of the open square that marked the village center. He dismounted and led his beast through the squat stone buildings toward the murmur.

The square was empty, save for a stone altar, a tall iron stake, and a small dirty building of weathered rock that leaned away from the sun. The altar was covered with road dust and old chaff, except where a few stalks of grain had been placed. The beggar tested them and found them fresh, as though they had lain there only a night. The stake stood behind the altar—tall, stark, charred, with old ashes circling the metal spike. And the building, only a few paces wide and long, bore iron bars in the few tiny windows.

The beggar moved on beyond the square. There, between two of the buildings, an old man huddled over a wooden framework, grinding grain. His eyes were closed, dark and sunken in their sockets, and his cheeks were hollow. The beggar could hear now a monotonous cough, a ceaseless rattle that drove quavers through the old man's gaunt frame, already rocking with the rumbling rhythm of the stone wheel.

The beggar paused in the shadows and watched until the grinder, aroused by some slight sound, opened his eyes and saw him. He loosed the handle of the wheel and the sound of the rolling stones died away.

"Ho, stranger." He focused first on the beggar, and then peered at the sky, as if seeing it for the first time in many hours. "You bring the rain with you."

"Aye. And you should bless me for it. All your fields are dry."

"Let them wither. They only bring me burdens I cannot bear. The grain comes here, and I must grind it."

"You grind alone?"

"I grind alone because I grind slowly." He paused to hack in the dust. "The wagons bring the grain in the evenings. We—the old ones—grind all night and sleep by day if we can. This is the spring harvest, and all the able are working in the fields." He waved a gnarled hand over the many sacks of whole grain stacked beside his stone. "This is left of my share from last twilight. I have turned the wheel all night and all day."

"And if you do not finish?"

"For those who can no longer work—or will not—the pit of stones is waiting." The old man shuddered as he reached to resume his task. "I bid you welcome, for myself, but I also give

you warning. If you have the strength, you would do well to pass on. This village holds no love for beggars, and it makes no room for hungry idle mouths."

"I do not beg for meals. But I accept freely, even as I give freely."

"And what do you give so freely?"

"To prove that my mouth is not idle—a story."

"Yes. Tell me a story, if you dare to stand idle. A traveler's tale may bring some ease to this weary old heart." He began to turn the wheel.

"In another village over the hills there was a man . . ." His words hummed soft and slow and soothing like buzzing bees in the warm, close afternoon.

The old man slept over his wheel, and the rolling stones rolled slowly into stillness.

When the old man started awake, he saw the sun lying far beyond the noon zenith. He grabbed frantically for the wheel, but he stopped when he saw the sacks of ground grain stacked neatly beside the framework and his own work bins now empty. The beggar had not moved.

The two men stared at each other while storm clouds grumbled in the corners of the darkening sky.

"I know who you are now," the old man said softly. "There were rumors of you, but not many believed. Unlike some who are not old enough to be wise, I have heeded what I have heard."

"And you believe now because all your grain is ground?"

"No mortal could grind all that in a mere span of hours. And I know you did not turn this wheel."

"You do well to believe, but you believe on shallow deeds. The grinding of grain is a small thing."

"In your eyes, perhaps, but not in mine. I am grateful for your gift."

"Then share your meal with me. Let us feast together."

"On what? I draw poor rations for grinding. Nothing else

is mine but a tiny room in the shadow of the walls. Little else will come to me. I have no food fit for the gods."

"Then let us eat this." The beggar rose and slung a sack of the fresh-ground meal over his patient donkey's back. "It will feed the three of us handsomely."

"It is not allowed!" the old man protested. "All the grain belongs to the village, until the elders hand it to those who need it."

"And do we not need it?" the beggar continued, fastening the sack in place with bits of old rope. "Is there no provision for wayfarers? Or for the hands that ground it? Even the workers eat the fruit of the orchard as it passes through their hands. And the oxen that pull the threshing sledge may browse the ground when the sledge is still. Come. We deserve this meal. Let us prepare a supper fit for the weary."

The old man and the beggar sat in the shelter of the tiny room. The graincakes were soon gone, slaying hunger in their passing.

"Soon," the old man said, "soon the wagons will come and I must grind again."

"They give you no rest."

"No. The greedy never rest. And neither may the poor."

"And the law of the elders?"

"Their law has freed the village from the burden of caring for those who cannot contribute. The aged, the infirm, the diseased—they are taken out to be stoned. It is what they shall do to me when I can no longer turn the wheel. Each night the task grows longer, and I weaker." He gazed at the doorway and wept inside his heart where he thought no one could hear. "I hear the wagons now."

"No. That is only the thunder that heralds the rain—and the rain will come before the wagons. But the storm is not yet upon us, and even the sun gives us a few hours. Do not the workers gather until it is too dark to see?"

"They come home at dusk." The two men watched the shadows lengthen across the doorway.

"You have heard tales of me," the beggar said. "And you believe. Yet you have asked nothing of me. Is your fear so great?"

"I have fear, yes. And also poverty. I am so poor that you have nothing to offer me."

"I gave you a story to warm your heart and rest your body. And now your heart cries out to me across the room. Name its need and I will fill you."

The old man wept openly. "I know of you. You bring life to the dead, and grain to the hungry, and wine to the thirsty, and strength to the faint . . . I desire none of those things."

"Have you no love dead and buried? No hunger? No thirst? No weakness? I cannot accept that you are a man without need."

"I have my needs. But it may happen that a man—especially an old man—may no longer desire to have his needs fulfilled." He stood slowly and led the beggar to the doorway, where they could see through the village, over the far wall and beyond to a river, with trees rooted deep into the banks. "I have my needs. I am always hungry. I thirst. I am weary of my weakness and even of my weariness itself. And I have my beloved dead." He pointed to the trees by the river. "I buried her beneath the willows," he continued softly, "and now she waits for me in the City beyond the rainbow."

"The rainbow?"

"We used to walk there beneath the trees by the water, where the sun sets like fire and diamonds over the mountains. When the rain comes in the evenings, the sun leaves a rainbow behind as its final shadow. Under the rainbow are those mountains, and those mountains are the end of the world."

"And beyond them? Nothing?"

"Beyond them must be the true West, where the City lies and the Elder God dwells. We promised to wait for one another there. One night, after the rain, while we wondered at the rainbow from this riverbank, she died."

"Has your grief passed?"

"My grief was small, and not for her, because I saw the peace of her passing. With my own eyes I saw the smile that came as the last pain was fading. She opened her eyes then, and they were filled with marvels as she gazed into a wondrous land I could not see. My grief for me was swallowed by my joy for her. I buried her there between the roots of the giant willow, our private place of rainbows. Even now, when the rains come and go, I may stand in my doorway and see the bright colors arching over her grave."

The beggar stepped down from the doorway. "I should be honored if you would walk with me there."

When they reached the riverbank, the old man broke the silence. "Why are you here in this town? One who comes here can only be coming here. There is only the one road. To the west are only the mountains, and on either side only our fertile fields. No roads point eastward save the paths of the great grain wagons.

"And you wake legends with your footsteps. It is said that strangers who come before the rain bring with them darkness and death."

"So I have heard. But is it not also said that a stranger who lingers after the rain brings a blessing?"

"So some say. But only if there is a rainbow."

The beggar traced circles in the grass with his foot. "Not all the old legends are true. And some are truer than you might imagine." He looked up suddenly at the old man. "And you, in your turn, are a strange man. You know who I am, yet you ask nothing."

"I know what you would have me ask, and I will not. *She* is the pain closest to my heart, yet I would not call her back to me. Some deeds are better left undone. What joy could she return to? The grainwheel awaits her, to drain her and steal her strength again, as it does daily to me. They would soon take her out to be stoned. No. Please do not impose such a kindness upon us."

They watched the ripples in the river.

"I hear the wagons," the old man said. "Or do you say it is only the thunder?"

"No. The wagons come. But you need not return to meet them. There is still time for you to seek a gift."

"I am grateful to you, but I desire nothing more."

"No secret dreams? No untold wishes?"

"Only . . . only one." He scarcely dared breathe the words. "Perhaps you are the only one who might understand." He gazed unseeingly at the mountains. "I dream often of dying here, here beneath this tree where she lies—of dying peacefully, and not under the hurling weight of many stones or in the heat of the hungry flames—of dying with her face in my heart and her name on my lips. But I would need gentle hands to bury me beside her, and I have no man to lower me into the embrace of the earth."

The beggar's next words hung like sunbeams in the air. "Many have sought a good life and more of it. You may choose a way which is better yet."

The old man let silence preface his words.

"Before I was yet this old," he began, "before this village grew complete in its corruption and enslavement by love of gold and grain, one day in seven was a day of rest—born from the word of the Elder God, I know, but by then little more than a tradition.

"On such days I would wake, weary, fearful, not remembering at first that no work would be required of me that day. And then it would burst upon me like lightning that more rest awaited me, that a prolonging of sleep was mine for the taking. And how often I longed to hold that glorious lightning in my hand and make it a lasting joy—to wake and find an eternity of unbroken rest at hand." He opened his arms wide to the mountains and the hidden lands beyond. "I believe that was what sparked her last and most lasting smile—the beck-oning, the rest, the peace, the waking in the west that makes all that has gone before a long and troubled sleeping." He dropped his arms and faced the beggar. "Is such a gift within your power?"

"It is. The one who gives forth may also withdraw his hand. Only the ones who are bold of heart may claim them both as equal blessings. I speak for him, for I am he. Ask what you will."

"I have seen the first blessing. It is the second that I ask from your hand."

"Then behold your rest! It comes for you with loving hands. Because you asked me not for small favors that perish, I give you the everlasting desire of your heart." Wooden wheels rumbled along the dirt roads behind them. "And you need not go to meet the wagons."

"If . . . If I may . . . I should like to enjoy this last rain, and see one final rainbow."

The beggar laughed, and the old man's unbidden tears shared that burst of joy. "By all means! Let there be soft rains and the light that arches over! And then, after the rain, I shall give you rest."

He waved his arms across the swollen sky, and beneath a new prismed curve of color the rain came to them over the fields like lambs running.

FIVE

Trial
by
Fire

Y OU WILL STAND TRIAL TOMORROW FOR THE SLAYING OF
the old man!" The young man jeered through the bars at the
beggar in the tiny stone cell. "But the verdict is sure. More
than one of us saw you bury him."

Grain wagons rolled through the streets outside, bearing
home a double load of harvest and weary people. The beggar,
eyeing the jailer as though they sat at table for supper and
were not separated by iron bars, spoke at last. "There is much
that you did not see. And much more that you do not."

"What is that to me? *You* are the one who will pay the price.
Do you deny the old man's death?"

"I do not. But you do wrong to call it murder."

"Let the flames decide your innocence. You will have your
trial by fire. And just it is, too, although I myself would chain
you to the wheel and let you grind your life away. Or cast you

into a pit and test your flesh with stones. There are others of the same mind as well. You anger many when you hinder the harvest."

"If all in this village work, how do you justify yourself? You are too lame to work in the fields."

Anger flushed the young man's face as he forced himself to his full height. "My leg is not too twisted to drive a wagon! Besides, this town would be poorer without me. I entertain them at night when their work is done. I am their balladeer, their poet, their historian, their jester, their teller of tales— and their law-binder and jailer when someone breaks the laws of the elders.

"I am Barid, and my brothers own the finest land here. I am not a man to be dismissed lightly!" He turned away from the bars and hobbled across the square to join a small, gathering crowd.

The beggar could see half the square from his window. There was a high metal stake set in the center, a few paces from the altar of the Elder God. Down a side street he could see the wheel that the old man had so wearily turned.

He watched the wagons passing, and noted the few who paused to throw a sheaf of grain down onto the basin of the altar. Barid's voice carried clearly to him, soaring and swooping, singing a rude and bawdy ballad to the cheers of sweaty men slaking their thirst with mugs of fermented grain. Barid possessed a fine voice, and the beggar reflected long upon him.

Later, Barid's face appeared at the cell's window. "Beggar! We would try you tonight, but the Harvest Feast is almost upon us, and we are weary, and there is much to be made ready. Perhaps tomorrow, as entertainment."

"Barid?"

Only a grunt came in answer.

"Do you not know other songs?" the beggar asked. "Any songs that do not dishonor the gifts the Elder God gave to men?"

45

Barid laughed through the barred opening. "The Elder God! I suppose you're one of those fools who would throw good grain to waste upon the altar!" The hardness in his eyes softened, and his voice gained a faint tinge of sadness. "I need no other songs, only new ones like those I sang tonight. They throw me coppers now, and sometimes silver for the choicer stories. There would be no payment for a sentimental ballad."

"Is it in your memory or your lore why you feast tomorrow?"

"For the grain, of course! The flood gates of our life have opened wide, and golden is the tide! Why should we not celebrate?"

"You do not remember why the Harvest Feast was first held? Or when? By whose command? Do you recall a time before there was grain here?"

"No. We have always held the feast. And the grain has ever been here. Go to sleep, old man, and enjoy it. You may not have many more wakenings."

The beggar spoke to the darkness where Barid had been. "You do not know these things? Your fathers did. And I shall remind you tomorrow." His eyes overflowed with sadness as he leaned back on the prisoner's bench. Barid returned later, full of spirits and mirth, and collapsed into sleep in the dust outside the cell.

* * *

The next evening Barid brought the prisoner to the center of the square and set him before the people. He read aloud the charges and turned to the beggar.

"The assembly has met and has decided. We do not know if you slew the old man. We do know that you buried him by the river. Therefore our judgment is this: you shall stand trial by fire. Here at this stake we shall bind you and kindle the flames. If you perish, you are deemed guilty, and justice will have been done. If you endure, you are innocent of the man's death.

"But if innocent, you will take his place at the wheel until the harvest is finished. We cannot afford the loss of a laborer." Turning to the people, he commanded them, "Take him to the fire."

They bound him there, and brought wood and kindling and oil.

But they could not light the fire.

The kindling dripped with oil, but the sparks sputtered out as though the brands had been thrust into water. The fire-striker muttered and moved away from the stake.

Then the beggar raised his hands and the bonds fell away. He leaped to the top of the altar. "Your fire is not enough!" He pointed his finger at the stake and the fuel flared in a single monstrous tongue of flame, driving the watchers back with its heat. The wood was consumed in a blink of bright fury. In a moment only the twisted iron of the stake showed above the smoldering ashes.

The smoke scattered on the breeze as the beggar turned to the cringing crowd. "You have brought judgment down on your own heads. Had you condemned me for what you supposed to be the slaying of a man, a free and worthy being, I would merely have walked away from you. But you have tried me for the destruction of that which you viewed as your own property—a nameless slave whom you yourself would have killed in sickness, a possession useful to you only in your service to your god. *Your* god, and not the God of your fathers."

He stared at them all, his eyes daring them to move. No one left, and he continued in a lower but even stronger voice. "I stand on this altar to the Elder God. Do you worship him?" He brandished a fistful of offered grain. "Some of you do. I hold your offerings and firstfruits, and I know your hearts and see your faithfulness. I know you sing songs of praise and thanks to the True God, to the One who ordained this feast and granted you this harvest." Then he named their names, one by one, and their hearts were strangely and suddenly

lifted as he called them to stand by the altar at his right hand. Slowly and cautiously, the called ones eased their way through the crowd and obeyed.

"I bless you for your faithfulness," the bold beggar said to those who had moved at his bidding. "Yet I have this against you: You saw injustice, greed, and the growing idols in the fields, but you said nothing and did not raise your voice in protest. Behold! You must share the ordeal of the others. But know that I will strengthen your hearts, and it will surely pass."

He turned to the small multitude of the ones who still stood on his left. "As for the rest of you, you have forgotten the faith of your fathers and unlearned their gratitude. This altar was built by zealous men in a barren land—men who prayed to the Elder God and waited patiently. Seven times they prayed, for seven days, and on the seventh day the Elder God turned their wasteland into fertile fields. This altar was here, built by their hands, before there was grain here. When the firstfruits were reaped, they were offered here. And on that day they declared a Harvest Feast to be held each year, that the kindness of the Elder God might not be forgotten.

"But you have forgotten. You remember not the Elder God but the false golden god who grows in your fields. Do you doubt me? Then look to the pain of your hearts as your god is put to the test of fire. For it is not I who stands here for judgment, but you and your chosen god!"

The sheaves of grain flared suddenly in his hands. "Behold the acceptable sacrifice! Behold the pleasing smoke!" A pillar of fire rose from the altar, wrapping the beggar in flames, yet not consuming him. The burning reached high into the sky and dark rolling clouds gathered around the pillar, spreading out over all the heavens. Thunder rolled overhead and on every side, smothering the screams that came unbidden to the throats of the watchers.

"Behold the judgment—and the death of your golden god!"

From the heart of the cloud, vast lightnings streaked the sky, striking again and again around them, forking the fields with flame. Fire raged through the standing grain too quickly to follow, consuming barns of stored grain in single deep explosions. The earth trembled. Where the fire had passed, the earth smoked.

Huddled together, the stunned villagers watched through their fingers, afraid to cry out, afraid to run, afraid to breathe. Then the lightning ceased and the clouds swirled backward into the standing pillar. Then the pillar collapsed with slow violence, leaving the beggar standing alone upon the altar.

"A trial by fire. And the verdict? Where is your god now to proclaim his innocence?

"And your own innocence? You grieve the smoldering earth." Only a few scattered stands of grain now stood unmarked. "Even the soil is lifeless. It has returned to the wasteland from which it came. Your god has abandoned you in his death, and with him goes your life as well."

He turned to Barid. "Approach the altar. I have not yet finished with you." Barid, afraid to obey, too frightened not to obey, crawled awkwardly to the foot of the altar.

The villagers trembled. The beggar dismissed the ones on his left hand, saying, "Go to your homes. You have not honored the Elder God, and he will not honor you until you repent of your hardness of heart. Never again shall this land bear fruit for you. Go, and make plans to journey on from this place."

Then he dismissed the few on his right hand, laying a blessing upon their heads as they went. When the square was once more empty, he turned at last to Barid, sprawled in the dust beneath the altar. "You have not honored me, but you shall. Stay here with the faithful, for mercy follows judgment, and I have not finished my work here."

During the next two days, wagons thundered slowly through the town, carrying not grain but households and goods and people away to the towns to the east. The old man's wheel sat unneeded and unheeded in the middle of the emptying village.

Only a few remained with the beggar to watch the exodus. And when the dust had settled behind the last wagon, they began to speak with him.

"We have done as you said. We bought all their fields. But why? Why did you bid us trade our last silver and remaining gold for worthless soil? And why were our fields not consumed? Forgive our boldness, but you have given us only commands and no answers."

The beggar gazed out over the scorched fields. "Yours is the right now to ask questions, because you have already obeyed. Your own fields were not burned because you had already offered your firstfruits. Your firstfruits ransomed the rest of your crops—that which was in the fields and that which is now laid in your barns.

"The others hated you. Why should they not sell you the land that would never yield for them again? They are not fools to pass by profit. Your gold and silver are honored in all the land—but even their soil was burned. And you have bought it now. By deed of law?"

"Yes."

"Witnessed by the elders?"

"Yes."

"Can anyone argue that you forced their lands from them?"

"No."

"Then the land is yours forever. No blessings remain for them. But the land will yet bless you when I return and bless the land."

"But what shall we do now?"

"Abide here. You have sufficient grain to survive here until the winter. There is none left to sell, but you have no pressing need either for money or for the things that money can buy.

"Await my return. I shall surely come before winter. Wait

for me. Wait with the same faith that has been your salvation so far. If any among you should lose courage and set out toward the towns and fields of the east, let the rest of you buy their land honestly from them.

"As for the land, let it savor its rest now. Greed has abused it, and only now shall it have peace."

Then Barid spoke. "And what of me? Shall I, too, wait? I own no land, I have no inheritance. It was only at your command that I did not board the wagons with my brothers. Shall I starve here?" he asked bitterly.

The beggar took the man's elbow in his hand and urged him away from the square. "It would not be an evil yoke for you to learn humility. The rest would feed you—but not for your twisted songs and tales. Indeed, I do not think you have the heart to sing such now. They would feed you in love for you and obedience to me, and that would shatter your pride.

"But I choose another way to break you, bind you, make you whole and set you free. Come with me." And they wandered toward one of the houses lying between the square and the willowed river. The beggar stood before the door and said, "You are one who wields power, yet you will not yield readily to my power. I know this, for I know all men. Enter this house with me, and see for yourself that high power need not always be terrible." They entered, and a child met them—a child with tears in her eyes, a child who stared with hope at the beggar.

Barid asked in low tones, "Does she cry for the loss of the grain?"

"No. She is too young to understand. But she is old enough to know other pains, pains that are larger to her than ruined fields." He bent down and spoke softly to her. She disappeared into the depths of the house. When she returned, she carried something in her arms.

"Behold the source of her tears." The beggar reached out and gently plucked from her arms a kitten. "The wagons, leaving, left more than simply tracks in the dust." Barid saw the mangled legs and the heaving flank and the pain-glazed eyes, and something hot and piercing flamed in his heart. His hand trembled against his own leg, and visions of other wagon wheels in another year danced in his memory.

"Loud words, and rude, are not all that move you," the beggar said, "nor are violence and destruction the only deeds that I do. Behold." He stroked the kitten, and in his hands he made it whole again. It mewed and licked his hand, and he gave it to Barid. "This is the first lesson. Give the child her beloved, and follow me." The child clung to her kitten and to the beggar's legs for a moment, gazing at him with wordless, open gratitude before happily vanishing into another room.

The beggar urged Barid outside and continued. "Are not ten kittens sold for a single coin? And a lame one tossed away? Yet not one of them is struck down where the Elder God does not see. And are you of less value than a kitten?" He led him to the river, where they sat beneath the willows.

"Is it always your business to interfere?" asked Barid.

"Yes, and it is my pleasure as well. I take delight in proving that the universe holds more than people believe—that there are indeed answers, if you choose to look in the proper places and ask the questions correctly.

"It depends on what brings you joy and hope." The beggar gestured to the west. "Look above you at the mountains and below you at the river. I know that these touch you with beauties that do not dwell in the songs you sing. What of the love of a small child for her pet? Or of the woman who walks arm-in-arm with her chosen husband? Why did you not celebrate the love they share rather than the desires of the women who idle near the alehouse?

"You have been given a fine gift, but you profane both it and the giver, and with them yourself. You know many songs to gladden the appetites of men. I have brought you here now to learn songs to gladden their hearts."

The beggar began to sing. And, after the first song, he told

Barid an ancient story, fascinating the man with his weaving hands. When he spoke, he gestured, and such magic was his as to bring life to the words and breath to the images standing behind. Barid expected, watching, to see worlds appear at his command. And then there was another song, and the fresh beauties in the beggar's words broke over Barid like a thunderstorm.

Barid wept, trembling, feeling old inner walls give and quake and crumble, and then walls within walls, both secret and known, until all his defenses lay in ruins. And still the beggar sang on, spinning stories, relentlessly grinding the shattered shards of hardness into powder and fine dust that scattered before the bright breeze of his words. The words carried wisdom so starkly true that his heart leaped, crying Yes! and was ever after changed. And Barid wept for grief for which he had no tears or words or outlet. He begged the beggar to stop and not to stop, for he could no longer bear either the flow of old truths or their cessation.

The beggar came to an end of his tales. He spoke to the weeping Barid long in healing words, mending where he had rent, soothing where he had sliced away, giving balm where his words had wounded.

"You have heard my songs and listened to my refrains. Do you now desire to learn them?"

"Yes."

"One who sings my songs may no longer sing the songs of the world. Do you still choose mine?"

"Yes. If you will give them to me."

"You cannot receive them until you bury your old songs. Bury them here and now, in this place beside the river."

"I do not know how."

"But I do. They will perish with your name. See you the ground where your tears have fallen? Write your name there."

Barid obeyed, inscribing his name in the dampened dirt.

Then the beggar scooped the earth into his hands and molded the moist soil into a tight ball. "Take it, and throw it into the river." Barid obeyed, and they watched it sink, dissolving again to mud on the river bottom.

"You have no name now, and no songs or tales. Prove to yourself that my words are true. Sing me a song from the alehouse."

Barid could think of none. There was only blankness in his mind, blankness overwritten by the words of the beggar.

"You see? I bring other healings beyond the merely physical. And can you tell me your name?"

He could not.

"Your name was Barid, and you belonged to yourself. You are Wordsmith now, and belong to Covenant, because I have need of you to do my work in my name. Come share my spirit, and no longer the spirits of the alehouse. Come keep not prisoners, but free men; write not bawdy ballads, but truest truth. Observe not fallen festivals with your people, but serve a living Feast to my own. I cannot be all places at once, and it is you I select to be with me and do my bidding. What I show you by night you will tell by day. The tales you unravel in secret, you will spin in the middle of the marketplace.

"Of the others, I ask hard things. Of you I ask harder things still. Do not wait. Do not test your faith with the patience of doing nothing. Follow me instead. Do not wait, but follow me. By my power I have forced your obedience—but I have neither your loyalty nor your devotion. That is why I have spoken to you these words of purest truth and unmixed beauty. I speak these things because I am their source and their lifespring. It is because of these things that I ask your loyalty and your devotion, and not because I have power and am to be feared.

"Will you come, Wordsmith?"

"I have not always lived in this tiny, forsaken village. I was born here, and I have returned here, for nowhere have I found that which satisfied me. Here at least I am among my own people. There are finer singers in Glory, and I was only one voice struggling to be heard in the multitude. But here I stand honored and alone."

"I promise you this: Your voice shall be heard by all and heeded by many, if you come and tell my tales for me. You have seen Glory and turned your back upon it willingly?"

"Gladly, even. It is a place of hollow wholeness."

"Then I bid you do a very hard thing," said Covenant. "Return with me to Glory, for it is there that I have established my house."

"I will—but I saw no house grand enough to hold such power. And I never heard your name. Surely you are well known there?"

"I have founded my house, but it is neither finished nor inhabited. I am well known to those who know their need for me, but not famous to all. But why will *you* follow me? Be sure you know clearly in your own mind. I have called you, but it is not written in the stars that you must heed the call."

Wordsmith drew a bottomless breath and stared at the sky that concealed those same stars. "I follow because you have touched me with the truth. I have found it nowhere else." He knew that the answers were already known to Covenant. He knew also that his responses must be uttered anyway.

"Then leave all you have to these faithful ones. Bring nothing with you, and you shall soon possess more than you can carry."

"I have vowed to you, but I do not even know your name."

"I am Covenant," he said. "But he who calls me Covenant must also call me Master. My name is Covenant, for I keep my promises. Even when you do not understand me at all, I will be faithful to you. You have vowed many times to do many things," he continued, "and you have withdrawn your word each time. This time I will hold you to your word. And you shall never regret it, though your own vows return to puzzle you."

"But what are you promising me?"

"My promise is nothing—or everything: nothing you be-lieve you've always wanted, but everything you've always needed." He paused, searching Wordsmith's face. "Have you further questions for me now? If not, then we shall leave in the morning."

But Wordsmith lingered to talk, and their words that night outlasted the shadows and outshone the stars.

─── SIX ───

Trial
Without
Fire

THE WARMTH OF THE COMPANY SHORTENED THE LONG road to Glory.

The two men spoke now and again, but there were long silences that neither chose to break. After their initial night of challenge and long talk, even gestures were enough to convey volumes. And Wordsmith learned from Covenant even in the silence. Covenant smiled and pointed much, moving his hands to underline the truth that had already been uttered. Wordsmith saw and understood. He thought much and wondered at the things that had happened to him in only a handful of days.

Wordsmith was weary, and he wondered if Covenant was tired as well. The beggar walked like an aged man with sore feet, but he did not speak of his pain or complain against the rough dirt of the road.

The donkey could not carry them both, so they walked and trailed the small beast behind them. Covenant seemed to be in no particular hurry, taking time to examine the flowers by the road and enjoy the birds wheeling in the air. Wordsmith too looked at these things, and he began to appreciate many things he had merely seen before.

The first night out, Wordsmith built the fire and curled between the flames and the rocks behind him, while Covenant curled up alone in the unpenetrated shadows away from the fire—alone save for Kingsburro, untethered, nodding, and seemingly unafraid. Wordsmith wished the beggar were sleeping closer to him; somehow he felt safe with Covenant—though he was still mostly mystified by the beggar and his enigmatic but unarguable ways.

He wondered again about wild animals. He had seen nothing large, but he thought the small animals were exceedingly abundant. All day they had flashed across the edges of his vision, appearing at the edges of the trees to peer at the travelers. Now he could sense their comings and goings around the perimeter of the tiny campfire.

In the morning, he awoke after having slept poorly, suffering from the one-sided heat of the fire and the vigilance necessary to keep it burning. Covenant seemed rested and warm. Wordsmith did not understand how the beggar could sleep so soundly and without fear through the hours of darkness.

For Wordsmith, the second day of their journey faded to a timeless wandering, their way becoming as much a goal as their destination. He was often filled with curious wonder, but he could not easily form his questions into words.

The second night passed like the first. Covenant did not suggest a fire, but he allowed Wordsmith to build one for comfort.

But on the third evening, after a third day of tiny marvels, Covenant stopped Wordsmith as he began to gather wood for the night. "We need no fire tonight," said the beggar.

"But the nights are still cold!" objected Wordsmith. "Summer is not yet here."

"The nights are indeed still sharp, and I feel them as keenly as you do. Nevertheless, I ask you to wait. There are other ways to be warmed than by the fire."

"But what of the animals?"

"What of them?"

"Are you not afraid?"

"I have no need to be afraid. You are afraid and do not sleep, while I fear not and sleep well. You should follow my example. You have already obeyed me—now you must learn to trust me as well. Hold back your hand from the wood. Let the sun warm us a final time before it sets. Then let the darkness come."

Wordsmith sat with Covenant and watched the final fingers of day withdraw from the sky. He was cold. He could feel the fear of the night draw closer, but he made no move to spark a flame in the gathered pile of sticks and dead brush.

Covenant stirred, and said, "Now you shall see. Or rather, you shall *not* see. You have obeyed me before from lack of other choice. Your obedience was born of fear—or awe. Now let your obedience be born of trust. Let the fire be, and what will happen then will be a miracle."

"You will show me another miracle?"

"You will see it, but not all of it. You will feel the rest." He said no more than that.

"All right," said Wordsmith at last.

In the twilight, the small animals came first. Foxes, squirrels—together—and rabbits, badgers . . . *were those wolves?* They all came quietly to Covenant, making only snuffling noises. They settled at his feet and on each side of him, nosing his hands for a few moments before settling down watchfully. The drift of animals deepened, and soon the beggar was nearly covered in a fur blanket that had a life of its own. Their small black eyes watched Wordsmith—not fearfully, or with won-

der, but with interest and, perhaps, amusement.

"You see?" asked Covenant. "The animals are not a danger, if you know how to call their names. You have seen. Now you shall feel."

Complete darkness fell, and Wordsmith tuned his senses to the shadows. Even so, he did not see the beasts approaching, and the first he knew of them was the rasp of their claws in his ears and the blast of their breath in his face. He did not—dared not—move. A giant warmth bumped him from one side; a matching bulk pressed against him on the other side and poured its heat into his needy body. A host of smaller, squeaking animals filled in the gaps before him and behind him.

Still trying not to move, Wordsmith fell asleep. He dreamed of bears and lions, but only rabbits and squirrels were left when he awakened. Many pawprints—both great and small—had been scampered in the earth. A blend of heavy, warm scents lingered in the air, and he traced his fingers across the enormous indentations in the soft ground beside him.

Neither man spoke until the road was once more under their feet. Wordsmith did not know what to say; Covenant needed nothing to say.

Wordsmith was never sure what kind of great animals had flanked him as he slept. He chose not to ask the beggar, lest he tell him not only what kind of animals but their very names as well. Even without that knowledge, the road gradually changed from a dusty ordeal into an unwinding revelation of the work and delights of the Elder God. And when they drew near to Glory, Wordsmith's world held more beauty than when they had left the village.

Only one sight arose which threatened to sap the joy from Wordsmith's revelations. From one point on the road, they could just see the edge of the village of the lepers. Covenant gazed upon it, but made no comment and did not move to alter his path toward the distant walls.

"This place is a misery," said Wordsmith.

"There is much misery here," answered Covenant. "I will send someone to ease their pain when the time is come."

"Is not this place ripe for a miracle? This, of all places?"

"No. There is suffering here, but there is no hope. Where there is no hope, there can be no miracle."

"There is a time for everything."

"That is a true saying, but you speak it lightly. Do you think the Elder God can look upon any place of suffering without sorrow?"

Wordsmith did not reply, and they moved on.

Later that afternoon, Covenant said, "We are nearly there."

Wordsmith had not, for the last few hours, even been thinking about Glory. His enthusiasm had vanished, but he answered, "Yes, I remember the road." He recalled the town clearly but with little warmth. He wondered what lay ahead for him now.

Even though Glory sat on a hill, travelers from the south came upon it suddenly. Even to those who lived there, it was always a surprise for the eyes. Covenant and Wordsmith turned the last bend in the road.

"Behold Glory, the center of all the earth," declared Wordsmith flatly.

"It is, even more than you can possibly imagine," answered Covenant.

From a distance, Glory seemed marvelous indeed. The high walls gleamed in the sunshine, and the roads led straight and immaculate through the many gates guarded by the massive white towers. The beginning of the maze of streets was just visible, masking the hills and springs, peaks and pools that Wordsmith knew lay within the walls. Glory was etched clearly in his mind. He knew the quiet areas where the houses stood grandly, far apart and almost isolated on broad streets, and the other parts where old crumbling buildings shouldered each other for air along tiny crooked passageways.

Deeper in, on its own triumphant hill, alone in its splendor, stood the palace of the Hermit King. Before and below the palace lay the Standing Stone, the Pool of Wealth, and the great amphitheater in the midst of the wonders where the Hermit King, upon rare occasion, addressed the inhabitants of Glory. Even though the palace lay within the walls, it was silent, still, and almost remote. Beyond the palace, beyond the walls and nestled in the hazy distance, more hills swept up to the foot of the Lonely Mountain—unclimbed and unclimbable, unknown and unknowable, shrouded in fog and wreathed in mist.

Covenant and Wordsmith continued to gaze at Glory. The donkey drifted aside and began to graze in the grass, being little impressed by the beauty of stones arranged by humans.

"You look as though you had never seen Glory before," said Wordsmith.

"I have seen it many times," the beggar replied. "I saw it before it was built—and I shall one day see it leveled." His eyes were moist, as he stood with folded arms. "I weep for Glory," he said, "and someday you will understand my tears."

"I understand the pain of illusions shattered," replied Wordsmith. "You cannot see the cracks and the corruption from this distance."

The beggar nodded. "Most who come here prefer not to notice. But for those who reject reality, the illusion is all they have, even if it exceeds the reality of the town. The eye will see what it believes it should see. But to me it is like seeing a living ghost, a ghost that does not yet know it is only a shadow. Once there was healing here. Now even the healing has died."

Wordsmith's eyes, gazing at the palace, betrayed his thoughts to his companion. Or perhaps he already knew them.

"Do you believe there will be an end to kings?" Covenant asked.

Wordsmith shrugged eloquently. "The king is old and heirless. Who will come after him?"

"Many wait in the shadows of the throne."

"Why should anyone want to be king? His men ensure the peace, but he does little besides. He is seldom seen and less frequently heard. He leaves us alone and is left alone. There is no circle of power in that throne, no tribute, no honor."

"Perhaps not to your mind. But is that the fault of this king, or the kings that have come and gone, or those who pretend to kneel before them? People are foolish, and will choose for themselves a king, even though they neither want nor intend to obey him."

The sun began to set behind them as they walked the last few miles into Glory, trailing the donkey behind them. The gates stood open, but attended. The guards did not stir at the travelers' approach; they were there to guard against wild animals, and at dusk they would close the gates behind them.

Covenant, Wordsmith, and Kingsburro walked directly beneath the archway into Glory. The town spread out before them in every direction. Wordsmith did not know whether to be elated or grieved. Glory held many memories for him; not all of them had been pleasant ones.

They walked a few hundred yards along the great broad street, and then Covenant stopped before a shop that displayed all manner of goods from the corners of the land. The curious, the rare, the unusual, the unobtainable were here. The shop was not large but, like many other shops, there were tiny rooms built above for living.

A peculiar carved sign was fastened over the door.

"Whose mark is that?" asked Wordsmith. "I have not seen it before."

"It is mine," answered Covenant, "fashioned with my own hands and hung here at my direction. This is the house of Candle," he continued. "It is our destination, for now."

There came a shout from within the shop. A few men and women came outside to meet them, eager to see Covenant but uncertain of the words to say.

Wordsmith saw a young man with an infant cradled in his arms; scars on his face were only partially hidden by a great billow of hair and the beginnings of a beard. A man and woman held hands, while an older woman hovered nearby.

Covenant introduced Wordsmith to them all. "Lionheart, with Woodswaif. Candle and Moonflower. Trueteller. This is Wordsmith. He too shall be one of us."

They greeted Wordsmith courteously, but their eyes returned again quickly to the beggar, showing both anxiety and awe, seeking more words from him.

"We came," said Candle.

"We waited," added Moonflower.

"We are here," announced Trueteller.

"And what shall we do now?" asked Lionheart.

"We should eat," said Covenant calmly. "Are we in time for the meal?"

They were. Trueteller, seeing her old friend the donkey, led him away behind the shop to the tiny stable where Roadreeler already dozed.

Covenant did not join in their conversation as they ate, and after the meal he disappointed them as well. "I will return by morning," he said. "Wait for me here, all of you." Then he was gone, absorbed into the river of people flowing through the streets.

Lionheart eventually broke the awkward silence, as Woodswaif lay gurgling and content at his feet. "We have been living in the rooms above Candle's shop," he said to Wordsmith. "We have prepared a bed for you as well."

"Thank you. Will Covenant sleep here as well?" asked Wordsmith.

"I do not know where he will sleep," said Candle.

"Or even if he does," added Moonflower. "He is a man of many strange powers."

"Who *is* he?" asked Lionheart.

Shyly, they began to tell each other their stories before the kitchen fire, with the absent Covenant present in the midst of all their words. Shyness thawed in the warmth of strange things revealed, and laughter came. After the laughter came yawning and sleep, and then puzzled peace reigned in the house of Candle.

Only Trueteller was still awake when the beggar returned. "Covenant?" she asked, trying unsuccessfully to sleep in the massive wooden chair. "This is very crowded and uncomfortable. How many more do you intend to gather under your wings?"

"I will multiply this company many times. But I also assure you they will not have to squeeze into this house."

"Then where? There is no place in Glory to hold a multitude all at once."

Covenant nodded, smiling. "Then we must build one."

SEVEN

This
Shall Be
My House

T HE NEXT AFTERNOON, COVENANT GATHERED THE COM-
pany of those he had called, saying, "The time has come to
build my house." At Covenant's bidding, Candle shuttered the
shop and they all trailed after him into Glory.

Trueteller carried Woodswaif, but only because she actually
had hips, and Lionheart was far too lean and bony to offer a
comfortable perch for the baby. Nevertheless, his eyes rarely
left her for long.

They left the streets of shops behind them and slowly
passed from prosperity into poverty, winding their way deeper into parts of Glory neither Wordsmith nor Candle recognized. The streets narrowed and filled with old clutter and
shadows. Rats (or something else small and ferocious) scuttled
in the gutters. The walkers drew close to one another, and

closest of all to Covenant, though they saw few people. Many of the buildings had fallen from neglect or from the shaking and sinking of the ground, and they had been ransacked for stone and brick and wood. Those buildings which had not altogether crumbled were too quiet, conveying only hopelessness.

Covenant halted them all before one of the grandest ruins of all.

From the outside, it looked like the other dusty stone shells, stained with age and marked with neglect. There were no doors or windows left intact. Inside they saw nothing but rubble. How the walls continued to stand was a mystery; though the stones were thick and solid, and their mortar still held firmly, there were only a few cracked beams left to brace them.

The small company mounted the ruined steps and entered the gaping doorway—Covenant boldly, the rest with caution. They stood in vacancy and watched the walls crumble.

"You shall live here?" queried Wordsmith. His whispered words echoed from one bare stone wall to another.

"We all shall!" claimed Covenant, his words waking brighter echoes.

"This is only a shell from which the life has flown," said Trueteller.

"Then life has come to it again," answered Covenant.

"What was this place?" asked Lionheart.

"At an ancient time," Covenant said, "it was a holy house to the Elder God. But he was neglected, and then forgotten. This building has met a similar fate."

"And what shall we do with it?" asked Trueteller.

"We shall rebuild it with our own hands."

Covenant's words were met by shocked silence.

Wordsmith eventually found his voice. "There is little left here to build with but rubble. This is a ruin—all that can be carried away *has* been carried away."

"At least it is honest rubble. And it was once holy, hewn from the hearts of the mountains and carried here with the sacrifice of sweat."

"Why did they build here?"

Covenant ushered them to the edge of an old pit that sank down along one wall. "Many times before us there have been seekers here who followed rumors of treasure. Someone has dug by this wall, quitting when they reached the great rocks." They all could see the stones, too deep in the earth and far too vast to have been quarried and moved by human beings. "The seekers left, disappointed, not knowing they had found a great treasure indeed." Covenant, working his way deeper into the pit, knocked his fist against one of the massive stones. At his touch the rock boomed with a deep softness like a solid bronze bell, an element of the earth that lived but could not be moved.

"These stones," said Covenant when the echoes had faded, "are the last foundations of the City that once was here and shall be again. They are old—not carved by human hands—and part of the rock that has always been here. People guessed long ago—and dug and delved in the earth, and they were allowed to find this foundation—that they might build this temple. But in the ages that followed, they forgot what they had found. Or at least they ceased to understand it.

"Here, indeed, was the gate to the City," Covenant continued. "What was left behind has been removed, and what people built after their own fashion has fallen. We will build on this very place once more, and we will use the stones that are here."

"Covenant," said Lionheart, "this is far too grand for a handful of people."

"There will be others." Covenant smiled a smile that was born in a nest of good secrets.

"Others? Are they all following you to Glory?"

"No, there are others whom I have called, but not called to be here. Not yet. And there are many whom I shall call, either

to come or to go. And the more I call, the more room there shall be, until we have many, and all have enough."

"How are we to build such a place?" asked Candle. "We have no army at hand."

"We are enough," answered Covenant. "You need do only the tasks I give you—the jobs that lie to your hands to do. The other work will follow. There is a very old saying you all should ponder: *Complete the possible, and the impossible will follow.*"

Covenant would say nothing more. They followed him back to Candle's house for the night, where he left them again to carry out his lone and unspoken pursuits.

The next morning, they came together to the empty stone shell to begin their work. Covenant divided their labors immediately. Trueteller and Lionheart began to scrape the drifted earth from the tiles, with Woodswaif in a basket on the floor between them. Moonflower and Candle pulled weeds and shrubs that had grown unwanted but unheeded in the corners. And Wordsmith stacked splintered blocks and bricks collected from the floor.

Uncalled urchins gathered behind them and played in the far corners. There were mocking words, but Covenant did not chase them away.

None of the others aided Wordsmith with his appointed task, but it seemed to him that unseen helpers worked behind his back. The stack grew much faster than he had imagined possible. And the blocks, when he bent to inspect them again, no longer seemed so fragile. The corners were square and firm, where moments before there had been only weakness, air, and crumbling stone.

"Covenant?" he called, not sure how to express his wonder in words.

If he was listening, Covenant was not answering. He spoke to Lionheart and Trueteller instead. "Wash these slabs," Covenant suggested, "and see if more than the dirt comes away."

Their efforts were rewarded immediately. Where they

scrubbed, the pits and cracks seemed to come away with the sponge, leaving the floor whole and smooth and glossy once more.

"This is not an ordinary house," said Trueteller.

"It was never meant to be," answered Covenant.

Later that day, Candle beckoned the beggar aside. "Covenant, what of my shop? How can I serve both you and my customers? Is this to be my home as well, that I must work upon it?"

"Your business is doing well."

Candle was not sure whether Covenant had answered the question, asked one of his own, or merely made a statement.

"Yes," he agreed, to be safe.

"Then let it close for a few days. It will do even better as you learn from me, working with us. When you begin to see people as more than their money, people will come to you in loyalty and friendship as well as in trade. You shall keep your shop, and you will find that your shop will keep itself. You will indeed come to live here, for you will soon need all your present rooms above for your wares. There will be abundant room for the three of you here."

So the days passed, and the house continued to grow beneath their hands. Each had a task, though the task changed from day to day. They often worked in pairs and multiplied their labor, each one wondering if the other was doing extra work unseen. And each night, they slept the sleep of the righteously tired.

Yet there were parts of the house that Wordsmith never labored on, nor did anyone else that he could discern. The shell of a great five-sided tower still loomed above the back of the house, and it was being restored day by day with no obvious labor invested.

It was several days before Wordsmith realized that the tower was apparently being rebuilt from the top down. Wordsmith could see the work progressing far above him, yet there were no stairs or ladders within or without by which one could reach the work. Wordsmith could not have wandered there, even if he had so chosen.

He inquired about the tower's progress, but Covenant only said that the tower was not ready for others to see. "You shall be the first of the few who will see it, for it is being built for you. This tower reaches rare heights. It cannot be climbed by just any man."

There were many other things Wordsmith could not explain. He was never quite certain how the mammoth beams had been relaid for the floors, nor was he sure of their origin. The oak columns had simply been there on the ground one day; if anyone had actually lifted them into place, Wordsmith could not determine who it was.

A maze of walls had slowly grown within, and there seemed to be no end to all the rooms. Wordsmith was convinced they had not built so many as he now found. He had carved and carried doors himself, but not this many. The wood was darker and richer than he remembered, and he traced his fingers along the delicate embellishments and wondered how he had even imagined them, much less fashioned them himself.

Wordsmith toiled patiently, continuing to watch the tower. And at last, one afternoon, he saw that the stairs now reached the ground. He began to look for Covenant, but Covenant found him first.

"Your touch can be seen in any room of this house," said the beggar, "but not here. This tower has been made for you, and you alone. You could not work on it, for it is empowered beyond your capacity to gift it. It required the touch of my hands. You have labored enough on the house. Now I will give you a different task—more difficult, more demanding, less common. The steps to the tower, and the tower itself, are finished. Let us climb together."

Wordsmith paused with one foot on the lowest stair. "You have not asked me to sing since I returned to Glory," he stated.

"No, I have not."

"Shall I ever sing again at your command?"

"For now, it is my command that you refrain from singing. You thought your voice was your gift to the world, but it is not. You shall indeed sing again, but not alone. Now is not the time to sing; it is the time to see and think and do and write. I have other voices to sing for me—some which you have heard already, but do not know it. I have only you to write down the tales of the City."

They ascended the stairway.

Several hours later, Covenant descended alone. "You will not see Wordsmith again for several days," he told the others, "but all is well. He has begun a new task."

Before many more sunsets had passed, the others finished their tasks without him. Proud, hot, and happy, they stood in the cool street with Covenant and rested in their handiwork.

"Surely we did not do this work," said Trueteller. "It is far too fine for the fruit of hands such as mine." The others agreed. "Shall we repair the outside now?" she asked Covenant. "The inside is ready."

Covenant shook his head slowly. "No," he said, "we shall not. Whatever is outside now, let it be as man has left it. Whatever is inside, let it be beautiful and clean. This house shall become known for what is inside it, and not for its own appearance. Let the world that looks for outer beauty look elsewhere."

"What shall we do now?" asked Candle.

"Let us clean the last dirt away from beneath our feet," answered Covenant. "Then the need will present itself."

The others began to sweep the steps for a final time, while Candle moved to the far side of the door to stack extra lumber.

As she swept, Moonflower brushed away a drift of wood shavings and shrieked with surprise and delight. She scooped something from the dirt and yelled to Candle, "I found your pledge!"

He, moving aside an armload of wood, gave her a like

answer: "And I have found your half!"

They met on the stairs, sharing their speechlessness and matching their medallions.

Only after a moment did Moonflower say, "Candle? These cannot be ours! Look at our names here!"

"They are our names," he said, not comprehending.

"They are our *new* names," she replied simply.

And then Candle was struck by another realization. "And these are gold, not silver. What does this mean?"

"Do you remember when Covenant asked us what we had lost—and then he spoke those words about our pledges? He called them 'silver ornaments.' But how did he know they were silver? He never saw them."

They turned to Covenant, who stood amused at the bottom of the steps. "What is the meaning of this?" asked Candle, holding the divided gold medallion high.

"It is the answer to the question as to what we should do with this house," Covenant announced. "First we shall have a wedding."

EIGHT

The Book
& the
Burden

"YOU HAVE GIVEN ME WONDERFUL TALES TO WRITE," WORD-smith said, looking at the piles of parchment littered on the table. He stood and stretched, as if to throw off the weight of the night. "Now I must turn and tell them again. But who will listen?"

Covenant looked at him from his seat beside the table. "There are hungry hearts and willing ears here in Glory, as well as all the villages beyond. You cannot count them—but I can, and have. I know that they are waiting for your words, though some will not know what their hunger is until it has been satisfied."

"My heart is so full that it quivers," said Wordsmith.

"Are you weary?" Covenant asked.

"My eyes are tired, and my arms are tired, and my back is

tired, but my heart and mind will never tire of this."

"Is that all that pains you?"

"My stomach aches as well."

"You have missed many meals," remarked Covenant. "Your body needs food as much as your heart."

Wordsmith nodded, motioning to the five great windows in the room. "Day comes and goes, night follows and fades, but all time seems the same up here when I watch the fifth window. From the other windows I can indeed see in all directions, but I cannot see straight down. What is happening below?"

"My house is finished. You are sitting now at the crown of the beggar's haven."

"Have I been here that long?" asked Wordsmith, astonished.

"Long enough," said Covenant. "This house is ready, and a wedding feast is being prepared."

Wordsmith did not seem surprised.

"It is time," continued Covenant. "They have waited long for this and worked hard for it. Now that your present burst of imagination is spent, you should descend among us again. There is work to be done there as well."

"What manner of work?"

"If you are to preside over this house, you must see what it is you are steward of."

"Steward? *This* task is enough!"

"Does not the work with the pen delight you?"

"Yes," Wordsmith said, "more than I ever thought, though it exhausts me as well. Before, my singing was all that I ever wanted to do. But you know how I fared in Glory when I came to sing."

Covenant nodded.

Wordsmith turned toward the windows. "I was nothing here—a good but untrained voice among many both fine and trained. My betters wrestled with one another to gain a few coppers singing in the inns. What chance had I? I came, and I failed."

"But you did come, and you did dare your dream. Not many have done even that. Besides, not all failure is evil. One must test doors to see if they are unlatched. One must follow some paths to see if they lead anywhere at all. And your failure has honed you for the task I have set ahead of you. Only a man who has known the death of a dream will be strong enough to survive the days ahead."

"What do you mean?"

"I will tell you more at another time, when you have been made more ready."

"Must I be made and remade again? You seem to be always shaping me."

"It is not that I am making of you a different man. I am only remolding the man who was there from the beginning. You have been growing away from yourself all these years, and now it is time to grow back. You were born for these stories, and not for singing. You shall sing again, but not for the crowds, not for honor, not for Glory. You shall sing again, but for love and for love alone. Until then, you will have the stories that come to you here in the tower."

"The stories—" Wordsmith began. He paused, then began again in earnest. "In every story there is good against evil. But where does evil come from? I do not mean simply greed and selfishness and a bent to pleasure, or stupidity and fear and sloth. I can find those in my own heart without any help. But where does the higher evil come from? Why do we make slaves of each other, and agree together in cold blood to destroy and ravage? Why are children cruel and women cold? Why do our hopes fail us? Why does the world grow darker every year?"

"You have seen the story of the City," replied the beggar, "and written it down. Do you recall the one who played strange music in the wilderness and drew people away from the One who had made them? That one is still alive; I know him by one name—Twister—though he is known by many

79

names. His only desire is to destroy, and to rule over that destruction. So far, he has been prevented." Covenant smiled an odd smile, as though he were thinking of other times and other places far away in distance and remote in time. "He is old—older than you can imagine. In all those ages he has become very clever, but he has not become wise. You should look to him for the root of all evil."

"Has he put blackness in the hearts of all everywhere?"

"He planted those dark seeds in everyone whom he lured away from the safety of the City. He has done the same with everyone born into this world since."

"But has he so corrupted you?" asked Wordsmith.

"No." Covenant smiled again. "He does not have that power."

"But why should Twister do all these things?"

"Why should he not? There is none to stop him but the Elder God. It is Twister's chosen nature to sow evil. After all, it was Twister who opened the fateful path into the wilderness, with full knowledge of what could follow."

"So he is my enemy as well as yours."

"Yes, but he is far too strong for you. Do not confront him."

"Is he too strong for any of us?"

"He is stronger than any person who now walks this earth."

"Is he stronger even than you?"

"You will think so, when the time comes."

"But who shall conquer him? When will the Elder God cry halt to this evil?"

"You shall have to wait for the voiceless child. But do not be dismayed at anything that comes before; Twister will indeed win many battles—but he cannot win the final war."

"Covenant," said Wordsmith, after a moment's reflection, "I have asked you many questions this morning. Yet I am still confused, for you have answered none of them directly."

"Do my answers seem more like deeper riddles?" he asked as he stood and beckoned Wordsmith down the winding stairs.

"They *are* answers, but you are unable to hear them. Remember that *I* am your answer, in and of myself. I need not answer any of your questions, but I have chosen to do so. And now I have given you all the answers that will fit in your mind. Come and eat, and then you and I will survey this house."

They went immediately. At the end of two hours, Wordsmith's legs were weary, and he sat heavily on a chair in one of the backstairs rooms. Covenant stood lightly beside him, untired by the many stairs they had climbed and the rooms and passages they had explored.

"I do not understand where all this splendor came from," said Wordsmith.

"You all built it with your own hands."

Wordsmith shook his head. "Not this. This is grand beyond our imagining, exquisite beyond our skills. There is nothing lacking."

"Everything that is needful is here," said Covenant. "Tables, chairs, beds, clothing, dishes, pots . . ."

"I do not know where you brought it all from," said Wordsmith.

"I will someday soon show you more of this house's deeper secrets."

He handed Wordsmith an ornate key on a chain. "There is only one key," he said, "for there is only one lock in this house."

"The door to the street?"

"That door has no lock, for it is open to all at all times."

"Do you not fear thieves?"

"A thief is only a threat if your treasures can be stolen," he replied. "The lock is on the single door you have not yet seen—the door which leads to the path which leads to the City."

"The pathway is *here?*"

"Yes, as I promised."

"What is it like?" Wordsmith asked quietly.

"You shall see for yourself, directly. Come. We have one last

adventure this day. The path inward to the City is not difficult; the difficult part is coming back. I will give you that
choice. But I warn you: No matter whether you say yes or no
to my offer before the City, you will never be the same again."

"Will it be a good change?"

"One leads to the best of all possible changes—and the other
leads to something even better."

"Then I am not afraid."

Covenant led Wordsmith down the hall to the final door.

NINE

Proven
Metal

T HAT EVENING WORDSMITH ATE SILENTLY AT THE TABLE, his mind far away in worlds no one else could yet imagine.

"Wordsmith?" asked Trueteller. "Are you all right?"

"I don't know," he answered abstractedly. "This has not been an ordinary day."

"What day of ours has been ordinary since the beggar came to us?"

"If I could put into words what I have seen today, you would not believe me."

"I would believe almost anything," she replied. "Remember, I have seen the once-dead burst forth from the grave."

Covenant stepped into the room, looking for them. "Come," he said, "There are proclamations to be made in this place."

Wordsmith and Trueteller followed him to the great hall

where Candle and Moonflower stood beaming at each other and waiting for the company to gather. Lamps and candles stood in every available space, and the house was awash with soft light in the dusk.

The newcomers took pillowed chairs (where Lionheart already held Woodswaif), and Covenant moved to stand between Candle and Moonflower and in front of them all.

"First," he said, "I proclaim Wordsmith as the steward of this my house. I shall not always be here, and when I am away he will speak for me. I have shown him the ways of this house and the wisdom hidden in it, and each day he gains more. He—and under him you all—shall administer comfort, serve food, and offer shelter to any who have need of it."

They applauded Wordsmith, though he did not know how to accept their praise for something he had only begun to do. To his relief, they soon came to the second proclamation.

In solemn joy they all watched as Moonflower and Candle matched the tokens once more. They spoke then the words of promise that would bind them to one another. Afterward, Covenant took the rendered metal pledges from their hands and held them high in his right fist and invoked the name of the Elder God. There was a flash of golden flame. When he drew down his hand and opened his fingers, his palm held two complete medallions on gold chains. "Place this one around her neck," Covenant directed Candle. "And place this one around his," he told Moonflower. When the two performed their actions, he smiled at them and said, "Now you belong to each other."

After the ceremony, they all ate at their leisure, and laughed much, and cried some, and talked at length of the new futures that had been given to each one of them by the beggar. Woodswaif fell asleep on Lionheart's shoulder; he would not lay her down, and so he ate as best he could with only one hand.

Moonflower and Candle held each other close, and Moonflower fitted her face against her husband's neck. After a moment she pulled back and held up his medallion for him to see. "Look," she said, "There is a new marking on the back. Covenant's mark."

"I am no longer surprised by anything he does," murmured Candle, "but he has brought us nothing but good."

Later, Covenant led the pair upstairs to a set of rooms they had not seen before, where there were chairs and lamps and pillows and a curtained bed. And there Covenant left them to each other, while he returned to the feast below.

TEN

The Woes
of the
World

DRAWN BY A MISERY EVEN GREATER THAN HIS OWN, A
hunchback staggered down the tangled back streets of Glory.
Every twitch of his muscles betrayed his pain. His face was an
uplifted agony, and all his bones were warped.

Yet where he stopped and touched the sufferers in the
shadows, their pain paled and healing came and lingered, and
the unseen weight on the hunchback's shoulders grew heavier. With each pause and each touch he groaned anew, but said
nothing else aloud.

The hunchback crept along the gutter and humped to a stop
in front of one of the undistinguished structures in the dry
backwaters of the human wash. The house was old and tall
and once grand. Now it was tattered on the outside, though
still kept clean.

A beggar sat on the step of the house and eyed the hunchback. "I have been waiting for you," said the beggar. "I could feel you drawing near."

"I have come to take away your pain," said the hunchback.

"Then you have come in vain," answered Covenant. "Indeed, you carry the woes of the world, but you cannot carry mine. And now your strength is gone. You must rest here in this house if you hope to take another step in this life."

Weary and surprised by his own rising weakness, the hunchback nodded and began to obey the beggar's summons. But he could walk no farther, and he collapsed in a twisted ruin on the street. Men came at the beggar's call to carry the fallen one inside.

Later, the hunchback drifted up through clouds of horrid encoiling dreams to find himself in bed. The bedroom was not splendid or elaborate, but it was clean and sweet smelling. A thick woolen blanket covered him, and he had not at first the strength to pull it back. He turned his head slowly and saw the beggar sitting patiently in the corner.

"Welcome to my house," said the beggar. "My name is Covenant."

"And my name is best forgotten," croaked the hunchback, turning his face toward the wall.

"You may let it fade, if it pleases you. I will not call you by the name with which you were born."

"Few know that name."

"Few do," Covenant agreed.

"That name is a curse. Do not shame me with it again. I have no name. I need no name. I am nameless."

"You are not nameless. Every being has a name, whether it knows it or not."

Silence ruled the room until the hunchback murmured his first question. "What manner of house is this?"

"This is an ancient and honorable house," said Covenant. "It is only from the outside that it seems ancient and dishonorable."

The hunchback flinched at the word *dishonorable*, but Covenant continued without pausing. "I know you, I know your gift, and I know as well what goads you on."

"You are a healer too," whispered the hunchback, struggling to push back the blanket and sit up. "I can feel it."

"We heal for different reasons, perhaps. A man can be motivated by more than compassion. You are a driven man," said Covenant. "I have need for you in my service. The weak and wounded come here daily and have need of help."

"I must stay, it seems," the hunchback answered, "unless you carry me back to the door. If I can help you, I will."

Covenant nodded, content. He rose to leave, and then said, "Since you acknowledge no particular name, I shall give you a new one: Woebearer. You have been Woebearer for many; I shall do the same for you, when you have confessed the second half of the great secret. You have discovered that you may bear the sorrows of another, but you have not yet discovered that you cannot bear your own."

Covenant met Wordsmith outside the door, who pulled him aside. "This man does not belong here. He is ignorant of you and does no work in your name."

"He does all his work in my name," rejoined Covenant, "though neither he nor you realize it. Let him remain and let him heal, that he may heal again. He hurts no one and helps all. He will learn the needful lessons when his time is come."

"Who is he?" pressed Wordsmith. "How is he doing this? What warps him so?"

"He has done a foolish evil in his life and caused much suffering under another name. He thinks in vain that if he wrests enough suffering from the backs of others and carries it himself, he will be set free from the distress of his own guilt. But those are chains he cannot break and can never shed unaided, no matter the strength in his hands. Remember the rule of this house," Covenant added. "It does not matter what he has done. It matters what he will be."

"And what will he be?"

"You shall see soon enough."

The beggar's words came true with the dawn. A renewed Woebearer bounded downstairs to Covenant's table, clutched the beggar's shoulder, and cried, "Look! Last night, while I slept . . ."

Wordsmith and the others at table stared at the transformation. The work of the night was plain: the intolerable weight on the man's shoulders had been lifted. His back was almost straight, and his pain had receded. His face had straightened now, though still grooved with the tracks of old tears, and some of his bones had unbowed.

He was the same man, but he was not the same man.

Woebearer continued his incredible tale. "Last night, for the first time in many years, I had no dreams!"

"You mean you had no nightmares," countered Covenant calmly.

"They are all the same to me."

"You will soon remember the difference," promised Covenant.

"How did this happen? Is this a magic house?"

Wordsmith answered first. "This is indeed a magic house. I am no longer startled by any good thing that happens here."

"Was this *your* doing?" Woebearer asked Covenant directly.

"Yes," Covenant said. "You would have died had your burdens not been lifted from you. You have worn your body to the very bone by following the trail of others' miseries. The shadow of death hovered over you even as you paused at this door."

"But now I am not dying!"

"You are still dying, but much more slowly now. Your death has only been delayed. I will not take your gift from you, even though I believe it is more your burden than your blessing. But you will not survive yourself on your mission unless you sleep here each night and eat the food that is served at my table."

"I cannot leave?"

"You may leave any time you like," said Covenant, nodding to the streets. "If you are a prisoner here, you are a prisoner of your own need to be needed. Here, and here alone, will you find untroubled sleep and the nightly lifting of your burdens. If you leave this house to wander again you will surely die, and you will suffer evil dreams until you do."

The hunchback pondered. "If," he said, "if I go and draw another load of misery, would I be healed again tonight?"

"You may."

"Then I must go and see!" Woebearer leaped up and plunged out the door into the streets again.

"Will he be back?" asked Wordsmith in the sudden hush.

"He will be back," answered Covenant. "He believes he has found paradise here. He is right, but for all the wrong reasons."

ELEVEN

The Bright Flower

SHE WAS BEAUTIFUL AND HAD LONG BEEN DESIRED ABOVE all other women in Glory. Her likeness bloomed in drawings hung on a thousand walls, and her image hovered in the hearts of many men.

Her name was Beauty, and word of her footsteps in the streets swept on before her, drawing watchers from all manner of people. Among those who came to see were Covenant and Woebearer.

Covenant turned his face toward hers, and she saw it first among all the crowd. It was not a remarkable visage, but it drew her. And then she saw the contorted face and body of Woebearer, and in fascination she continued to stare. Covenant was not waving or cheering or trying to attract her attention. He was merely gazing at her and smiling. But his eyes compelled her to return his gaze.

She should know him, she thought. He looked at her without appraising her—an incident that disturbed her at first. She could not readily break its power. For a moment, in all that crowd she could see only the two men.

"She too carries much pain," said Woebearer, "but it is sorrow and loneliness, not suffering."

"There is more to come," answered Covenant. "She has not yet been abandoned."

Then there appeared another face to draw her eye away: a handsome gentleman, standing at ease across the street from Covenant and Woebearer.

"We are not alone," said Covenant. "He, too, has come to behold this Beauty."

Beauty passed on, and the crowd melted away, leaving only the three men on the street.

"You know this man?" asked Woebearer.

"He is my enemy," replied Covenant, "and therefore yours as well. In everything I do, he opposes me. And in everything he does, I oppose him. We have met before. We shall meet again many times."

"Soon?" Woebearer wondered. "Now?"

"Later. Much later. You see, his plan is to rule Glory. He must be content with that, for the way to the City is forever closed to him. He lived there, once, and was exiled to this land until the City reappears. And then he will be judged. Once he was the keeper of the door. It bitters him now, for there are marks on the door where we struggled, he and I. I cast him down and banished him from my house."

Woebearer pondered. "What is his name?"

"He has many. Some know him as Twister, others as Fame or Fortune, or Mesmer, Mummer—whatever suits his purpose. But you see, I know his true name."

The air chilled momentarily. Twister—or whoever was behind that name—turned suddenly and stalked off.

Later that same morning, Wordsmith pressed his way

through the crowd around Beauty and presented her with a book. "These words were written for you," he said. Beauty, who had received many such tributes, nevertheless thanked him graciously and glanced politely at the first few pages. When he had gone, she gave the book to one of her attendants, and promptly eased the memories of all four men from her mind.

None of the four men forgot her.

— TWELVE —

The Wondrous Wine

THE FALL DEEPENS," SAID COVENANT, LOOKING OUT THE door past the streets of Glory, "and I have a promise to keep."

"To my people?" Wordsmith stood near the fire.

"To your people. The drought has nearly slain them, and when the snow comes, they will have no grain. And no hope for more." He gathered their cloaks from the peg by the mantel. "And now is the season before the snow. We will be in time if we go now."

The two left the warm house behind and turned from Glory over the falling leaves, the one walking slowly to keep pace with the other's uneven steps.

"We came to Glory by the short and lonely way, where few tread. We shall return to your village by the long and winding way, where people live. When we journeyed before, we talked much and kept our own counsel. Now we have other tasks to do, other reasons to be on the road."

"Will I always walk like this?" asked Wordsmith wistfully, after a few halting miles.

"Some day you shall run again, like these leaves before the wind. I know my kindness bewilders you, but I ask you to be content and patient. Some day you will understand. You have accomplished much this summer," he added.

"And I have learned more."

"That is why you have accomplished much."

When the day's light failed them at last, they sheltered in a town that had little food to spare.

"The drought," the innkeeper explained. "It has destroyed us. There is no water in the river that flows from the mountains. Our grain and fruit wither in the fields. Nor is there any grain from the west this year. The Elder God has failed us. He no longer hears our prayers."

"Do you still have one who intercedes at his altar? I saw the stone as we entered the town."

"Yes. The head man of the village prays there daily. He is the one who has kept our faith alive."

"In the morning, as soon as there is enough light to tell one face from another, you should find him and bring him to meet us at the altar. And bring the people of the village as well." Leaving the puzzled innkeeper in their wake, Wordsmith and the beggar went gratefully to bed.

And in the morning, before the dawn, they rose and walked slowly out of doors to the altar. The innkeeper joined them within a few minutes, drawing behind him an old man still banishing sleep from his eyes. "I had a dream," he was saying, "a dream of harvest and good fruits on the edge of winter. There was a beggar carrying grain, and a cripple laden with ripe fruit. They came to our village—"

He saw the travelers, and stopped and stared.

The beggar spoke first. "Behold, old man of durable faith.

Your daydream stands before you. Are our images fresh in your mind? Then hear us, for we come in the name of the Elder God."

The old man spread wide his arms. "We are at your mercy. And at your service."

The beggar looked around at the growing crowd. "If you would see the end of this drought, then command each man in all the village to scour every house and bring me the grain— the whole grain, the kernel, everything that has not been ground between the stones. Put it here, before the altar." The old man moved, and ordered, and the two travelers had but to stand and watch the baskets and pots of grain grow at their feet. There was not much to be gathered.

"Is this all?" Wordsmith asked. "You may forfeit the blessing if you withhold any." The old man gazed into all the faces about him, questioning, until a woman flushed red and withdrew a tiny pouch from the pocket of her cloak. She tossed it on the pile, and the sad rebellion in her eyes declared it to be her all.

"Place it all in two sacks," the beggar ordered. And two sacks were filled, each one no more than a fair burden for a strong man. "You have fruit still?" he asked. "Enough for three days? Then keep it, and share it generously among yourselves. We shall take these sacks with us, and in three days your harvest will be upon you." He handed one sack to Wordsmith and led the way to the westward road. Despair came to roost in the village, but at the word of the old man no one stood in their way.

"Three days," he muttered to himself. "Three days. Grant us the strength for such a span of hours."

Out on the road, Wordsmith asked, "And what of their harvest? I do not understand. Is this all?"

"No," the beggar said, "it is not."

The day grew hot again, and Covenant and Wordsmith grew quickly tired with the burdens of grain on their back. The arrow-straight, shadeless road had driven thirst into their

throats, and they had long since shed their cloaks. The squat, shabby, stone-and-mud structure before them was neither pleasant nor inviting, but it was the only travelers' shelter they had seen for miles. A few old men and children panted in its shade, their faces and tongues as dusty as the weathered way.

"Have you any water here?" asked Covenant.

"We have waterskins and wooden barrels, jars and bottles to spare," said one of the men, "but we have no water. The long drought has left us nothing fit for the mouth of any living being, save the wine inside—and it is too dear to drink. We have only ancient mud, and our merchant has only aged wine."

"You are thirsty?" another man asked with a knowing smile.

"We are," replied Covenant. "Though possibly not so thirsty as you have been."

"Then I shall warn you that the keeper here is a very rude and greedy man. He will not even notice you unless he sees the gleam of your coppers."

"I have a few coppers in my bag," said Covenant. "And if there is no water, then we must drink the wine instead. He will not share?"

"He will only sell."

"Perhaps I can change his mind."

The two travelers entered, and the rest came after, hoping that inside was cooler than the shade, thinking that perhaps a wanderer would share what a merchant would not.

"Bring me a cup of your best!" commanded Covenant, rattling a few coins down the length of the first wooden table.

The merchant brought a bottle of wine and a cup, with many praises for its taste and clarity. "This is a truly wonderful wine!"

Covenant drank, and then put the cup down with a gesture of irritation. "Is this what passes for wine here?" he asked. "It tastes like water to me."

"Here—let me taste it," barked the merchant. He snatched the cup away and swallowed a mouthful. Surprised, he spat it out and poured another cup from the long bottle. It, too, was only water. "Take this away!" cried the merchant, as he disappeared into his cellar again.

"The boy will do it for you," called Covenant after the confounded man. He beckoned to one of the children in the doorway—a boy who looked to the beggar to be wise beyond his years. "Take this outside and dispose of it properly." The boy eagerly lifted the bottle off the table and lugged it outside. Covenant winked, and some of the others followed the boy, new smiles concealed under the dust of the day.

The merchant returned with more wine, uttering great apologies and greater promises.

Covenant tasted again, and his face filled with disappointment. "Take this, too, away." Covenant waved the second bottle outside with one hand and dazzled the merchant with the clink of coppers in his other.

"You test the next bottle, Wordsmith," said the beggar quietly.

It, too, was only water—as were the next ten bottles. They all had a chance to test the vintage. On the point of collapse, the merchant asked frantically of the heavens, "Is all my wine ruined?"

"It cannot be ruined," said Covenant, "if it is not wine." He stood up. "Keep the coppers. You have found us no wine, but you have, at length, quenched our thirst."

"But there is still one bottle . . ." his voice trailed off into uncertain silence.

"Here are more coppers," Covenant responded. "You shall keep this last bottle—whether of wine or of water—until I send for it. Keep it there upon the mantel where all can see and ask their questions, but keep it safe and unhandled."

"How will I know when you need it?" the confused merchant queried.

"I will send a boy for it, and he shall bear this token." Covenant plucked up the top coin on the pile of coppers and snapped it in two like a withered leaf. "He shall bear the other half of this coin." He tossed the broken copper to the dazed merchant, who could only stare wordlessly as they left.

Outside, Covenant remarked to Wordsmith, "That was truly a wonderful wine. See? No one is thirsty now."

THIRTEEN

Before Winter

WHEN THE TWO TRAVELERS CAME AT LAST TO WORD-smith's village, they found that hunger had settled there before them. The few people left behind came to meet them with smiles, fear, and many words—words of waiting, of drought, of hardship, of rejoicing.

"We ate the last food yesterday," they complained. "It was hard to await you. We feared the snow would come before you."

"You see that it has not, though clouds follow hard upon us. Have all waited?"

"No. There were four who left. But we did as you said, and we have purchased their land." The one who spoke showed him the deeds.

"You have done well." The beggar opened one of the sacks.

"And here is grain."

"You have brought us food! But how will it be enough? And for how long?"

"It is not to eat. Not now. You have believed that the hard part of your trial was to wait—but now I ask you to do a harder thing yet." He called the people to arrange themselves by families and come forward. To each person—child, woman and man—he gave a handful of grain. "Take this to your fields and scatter the grain. All of it. Spread it in equal measures upon the good soil and the sour, upon the untouched earth and the scorched. Do not withhold any of it, nor eat of it, nor bring a single seed back with you."

They went, all of them, save Wordsmith and the beggar. "I begin to see," said Wordsmith, "the depth of your ways. I shall write of this, too."

"You shall."

The two men stood, then, and silently watched the sowers.

When each family returned, the beggar asked them, "Have you obeyed my word? Have you scattered it all, without judging the ground?" They all answered him alike. And when they all were done and night was falling, he bade them build a fire in the square and sleep around it.

Rain came in the night, soft rain, falling only in the fields and coming not into the village. No lightning flickered in its midst. The sound of the waters was music to the withered land.

And in the morning the people beheld great waves of grain about them, and they ran rejoicing into the golden depths. The beggar followed and moved among them, taking each one aside and reminding them that the land was now theirs in everlasting trust, and that none should take it away save the Elder God. And he bade them remember how it was that the land had first been given and then taken from those who had not devoted the firstfruits.

He came to one man who stood bewildered in his field. The

grain had grown there, but not tall, and there were many patches of bare ground. The man turned his troubled face to the beggar, who watched him with sad eyes.

"Your grain would have been like the others had you obeyed me. But you held back the grain, you or your family."

The man nodded mutely.

"Small is the price of your lesson. You will have enough here for your needs. But not until the next harvest will you have any to spare or sell."

He gathered the people together and brought them back to the square. "You have learned the way of the covenant. You have taken humility upon your shoulders. You have obeyed, and I have spared your fields and homes and goods. I made the proud and greedy and unyielding your benefactors, for now you own what they labored for. But you, too, will be unable to hold it if you neglect the old laws and forget the Elder God.

"Your faith has been rewarded. But there are others in the land this night who have given their faith and have not their answer. Not one of you has asked me where this grain came from. It was a gift from others—given to you in my name, at my command. They have blessed you, and it is time that you bless them. Take buckets, all of you, and pots and pails and wineskins. Fill them here at the well and follow me to the river."

They assembled again at the riverbed, still dry now where once rainbows had rippled in running waters.

Wordsmith asked Covenant, "Why is there water in the fields, and not here?"

"It is not here because it all fell in the fields," he answered.

Then the beggar beckoned the man whose faith had wavered as he sowed. "Pour your bucket into the river, and then return for more. And the rest of you after him."

Then he sat beside Wordsmith on the riverbank and watched the procession. Many looked in wonder at the beggar, and one called out, "How can we fill a riverbed from a well?

It seems to me folly!"

The beggar roused and said, "Nevertheless, it is the folly I have given you to do. I have rescued you twice. Do not doubt me for a third time." And he turned again to watch the dry river. His eyes noticed too the two graves lying beneath the thirsty willows.

At the end of an hour, he bade them stop. "Look downstream. Behold the river, and see the fruit of your obedience." They looked, and they saw deep waters swelling from the mud and flowing eastward away. "You may stop now, for you have repaid the blessing. You should harvest your fields at once, for the snows are not far behind me.

"And do this: Keep one bucket full of this water, and place it on the altar of the Elder God. There the sun will not dry it, nor will the birds come and drink of it. When your harvest is nearing an end, and you have need of more water than your well gives you, take that water and pour it into the river. It is my gift to you. But do not use it until your wells are low and you have need of much water for the harvest. Then this river which is the life of your grain will flow for you again. Go. Your fields are calling."

Covenant watched them go, and then turned to Wordsmith. "This gentle flood will reach the other village this night. There it will swirl through thirsty fields, reviving, ripening."

"You need say nothing more," said Wordsmith. "The river speaks for you."

FOURTEEN

A
Price
of Tears

STALLS OF MERCHANDISE LITTERED THE WINDING STREETS of Glory—women and men selling cloth, fruit, meat, and jewelry, competing for the attention of the hordes. Unlike the other merchants, who shouted the praises of their goods and jostled for attention, Wordsmith stood patiently as all of Glory streamed by. In and atop a box on a wooden table before him were a handful of books, no two the same. Some were small, some large, some thick, and some thin.

Few browsed, but one man lingered and looked. "This is a handsome book," he said at last, pointing to the most ornate of all Wordsmith's wares. "How many coins will it cost me?"

"Coins cannot buy it, nor will I give it away," answered Wordsmith. "It was written with weeping, and I paid a price of tears for every word. And as I cannot sell it for less than it cost me, the price to you is also a price of tears."

"What foolishness is this? Do you take me for one who mourns at will, or for a fee? This whole world is not worth a tear!"

"This whole world is worth much more than a tear—it is worth blood. But you are not ready to understand that either. Yet this book is to be yours someday; it was written for you." Wordsmith opened the book and pointed to the inscription inside.

"It has my name in it!" exploded the man. "What sort of sorcerer are you?"

"I did not know of myself that your name was Ellard, though I myself wrote it there. It was told to me by someone who does know. You see, some books are written for the many, some for the few, and a handful for one reader alone. This book was written for you—but you may not claim it until the full price has been paid."

The man stood bewildered as Wordsmith continued. "You have many other books already."

"Many—as some count many," the man countered. "Perhaps not so many as I would count them. But what I have are exceedingly fine and difficult to come by. All have been made with care. They are works of love that bring delight at every viewing."

"But you speak only of the bodies of books. What of their souls? What of the truths they contain?"

"Some of the books must contain great wisdom indeed," the man said, "for the words are so high and flowing that I scarcely understand what they could mean."

"Then they probably are not true. The truth is easy to see, and it is not hard to understand, though it is often very hard to accept." Wordsmith pointed again to the book in his hand. "But even so, these words would be utter foolishness if you were to read them now, for you would not yet understand why they must be written, or why anyone would need with all their aching heart to read them." Wordsmith set the book down on the table, along with the others. "Go away for now. But come back to me, without fail, when you have learned to grieve. When your heart has been broken, and your hopes are gone, you will be ready. Then and only then shall you have this book."

Ellard went away seething, yet wondering greatly at the ways of the man with the cryptic sayings.

Wordsmith continued to display his books to the unheeding crowd until the hot sun thinned the streets of people.

That same night, Wordsmith was in the highest room in Covenant's house when the earth trembled for a score of heartbeats. Throughout Glory, dishes toppled and walls warped. In one part of the city, a house fell in upon itself and perished in flames sparked by the fire on the hearth.

Wordsmith watched from the window in his tower study and descended the long stairs seeking Covenant's face. "Is this the disaster you have spoken of?" he asked urgently.

"It is," answered Covenant. "Come, we have a visit to make. Woebearer has already gone where he is needed; call Candle and ask him to come with us."

Together the three traversed the streets of Glory, winding their way toward the scene of destruction. They came to the place where the restless earth had brought the great house to its ruin.

"This is where Ellard lives," said Covenant, as the three mingled with the gathering crowd.

"Until this evening he did," added Wordsmith. "No one can live here now."

One man knelt close before the ruins, gazing in anguish at the rubble, blood staining his hands and face. Two children lay crumpled in the dirt at his feet. The buzzing crowds held back, but Wordsmith and Covenant approached and knelt beside Ellard.

"Buildings fall," murmured Covenant, "and belongings

burn. It is not a new thing, and neither is death. Why did you rescue the children and not your books?"

"I do not know," replied Ellard, staring into the final flames with hollow eyes. "They were trapped beneath the bricks. There was no time left before the fire began to spread. Are they dead?"

"No, but they will die if they are not cared for."

"Who are they?" asked Wordsmith.

"I do not know their names," admitted Ellard. "Two urchin brothers who lived in the shadows behind the house. Sometimes I gave them scraps from my table."

"They have no one, then?" inquired Wordsmith. "Even though they have been battered by the stones and scorched by the flames?"

Ellard shook his head slowly, unaware that Covenant was doing the same.

"You pulled them from the rubble," said Covenant, "and now they are yours. I will give you all food and a place to sleep in my house, but you must care for them yourself."

Wordsmith glanced curiously at Covenant, knowing that a full cure was less than a word away. He began to speak, when Covenant motioned silence with a wave of his hand.

Without further conversation, the two men pulled unburned boards from the wreckage and eased the brothers' prostrate forms onto them. With Wordsmith in front and Covenant trailing, they carried the first boy away. Ellard, still numb with shock, grasped one end of the board and helped Candle bear the second child away.

Woebearer returned after them from the streets, feeling the presence of pain in the house. He found Covenant and pressed him for an explanation. "You have never allowed suffering in this house! Where are they? I must see them at once."

Covenant gripped the hunchback's shoulder and sat him down firmly on the stairs. "Woebearer, my friend, I have given you much and restored your strength nightly. In return I have

asked little of you. Now I ask of you a hard thing, a desperately hard thing. Do not heal the boys. Do not go near them, do not speak to them, do not let their suffering summon you to their side. They are Ellard's burden, and not yours. It is his task to apply herbs and wrappings and soothing words. This is a load you may not yet carry."

Woebearer began to protest, but Covenant cut him short. "Each night you return smiling and suffering to my house; each morning you rise refreshed and unburdened to plunge into the limitless pool of pain called Glory. But have you truly healed? Have you erased the agony and sent it away into the outer darkness forever? No. You have not. You have merely shifted the pain from the shoulders of the sufferers to your own. The mere transfer is noble, but falls far short of destruction and obliteration.

"It is an ugly law: there is no healing without suffering. By the wounds of another we are healed; only if someone suffers for us can we find healing. Pain cannot be undone. It may only be carried by someone else, until it is all destroyed by the one who made possible the pain.

"I heal the outside of you—nightly, and temporarily. When I heal the inside of you, it will be forever. But he who truly heals must drink the bitter brew that tastes like blood and death.

"I have given you this command," Covenant said, "and there is nothing else to say for now. If I thought you would understand the reasons I forbid you, I would tell you plainly. You have more power than you have wisdom. You see suffering as only an evil snake to be snuffed out wherever it is seen. It is a snake and it *is* evil, but it may sometimes be put to good use."

FIFTEEN

Words for the Wounded

ELLARD CAME INTO THE ROOM WHERE WORDSMITH WAS writing. The writer looked up and asked, "How are they?"

"They are not dying," Ellard said. "If their wounds were mortal, they would be dead by now."

"This is the third day."

Ellard nodded. "And I have been at their side for all of them. Mercifully, they have mostly slept and moaned, and not wakened often to the fullness of their agony."

"And your own wound?"

Ellard absently touched the small bandage on his head. "It is nothing."

"It is more than you think. It is the first blood you have shed for the world. Much has changed since first we met in the street," observed Wordsmith. "You have lost your old loves and gained new ones."

"I did not know the children, for I did not care for them. But by caring for them, I have come to know them. In knowing them, I find that I am beginning to love them. It is a strange thing."

"You should love them," said a new voice, "for they have cost you dearly." Neither man had seen Covenant enter the room, holding a bag at his side.

"You were not a fool to rescue them," he added quietly. "You would be a fool if, having rescued them at the price of your old treasure, you now turned away from them. If you had tried to save your collected wealth instead of the boys, you would have lost everything: all the books, your house, and your own life as well. Instead, you gave mercy. You shall receive mercy in return."

"Will they live?"

"They will live, and they will need you."

"How can I help? I am no healer."

"You can bring them stories to ease their agony and mend their minds."

"They cannot read."

"True, but they can listen. And to bring them that solace you will need the help of some old friends."

"Old friends?" he questioned. "I have none. All my companions perished with my house."

"Perhaps," said Covenant, "and perhaps not." He reached into the bag at his side and carefully stacked the corpses of a dozen scarred books on the table.

Holding his breath, Ellard took the uppermost volume and cradled it gently in his hand. The binding was torn where bricks had scored it, blackened where flames had scorched it, and swollen where water had dripped upon it. The papers were loose and would ever smell of mold and damp and fire. But all the pages were there.

The others were in similar condition—ruined but not destroyed.

"There are other uses for books than to please eyes and fingers and intellect," said Covenant. "You shall discover another one now. Take this book and read it to the boys. They will wake soon, but they cannot rise; they will need kind words of many kinds. This is a lesson for you: the bodies of these books have been destroyed, although their souls have been spared. I know that wounds you, but I counsel you to consider that *every* body is perishable, though *any* soul may endure."

Covenant left the tower, and Ellard sadly contemplated the remains of his fallen but uncomplaining friends.

"They were, I believe," said Wordsmith, "the only books from your collection that Covenant found of much value."

"But these are all children's tales!"

Wordsmith picked up a battered volume and carefully turned the pages as he answered. "Most likely the rest were full of wind and not wisdom—folly, and not philosophy. They pretended to hold the truth but sheltered only lies instead. These," he said, elevating the book in his hand, "do not pretend to have the truth, and so have many truths in them. You kept them, I think, because of their fine binding. They look as though they were handsome once."

Ellard nodded, genuine tears brimming his eyes.

"You may now discover their true value," added Wordsmith, surrendering the book to Ellard. "You will find that Covenant has a taste for true stories—stories that are always true, stories that once were true, stories that should be true." He smiled before adding, "And stories that one day shall be true."

SIXTEEN

The Hope
of the Healer

AN ANGRY ELLARD, TRAILING WOEBEARER IN HIS WAKE, AT
last found Covenant in the house. The beggar was speaking
with Wordsmith in the tower. "We have spoken together for
the first time, Woebearer and I," Ellard began. "I did not know
that you were a healer, or that another healer lived under
your roof. Why then have the children been permitted to
suffer? Why have you forbidden this man to come to us?"

"For reasons of my own, I have neither healed them nor
permitted them to be healed," responded Covenant slowly.
"They will hurt, but they will not die." And again, smiling
sadly, he walked away, beckoning Woebearer to follow.

"These boys will continue to break your heart," continued
Wordsmith, after Covenant and Woebearer had departed. "So
Covenant has said. But why it will be better this way, I do not
know."

Elsewhere, Covenant said to Woebearer, "Hold your healing. This pain is not yet yours to destroy. It is a cruel thing to say, but sometimes suffering is necessary."

"For the children? What have they to learn?"

"It is necessary for you. I must arrest your gift for a time until you learn that it is not your salvation. Neither is it your burden to the grave. It is a gift. In your belief alone is your salvation. When you see that, you will know that all your wretched burdens have long since been lifted from your shoulders. Know too," Covenant added, "that their suffering is also necessary for Ellard."

And Covenant would say nothing beyond that.

The next day, Ellard confronted Covenant and Wordsmith again. "Why? Why are you letting this go on?" he thundered.

Covenant stood silently, though not without compassion.

"WHY?" screamed Ellard, as tears trickled down the new furrows that had come in recent days to seam his face. "For days now they have been crying for relief, finding none save in my voice."

Covenant turned to Wordsmith and said simply, "Behold his anguish. It is time."

Wordsmith nodded, and Covenant left while the unanswered challenge rang in the air. Wordsmith pulled a thick, richly bound book from his pocket and handed it to Ellard.

"It is yours now. You have earned it, for you have proved the lie of your own words about the worth of the world. When you were crying for your books only, your tears availed you nothing. But I said that you might have this book when you had learned how to grieve. You could not have it before this, for you had failed to understand the heart of books, though you loved them. Your eye was enchanted by the binding, and not by the truth of the words within."

That night, as the boys finally slid into troubled sleep, Ellard read the book silently by the light of the smoking lamp. He kept the words to himself.

Long before the dawn, Ellard sought Covenant but could not find him. Wordsmith was at hand, still awake and writing, and eager to speak with him.

"Have you finished the book yet?" Wordsmith asked.

"Yes," said Ellard slowly, as if still half in a dream. "I came to the end of the book but not the story. It ends in the middle of a sentence . . . rather painful, even, for I so wanted it to go on and on and on with never an end, and I do wonder what happened."

"Perhaps you will be granted a glimpse of the knowledge of the rest of the story, though you will never come to the end. It is a true story with never a final chapter."

"The words were new to me, but the story stirred ancient memories." He spoke tenderly, choosing his words carefully, a faraway look in his eyes. "I must have heard it a long time ago—so long past I can scarcely remember."

"It is an old story," Wordsmith nodded with a smile, "and the greatest one of all. There will never be a time when that tale is not remembered, recounted and enjoyed."

"I cannot believe that you, a mere man, wrote those words."

"I did indeed write these words, but they are only echoes of the tales from a book that Covenant keeps hidden away. I have seen that book and would lose my life to save it if it were necessary. But it will not be necessary, for it is the book that saves me and not I the book. That book cannot be spread abroad yet. Someday, all people everywhere will know its stories by heart. Until then, I am permitted to write ghost echoes of its beauties, to draw people to Covenant and this house."

Wordsmith wandered to the window, and a long silence came to dwell in the room. It endured until Covenant appeared.

"Do you still demand that they be healed?" Covenant asked Ellard directly.

"No," he said finally, with a mixture of resignation and peaceful enlightenment. "I see now that there are other matters that matter more. Thank you for the book. It is the first book I have ever held whose soul was more beautiful even than its body."

"You have long kept books, but now this book will keep you. And so I rename you as I have renamed almost every person in this house of mine. You shall be known as Binder. And I think such a book as you now have should be read to your charges—the sooner the better. This will be the best of all medicines for them, as it has been for you. It is fit that they hear it first from your lips."

Binder obeyed, and sought his suffering friends.

*   *   *

Later, at the midday meal, Covenant found Woebearer and Wordsmith and nodded to the hunchback. "You may go to them now," he said simply. And food forgotten, Woebearer sprang away like a honed arrow to its mark.

After a moment, Wordsmith asked, "Was all this delay truly necessary?"

"It was," said Covenant. "Someday you will see the secret purpose behind all mysterious things. Come."

They followed Woebearer's footsteps and came to the room where the children lay. The sound of laughter spilled from the room. Binder and the boys embraced, and Woebearer embraced them, and then Covenant embraced them all. Although there were more new lines carved into Woebearer's brow, he did not seem to notice.

"Their pain is gone now," said Covenant when the laughter subsided to joyful smiling. "But their strength will return only over many days. There are still stories they have never heard."

"But I have no more books—and no more stories!" protested Binder. "I have read them every word of this wonderful volume, but they do not seem to understand it."

"Perhaps it is because this book was written for you," replied Covenant. "Perhaps they shall understand it when they are older."

"That is why we shall be good friends," said Wordsmith. "I write books, and you read them. It is such an excellent combination. You may read more of my stories to them, and then it will be time to create your own and write them down. Then you will have the privilege of learning the true delight of books. For I have found that the one who writes a book learns more than the one who reads it."

The weariness of relief swept through the room. What had once been sleepless pain became painless sleep for the boys.

The four men stood quietly by and watched them slumber.

"They are much alike," said Binder.

"Their two hearts beat as one," answered Covenant. "They will not be stopped in anything they do. In fact, they barely will be guided." And Covenant blessed them, calling good fortune and honor down upon their heads. And at that moment, he named them Firecolt and Flamerider. "You have always been together," he whispered to them. "Never shall you be parted—in this world or the next."

SEVENTEEN

Beauty
& the
Feast

BEAUTY HAD KNOWN FAME, REWARD AND THAT WHICH WAS said to be love. And then in the space of a summer she had faded from splendor as the masses turned their attentions to another who was fresher and more fair.

Now she wandered alone through the places where once she had gathered crowds; weary and sleepless where once she had the offer of a hundred beds; rejected and forgotten in the midst of the congregation that once had mouthed her praises.

Beauty heeded not her footsteps until she raised her eyes and saw before her a pair of gates she did not recognize. The gates stood open, and the road beyond beckoned with a peculiar urgency. She followed the path into the sandy wilderness of the desert, content for now in the knowledge that the great town could do nothing but dwindle behind her back.

One mile beyond the gates the road divided, arching away to the left and the right. A high flat rock slumbered in the notch of the fork, and two men sat on the rock. The man on the left was tall and fair, cloaked in white silk unsullied by the dust of the earth. His skin was smooth and lightly tanned, like many of the high gentlemen she had known. The man on the right was neither short nor tall, neither young nor old, and his beggar's coarsecloth was marked with the dust of the highways and the darker, thin grime of the unwashed streets. His work-gnarled hands and lined face had long been bronzed and cracked by the sun.

Both men seemed to be waiting for her. She stopped and stared uneasily at them. She dimly remembered their faces, seeing for a brief instant the images of two men standing against one another on a wretched side street.

The gentleman spoke first. "You are a long way from home."

She nodded, looking up. "It is my choice. I leave it behind of my own free will." The sound of her own voice encouraged her.

"And why? Where would you go instead? Is not this town the center of all the world?"

"I have lost the fame that was mine. Perhaps I will find it again in another place which does not count itself so civilized. Or perhaps I will find the City, if indeed it exists. Some say it lies this way, or that, and that one may find pleasant things there."

"Who are you to seek these things?"

"My name is Beauty. Who are you?"

"I am Fame. I am the Master of all that is glorious. Honor and Fortune are my servants."

Then the beggar spoke. "I have many names. You may call me Covenant."

"Is that your true name?"

"All my names are true."

121

Fame spoke again. "How fortunate that you have come to me in your seeking. The City, indeed, lies before you—there!" He pointed down the road to the left, and Beauty thought she saw the way straight and golden, with tall towers and bright banners at its faraway end. He dropped his hand, and the vision faded into the shimmer that always bathes the desert horizon. "The way is open and needs only your feet upon it."

The beggar broke in. "That way is an illusion, and the path a snare. The true way to the true City lies through the very heart of the town you have abandoned. I have set a man there to guard the way and hold the key to the door. If you wish to find the City, you must return and find the man who serves me.

"To go onward leads only to the realms of Fame. Beyond this rock that road is one way, leading not to the City but to desolate lands that have long forgotten the sun. Fame sits here, guarding not the path beyond but the way back.

"His kingdom is made of false towers," Covenant added, "with hollow lands behind. The grand gate at the base of the towers is the Doorway of Deceit. Return with me to the town and the City within. Fame lays a trap for you, and all other quests are in vain."

Fame interrupted him, shaking his head. "The foolish words of a beggar. He offers you nothing. I offer you love. How many husbands have you had?"

"Five. No, six."

"I can promise you many more—husbands, or at least men to love you freely."

Covenant spoke again. "A worthless gift that will leave you as unfilled and aching as you already are. I offer you the hope of only one man—if he chooses to have you, and you him. A man who is mine and changes not from day to day, except that he is free to respond to those who have need of him."

"What manner of offer is that?" countered Fame. "I give you a feast! Wine, song, laughter, crowds, honor."

"But I offer you a different Feast. Food for your spirit. A song for your soul. The laughter that heals the heart. The company of a few. And the honor of serving one who serves a holy cause."

Fame's hands moved in the air, as though stroking Beauty's face. "And what of the glory of your face? The flesh! So easy to mold—a touch here, a stroke there, and you will be more striking than any the world has yet seen. Your first beauty was your own and was mortal, but what I give you shall be unearthly. All will fall anew at your feet. You shall be high and lifted up, and men shall once more fight to serve you."

Covenant's eyes met her own. "I give you not beauty renewed but the knowledge of yourself, and a new chance to be what you might have been had your beauty not hindered you. The one who serves me shall give you leave to serve him; he shall not lift you up, but you him, and he will give you honor but not worship."

Fame countered, "You have tasted fading glory in a place that will also fade. Do you desire eternal fame?"

The beggar interrupted. "He offers you eternal *flame*. Do not listen to him. All his words sound too like one another. His words build a grand illusion—and a fatal one, for his touch brings decay."

She wept. "You confuse me," she said, shaking her head and turning away. "Both of you—go away and let me be."

Jumping down from the rock, Covenant answered her with quick yet gentle words. "No. That we cannot do, for you have come to us and must walk one or the other of the ways that we guard." He pointed to the left, while peering into Beauty's eyes. "His road leads without turn to his own realms, and my road turns here upon itself to lead you back through the town." He gestured to the right.

"Can this Fame do what he promises?" she asked. "Can he return to me all that was mine?"

"He can restore to you—for a time—the illusion that you

had when you claimed those things for your own. I offer you more, but you will not know it now. I offer you the loss of all you hold dear and the gain of all you think you never wanted. You are empty, because you have already lost. Do not seek to retain what you cannot keep." He paused. "You are tired, and I shall bring you to a place to sleep. The house of Wordsmith is open to you this night, if you will come."

"Wordsmith? I think I have heard that name."

"You have," Covenant said, gently reaching his arm around her shoulders. "And you have laughed at him. Wordsmith is his name now, but he was not born with it. He was a great man once, as some reckon greatness. But I claimed him, and he took my yoke upon him and became mine. He accepted the fire of my refining, the piercing of my breaking him—and gave up all he once had. Now he sits alone, and sees far visions, and thinks hard thoughts, and writes the unchanging words that I put in his heart, and serves a Feast daily. His words and his service have spread farther than his fame. You were given some of his writings, but they gathered dust on your costly shelves, and you did not heed the weight of his words. It would have been better for you if you had."

She blinked away the last of the tears from her eyes and looked up to the rock again—catching Fame in the last split-second of an ugly scowl. It had not been directed at Covenant alone, but at her as well. It was gone in a heartbeat, replaced by the smile that now seemed so false.

Covenant looked at her, knowing what she had seen. "This is my way," he said. "Any who stand by me long enough come to see the truth behind everything."

On an impulse she would question many times but never regret, she dismissed Fame with the wave of her hand. Then she followed Covenant silently back along the beggar's road to the town cloaked in twilight.

They passed through Glory's gates again and journeyed past the places she had abandoned, past the entertainment halls, and past the places where the people crowded together noisily. They left the torchlights behind them and wound their way deeper into the older and shabbier districts of the town, between the buildings where rats rustled and children cried and the buildings themselves towered ominously in the darkness. There in the very heart of the squalor they stopped before a door. Covenant bade her sound the knocker. Then he left her.

When the door opened, the gift of speech was taken from her, and Beauty stood mute and frightened and needy on the doorstep. Wordsmith drew her inside, gently, and his face showed no surprise. *His words have always borne fruit*, thought Wordsmith, *but I never know when to expect a harvest.*

The door closed behind her, and her helplessness rolled over her in thrashing waves. Weak, hungry and weary, she could no longer find the strength to bolster courage, the fierceness to defend herself, the power to resist, the voice to question or cry out. She was in the hands of Wordsmith, for good or for bad, both vulnerable and dependent. She trembled, and he soothed her with a word and led her to a table laid for a meal. It looked as though many others had recently eaten there, yet there was food in abundance. He held his hands out, palms downward, and proclaimed a blessing.

She sat, and ate with a hunger she could no longer conceal. The food was excellent and plentiful, and the very act of eating increased her desire. Wordsmith moved slowly about elsewhere in the house; she heard the faint sounds of doors opening and closing and water gurgling from stone jars.

When she finished, he led her to a place where a bath was drawn, and left her. She bathed and dressed herself in the new clean coarsecloth lying there. Then Wordsmith came again and led her to a room where a bed stood freshly made. And she grew sad inside, expecting to pay for his kindness with her favors. But Wordsmith only bade her good sleeping and left her alone. She slept, unaware that he returned in the middle of the night with more blankets, or that he stood long in the

doorway and gazed at her, wondering what manner of woman slept within her.

For two days she lingered speechless in the house, sharing with open eyes the Feast given daily by Wordsmith—plain banquets opened to the homeless, the hopeless, the destitute discards who crowded in hungrily to the laden table, yet who showed their respect for the master of the house.

She discovered many things that she did not understand—doors that would not open to her, doors that she could not shut, staircases that had no landing and no end, mirrors that reflected nothing or frightened her when she looked into their depths. And though the door to the street opened freely at her touch, yet she stayed. If any had asked, and if she had possessed the voice to answer, she would have said that she stayed of her own will and choosing.

And she came to see what she had not noticed the first night: Wordsmith was lame, though he moved with slow grace and did not always use a walking stick.

On the morning of her third day in the house, the freedom of her tongue returned to her. She came first to Wordsmith and thanked him for his kindness, asking him why she had received so much care and yet so little had been demanded of her.

"Why should I ask anything of you?" he answered, laying aside his work. "I am here to serve Covenant."

"Why do you keep this house and serve this feast? Who are you, and who is Covenant? I have met you both, but I know neither of you."

"This is not my house," he said, waving her to a chair. "It is Covenant's. This world is Covenant's. He walks unseen here. It is his Feast that I serve here, to the people whom he has touched with his care. I am his servant, his anointed houseman. He it was who turned me from the greed of the world, from the worship and celebration of things that perish, from the living of a life that held no promise but unholy fame."

And Wordsmith told Beauty the tale of the night he had met Covenant—of the dusty beggar held for the death and burial of an old worthless man who was needed only for the grinding of the harvest—of a verdict of death, of the fire that could not be kindled and the greater fire that could not be quenched.

"I lived in Glory once," he said, "and left it behind me because of all the falseness and misery."

"I too have known misery. Has Covenant changed Glory, that you can live in it now?"

"No. He has changed me that I might live in Glory. He promised me that—and his name is Covenant because he keeps his promises."

She motioned to the room in which they sat. "But why is this house here?"

"Of fourth importance, it is a house for Covenant's servants.

"Of third importance, it is a house of healing for those who suffer from the sickness unto death, the wounds that come from the weight of a world broken upon its own altar.

"Of second importance, it is the place where a Feast is laid daily for any who will come.

"But this is the first meaning of this house: Behind a door in this house is the path to the City."

Her heart jumped at his words, but he continued before she could speak. "That is why Covenant turned your feet from the path that is drifted deep with the dust of death. Your eyes were blinded, as they always have been. Even now you see only dimly, as though you peer into a mirror never cleaned and never purged of old, deceptive images.

"The door to the path to the City lies behind you," he continued, nodding toward the long corridor. "And Covenant bade me show you the way whenever you desire."

"Yes, please! Even now!" She left the chair tilted behind her and caught herself at the door.

"You may go if you choose," he said, "for there is none to

stop you except yourself. But hear my words first."

She turned and looked at him.

"I do not advise that you go to the City now," he said. "You could not stand there unaided, or withstand the weight of joy unrestrained by sorrow. Remember that as there are lights too bright to see by and sounds too loud to hear, so there are glories too high and lovely to behold with unredeemed eyes. And redemption lies only in this house.

"The bright shadow of the City is here in this town, if you would but see it. Do not go to the City now. Not yet. Linger here instead—tarry, stay, enjoy—and learn to both see and endure the lesser glories before you expose yourself to the Life of the City, which is health and nectar to those who have both the desire of a new heart and the endurance of courage renewed. It is overwhelming pain to those who have neither."

"I am ready to journey now. I have seen too much of this town," she said, gesturing to the streets beyond the window.

"So you think. Perhaps you have not seen enough. But go, if you will. I will open the door for you, and Covenant will meet you along the way." He led the way through the winding halls to a door in one of the walls—a door she had tried on her own once before. It had been a door that she could not open, a door that should have opened into the back of another room. The hand-hewn wood bore ancient marks in odd places, and she could not name the dark stains lying deep in the grain.

"The path will turn long among the mountains," Wordsmith said, "and darkness will rise up to surround you. But the sky is clear, the morning star will guide you, and you will see a few steps before you and a few steps behind. You will be frightened, but you cannot be harmed. And then . . . then, you will come to the peak and see the City before and above you, and the night will be forgotten. If the City draws you gently, but the rush of beauty and holiness does not break your heart, then you should go farther. Journey on until your heart remembers its early thirsts.

"But when you have drawn close enough and your soul is suddenly drawn with the raging thirst that can only be quenched by the waters in the fountains before you—then return to me, for you will have motive enough and memory sufficient to aid me in my work here." He saw that Beauty hesitated. "Go on, go on," he urged, "and gaze upon the City. Fear not. The path from here is steep but certain. The hard part, the perilous way, is to return in obedience."

"I shall not return," she stated flatly.

"If you do not return, I shall understand, and all will be well. If you do return, I shall also understand, and all will be better."

He opened the door with a twist of his key and by speaking Covenant's name. She looked through the archway upon a path winding among tall mountains under an endless starry sky.

*　　*　　*

Wordsmith was preparing the table for the evening Feast when Beauty slipped softly into the dining hall. She nested silently in one of the chairs and gazed at him. Not all the tears had dried from her face.

He ceased his labors and drew a chair near to hers. "Words are painful now, I well know. I will not ask you to speak. But I will tell you how it was.

"You saw the City, did you not? And Covenant met you on the way?"

She nodded.

"How well I remember," he said. "To see the City is to seal one's desire to dwell there. But it is not like any earthly desire. It is not a consuming passion that one feels must be filled at once, before all else, without reckon of the cost. No, it is certain, safe, durable, everlasting. And most who see it are content to return here, to abide, to serve faithfully the beggar who is himself faithful to the High King of the City." He paused, searching her face. "Did Covenant ask you to return?"

She nodded again.

"He did not command you?"

This time she shook her head.

"And you do so willingly? To serve me as I serve him?"

Another nod.

Wordsmith nodded with her. "Once one sees how solid is the City, one is content to do other things first. Come. I accept your service, as he accepted mine. Aid me with this table now, and tomorrow I shall teach you the inner ways of this house."

EIGHTEEN

The Marvelous Mirror

ONE DAY BEAUTY FOUND THE NURSERY. SHE LINGERED long there, fascinated by the odd mixture of infants and ancients. A dozen old men and women happily tended to a noisy gathering of babies; some fed and changed their charges, some played on the floor, and some too frail to move about simply sat and held the small ones. All looked worn by time, but not defeated by the demands of their children.

Trueteller was among them, holding a baby on each arm and talking to a young man on whose face a glorious tawny beard had begun to blossom. He, too, rocked a child firmly but gently in his arms. They did not see Beauty, and she did not distract them as she left.

"Lionheart is the father of them all," smiled Covenant. "Though they had many fathers, now they have only one.

Young and old alike were betrayed, and now he has brought them together to mingle the old wisdom with the young innocence."

"I do not understand. Where did they come from? Why is he called Lionheart?"

"That story should come to you from his own lips."

Later, she asked more questions of Wordsmith, but all he would say was "Covenant's advice is good—for Lionheart, too, is a good storyteller, and he is a very patient man."

She thought for a moment, and then asked, "Why do all of you stay?"

"Our work here is founded upon the power of paradox," Wordsmith said. "We who keep this house have all seen the City. Even as our desire grows to journey on, the more our strength and yearning grow to serve Covenant here."

"I shall serve as well," she declared. "Where do I begin?"

"At the beginning—as we do each day." He led her into the long hall beyond the Feast table. "Have you seen this mirror?"

"Yes! I despise it, for I looked into it when first I came here. It showed me horrid things."

Nevertheless, fascinated, she raised a finger to stroke its intricate frame.

"It showed you only yourself as you were. It is not a mirror that has been fashioned by hands of this world. It is Covenant's command that we each stand daily here, alone, and see ourselves without pretense in its glass."

She looked, and beheld herself as a hideous, twisted, weak creature—grotesque and hardly human, defiled and deformed. She cringed and turned away from Wordsmith. "That is not me! It cannot be!"

"The mirror does not lie," he said. "Look again, for you have not seen enough."

She looked again, fearfully, and saw this time that hideous reflection swathed in a robe the color of new snow. She turned to Wordsmith in wonder.

"Look again," he gestured with a broad smile. "There is more."

She looked yet one more time, but now she saw Covenant's face beside hers in the glass. She felt his arms join around her waist and heard his voice soft in her ear. She laughed, basking in the flood of sudden warmth. Somewhere deep inside her she heard a sound like old frozen chains shattered by a great flame.

"Wordsmith! He loves me anyway!" The radiance of the embrace faded, and the mirror shaded into featureless gray.

"Yes. And that is the mystery. We must be reminded daily of both our low stature and his high love. Our answers lie only in Covenant and his choices."

They walked slowly into the kitchen.

"Then our work begins," he continued. "We need food for the Feast, and today you will gather it for us."

"Where do I buy it? For how much? And with what?"

"You do not buy, neither will you beg, or steal. You must go, and wait; be found, and receive. Take this basket and walk through the streets of the town. Do not hail those you know—if indeed any of your former friends would recognize you in these common clothes. Wait, hurry slowly; tarry, but do not stand still. Covenant has prepared the hearts of some to see you, to give you food and fruit out of their abundance. Take, accept without question. Do not test the quality of what is given you. Count not the outward appearance, but bring all of it here when the basket is full, and bless it in your bringing. Covenant shall then make the one basket suffice." He picked up a large, sturdy, but well-worn basket. "Do not speak, do not multiply your thanks, but bow gracefully and move on. We do not walk the same path twice in a week, nor the same path on the same day of each week."

"It all sounds so . . . uncertain."

"So it is, in our eyes. But not in his." He gave her the basket. "Go now, and return when the basket is full."

She paused at the door and turned back. "Will you not go with me?"

"Not today. There is no need, for there is nothing to risk but your pride, and nothing to lose but your independence. You walk under the protection of Covenant, for your work is done in his name. And for the time that you are away, he has given me other work to do. When you return, seek me on the topmost floor at the end of the farthest stair."

Beauty stepped outside and carried the empty basket away into the swarming town.

NINETEEN

The
Five
Windows

BEAUTY STOOD AT THE FOOT OF THE STAIRS AND GAZED upward. These were the stairs that had frightened her when she had first tried them, for they seemed without landing and without end. But she ascended, and somewhere on the heights Wordsmith heard her footsteps and came to meet her.

"You did well," he said.

"How do you know? You were not with me!"

"Ah, but in a way I was. Come, see the secrets of this upper room." He drew her up the last steps into a room with five great windows. Four of the windows peered out over the town—four windows glazed with clear crystal that offered no reflection.

"From here one can see everywhere within the town—and beyond. Look there: It is the road you followed to your meeting with Covenant—and the road by which you returned."

She peered through the window, seeing a far road and the flat rock dwarfed by distance. Then it grew closer and larger, until she saw the stone seat as though it were only a pace away. She turned to look at another window, and when she looked back the first view had once more receded into the distance.

"This is how I knew your basket to be full," he said. "One who stands here may watch closely anything he or she desires." He turned her to the fifth window, which until now had been featureless and gray, like storm clouds brooding at dusk. "This is my appointed station," he said. Then the gray faded and a field of stars unfolded like flowers before her. Galaxies gleamed in the sable sky. Comets whirled through blooming constellations.

"Behold the Fields of Arbol—the realm and handiwork of the Elder God." Then the stars were gone, replaced with a glen deep within the center of a green and peaceful forest.

"This is Covenant's window, even as this is Covenant's house. He built this window for me with his own hands. It was his gift to me that I may do the writing he bids me do." The forest faded, and, within the opening, colored shadows shifted and swirled in quiet glory. "I recline here, upon this couch, and watch the visions come and go. And when I have seen them, I fashion them into stories and put them into books. Then I go to the marketplaces and the corners and other towns, and I place my books where they belong, and tell these stories, speaking always of Covenant and the City, and inviting all who will both hear and hearken to come to the Feast.

"Look into the window, Beauty, and see a story for your eyes. I cannot tell you what we will see, but what Covenant reveals here is intended to help you."

The whirling colors ceased their play, and Beauty saw a woman descending steep unlit paths to a dark and sprawling castle where shadows lay like rancid filth in the passageways.

False towers framed the open gates, and every winding stairway led downward to the same deep dungeon.

"That is you, as you might have been," Wordsmith explained. "And those are the realms of Fame. You saw them once, as Fame showed them. Now you see them through Covenant's eyes."

She covered her face with her cloak and the view vanished. "But you are secure now. You need only stay to be redeemed." Soft silence fell as he stared at the window. "Too long have I neglected the tasks of watching, hearing, and writing so that I might bring order to the Feast. I ask you to free me from the kitchen's burdens that I may linger here. There are many sleepless nights, long midnights when the window scrolls and speaks ceaselessly, without regard for the sands of time, hours when I will be grateful for any food or drink you may bring me, and for any weight you may lift from my shoulders. Mine is a lonely task; you cannot join me in it, yet, you can be my solace and my company."

"I will," she said. And then she added, "For once, I have no shame in giving another my service."

They turned away from the window.

"Wordsmith?"

"Yes?"

"If Covenant has healed so many . . . why has he not healed you?"

"When he summoned me, he made my healing no part of the bargain. And it was many months before I grew wise enough to understand his wisdom. Covenant took from me my old name, my old songs and tales, and he gave me new ones instead. He has left me my lameness to remind me of what might have been—to grant me a humbling affliction—to prevent my exaltation in my own eyes.

"He is sufficient now, though I did not see it then. Not all ills are cured by making the body whole. I have seen Covenant heal a broken kitten, yet he has not healed me—at least on the outside. His surgery began quietly on the inside. Someday it may conclude with fanfare on the outside."

"Then who *is* Covenant?"

"Covenant is but one of his names. It is his true name, but it does not contain him. No single name can. In some places he is known only as the Beggar, even though he rises higher than the King. But he is not famous, except among those who have tested all other champions and found them lacking. He comes to those who call for him and to those who do not even know their need of him. Women wake to find sick children well. Poor husbands rouse to find gold beneath their pillows. Starving towns turn and find new fields of grain. The thirsty claim water in his name. The desperate find rest in his hands. The hungry come to his Feast at his invitation. It is he who provides the food, though you carried it. It is his generosity that sparks other hearts to grant the food, and his voice that woos other souls to come and partake of the gifts."

He led her away down the steps to the kitchen, where the unready Feast awaited the touch of her hands. He continued speaking as they walked. "He breaks the proud and shatters unworthy gods. He casts down the prayers of people who seek high things for low reasons. He orders the rainfall and draws the lightning. All these things are from Covenant, and through him, and he comes in the name of the Elder God. Let your own heart tell you who Covenant is—who he must be, who only he can be."

As Beauty worked in the kitchen, she knew as she portioned out the food that none could name it good. Yet the ragged guests at the Feast seemed not to notice. Some tarried after to speak with Wordsmith, and some slipped away into the murky streets, while others stayed to sleep in tiny rooms that opened from the side halls.

After the Feast, Wordsmith took her to meet the others she had seen working in the house, doing other tasks. They all made Beauty welcome, and she was both comforted and, yet, disappointed. There still was something within her that cried out for recognition, but she stood relieved that none spoke to her of her past.

In the evening she tended Wordsmith before his window and watched with him. After the window had paled to gray, they talked until the new day was born.

"Is Wordsmith a true name? Or Woebearer? Your names do not seem proper."

"Covenant gave us our names. Our old names died with our old lives."

"He has not given me a new name," she said simply.

"You have already abandoned the name first given you—and the one you have adopted suits you well enough for now. The best names, the true names, are not yet ready to be revealed. Someday we will hear them from Covenant's own lips."

After that, the time passed in pleasant cycles of hard work and deep sleep, of Covenant coming and going like sunshine through the rainbow and wind across the grass. Again and again Beauty sat with Wordsmith in the marketplace, hearing his tales and teaching, and turned to help him in the long evenings, bringing him food before he asked. Sometimes she wrote down for him the words he chose to fit the visions, and sometimes she simply listened to his wisdom.

"Wordsmith?"

"Yes?"

"It is an odd thing—I am more of a queen here, serving, than in all those houses past where I was served. And I did not know love, although I heard the word often, until I came beneath your care. Yet you have never sought to touch me or fed me sweetened words."

"There is much honor in this house. It falls on all who are humble enough to lay it aside. Do not seek it and it will be given to you."

"It is fortunate for me that you do not see me in the mirror.

Could you do so, or had you seen me so that first night, you would turn me away."

He turned to stare at her for a long moment. "Did not Covenant tell you?"

A puzzled look creased her brow.

"I did see you as you are in the mirror. And I still do. But I also see the white-robed lady with the radiant face. It is like seeing thrice with a single glance—the one inside, the one outside, and the one waiting to be revealed. This way of seeing is one of the gifts he gives the ones who serve him long."

Shame and wonder flooded her soul and peered out through her eyes. "And still you took me in?"

"Certainly. I had no reason to turn you away." He paused, and then continued in softer tones. "Do not forget that I, too, stood before the mirror with a naked heart. And what I beheld there was a foulness you will never approach. You were vain. I was evil. But I will not judge you now. You must judge yourself before him and then accept his judgment."

"Might I someday stand with you at the mirror, then? I would like to see you as you will be."

"If Covenant so grants. Until he allows otherwise, the reflections in his mirror are a private vision."

"The reflections. Wordsmith, it also seems—and perhaps I deceive myself—that when I look into the mirror each day I am less foul than the day before. Is my . . . beauty . . . returning?"

"Yes, some of it. Some of it is merely the dirt coming away. But do not misunderstand—its source is not in you. It is because you dwell in the very shadow of the City, and because Covenant loves me, and I in turn love you. Other men gave you love because you were beautiful; here, you are beautiful because you are loved."

Now answered, she left him to his appointed vigil.

TWENTY

Old
Promises

BEAUTY WAS EYEING A SPOT ON HER CLOAK WHEN WORD-smith found her.

"Wordsmith?" she asked. "I cannot clean this cloak any longer." She dropped the fold back into its place and eyed Wordsmith's cloak. "Why is yours always so clean? And the others' clothing as well?"

"I know the answer to that mystery," said Wordsmith, "but I do not pretend to understand it. The cloak you wear is fine indeed, but it is the one you wore when you left Glory for the wilderness. It is Covenant's wish that, when you realize the poverty of your old clothing, you make a new garment for your own—as all in this house have done."

"I do not know how to sew."

"You can learn. The rest of us have done so before you—

behold my own creation!" She looked more closely at his cloak. "I did not choose the pattern," he continued, "or find the material, but my stitches hold it together. It is good enough for now; I am working on a second cloak which will be better. Then I will unsew this one and refold the cloth and leave it for another to use."

"But how does it stay so clean? I have seen dirt upon it at one hour, and the next the stains have disappeared—and you have not had time to clean it."

"That is because it has been made from Covenant's cloth and then scrubbed upon the rock in the river," replied Wordsmith. "And you must do the same with yours when you have finished."

"I don't understand," she said. "It is winter, and the river is not only filthy but frozen."

Although she did not comprehend, she began to piece and sew with the fabric he brought her. As the cloak she wore grew duller and darker and less fit for wear, her new one began to take shape under her fingers.

"This is strange fabric," she said. "It is not any cloth that I recognize."

"A bolt of this was here in the house when Covenant gave me stewardship of it. I do not know where it was made, or how, or by whom, or even what manner of cloth it is. But it is very beautiful, and it is durable if treated properly."

When she was finished, Wordsmith admired her handiwork—clumsy and unpracticed though it was in places—and bade her take it to the river and wash it there.

"But the cloth is not dirty yet."

"If you do not preserve it by scrubbing it upon the rock in the river, it will soon stain and never come clean again. Then your effort will be wasted, and you will have to begin again.

"I would gladly do it for you," he continued, "but this is one thing you must do for yourself. Come, I will walk with you to the river."

By the water he pointed out the rugged rock, crystalled with ice and glittering in the sun.

"I feel foolish doing this," said Beauty.

"You are foolish. But every time you play the fool by obeying Covenant's commands, even though they bewilder you, you become less of a fool than before.

"The river looks dirty and foul to me as well—but it is Covenant's river, and it carries out his wishes when we do the same."

She went, gingerly treading upon the ice and chopping through the frozen crust with a stick to reach the surface of the rock. There she scrubbed her new cloak in the frigid, murky water and pounded it flat again with a stone.

When she picked her way ashore, her fingers were cut and bleeding and blue with cold. "A little of your own blood will not hurt the cloth," said Wordsmith. "Indeed, it will make the seams—the only part which you have made—all the stronger and all the more lovely."

As Wordsmith and Beauty walked back from the river, Covenant came to Woebearer.

"Your body is worn beyond your time," he said to the hunchback. "You have suffered much that was not your agony to begin with."

"I have," answered Woebearer, "but has it been in vain?"

"It has not. You have helped many."

"But now?"

"But now it is time to make you a whole man at last. That I cannot do here in Glory."

Woebearer nodded. "My feelings fight within me. The City will be pleasant."

"More than pleasant—it will be *right*. For the first time in your life, you shall inhabit a world for which you were made."

"When must I leave?"

"Before the sun hides from the world again. I shall leave the time to your choosing, if it pleases you. You may go this very moment, if you desire. You have nothing to do before you go?"

"I cannot leave now—not just yet. I have strength left in my shoulders, and no weight upon them!"

Covenant smiled, and waved his hand toward the waiting streets. "Then go to the streets one last time. Your deeds cannot save you, but neither will they go uncounted."

They all went about their daily work, knowing that only as the sun fell down the sky would Woebearer return from his final reckless swing through Glory, slumping beneath the staggering weight of his collected sorrows.

*   *   *

That evening Beauty had good reason to test her cloth. After helping serve the Feast, she found new stains upon the fabric. She rubbed them with her finger and waited for the marks to go away. When they did not, she sought Wordsmith and showed him the stubborn blots.

"Perhaps," said Wordsmith with a smile, "you should go and ask Covenant about this."

She found the beggar and asked him, "Why will this dirt not come out? Wordsmith said it is magic cloth and will clean itself."

"What dirt? I see no stains here," said Covenant, peering carefully at her cloak.

She looked down again to point, but found nothing to point to and nothing to say, for it was spotless. It looked as fresh as the day she had first been handed the fabric.

"I think you should ask Wordsmith for a fuller answer," Covenant continued. "He knows more than he has chosen to tell you."

She hurried back to Wordsmith and demanded an explanation.

"You have understood most of it correctly," he said. "It is magic cloth—Covenant's own kind of magic—and it does renew itself. But time will not erase the stains, nor will anything else but one single act remove a smudge: You must only go and see Covenant. The cleansing only comes when we spend time with him."

Her contemplation was set aside by the arrival of Woebearer. They could all hear him dragging himself joyfully down the street. Wordsmith, Binder, Beauty and Candle met him at the door and helped him down the long halls to the ancient wooden door where Covenant stood waiting.

"I cannot walk another step, my friends," said Woebearer. "I have grabbed more griefs than I can bear."

"I knew you would," answered Covenant. "That is why I have come to carry you myself." Covenant aided the crushed man onto his back and opened the door to the City with one hand. They stepped through, and Woebearer looked back at Wordsmith and the others. For the first time in all his life, joy and full pleasure flushed his face and began to reign there.

All in the house slept well that night, not waiting for Covenant to return. But on the following morning, Beauty sought him, realizing suddenly that she had never seen him standing alone—save those times when she desired to speak with him privately. So once again she made her wish, and it was answered when she came into a side room and found him waiting there—patiently sitting as though only Beauty existed and Covenant had all the time in the world for her.

And Beauty asked him, "You told me once that I might have the hope of a man—you called him 'a man who is mine, who changes not from day to day, except that he is free to respond to those who have need of him.' "

Covenant smiled. "I see you have not forgotten my words."

"How could I fail to remember them? Your promises have a life of their own, and my life has a before and an after because you met me at the rock of choosing."

"I know your question. Yes, Wordsmith is the man who is meant to claim you, and it is within his heart to do so. He has not yet spoken, but I have, and I call it not good that he should

be alone. But do not press him, and do not hurry the time. Each moment comes only in its own season."

Then they climbed to the upper room and joined Wordsmith there, and she was content to stand between the two men as they looked out over the length and width of Glory and all the land beyond, as far as the shores of the sea and the mists of the mountains.

It was Beauty who first spied the wan figure on the nearby path leading into the wasteland, and first called out the name of the most recent beauty, the newly dethroned queen of fickle hearts. Fame was already at the rock, waiting to fill the young woman's empty ear with the illusion of promises and the promise of illusions.

Beauty called to Covenant and asked if she might go with him to meet the one who must, as she had once done, choose one or the other of the roads that go on forever. He smiled, and blessed her, and then the two descended together to the place where the outward road divided in the wilderness.

TALES OF THE FORGOTTEN GOD
BY DAN HAMILTON

THE BEGGAR KING
THE CHAMELEON LADY
THE EVERLASTING CHILD

TALES OF THE FORGOTTEN GOD

THE CHAMELEON LADY

Dan Hamilton

Illustrated by
Jack Stockman

InterVarsity Press
DOWNERS GROVE, ILLINOIS 60515

InterVarsity Press® is the book-publishing division of InterVarsity Christian Fellowship®, a student movement active on campus at hundreds of universities, colleges and schools of nursing in the United States of America, and a member movement of the International Fellowship of Evangelical Students. For information about local and regional activities, write Public Relations Dept., InterVarsity Christian Fellowship, 6400 Schroeder Rd., P.O. Box 7895, Madison, WI 53707-7895.

Cover art: Jack Stockman
ISBN 0-8308-1672-0

Printed in the United States of America ∞

Library of Congress Cataloging-in-Publication Data

Hamilton, Dan.
    The chameleon lady/Dan Hamilton; illustrated by Jack Stockman.
      p.   cm.—(Tales of the forgotten God)
    ISBN 0-8308-1672-0
    1. Fantastic fiction, American.   2. Christian fiction, American.
I. Title. II. Series: Hamilton, Dan. Tales of the forgotten God.
PS3558.A4248C48   1994
813'.54—dc20   94-16541
                                      CIP

17	16	15	14	13	12	11	10	9	8	7	6	5	4	3	2	1
08	07	06	05	04	03	02	01	00	99	98	97	96		95		94

For Jennifer Elise Hamilton—
daughter, friend-in-miniature,
beloved shadow, and future lady

—CONTENTS—

—PREFACE—

Once there was a City where dwelt the Elder God and the men and women and animals and wonders he had made. All shone, all had joy, and all were loved.

But there were ways to leave the City—paths that were still forbidden to the people though left open to their feet, avenues made not by the Elder God, but by his old enemy who hated good things everywhere. All that the people needed was given them freely, but they were not content as long as the untrodden paths to the unexplored wilderness shimmered in the sun. So they left one day, first by ones, and then by groups, until they had all left the City to see what lay beyond. The Elder God called after them all, but curiosity deafened them and stopped their ears.

First the wilderness lay before them, then beside them on either hand, and then it surrounded them. And the wilderness terrified them, for there were lions there, and wolves, and fierce things that lived in the sea. Darkness fell upon them, and rain and thunder—the sad voice and tears of the Elder God. The world was changed in a great shaking and windstorm; the people turned, but could not find the way back to the City. And too late they understood that the roads would have been theirs to explore, and the wonders beyond theirs to conquer, had they waited until they had been tested, approved and empowered. Instead, they went in their own strength to conquer the wilderness, and it was the wilderness which conquered them.

The City was never lost; it was only removed from the face of the earth and still was—somewhere. But the people were lost, and it was the path back to the City that was forfeit.

The people made themselves a king to remind them of the Elder God, but no man falsely exalted could truly fill the empty throne. The people built Glory where they believed the city had been, but it was only a wicked and flimsy shadow. Some thought there might still be a secret door, and behind it a dark and dangerous path to the City, winding its way back if only one could plumb its mysteries. But if there was a door leading to such a path, it was hidden, and no one knew where it was. Each year fewer searched for the fabled door, and then the people lost count of the years. Glory endured and they still crowned kings, but the memory of the Elder God largely faded from the land. In few places was he still worshiped; in no place was he altogether without a witness.

And then the beggar came. Covenant. The beggar who reigned as a quiet king. The dusty man who spoke for the Elder God and changed lives around him frequently and forever. The one who bent the twisted world around him so that those who stood with him could see its true shape. The man who raised the dead to life again and granted rest to the bone-weary. The traveler who defeated fire and fired the defeated to new heights of courage and honor. The patient man who sifted the refuse of the world and recovered men and women and children (and even animals) and made them whole again in the midst of their imperfections.

Those he redeemed he called to his house in Glory. The old stone ruin was weathered and unremarkable from the outside, but on the inside it was a wonderful warren of comfortable rooms and kitchens and places to meet and eat and heal. And behind one particular door lay the path to the City.

The City is still the center of all the universe—it is there that the Elder God reigns in unapproachable holiness. The City has a heart and a name, and that same heart beats at the core of the earth and clocks the candling of the stars.

This part of the story was told in *The Beggar King*.

ONE

The Face in the Shadows

WORDSMITH GRASPED BEAUTY'S ARM AND POINTED through one of the tower windows. "Watch—there, in the street below us."

She looked and saw nothing.

"In the shadows," he continued. "I think she is coming here."

"She?"

"I saw her face in the moonlight just now."

"Who is she?"

"I do not *know*," he said uncertainly.

"Who do you *think* it was?" Beauty asked.

"A woman dead many years," he answered quietly.

She dared say nothing. *Anything is possible in this house*, she thought. *Anything.*

They both gazed down, where the woman was only a shadow in the dimly lit streets of Glory. Unheeded in the darkness, she wound her way to the gray stone house where the door was never locked.

A moment later they heard the ghost echoes of a knock. Binder appeared from the corridor and opened the door; he was already drawing the woman into the candlelit front hall as Beauty and Wordsmith approached. The woman looked up at them, and Beauty gasped. All their eyes fixed themselves upon the stranger's face.

"So I remind you of someone?" the newcomer asked softly.

"Yes," said Wordsmith.

"Yes," said Binder.

"Yes," said Beauty.

"Who, then?" she challenged gently.

"A woman from a long time past," answered Wordsmith.

"A girl I knew in days before," said Binder.

"A child I used to play with," said Beauty.

"Then tell me the color of my hair, and my height, and the shade of my eyes," she said.

"You are tall," said Wordsmith, "with long black hair and dark blue eyes."

Beauty looked at him with widened eyes. "What are you saying? Her hair is red, and her eyes are green, and she is the size of a mere child."

"You are both wrong," said Binder. "Her hair is the color of the sun, and her eyes are brown, and she is my height less an inch."

The woman smiled sadly. "You see?" she said. "I am the Chameleon Lady—my image lies solely in the eye of the beholder.

"What am I wearing?" she continued.

"A cloak the color of the doves that flutter in the dust," answered Beauty promptly, "with purple piping and a purple lizard embroidered upon the collar."

Wordsmith nodded as Binder spoke his agreement.

"You see?" she said. "My cloak remains the same, but the rest of me is ever shifting."

"Then who *are* you? What *do* you look like?" asked Beauty.

"I no longer know," said the stranger. "My mirror lies even to me."

Beauty looked thoughtfully at Wordsmith. "There is a mirror in this house that does not lie," she said.

Beauty drew the woman after her along the hall and stopped before a large mirror mounted on the wall.

"See here," she pointed. "This is a magic mirror."

"I have had more than enough of magic," moaned the newcomer. She shrank back from the mirror and would not open her eyes to it.

So Beauty looked instead—and saw nothing, not even herself in the depths of the mirror. The silver that ever shimmered was now lifeless and still.

Wordsmith, standing behind them, said quietly, "This mirror never lies. But it does not always speak." He faced the strange woman squarely. "I think you should abide here until Covenant returns. Though the key to some of its secrets has been trusted to my hands, this is his house, and a mystery too deep for his mirror will not be too deep for him."

"Thank you," she said. "I came here because I heard that this door is never locked and there are always kind words in abundance."

"That is our task," he said, "and our joy as well."

"And I have also heard of a beggar," she added.

"You have, and he is Covenant, and he is real, and he is the heartbeat of this house. The question is not how we will treat you, but what Covenant will do with you. We are only human; though we have learned not to decide too quickly, even our opinions in the end mean little. Covenant's judgments are lasting and leave no room for argument."

"And who," murmured Beauty, "would argue with mercy?

"Come with me," she continued in a louder but still kind

voice, "and I will find for you a bed."

Wordsmith smiled to himself, remembering the night he had spoken those same words to a lost and voiceless Beauty. Now she was in turn extending that kindness to another, and the circle of compassion had completed another turn.

"You will need help," Binder said. "I will send Flamerider and Firecolt to warm and fill a bath for you."

Wordsmith, knowing all things were well in hand, ascended to his study and turned his pen to paper again.

The first vision of this night has come true already, he thought. *Now I have seen the woman without a face. Or does she have too many faces?*

The crown of the old stone house in Glory was Wordsmith's tower, a room with four windows that looked out over Glory and beyond, and a fifth window that opened upon somewhere altogether different. Beyond that pane were constellations and whirling planets, darkness and intricate patterns, subtle plays of light and shadow that either were stories themselves or triggered tales in the mind of the watcher. Wordsmith sat before the window and saw the things that unfolded there, and hunched over paper in the mostly magical and faintly futile attempt to record the dreams and visions of the night.

This deep into the hours of darkness there was no other motion elsewhere in the house. The only two awake were in the tower now, as Beauty ascended the familiar winding stairs and came to the secluded room. She stepped softly behind Wordsmith, thinking him unaware of her arrival. But without taking his eyes from the swirls and stars that shimmered in the fifth window, he reached out his hand for hers. She took it silently, and their fingers spoke for them, and the warmth of each renewed the other.

Their entwined fingers mirrored the joined pledges on the chains about their necks. She had made her promise to stay with him, and he with her, and the metal of promise was a comfortable burden that each shouldered well.

The words of Covenant still echoed in Beauty's ears, joining them together in both time and eternity. Still it was a wonder to her, that of all the men she had known she should be united with the one man who had shown her the most kindness, who had been drawn to her not by her great beauty and former fame but by her poverty, isolation and suffering. He had not demanded her love as a price for his own care, but had accepted her as a prize won by his care for her, and had taken her needs as his own.

Covenant's care was at the core, for Covenant—the beggar—had changed their lives. They thought often of the strange and splendid man who had burst into their lives to bring them to this house in Glory and together.

Wordsmith once was a drunken bard, bitter with the taste of a crippled leg and the weight of failed dreams. Now he stayed up with the stars and wrote down visions and truths, copying them in books to sell in the marketplace to anyone who would buy.

Once the fairest flower of Glory, Beauty had been left behind by fame in the drift of time. Once all men had been hers, and she was never content. Now, only one man sought her love, and she was more than satisfied.

Wordsmith had then been named steward of the House of Covenant. But his first place was still before the windows, and Beauty was content to join him there. Indeed, she knew no reason to leave his side for long. Many had joined the fellowship at the House of Covenant, and now other hands did the main work of laying the Feast daily for the homeless and the hungry and all who would come to the rebuilt ruin in the back alleys of Glory.

"What have you seen tonight?" Beauty asked her husband.

"Little that I can make sense of," Wordsmith answered. "Many strange things that I wish Covenant were here to explain. I have seen an ancient book with a sword growing from its pages, while a young man pores over the words and his spirit blazes within him. I have seen a woman with no face riding a lizard. And I have seen a man in chains suddenly sprouting wings and clawing his way upward across the rocks."

"Your dreams are always strange," she said. "But they always mean something, and we have seen the lady with no face riding her curse."

Wordsmith nodded.

"Where is Covenant?" she asked. "And how long will he be gone? He has not been here for days."

"I have seen him, too," he answered. "He is a long way from Glory."

"Has Lionheart left as well? I saw him early tonight buttoning his cloak in the hall."

"Yes. He has far to ride tonight."

"How swift are his beasts? I have never seen them running."

"Swifter than horses, and always fast enough. I watched him in the glass as he left," he said, gesturing to the window that overlooked the west edge of Glory. *I am always thrilled when they come to his call*, he thought. *Nothing can be seen in the trees until he roars, and then at his voice the lions are suddenly there.*

Wordsmith was unsure they were always the same ones, though there generally seemed to be two—a great male and a smaller female. Lionheart said he often rode the female while the male ranged ahead and beside them as a guard. "But when speed is more useful than caution," Lionheart had said, "I ride with my face in his mane, and we outrun the wind."

Though Wordsmith could see many things at a great distance through the magically magnified windows, he could not see where the sun did not reach. He saw very little of Lionheart's nocturnal doings and did not understand how Lionheart knew when to go and where to seek. But go he did, and the more intimate secrets of his calling remained between himself and Covenant.

"He should be home soon," said Wordsmith. "Shall we go down and meet him?"

They descended and were met in the front corridor by a roar of laughter that lightened the house. Lionheart still carried the tang of a wild animal; Wordsmith could not guess how many leagues he had ridden that night in rescue.

But Lionheart held two infants in his arms, and close behind him tottered an old man nearly blind with age and withered with weakness.

"Good hunting?" asked Wordsmith, more as a ritual than a question.

"Very good hunting," answered Lionheart, brushing back his great mane of hair and shaking the weight of the night from his weary shoulders. "But then it is easy to pluck the fruits that are left unwanted in the orchard."

He moved away down the hall, the old man clinging to his belt for guidance and support.

* * *

All those in Covenant's house heard the strange lady's story the next morning.

"What is this curse upon you?" asked Beauty gently. "We have seen many remarkable things here in this house, and this must be numbered among them."

"It is the curse of the chameleon," she began. "I have sewn the figure of a small lizard on my collar, and I am burdened with a necklace fashioned in the shape of a chameleon. I do not know who I really am."

"Why is your necklace a burden? Can you not take it off?"

"This necklace will never come off," she said. "And even if I could take it off, I would die. So runs the curse."

"What is this curse?" Beauty asked again. While she alone was speaking, Wordsmith, Binder and the rest waited for the stranger's answers.

She sighed and began an old tale many times told, and no less painful for its familiarity.

"I deceived a man, and he cursed me, and his words came true."

Beauty reached for her hand. "I, too, have suffered from the words of men—and their deeds."

"But did their curses ever come true?" Something blazed in the woman's eyes for a moment and then died down again.

"It was not their curses that came true," Beauty said evenly, "but their blessings that were false. Many men praised me, honored me, showered promises upon me and adored me, but none of it was of any value in the end. Their loyalty failed, and they turned their attentions to another who had not yet been ravaged by time." Beauty's voice softened. "But that is a tale for another day, and I will not interrupt you again."

The newcomer stared at the wall for a long moment before resuming. "I had a sister whose lover would often come to her by night and meet her in her darkened room.

"My sister was beautiful, and I was not. One night I tricked her into seeking elsewhere for her lover, and I hid myself in her unlit room to wait. There he came to me, through the window; he slipped this pledge around my neck, and we said nothing, letting our passion speak for us. But he soon realized the deception, and he lit the lamp and beat me and cursed me.

"My sister called him a 'magic man,' and so he was. I learned too late that he could throw spells and do dread deeds with a power I could not understand."

"Perhaps he was a servant of Fame," Wordsmith suggested. "Fame may be false to the very core, but he is not without power and gifts to those who follow him."

"Whoever he is, he turned this necklace into a pledge of punishment. My sister found me and cursed me as well. She drove me out and left me friendless and homeless. I have drifted through Glory and the land around ever since."

"Is there any way to break the curse?" asked Wordsmith.

"Her magic man said that there was a cure for the chameleon curse," she answered, "but that another man of power would have to pay the price himself. He said that I would never find one who both could and would make me whole again."

Even as Wordsmith gazed, her image slowly changed from one old memory into another. She glanced up at him and smiled wearily. "I know that look," she said. "Another memory. Each time you see me I am different, both strange and familiar at once. Everyone remembers me, but no one knows what I look like."

He could see the bond forming between Beauty and the Chameleon Lady. *I know what it is,* thought Wordsmith. *Both of them have been trapped behind their faces, prisoners of others' ideas of beauty. Covenant set my lady free and gave her to me, but what of this one? Who is she, and what can be done for her?*

Her face dissolved and rearranged again as she fingered the embroidered design on her cloak: a purple chameleon turning tightly in the confines of a black square. "It can't find its way out," she said sadly. "I saw the design in an old book, and I thought it true enough to bear as my own mark. This is how people know who I am. You cannot describe my face and stature so that anyone will recognize me, so perhaps you should continue to call me as I have called myself—the Chameleon Lady."

"With any shape, behind any face, you are welcome to stay here," said Wordsmith. "I am the steward of this house, but the true master is away. When he returns, you should meet him and tell him your story."

"But do not be surprised if he knows it already," cautioned Binder.

"No one will ridicule you here," added Beauty. "We have all borne our share of sorrows, and we have no wish to add to your burdens. Come and go as you please. Though we will know you by the device of the chameleon, we will not use that name for you if you wish it."

"Then what will you call me?"

"Perhaps," said Binder, "we should simply call you our friend. When Covenant returns, he will no doubt have a better name at hand."

"That seems to be his specialty," added Beauty.

"Where did Covenant come from?" the Chameleon Lady asked.

"Even that we don't know," admitted Wordsmith. "Trueteller was the first of us to meet him, but even then she had heard rumors about a man who gave away gold and raised the dead to life again."

"The beggar?" Her eyes widened. "I have heard of him. And before that?"

"Nothing that I can discover. He has merely appeared among us, as though he has come a long way for a purpose he will not yet reveal."

"How old is he?"

"I don't know if age is even a proper term to lay upon him. I often wonder if he was ever born, and I am convinced he will never grow old and feeble. How can we know? No one has ever come to us from the Elder God before. We have no standard to measure him against."

TWO

The
Black
Banner

L EAGUES AWAY FROM GLORY, IN THE LONG SHADOW OF THE afternoon, the fishing fleet returned to the weathered village of Graycove. A gathering of salt-battered houses and open fishing sheds clung to the rocks and the sand by the untracked ocean, where two separate domains collided. These people were bound to the sea, but bound by the land—of the sea but not on it, and on the land but not in it. Had the waves been solid enough, they would have built their homes on the foam.

Each boat in the oncoming flotilla bore its share of the harvest of the waters, with bright flags atop the masts signaling a good catch. The brighter the flags, and the more of them flying, the better and more valuable the catch aboard. At the rough wooden pier, men, horses and wagons waited impatiently to buy and carry. The fish would be sorted, haggled over, paid for and packed in cold wet seaweed for the long journey to Glory.

Women gathered on the shore and chattered excitedly as they numbered the boats and their banners, but they suddenly stilled when they spotted the last boat, trailing the others by a few hundred yards. No bright flag flew upon it, only a single midnight slash of fabric. One waiting woman recognized the *Childsbreath* and uttered her name aloud. The others echoed the name in whispers, and two of their number began to cry—the half wail that is born in sudden fear and is fully loosed only when dark suspicion is confirmed as truth.

Unwatched now, the other boats passed by the women; the trailing boat drew onto the sloping sand, coming ashore directly before the village and away from the fishing sheds. A tall fisherman splashed down from the deck and gently hoisted the body of a boy to the sand, while another man stood silent in the shadow of the sail.

"He fell into the water," the fisherman said into the breathless hush, "and was caught in the nets. He drowned before we could fight to him and cut him free."

For one woman, grieving began in earnest. The others helped her cry.

The boat did not linger on the sand. "There are a few fish to sell," the fisherman said, "and the buyers are waiting. He caught a net full of fine fish before he died, and I cannot allow his labors to be wasted." He waved to the man still on board, who turned the *Childsbreath* about and set after the other boats.

Soon the rest of the women drifted away to their own men in their own boats and to the fish they might yet redeem from the bargaining pile. Only three, and those beyond speech, were left on the sand. The fisherman stood stiffly in the breeze; tall and lean, the salt winds had long since scoured away any extra weight, and the sun had burnished his skin like old leather. His wife, short and lean, whittled by worry and trimmed by toil, cradled the body of her boy in her arms, rocking him as though he were once again the infant in need of comfort. Her sobs were echoed by the keening of the gulls overhead.

And then the beggar came to them, and they were no longer alone. Where there had been sand and silence, there was now an unobtrusive presence beside them. He was an unremarkable beggar in a dusty brown cloak of many patches. He was neither old nor young, short nor tall, but the traces of countless miles were plain on his countenance.

The beggar reached down and boldly stroked the dead boy's hand. "He is only asleep, you understand. This kind of death is not forever."

The fisherman turned to the beggar with an angry fist clenched tightly at his side. "What *kind* of death?" he challenged. "Death is *death!* Do you not know it even when he gapes before your eyes?"

The woman said nothing, only crying softly and gripping her boy, and staring out at the sea, her endless, eternal enemy: strong, unbeaten and ever hungry.

"I know your mind," the beggar said softly to the woman, ignoring the man and his anger for the moment. "No enemy is truly eternal, though it may seem endless. It is one thing to be undefeated, and another thing entirely to be undefeatable. Perhaps in the end you shall see this ocean burn."

The beggar shifted his stance, and the fisherman saw his face clearly for the first time.

"You!" he exclaimed, and then his voice dropped to a whisper. "Your face has haunted my dreams."

The beggar peered intently into the eyes above his own. "You have seen me many times when your eyes were closed. Open your eyes now, and behold me in person!"

"Who are you?" he asked uneasily.

"Who did you expect from your dreams?" countered the beggar. "Did not the man who haunts your dreams come with a message from the Elder God?"

"Then you came with lightning and with power," he replied, "but I see now you are no strong man."

"Strength can be measured in many ways," the beggar answered, a smile playing at the corners of his mouth. "Miracles do not depend upon muscle but on a higher might."

"A miracle? You are too late. I sought a miracle this morning."

"You will have more than your fill this evening."

"And what is the name of the man who makes me this promise?"

"There is more than one answer to that question," replied the beggar, "for names are a subtle business. Perhaps it is best if you call me Covenant; for I am a man of many words, and all of them are true. I give promises, and then I keep them."

"I am Seareaper," said the rugged fisherman, more gently now. "My wife is Wavewatcher. The boy is—was—Foamrider." The beggar only nodded, as though hearing old facts confirmed. "He had only us, and we had only him."

"And now you are desolate?"

"No! I will wrest from the sea its treasure, as I always have!" he shouted fiercely, gesturing at the dark water with clawed hands. He had finished his crying already, through the long day at sea, but his anger still burned in the approaching dusk. He was thinking of the treasures he had already given in exchange.

"The ocean and I are old enemies," he continued, watching the restless waves vent their energy on the sand. "My brother, too, was taken by the sea. He, and our father before us and my wife's father before her." He turned to Covenant. "The sea is not a kind companion."

"Many things are your enemy in this world," said the beggar, "but not the one who stands before you. My name is Covenant, and I practice the impossible. Do you dare to hope in your darkness?"

Seareaper remained silent, and spoke for his wife as well.

"I did not think you would," continued Covenant. "I know you to be a skeptical man, who believes in nothing that he cannot see or taste or hold in his hands. I have come to change that. I bring you a challenge," he said. "Give me your boat, and I shall give you back your boy."

Wavewatcher could stand their conversation no more; she stood with her boy's body in her arms and began walking wearily toward the village. Seareaper watched her tenderly, but could find nothing to say to her.

When she was many yards away, the fisherman laughed sadly and turned to mock the beggar. "I have lost my boy. Must I lose my boat as well? Get out of here," he said bitterly. "We have little use for those who do not earn their keep."

"I may or may not be a beggar. Is he a beggar who owns everything and keeps nothing? Trade me your boat for your boy," he repeated, not mockingly but as one issuing a dare. "Someday, I shall have a voyage to make from these coasts."

Seareaper stared out to sea and answered with defeat ringing hollowly in his voice. "Why not? I can always build another boat." He gazed after his wife fondly but sadly. "And we are too old to build another boy."

"Then let us go aboard the *Childsbreath,* you and I," suggested the beggar. "She is a chosen vessel and may show us a wonder or two."

Curiosity and grief tumbling in his heart, Seareaper began to scrape his tired body across the sand to the crowded pier, bustling with buying and business. The beggar followed but did not cease his questions as they walked. "Names are important. Tell me where *Childsbreath* comes from," he prompted.

"You seem to know everything; you should know that as well."

"I know that your boat has both an unusual name and a figurehead," said Covenant. "The others have only names, and those more common."

They could see the figurehead clearly now, the wooden image of a child with compelling eyes and outstretched arms.

"I carved it myself," said Seareaper, "for I could describe it for no one else to carve. Only my mind's eye saw it well, and even so this is a faint wooden reflection. I have seen it only in my dreams, but then many times. I would know the child if I saw him."

"And the name?"

"*Childsbreath* because this tiny child in my dreams came to me and breathed on me gently. His breath was very, very sweet and left me aching and fulfilled at the same time."

They began to wade from the shore into the shallow water. Most of the boats had unloaded now, and only one other boat remained at the pier in front of them.

"Why do you ask these questions?" queried Seareaper. "You are only playing with me, for you know the answers already."

"I do, but it is you who must voice the answers aloud."

"You were in those dreams as well. I saw you standing together."

They reached the *Childsbreath* and clambered aboard.

"Go on home," Seareaper said to his friend at the tiller. "The hard part is done."

The friend departed, and Seareaper turned his eyes ahead.

Riding high and light now in the water, the last boat before them eddied away from the uneven pier into the harbor. There were still five empty wagons, with impatient and frustrated buyers, each envisioning a wasted night and day before the empty boats could go and return laden.

"So few fish," Seareaper muttered, "compared to the other catches. It hardly seems worth selling them now. Perhaps I should keep them and dry them for another time."

"Fish do not keep well," said the beggar. "They were never intended to leave the sea. You would be better served to sell them to those who would buy, or, better yet, to give them away to those who cannot buy." He gestured to a ragged company of women and children who stood forlornly a few paces from the wagons. "There are hungry people in your village. Why do you not feed them first?"

"The buyers have more money," replied Seareaper curtly. "As always, those with no money may have the fish worth the fee." He pointed further along the shoreline, downwind from the village, where long-winged gulls wheeled over piles of dead and rotting fish—bony fish, gnarled with impossible scales or filled with poison and agony, discarded for the birds and the poor to pick over. "All the spoils of the sea go to Glory," he said bitterly. "We keep only what they do not buy and need not be left for the scavengers."

"Have you any fish?" One of the fishmongers called from beside his wagon.

"A few," Seareaper called back disconsolately, readying a hawser to be tossed ashore.

"I'll buy all you have," said the man as he grabbed the rope and made it fast to the pier. "High prices for good fish!"

Seareaper looked down at the few dozen fish heaped in the bottom of the boat. "It won't take long to load them," he said only to himself and the following breeze. "Or much money to buy them."

He was wrong. He unloaded fish from the boat onto the buyer's scales until the wagon was piled high and deep and his back ached. Each time he reached in for what must surely be the last fish, he felt three more beneath his groping fingers.

The sun slid further and further down the sky, but still there were fish in the boat. One fishmonger had already tired of the wait and gone away for the night. The remaining three buyers vied for the fisherman's attention and succeeded; Seareaper's final fish filled the final wagon, and the *Childsbreath* rode like a feather at the empty pier. The wagons creaked away behind a storm of curses, and there were none left on the pier save a few ever-hopeful beggars and a handful of men who had heard of the miracle of the fish. Seareaper counted the coins cupped in his hands and would not look at Covenant.

"Why is there more money here in my hand than was paid me? Another one of your tricks?"

"Perhaps. There were those in the wagons who weighed with light scales and paid with lighter coins. I do not think they will all profit from their unworthy trade," said Covenant. "Tomorrow's wind may be ripe with the reek of rotting fish on the road to Glory."

"This is a miracle, but it is a miracle that cannot heal tragedy. It is still blood money! Take it! I cannot keep this in exchange for my own flesh!"

Covenant shook his head.

Seareaper clutched only what the fish were worth in his eyes and scattered the rest of the coppers to the ring of hungry and puzzled watchers. "Then *you* take it! I cannot keep blood money!"

They scrambled for the coins even as other villagers arrived. Word of the miracle of the fishes had spread quickly, and news of the overflowing coppers was soon added to the rumors.

"Would you see another miracle?" the beggar called to the gathering people, although Seareaper saw the beggar's eyes fixed on him alone. "All you who caught no coins, go to the place of the worthless fish and gather all that you can. Those fish may be despised and discarded, but they shall not be worthless to you. Each of you take as many fish as you can carry in your baskets. Take everything—the meatless, the poisonous, the disgusting. Bring them back here, all of you, and I will show you a third miracle."

A very few went. Some laughed openly. The rest made no motion at all.

Not knowing what else to do, Seareaper huddled at the bow of the *Childsbreath* and cradled his head in his arms.

Everyone waited for a spectacle, some less patiently than others, and they were not disappointed. When the desperate few returned with the long-dead fish, the stench came with them.

"Their reek rises to the heavens," grumbled Seareaper.

"They were not meant to rot," Covenant answered, "for they were never meant to die." He gestured at the ancient graveyard further up the hill. "Nor were they. And the day shall come when they will never be dead again."

Seareaper's response burst from him unchecked even by politeness now. "First you talk of death that isn't, and now you give us this: a parade of fools, worthless men bearing even more worthless fish! You laughed at death while we cried, and now you are solemn while we laugh at you! You do not fit in this world."

"Perhaps it is this world which no longer fits around me. As for worth, it is not your task to assign value to men." Then Covenant spoke to a boy standing close before him, holding a long-dead fish at arm's length. "Open its mouth," he commanded. The boy did, and shook a copper coin out into his hand. The rest pried dead jaws apart and found similar gifts. Murmurs exploded into a riot of sound.

One family, who had gone with more children and so carried back more fish, poured their copper coins together in a jingling mass. Other villagers ran to rummage and dispute over the distant piles of discarded fish, looking for more coins that were not there. It was far too late for them. They found no coppers, no wondrous fish, only smell and stench and rotten meat and decay that would not easily wash away.

Covenant spoke again to the boy, still standing open-mouthed before him on the pier. "Now throw your fish back into the water." Unwatched in the confusion, the boy hurled the rotting carcass into the waves. The fish swam away, diving down and then arrowing up into the air to show its perfect gleaming flank in the last rays of twilight.

Covenant looked up to ensure that Seareaper had seen the splash and what followed after. Then the beggar stepped onto

the dock and tugged the rope away from the post on the pier.

Seareaper let the foaming water nudge the *Childsbreath* away from the dock toward her anchor in deeper water. On the pier, the disappointment of the remaining villagers turned to anger. They sought the beggar, but he was not there. No one seemed to know where he had gone.

THREE

The Face Between the Pages

W HERE IS COVENANT?" ASKED BEAUTY.

"Where he has chosen to be," answered Wordsmith. "Come and see, if you wish." He drew her to the west-facing window of his tower, and they watched as the view steadily magnified itself, over and over again, to show the figure of the beggar walking along a lonely seashore.

"In all this land," said Wordsmith, "I have seen no corner that is not his."

"But not all hearts are his."

"No, but remember that I can see only places here, and things, and not into houses or hearts." He gestured to the fifth window. "Only there may I see things that are not to be seen otherwise, and I see through that window but do not control what it shows."

"Or always understand it," she added softly, moving her hands along his arm and kneading his shoulder. He bent his back to her ministrations and cradled his head on the table, nudging the litter of papers and leather to one side.

"I have been watching him," murmured Wordsmith from between his hands.

"What is he doing?" asked Beauty.

"I am not sure," shrugged Wordsmith. "I can see many miles from this window, but sound does not carry here. Death is there, and now sadness and anger. I will not know the full story until I meet him again. When he has finished in this village, I am to leave here and find him along the road to another place."

"So many things you have seen figured. Are all of those people coming here? Who will be next?" she wondered. "They continue to come even when he is not here."

"It will not be long. Covenant said before he left that our company would grow before he returned."

The shadows fell along the seashore, and they could see no more from the window. Only the strange fifth window continued to swirl and bloom and reveal marvels to the man appointed to see its secrets.

* * *

Beauty descended and found the Chameleon Lady in one of the lower rooms.

"Are you in need of anything I can bring you?" Beauty asked.

The face before her blurred before settling into yet another countenance. "No, there is nothing you have the power to bring me. If there were, I'm convinced you would have by now." She looked up and smiled. "You have been most kind to me. You treat me as though I am still the same person you saw yesterday."

"Aren't you?"

"Not to your eyes."

Beauty shrugged. "I try to look for the person beneath the face anyway. It is not impossible with you, just harder."

"You have given to me freely and have asked nothing of me. Why?"

"I spoke those same words when first I came here," Beauty said. "We can give kindness and mercy only because we have received the same here ourselves—from Covenant."

"Tell me more of Covenant and this house."

"I have been here only a handful of months, and yet there is so much to say that I do not know where to begin."

"Start with yourself, if you please. Why are you here? You are beautiful enough to be celebrated in Glory."

"I was," said Beauty softly, "but Glory turned its back on me, and I turned my back on Glory. On a road into the wilderness I came upon a beggar and a handsome man, sitting on a rock and awaiting my footsteps. Each one gave me a road to choose with promises at the end. Even though Fame was attractive, I did not trust him. He offered me more of the same life I had tasted in Glory and had grown weary of."

A troubled look spread over the lady's changing eyes. "I have heard of Fame, but I have never seen him."

"I have seen him several times since that day . . . It is often hard to remember that though he is handsome and tall and powerful, his image is a mask. He means evil to anyone who seeks Covenant."

"Why should he hate Covenant?"

"I do not know the details," Beauty admitted, "but they have long been foes. Theirs is an ancient feud, going deeper than the bone."

The Chameleon Lady's next question was followed by another answer that raised more questions, and they talked long over the glowing fire.

*　*　*

Far from Glory, and far from Graycove, another fire burned late in a dwelling in one of the smaller villages. There, wrapped in his own solitude, a young man turned the pages of the ancient book again and wondered when its prophecies would come true.

" 'The greatest warrior of all will come,' " he murmured, remembering and only half seeing the words.

It is time, he thought, *to see if these promises have come true. Someone in Glory must know the truth behind the rumors of the man who sells written wisdom in the marketplace and invokes the name of the Elder God. I must go and see if he is the one.*

" 'When the hour of need is greatest,' " he recited aloud to no one but himself and the shadows, " 'the great warrior will appear, though only one will know him when he comes . . .

" 'And he will wield the sword of justice and the blade of righteousness,' like *this* . . ." He gestured in the darkness and prayed that he would live to see this warrior.

The shadows fell thickly from his thin body, and for a moment the shape of a giant danced upon the wall.

Then he sank back into himself, banked the fire and slept. In the morning he put on his cloak and wrapped his book in a leather pouch. Then he went out into the light and began the day's walk to Glory, seeking the man in the marketplace who stood and sold his curious books.

He found Wordsmith there on one of the street corners, gazing at the crowds but not seeing them. The expression in his eyes hinted that he watched the dance of distant planets rather than the parade of people.

The young man peered closely into Wordsmith's face. "You are not the one," he said disappointedly.

"I am Wordsmith," he answered. "Who are you looking for?"

"I am looking for the light of an old promise. I am looking for the mighty warrior who is to come."

"I am not a mighty warrior; I am a hobbling scribbler who dreams dreams and sells the words in the market."

The young man's face lost its disappointed look. "Do you sell wisdom, then?" he asked.

Wordsmith regarded him with open curiosity. "I sell the wisdom of the Elder God," he answered. "These books hold my words, but it is not my wisdom."

"I believe," said the young man, "that you may know the man I have been seeking." His eyes gleamed with a fierce and sudden light, and Wordsmith knew that he had seen this face in the visions of the fifth window. "You must tell me the secret of an old prophecy."

"What secrets I know, I share gladly," said Wordsmith. "But there are countless things I do not understand, and prophecies are the deepest of mysteries."

"Yet they are true."

"If real prophecies, then very true indeed. But they remain dense and dark, and often not understood until after they have come to be."

"I have here an old book," said the young man. "I would ask you a question about it."

Wordsmith examined the book, probing the pages with his fingers. "I know nothing of this book," concluded Wordsmith, "save that it is very old and that the script is tiny and hard to read."

"I can read it well; I know it by heart."

"Tell me the story," asked Wordsmith. "Perhaps I have seen this book in a dream, but I do not know what is in it. Is there a sword? And a warrior?"

"Then you do know of the book!"

"No, but I am shown many things that I do not understand until they happen. Come, the day is almost done and there are few buyers here, so let us pack these books away and go to the House of Covenant. We may talk there and have no interruption."

"The House of Covenant?"

"Covenant is the reason I am here. He is not in the City just now, but when he returns, he can answer your questions. His answers, however, may give you new questions. Every word he says is true, but not every word is clear at the time it is spoken. He seems to know all and see all, but he tells only when it is time."

* * *

The two men sat in one of the small rooms in the house in Glory. The remains of a meal littered the table between them.

"I have had this book for many years," the stranger said, "and my fingers have almost worn their way through the pages. This book has been my secret because I have heard few mention the name of the Elder God. But that name I have heard from your lips, and I was told it is here in your books.

"When I look at the book long enough," he went on, "and gaze at the words, and try to peer behind them, I can begin to see a face appearing between the pages."

"A face? Whose face?"

"I wish I knew him. It is the Warrior of the Elder God, Dreadnought the Freeblade, the mighty fighter who will come. I believe that I will see his face before I die, and if I can find him, I will offer him my service."

"The Warrior of the Elder God?" asked Wordsmith. "I know of the Elder God, but not this Warrior."

"The High Warrior, one who will be an earthly fighter on behalf of the Elder God, a mighty man who will walk with him, talk with him, obey him and be a sword of justice for him," recited the young man.

"And it is this face you are looking for?"

"Yes."

"You were disappointed when you saw me. You had heard of me, and you hoped to find that face upon my head?"

"Yes."

Wordsmith shook his head sadly. "I am sorry to have disappointed you. However, there is another here who knows much of old books," he continued. "Let us seek his counsel as well."

Wordsmith left, sought Binder and returned with him.

Binder lovingly perused the pages, well-worn by gentle handling and incessant turning of the vellum sheets. "It is not a book I have seen before," he said, "nor am I familiar with this sort of binding. It is old—very old. How long have you had it?"

"Two dozen years. It was given to me at my birth by an ancient woman who lived in the village."

"And there was no message left with it? No prophecy?"

"The book itself is the prophecy, and the message. I have read it, and I believe it with all my heart, and I almost understand it."

"Read it to both of us," urged Wordsmith, "that we might hear it and tell you what we know."

He laughed. "I need not *read* it! I know every word by heart."

He recited the full story, and after that they were silenced by wonder.

"The one who should answer you is not here," Wordsmith finally said, "but you are welcome to wait here until he returns. Tell us your name, that we may tell Covenant who waits for him."

The young man looked away from the flickering candle into the dancing darkness. "I am called Fearshadow," he said in a low voice, "but I despise that name."

"Then your name lies dead behind you at the door, if you wish it," said Wordsmith. "The master of this house gives good names to all who come here, and old names are quickly forgotten."

"But why not keep my name?" asked Fearshadow bitterly. "I have lived down to its meaning all my life, trembling at every hint of darkness, shunning all possible pain . . . I am not a brave man. Perhaps that is why I seek the company of the brave."

Wordsmith lifted his hand in surrender. "As you wish. I have no authority in this house to take names away or give new ones. Covenant will have the final word with you when he returns."

"And how long will that be?" asked Binder.

"I do not know," answered Wordsmith. "He is a long way from Glory, and I leave tomorrow to meet him in the wilderness."

"May I go with you?" asked Fearshadow eagerly. "I would see if *he* is the one."

"No," replied Wordsmith. "He has bid only me to come to him. I know where I will meet him, but I do not know what we are to do or where we will go from there or when we will return."

"He has not told you these things?"

Wordsmith eyed the young man for a moment. "He has not revealed all his thoughts to us, but he has revealed to us himself and his power as well. And to know him is to trust him and to follow at his command."

Fearshadow failed to find a reply.

"Think of this, Fearshadow," continued Wordsmith. "You have sworn allegiance to this warrior, even though you do not know if he is alive or even real. I have pledged my loyalty to Covenant, because of all men he is most real, and his call is to be trusted."

"But I would see if this Covenant is Dreadnought the Freeblade himself. How could it be otherwise? Look at his power and at the words of the prophecy."

"Covenant may or may not be the Freeblade. He has many names, but that is not one he has revealed to us. He already carries the words and the grace of the Elder God, but I cannot envision him with a sword in his hand.

"The hardest duty for the faithful is to wait patiently. I saw your book and your face in my dreams, and nothing is shown to me there in vain. Wait here, and learn the ways of this house. We shall return, and then you shall have your answer."

— FOUR —

The Boy
from the
Sea

A LATE FIRE BURNED IN SEAREAPER'S COTTAGE. THE FISHER-
man sat crumpled in a wooden chair, watching the flames
devour the splintered wood. Covenant leaned against the
doorjamb, half-concealed from the flickering light. He could
see Wavewatcher standing useless vigil in one darkened room
behind.

"You charmed the fish we caught," said the wrinkled, leath-
ery fisherman.

"I did," said the beggar.

"And you doubled the weight of my coppers."

"I did."

"And you made magic with the fish that perished long ago."

"That too."

"You offered me my son, but you have not given him."

"I have been waiting for you to challenge my words."

"Why are you still here? I am not poor any longer. You saw to that."

"Not poor in pocket, at least. But you are still poor in other things."

"You speak riddles. If it were not for what you have done already, I would wish you to go straight away."

"I know that too. That is why I multiplied your fish, so that you would talk to me now. You are a hard man, believing only what you have seen and examined and held in your hand. I bring you knowledge of a different sort, as well as a challenge to believe that which you have not yet seen."

"Who are you?" Seareaper asked solemnly. "You have told me your name, but not who you are. I would not choose to have one such as you angry with me."

"You have earned only my disappointment, not my anger. That could come another day. You have done some tasks at my bidding, but you will not believe until you have seen. Now, have you not seen four miracles in a single day?" inquired Covenant. "Surely if I can turn fish long rotted into fresh, I can bring new life to a boy not yet buried."

Hope and sorrow fought behind Seareaper's eyes. "No one comes back from the dead," he spat, leaving his words in the air like a dare.

"No boat the size of yours can fill four wagons, but yours did," countered Covenant. "And no fish was ever spawned that spewed coppers from its mouth, yet you held one in your hand. And can you explain coppers that multiply themselves in your hand?"

"I had heard of such things before—empty tales. I did not believe the ancient stories."

"Why? Because they were ancient or because they were stories? Haven't you had your measure of miracles? What more do you want?"

The woman spoke for the first time, her voice flat as she

drifted in from the next room. "Today has been a day of night-mares," she said, "and the only cure for nightmares lies in our wildest dreams."

"And what is your wildest dream?" returned Covenant. "There are as many dreams as there are dreamers."

"We both want what we dare not ask for," she retorted, moving out of the darkness into the firelight. "How could our need be plainer to you?"

"Those fish were despised, worth nothing to you, to the others, even to the birds," said Covenant. "Yet I found it worthwhile to give them life anew. Is the boy of your heart worth less than a poison fish that no man will ever see again?" He did not expect a spoken answer, and received none. "Do you believe?" he continued.

"I begin to believe," said Seareaper slowly, "but I do not understand at all."

"Belief and wisdom are not the same thing. Behold!" He pointed through the inner door.

Behind them, the boy came sleepy from the shadows.

"He will be hungry," said Covenant. "He has not eaten for a long time."

* * *

He ate in contented silence. The boy watched his father, and his eyes were full of questions. The father watched the beggar, and his eyes were full of gratitude. The mother's eyes were full of her son, and Covenant watched them all.

Not until they had finished did anyone speak again. "You have given us much," said Seareaper, "yet you have asked for nothing." He offered his words as a statement, but the wonder in his voice was not veiled.

"I claim your boat—not now, but for a later service."

"The boat is yours."

"Keep her for me."

"The boat is yours," repeated the old fisherman. "I keep my promises too."

"I give her back to you again. Use her well. Someday I shall return for her. That again is my word. And when I return, perhaps your son will journey with me. He, too, may see some wondrous things."

"Wondrous things, indeed. The village will not soon forget this night, for all saw Foamrider lifeless on the sand, and all will see him alive again tomorrow."

"They did and they shall. But I say that you should call him Foamrider no longer; let Seaswallower be his name. That would do nicely for a boy who has inhaled the ocean and yet lives to sail upon it."

"New names come hard to the tongue."

"Nevertheless, it pleases me to bestow new names on those who encounter me. Names mark both power and privilege. And there are better names for you as well, if you will receive them."

"You have earned that right," the fisherman admitted. "Name us as you will."

"What should I rename you?" mused Covenant, while they awaited his decision. "I shall call you Deedtester, for you have tried my works and found them true." He turned to Wave-watcher. "And you shall be Joykeeper. I have overcome your ancient enemy for you, and never more shall you despise and fear the sea."

"Will you tell me again why must you give us new names?" she asked.

"There are reasons beyond your imagining," said Covenant. "Everyone has a name, at least one name. And one name will be better and more suited than the rest. Your first names were only guesses and high hopes, or darkness seen and curses. Now your names tell what you do. When the time is at hand, I shall give you the names you have possessed all along and never heard spoken. Your hearts will leap when I name your true names, and no earthly title will ever satisfy you again.

"Your final names shall say for all to see who you shall be

44

then. Some names will be given in shame, for shame, and worn for shame forever. Blessed are you who are named with good names. Twice blessed are you who are renamed for the tasks you are called to do. Thrice blessed are they who are renamed a final time forever, by the mouth of the one whose hands made them."

In the awed silence the man finally spoke. "Then only my boat has its old name. Unless you would rechristen her as well."

"No," said Covenant, as his face showed the presence of warm memories, "I named her already in the dream I sent you. Let it remain the *Childsbreath*. There is both irony and prophecy in it."

After their meal, Covenant led the three others down to the pier. Deedtester strode beside the beggar, while mother and child followed together behind them.

"Tell me," Deedtester called to Covenant, "would he have drowned today if you had come yesterday?"

"No. That is why I did not come yesterday. Would you have believed in anything less than death undone?"

Again the fisherman let his silence answer for him.

They reached the weathered wooden structure creaking out over the water, scoured of coppers now but still strewn with the stinking remains of old catches. "This pier needs cleansing," Covenant said. "Let us try our hand as the boy did." He threw a dead and blackened fish into the lively yet blacker water. They heard it splash away and saw the phosphorescent trail blooming behind it as it headed for open water.

The boy began to gather the rest of the discarded fish, his excitement increasing as one by one they splashed, flashed and headed out to sea. The others helped, but the splendid sight was the boy dancing in the waves, a silhouette against the reflected moonlight.

His parents stood together in the darkness, holding hands

and marveling. When they turned to face the land again, Covenant was gone.

* * *

"We did not thank him enough," said Deedtester to his wife later, as they sat at each other's side and watched wild images dance in the fire.

"Perhaps we shall try when he comes again," she replied, "*if* there is a next time."

"He has promised a next time," her husband said as they stared into the waning fire, "and he seems to keep his promises. We have not seen the last of him."

─── FIVE ───

Words in the Wilderness

WORDSMITH HELD BEAUTY'S HAND ACROSS THE TABLE. "Covenant has called me to go on a journey with him," he said quietly. "He has said that he has much for my eyes and ears alone."

"Will you be gone long?" she asked, tightening her fingers about his.

"I don't know," he replied, "but whether a long journey or a short one I must go."

"I wish you could stay here, or perhaps take me with you."

"So do I," he answered. "You were my free choice," continued Wordsmith in a voice almost too soft to be heard, "and I would ever choose that choice again. But Covenant calls, and it is a call that must be answered."

She nodded, and a tear spilled down her cheek.

"Are you afraid that you won't see me again?" he asked.

She nodded again, and the twin of the first tear marked her other cheek.

"Then fear not, because Covenant has said that our work here is not finished. And when has Covenant's word ever failed to come true?"

* * *

Covenant and Wordsmith met in the high desert, and their friendship was rekindled.

"I asked you to meet me on the way," said Covenant, "that I might talk to you and to you alone."

"And you have two fresh puzzles awaiting you in Glory," Wordsmith said. He went on to describe the Chameleon Lady and Fearshadow and their quests.

"They will have their answers," the beggar said, "when they have learned to ask the right questions."

"And you will give them new names as well, I assume."

"Yes."

"Are Fearshadow's words true?" Wordsmith asked. "It is a most amazing story."

"You have walked with me, and you know some of my ways. Do you think his story is true?"

"I do not know," admitted Wordsmith. "It tastes of the Elder God, but it deals with events I cannot imagine. Why should we need a swordsman? We are in peace here, not peril. And where should we find this swordsman?"

"He will find us. Do you doubt my word?"

"I do not doubt your sayings and your promises. I simply do not understand them."

"Be content in your ignorance for now," Covenant said, "for when the veil of darkness is finally lifted, you will have much sorrow before you find your joy again. And that, my friend, is why you should carry this book always." Covenant handed him a tiny leather-bound book.

Wordsmith took the gift with pleasure and carefully turned

the bright, translucent pages. "There is nothing in it," he said. "The pages are blank."

"That is because you have not filled it with words," Covenant replied.

"What words?"

"The words I have not yet spoken to you," he answered. "I must tell you many things—more than stories, more than legends, more than wishful thinking. What I tell you now, you will not understand—but you will record it anyway, and when the time has come, you will turn to it again."

"Is this why you bid me come with quill and ink, but no paper?"

Covenant nodded, and waved his hand for Wordsmith to be seated on a rock. Then Covenant spoke, a timeless stream of words about righteousness, and long-dormant evil now approaching, and war, and Fame, and enemies pressing in on every side. And what Wordsmith heard he wrote down, and it filled him with both sadness and hope.

The hours passed as they worked, one speaking with solemn gentleness and the other writing as fast as he could. When the words were done and the book was filled, Wordsmith laid his head on his folded hands and said, "These are great and mighty and fearful words indeed—but I can scarcely remember a word now."

"You do not need to remember," Covenant replied. "The book will make sense to you only when it is time."

In the morning they began to walk back to Glory.

* * *

"Covenant," asked Wordsmith, "was this land always like this?" He gestured at the arid spaces and sterile soil and forbidding mountain ranges about them.

"No," said Covenant. "It has decayed to this. It was once magnificent, and unspoiled."

"It is still magnificent, even in desolation."

"Some things cannot be destroyed. The earth shudders, and

buildings fall. Rivers carve new courses, and old coasts are exchanged for new beaches sanded from the heart of the sea. This is a restless earth."

"This is a beautiful land," Wordsmith said, "even though it is stark and brutal."

"Someday it shall be even more beautiful again, for it shall cease to be merely stark. This land was created for peace and happiness, which cannot dwell undimmed in the midst of darkness, despair and death. The land crumbles where Fame rules."

"Again, I do not understand. Does Fame rule, or does the King, or is it you who rules in secret?"

"Yes," Covenant answered simply. "The King holds the reins of power, but Fame's hands guide the hands that hold the reins. The King is only a royal shadow, a puppet, a toy, a mask. But someday the King must fall ill and die, and who will rule in his place? He has no children, no heritage, no prince or favored counselor waiting patiently in the treacherous darkness behind the throne."

"Is Fame his true name?"

"Recall that his other name is *Twister*."

"Is that his true name, or one you have given him?"

"His first name shimmered and scattered light; then he chose Fame for himself, and was branded Twister by the Elder God."

"And does he have a secret and final name?" Wordsmith asked.

"He does—and it will be terrible to hear. He will have no joy when the words are uttered."

SIX

Rockhaven

COVENANT AND WORDSMITH STOPPED IN THE DUST OF THE thin road and gazed down into the valley that opened itself before them.

"What was this place?" asked Wordsmith, pointing at the rubbled rock ruins ahead. "Was it once a village? There is fear here now. I can almost taste it."

"I know," said Covenant. "That is why we have come."

They walked down into silence and stone disarray.

"Someone lives here," said Wordsmith, "but where? There is scarcely any shelter left."

A man and his child emerged from the rocks to meet the travelers. The man held a bow with an arrow already nocked; like his father, the tiny boy held a toy bow and arrow.

"I thought you were the wolves again," muttered the man.

"There are human wolves as well," said the beggar, "but we are not wolves of either kind."

"Where are the walls?" asked Wordsmith. "You should not have to worry about a handful of wolves."

"Once there was a village here, with houses, stables, a stout wall. There was shelter here," said the man, "shelter and enough—until the ground shook and the walls crumbled and most died beneath the stones. Those who survived left, except for us."

"And you stayed here alone?" inquired Wordsmith.

"The ground in this valley is fertile," the man said. "The weather is warm, and there is water in abundance. Why should I leave?"

"Yet you live in fear of the wolves."

"Could you ignore them if your protection had crumbled?"

Covenant did not reply, but only gazed at the fallen walls.

The man walked about uneasily. Where he strode, the child strode; where he stopped, the child stopped.

"There is more damage here than was done by an earthquake," said Covenant. "Many of these stones have been rolled away from the places where they fell."

The man nodded, but said nothing.

"Who moved these stones away?" asked Covenant.

"I did," the man reluctantly acknowledged.

"Where are they now?"

"Down there," he pointed. "They line my garden and give us shade where the pool comes down from the mountains. I could move the stones down the hill to build new buildings," said the man defensively, "but not up the hill to rebuild the old ones. Not by myself. You cannot defend a wall that has fallen."

"No, you cannot. Even less can you defend a wall which has been carried away."

An uncomfortable silence enveloped them before the man grudgingly asked if they needed water or a place to rest their feet.

Covenant accepted for them, and they ascended to a cleft in the rocks, a broad cave defended by only a few roughly placed boulders. Smaller stones and mortar had been pounded into the gaps; even so, it was barely worth the name of shelter. The cave was wide but shallow, with little protected room for a fire. A woman was struggling to create a flame in the broken oven, muttering over the crumbly bark and green wood. She looked up briefly and angrily, then turned again to the unborn fire. The spark from her stones was feeble, and Wordsmith did not think any fire would endure even a light rain.

Covenant looked sadly at their poor quarters.

"The wolves come every night," the man explained. "There is no other place to hide."

"If the walls were repaired, you would have no reason to huddle in the cave."

"If the walls were repaired," said the man sharply, "many of my problems would be solved."

"You have the child here," said Covenant. "Let him defend the walls."

"But he is only a babe!" snorted the man. "It is I who must protect *him!*"

"Against certain dangers, perhaps," answered Covenant. "There are some perils that perhaps only a child could discern, and some burdens that only a child could carry."

The man would not look at them now, but spat into a brittle shrub and began to shape the sand aimlessly with his foot.

The child, doing as his father did, spat dryly at the bush and drew figures in the dust.

"I have come," announced Covenant, "that you might re-build these walls. If you wish to survive the wilderness this valley has become, you must undo the damage that has been done here—both by nature and by your own hands."

"Who are you?" the man asked bluntly.

"I am Covenant," said the beggar. "This is Wordsmith, my friend and companion."

"I am Audin," said the man dully. "This is my child, Carlin, and there is my wife, Sabrin. Where do you come from?"

"There is a time for questions," Covenant said, "and there is a time for obedience. You must carry the first rock now. The rest may come later. Take the one that lies at your feet and lift it." He smiled. "It is more important than you can possibly imagine."

Reluctantly, Audin picked up a boulder and lugged it up the hill to the old wall. He thunked it into its former place and picked his way down the hill again, breathing hard.

"Now what?" he asked the beggar arrogantly. "Will the wolves be afraid of that?"

"Watch and see," said Covenant quietly. "You have done well. Rest for a moment, and have your eyes opened."

The child—doing as his father had done—selected a small rock at his feet, hefted it in his fists, carried it up the hill and laid it carefully on the remains of the wall.

"And again," said Covenant to Audin. "Grasp the largest stone you can lift and replace it."

He did so with enormous difficulty, and afterward sat panting on the ground near Covenant.

They watched as the child grasped a hewn boulder three times his own size and lifted it into the air.

Audin began to leap to his aid, but Covenant restrained him with one arm. "Say nothing to him," he commanded. "He does not know this is beyond his power. He does not know which work is impossible and which is merely difficult," said Covenant. "He is only doing what he has seen you do already."

The stone rolled into its rightful place.

"I do not believe what I am seeing!" breathed the man.

"You shall come to believe many things more difficult than this. For the childlike, nothing shall be impossible. Do likewise."

Audin bent to the stones before him and found them as light as the boy believed. Dizzy, he could not restrain a chuckle of relief in the face of wonder and power.

"If the two of you work diligently," said Covenant, "the stones will not weary you, and you may finish before dark. It would be a pleasant surprise against the wolves.

"Do not forget me," added the beggar, "or my friend here. We shall meet again. You live in isolation here, but I reassure you that your hopes still lie in Glory."

"Don't go!" said Audin. "I want to know what your power is."

"You will learn more of me in times to come. For now, behold what has happened, and accept my new names for the two of you: you are Stonesetter in my eyes, and the boy shall be called Featherstone."

Stonesetter's eyes accepted the command, though he did not understand. Covenant offered only his infectious smile for an explanation. With a warm wave he drifted across the hill through the passage to the open kitchen. There he bent to help Sabrin, still focused upon the stubborn fire. But she urged him away, saying roughly, "It may be a poor place, but it is my place, and I have always managed. You've taken up my man's time already, and I won't give you any of mine."

Covenant's offered assistance blunted itself on her suspicion and disbelief. He smiled sadly and let the rotten tinder crumble in her fingers. He abandoned her territory to her again and went outside to see a man at work and a child at play, and both rebuilding the wall.

"Doubt can be challenged and cured," he said to Wordsmith, "but there is no remedy for stubborn disbelief. The walls here are not the only things made of stone."

SEVEN

A Cure
for
Chameleon

WHEN COVENANT AND WORDSMITH RETURNED TO GLORY, Fearshadow was waiting for them on the stone steps of the house. He bounded down to the street to meet them, peering anxiously into Covenant's face; once again, he was disappointed.

"Do not be sad," Covenant said. "I know your quest, and I promise you that your heart's desire will not remain unfulfilled."

"When? How? Who?" he asked impatiently.

"Let us eat," said Covenant, drawing him along to the house. "Let us have our leisure with the others, and then we will talk. Beauty has prior claim upon Wordsmith, and you are not the only one who has come searching for an answer: there is a lady as well."

"Yes," he said, feeling suddenly ashamed of his eagerness, "she is inside. I hope that you can help her."

Their meal was happy and noisy, and the Chameleon Lady sat patiently observing, laughing here and there, until all were finished and only she and Covenant sat in the room.

"I have heard many good things about you," she began.

"All of them are true," he replied, his smile carrying away any offense that the words might have caused.

His candor surprised her; she hesitated, then spoke directly to her need. "Wordsmith has told you of me?" she asked.

"Yes, and I know more than he has told me."

"How many people have you seen in my face tonight?" she asked bluntly.

"Only one," Covenant said.

"Then you are not affected by the magic?"

"No."

"Beauty said as much. Is it, indeed, a true face, or does it shift from one image to another?"

"The face I see is the true one, but it is not the face you bear here."

"Is it a good face?"

"It is a very fine face, but it is hidden. You have been false," he continued gently, "and for now you must bear the burden of falsehood."

She fingered her necklace. "I have tested the metal," she said. "It will bend but will not break, and no tool can cut it. It shines like gold, but is more resistant than diamond."

She looked up. "Will not *your* magic melt it?" she asked hopefully.

Covenant traced his finger along the line of the necklace and shook his head. "Some magic is best cured by magic," he said, "and some magic is best remedied a better way. The highest kind of magic is neither angry nor violent," he continued, "nor does it have destruction as its purpose."

"Is there a way to unwind this chameleon curse?"

"There is, but it is not simple, and it is not easy to find. What has been cursed by a man must be cured by a man. If there is a powerful man who will place his pledge around this one and make you his own, he will end the curse. But even then he will not know what you truly look like until after the first night with you."

"Who would take such a chance as that?" she asked, expecting no answer and receiving none. She thought, and then said, "Will a man, indeed, solve my problems, or only cause more? Men have been the cause of my greatest griefs."

"Only he who has the power to bring you great grief can also bring you great joy. A man who cannot hurt you cannot heal you." He waved his hand in the air. "Nor is it written anywhere that you must find or even accept this cure. You are alive and well and need not have a man to be welcome and useful here. The flesh fades, and all faces change with time; you are not the only one who strives with a visage that is not the same from day to day.

"There is hope," he continued, "and there are promises, but now is not the time to talk of them. A better time will come later. Besides, I bring you not only a welcome but also a task for you, a task that no one else here can do."

Her eyes brightened. "What can I do that lies in my hands alone?" she wondered.

"You can deliver a special message to the King," answered Covenant evenly.

"The King!" she exclaimed. "No one goes there without invitation!"

"Or those who have the proper face, and your face just now is in the eye of the beholder. To the guards at the gates, you will be one of the servants. To the servants inside, you will be another visitor not to be noticed. And to the King, you will be his Queen."

"But she has been dead for twenty years!" she objected.

"She lives in his heart still," observed Covenant, "and her

beauty will never fade for him.

"He has many advisors, but they are weak; he trusts none of them. He hears their words, and he nods, but then he does what is right in his own eyes. But he will fall before you and beseech you to speak. He will hear you because he believes he has already heard her voice from beyond the grave.

"I have removed all obstacles from your path, and nothing can prevent you now but your own fears."

She pondered the idea. "But if I go, what must I say to him?" she asked.

"When you are ready to leave for the palace, I will teach you what you should say. The King dreams much, and even a forgotten god can still speak in dreams." He smiled again, and they went on to talk of other things.

EIGHT

The Search for Freeblade

FEARSHADOW STOOD IN THE HIGH TOWER AND MARVELED at Wordsmith's windows.

"Are these things true already?" he asked.

"What you see in these four windows is happening as you see it," Wordsmith said. "As for the fifth window, I am never sure. Things that could happen, things that should happen, things that will happen . . . it is hard to tell the difference until the reality arrives."

"All I see are blurs and strange signs and uncountable stars."

"Few people see things clearly there."

"And you are one of the special people?"

Wordsmith hesitated. "I would not call myself special—rather would I call this a very special window."

"And you see visions in its depths?"

"I do."

Fearshadow nodded. "I think I understand. I see a single vision, and that within the pages of my book."

"Does anyone else see that same vision there?"

"No."

"Then you understand perfectly."

They looked down at the street and saw Candle heading toward his shop.

"Is it Candle who supports this house?" Fearshadow asked.

"Some of his profits are used here, but this house does not depend on him or his work," replied Wordsmith. "He is a trader in fine goods, and he meets many who come to Glory for the first time and do not know where to begin to see what is here.

"Some find more than they expected," he added. "I have put all their stories in this book—at least, as far as their stories go. The endings are still unknown, though Covenant has given us many bright promises." He waved the stranger to a seat while opening his book. "Candle and Moonflower, first united in life and then in death, and now reunited in life again." He turned the pages. "Trueteller, the mother of Moonflower. Once an outcast and now a matron of much honor. Lionheart, a shaggy-headed young man with a harvest of infants and ancients abandoned as useless and unwanted in the wilderness, a man who rides lions through the darkness and roars with them in their wild and exuberant power." He smiled inside at the image and went on. "Binder, once a narrow-visioned collector of fine books, now a man who has found more value in the souls of humanity and in books than in their outward bindings. And Firecolt and Flamerider—the fire brothers—the two street boys Binder rescued from the flames that consumed his house after an earthquake.

"And there was Woebearer, the hunchback, who emerged from a mysterious and shameful life to spend the rest of his days absorbing other people's pains and carrying other people's burdens. Woebearer went ahead to the City when all the wax of the candle of his body had been consumed."

He gestured to the back of the house below them. "There are favored beasts as well, asleep in the stables at the back: Roadreeler the horse, who carried Trueteller and Candle and Moonflower to Glory, and Kingsburro the donkey, who served first Trueteller and then Covenant.

"All of these—men, women, children and animals—are the Company of Covenant. Covenant, the beggar who walks like a king and who comes in the name of the Elder God. All have been given new lives and new hearts by Covenant; most have been given new names as well."

"Covenant," said Fearshadow. "Why has he not spoken to me yet? He knows of my search, and he said only that we would talk of it later. Since that day I have scarcely seen him across the room."

"He has his own times and his own ways. I do not pretend to understand them, but I do value the gifts that he eventually brings our way.

"Bide your time—it is his time, too, and he seems to have an abundance of it."

*   *   *

The next day Fearshadow found Covenant sitting alone before breakfast.

"The one you seek is here in Glory," said Covenant without preamble.

The words burned in Fearshadow's heart like a welcome flame. "He is here? Where? Shall I see him?"

"You shall see him."

"May I serve him?"

"Not as you thought to serve, but you shall do his bidding. Go and search," Covenant said. "He is not to be found in the way you believe."

"Will I know him when I see him?"

"You will know his face," Covenant promised, "though you

63

will scarcely believe your own eyes. You must search diligently or you will not find his face."

Fearshadow was gone without another word. Late that night, and on each of the four succeeding nights, he returned in disappointment, turning to his book again by candlelight, seeking to refresh his memory of the face between the pages.

"I have disturbed everyone," he said to Covenant at last. "I have peered into every face in Glory and not found him. I have done all and found nothing."

"You have not yet peered into *every* face in Glory," said Covenant. "Perhaps you are looking too hard, and in all the difficult places.

"How long has it been since you beheld your own face?" asked Covenant.

"What do I care for *my* face?" responded Fearshadow, gesturing at his book. "I have been searching other faces to see *this* one."

"Look into the book again," Covenant commanded, "and tell me of the face you see there."

Fearshadow gazed into the pages and was silent for a while. "I see him again now," he said at last, "and clearly. He is not tall, or broad, but his eyes burn with holy fire, and he wields an unnatural strength that he does not claim as his own. His face glows with his calling, and foes quake at the sight. He is a bloody man and bowed with pain, but not defeated."

"What is a book?" asked Covenant.

Fearshadow, bewildered, spoke slowly. "A book is a group of pages bound together," he said. "There are words written on the pages, and the words make a story."

"A book can be much more than that," suggested Covenant. "You understand only the half because you see only the half: this is not only a book," he stressed, "but a mirror."

Fearshadow stared at him without comprehension. "A book reflects nothing save the spirit and intent of its author."

"It does reflect that, and more than you might think." He

took Fearshadow's arm and led him down the long halls to Covenant's mirror.

"Look into the mirror," suggested Covenant.

Fearshadow did so, and what he saw there staggered him.

He finally turned to Covenant. "Can it be?" he asked.

"It can," answered Covenant. "It can, and it is. *There* is the face you have been seeking. The words have soaked into your heart as well as your imagination, and shaped your face as well as your soul. That which you have yearned to find you have become.

"You have searched long for him; he was with you every step on every road, and yet you continually looked away. It was fitting that you did so, for you have learned to seek the best in others first. In futility you learned patience, and in meditation you have absorbed a noble countenance."

Covenant reached above the mirror, where a fine wooden sword was carved deep into the grain of the frame. He grasped it, and it came alive in his hands, a right blade, deadly, keen and sharp, a weapon that glittered even in the twilight of the hall and further heightened Fearshadow's awe.

"Kneel before me," commanded Covenant. The young man obeyed without question. "I know your old name," continued Covenant, "but now it is dead, as your old self is dead. Receive, then, this double name of honor. I name you Dreadnought Freeblade—Swordsman of the Elder God, Champion of the Company of Covenant and Defender of the Child."

He glided the gleaming flat of the blade over Freeblade's cheeks, and then commanded him to rise and take the sword.

"This is now your companion and your charge," Covenant said sadly. "I wish that you would never have need to pull it from its sheath, but you shall be forced to draw much blood with it."

Freeblade's tears dropped freely to the floor, but none of them were wasted.

"Has there ever been such a blade as this?" he breathed.

"No," Covenant said simply. "There has not and will never be."

"Is it enchanted?"

"It is holy—that is better yet. Worthy kings carried it, for it was set apart in honor, and it in turn was honored by them. Not all the kings were selfish, evil or withdrawn, and not all of the king's men were more interested in their own comfort than in the prosperity of the land and its people."

Freeblade looked up from the blade at last and met Covenant's gaze. "What must I do now?" he asked.

"No battles, for now. Read your book again, knowing this time that the warrior is you."

"Covenant," he said, "who wrote this book?"

"There were other dreamers before Wordsmith, faithful men and women long since dead. The woman who wrote this book had scarcely left her childhood behind when she filled these pages. She was mother five times past to the elderly woman who left it you as a legacy."

NINE

A
Measure
of Mercy

Trueteller came seeking covenant in the silence of the early morning.

"Do you believe in dreams?" she asked quietly.

"For some people I am only a dream," he replied. "Do you believe in me?"

"Yes. You know I do. I have more reason than any to know that you are real."

"Then you should believe in some dreams as well."

"Only the good ones?" she asked.

"No. Some good dreams will come true, but so will some nightmares."

"I'm not sure if this is a dream or a nightmare."

"Tell me, then, and we will see if it might hold a seed of truth."

She took a deep breath but found no easy way to begin. "He is alive, isn't he?" she finally burst forth. "I saw him again in my dreams. He is alive, and he is a captive."

"You have not asked these questions before," Covenant stated.

"No."

"But these dreams are not new."

"No. I have seen my husband many times in my dreams—often in chains, sometimes underground—but always alive, always in trouble and despair. I have had them for many years, but never so frequently as now, and never so vividly as last night."

Covenant smiled. "But you have never mentioned them to me."

"I thought them wishful thinking—a fantasy—a desperate hope."

"All hope is desperate when it is not yet fulfilled."

"But now I know that many true things happen before we are ready to see or accept them . . . and I hesitated to ask you, because you have done so much for me already."

"Is that not a good reason for asking further favors? One does not number gifts where love exists. All you need do is tell me what you would know of me."

She drew breath and exhaled slowly. "First, I would know if my dreams are true. Is he alive?"

"He is."

Her heart leaped; she squeezed her eyes shut and could not trust herself to breathe.

"Is he free to return to me?" she finally asked.

"No."

Again she held her thoughts for a span of heartbeats, choosing her words carefully, both wanting to know and not wanting to know the answer.

"Has he forgotten me?"

"He has never forgotten you. You are the strongest single

hope that keeps him alive."

She sat and wept for joy, and he did not bother her. When her tears slackened, she said, "I have never believed he was dead, even though he vanished nearly twenty years ago. *Can he be rescued?*"

"Not by any man—or any woman, for that matter."

"But you can."

"You cannot guess the source of his rescue," said Covenant, "but it may begin with the works of your own hands."

"I will do anything you ask."

"I ask that you trust and obey and give mercy while keeping silence. None of what you are told to do will make sense to you, and I will not explain it until all things are put right."

She nodded her agreement.

"Go out into the wilderness today," he said, "beyond the walls of Glory, and seek for a wounded animal that needs mercy. Then let your heart tell you what to do, even if you are afraid."

So she went out, images of a wounded rabbit or kit fox dancing in her head. She remembered fondly the many small wild animals that had ventured to her outcasts' cottage in older days.

But the sun reached its peak, and she found nothing.

The sun began its slide into the west, and she found nothing.

She was hot and hungry, weary of the search, but because of Covenant she kept on. What she did find left her breathless and very much afraid: a great eagle fluttered helplessly but angry on the ground, a long and wicked arrow lodged through the root of its wing. She gazed at the great bird for a moment, and it glared at her.

"Do not be afraid of me," she said suddenly. "I come from Covenant." *Do not be afraid of me?* she thought. *I am the one who is afraid. It could kill me with that beak and shred me with those claws.*

Its gleaming black feathers were matted thickly with recent

blood, and its eyes were glazed with pain.

She stepped forward, despite her doubts and in the face of her fears. The eagle drew itself up and hissed, but it did not give ground.

She began to repeat Covenant's name over and over, holding her hands out with open palms and advancing slowly.

Its good wing hammered the air vainly and it screeched at her, but it did not prevent her approach. She crept closer, afraid but still moving, until her shadow fell across the wounded bird.

Stretching out her hand, she hesitantly touched the arrow and shuddered as she felt the shaft grating against the bone. She drew back her hand, appalled.

"I cannot help you here," she whispered. "I shall have to carry you home."

She spoke to it soothingly for a long time, and at last she dared to touch it again. It consented to be caressed, and at long last was cradled and hoisted to her shoulder. It clung awkwardly and held its injured wing rigidly out over her head. Its talons pressed into her flesh, and she winced as a few trickles of blood began to inch down her arm.

But she moved on with both purpose and wonder, and the bird did not fight her.

Night fell before she returned to Glory, and no one saw her come through the gates with her peculiar burden. The dark feathers of the bird were only a smaller shadow in the vast shadow of the night.

Back at the house, Covenant's surprising hands snapped the ends from the arrow like straw, then deftly drew the shaft from the bird's flank. Trueteller washed the wound and packed it with spices and medicines.

"You might carry him to the roof," Covenant suggested. "He will find both comfort and privacy there, and no walls to close in his spirit."

"Will he fly away?"

"Not until he is ready."

On her way through the house she met Candle and some of the others.

"What is his name?" asked Candle, as they admired the great bird from a respectful distance.

"I do not know what his name is," she answered. "I did not know for certain it was a him. But Covenant knows such things, and he has not named him, so I shall call him Farsight."

"Why?"

"Because both Covenant and this bird see much farther than I can, and their ways are ever beyond me. And they are both part of a puzzle he has challenged me to untwist."

"A puzzle?"

But Trueteller would say no more. She gently carried the great bird to the roof and left the others standing below in the candlelit dark.

Once set down on the roof, Farsight tucked his head into the tangle of his wings and bandages and slept.

She lay down on the roof beside him and was soon asleep as well.

* * *

Farsight was already awake when Trueteller stirred in the light before the sunrise. He darted his head from side to side and hissed urgently at her, though without malice.

She decided he was hungry. At a loss over what to feed him, she returned with a basket of fruit and some bread. He tore at the bread, but was suspicious of the fruit until she sliced a piece and fed it to him. Then he hungrily gobbled the rest of that fruit, and more after.

Then she went to find Covenant. "And now?" she said to him. "I have done everything you asked of me."

"So now it is time to do something else. You must wait patiently until his wing heals."

"Covenant?" she asked as he turned away. "I have another question, but not about my husband."

"Speak it."

"Will I also have a grandchild of my own to hold someday? One child was a joy, but not enough."

"Some day," he answered, "and she will be a first to you and a first for many." He gently declined to explain further.

Later, she fed Farsight some strips of meat, and he ate, but was not satisfied until fruit was brought as well. He seemed particularly fond of cavada, soft purplish fruits that Candle often bought from a place many miles south of Glory, a remote valley village on the very edge of the kingdom.

"Eagles don't eat fruit," said Firecolt, who was standing near when she asked Candle for more cavada. Flamerider agreed.

"This one does," answered Trueteller simply.

TEN

Return
to the
Rock

LIONHEART WAS BUSY PLAYING WITH A CHILD IN THE NURS-
ery and did not see Covenant in the crowded room until he
spoke at the young man's elbow.

"Are you satisfied here?"

Lionheart nodded.

"Have not all my promises come true?" continued the beggar. "Did I not say that you would have children and parents
in abundance if you followed me?"

"Yes," said Lionheart, "all that and more." His eyes wandered fondly around the room of infants and ancients, frequently coming to rest on his tiny niece, Woodswaif. "I have
rescued them all," he continued, "at your bidding and my
pleasure." His voice softened. "But there is still one who is not
here, and so you have one last promise to keep."

It was Covenant's turn to nod. "Tonight he will join you."

The words sunk in, and Lionheart reached for his cloak, a blanket and a pouch of food. "Then I should have left already!" he exclaimed. "The sun is almost gone, and there is not time to reach the rock even before the morning! I was a full day on that road with Woodswaif."

Covenant stretched out a hand and stopped his rush. "True. But tonight there will be no need to ride gently or timidly. You have ridden the beasts many times, but have you ever raced another rider?" His eyes twinkled as he held forth the challenge.

"I would, indeed, race," Lionheart answered gladly, "if it would not harm the lions."

"Harm the lions?" Covenant laughed. "To make them run and roam and roar? Why do you think they were made? It is in their nature to be bold and quick and tireless, and it is they who have been gentle with you."

The two men passed through the house, the streets of Glory and the great gates, putting a field between themselves and the stone walls. They stopped in the deeper dusk beneath the trees, and Covenant called to the darkness. Suddenly the lions were there, looming out of the uncertainties of the shadows—not just two or four, but a dozen or more.

"They have all come," said Covenant, "to see this ride." He beckoned the two largest lions to him. "Behold the champions of the prides! Choose your mount. I shall ride the other, and the rest shall follow."

Lionheart could see that many more lions had arrived, more than he could number in the shifting shadows. The prides gathered—restless, eager, ready. Some were old and lean and purposeful, while others were young and excited and unsure of the occasion, hardly able yet to avoid their own feet.

They chose and mounted. Lionheart twisted his fist tightly into the mane before him, and with a single shout from Covenant they were off—a launch of lions leaving a vast roar behind them in the night. The rush of blackness blew Lion-heart's hair back, and he hunched down for safety and balance in the leaping madness. All were ready to run, but the two beasts beneath the men settled quietly to the fierce race. The others roared and called to one another, then slowly lapsed into a silence framed by the whorfs of their exhalations. He could not see where they were going, and his fear took time to fade, for this night he was not the master of the wild cats; he was not directing them, but being pulled along in their wake.

A river of great cats poured through the starlit land, ignoring the roads of man and needing none of their own. Their running was more serious now, silent and intense, less exuberant but every bit as joyful. Their feet pounded the earth, their breath exploded half-seen in the air, and their legs devoured the miles at a rate Lionheart could not guess.

There was no way to pace the passing of time, for even the stars blurred overhead in the swiftness of their flight. Lionheart soared unseated in the air as much as he clung with his knees; but even though the hills rose and fell beneath them and the way wavered from side to side, the ride was not rough despite its reckless majesty.

Lionheart drank in the power and the speed, and his heart was glad within him for more reasons than he could think to name.

At last the moon gave them a brief glimpse of their path, and Lionheart could see ahead a rank of trees he recognized. But any new thoughts were lost in the need to hang on as the two lions accelerated away in a final sprint. First one led and then the other, then neither could be said to be ahead or behind.

They plunged into the line of trees as one, branches crackling at their sides. Covenant cried "Well done!" and the lions sprawled heavily but happily in the clearing by the great rock.

The others, left behind in the final dash, spilled into the

clearing and collapsed wherever they found room to fall. Their flanks heaved like sea breakers and their lungs thundered like waves exploding against the rocks. But all were content, and more—exhausted with joy and joyed with exhaustion.

"Are we in time?" gasped Lionheart.

"We are well in time to rescue your father."

They leaned their backs heavily against the rock, and Lionheart waited for the spinning in his head to go away. "Who won?" he finally thought to ask.

"We all did," answered Covenant.

Lionheart looked around him, remembering their first meeting here. "It is good that he shall not die here. This is a cursed place."

"Our work has lifted part of the curse," said Covenant, "but there have always been evil places in the land because there has always been evil in the hearts of the people."

"Could we not make this a place where none would ever come again?" Lionheart asked.

"Do you have an idea?" answered Covenant, with his own question. "A little terror of the right kind would do no harm," he added with a smile. "But," he continued to say without a smile, "they will find other ways to be rid of the ones they will not keep. Denying them the rock will make no difference in the end."

Lionheart murmured a few more questions, and Covenant nodded, smiling again. Most of the shaggy company slept; some watched. All waited with the men for something to happen.

* * *

Within an hour there came a noise from the path. Covenant waved his hand, and the lounging lions faded away into the night. Lionheart saw them becoming one with the shadows, laying themselves low after their rest.

"Here they come," breathed Lionheart. Someone was drawing near, someone trying to make little noise but still sounding sharp echoes and snapping through the forest.

And there on the path a woman struggled under the burden of a semiconscious man, an old man, thin and pale, with the snow of the years upon his head. Lionheart stirred anxiously but made no noise.

On the woman came, unaware of the host of lions lying quietly all around them. She turned her back to the unseen men and lowered her burden to the rock.

Covenant nudged Lionheart.

Lionheart stepped forward, tilted back his head and roared. The mighty sound shook the branches of the trees and brought a wild and wavering scream from the woman.

She plunged headlong into the clearing and stopped abruptly. The moon showed her a glade filled with lions—all alive, all alert, all looking at her with glowing eyes. Her heart beat wildly, but she had forgotten to breathe, and her limbs were frozen with fear.

Then Covenant stepped out from the trees and spoke to her. "We have come because this is an evil place. It is an evil place because you made it so."

She trembled at his voice but could not turn her head to him. She had never dreamed so many lions could be found in all the forests of the land, and now they were before her.

"As you have sent others to their doom," Covenant continued, "so your doom is before you.

"But we give you a single chance, which is one more than you spared either your daughter or your father." He gestured, and the mass of lions parted a narrow way for her feet.

"Run," Covenant commanded. "Run, and let us see how swiftly you can find shelter. Run! Or there will be no mercy for you at all."

She ran.

Not a lion twitched, though they watched her unblinkingly until she passed through the terrible, patient circle and reached the edges of the trees.

Then Lionheart roared again, and the lions leapt after her, with a single voice of outraged majesty and a multitude of angry feet.

She screamed as she ran, feeling their breath on her legs and their claws tearing at her clothes and their massive bodies snapping the branches aside.

The chase disappeared from sight, and Covenant said calmly, "She flies to her hut, where her man waits, but even he cannot grant her safety. He shall flee as well. He did nothing to stop her evil, and he will suffer with her. Terror is theirs this night, and teeth and tearing on every side, though they will not be harmed except through fear. They will be an agony of miles from here when the lions tire of the chase and begin to wander home."

"It is good that they should learn fear."

"If they do not learn a little fear now, they must learn more later." Covenant turned to watch Lionheart, who had picked up the limp form of his father. "Your sister will never return, either to this forest or to her home. No one will blame her.

"Long will the lions remember this night."

"And I as well," said Lionheart, embracing and supporting the unresisting form of his father. "All your words have come true."

"All the promises I gave to you are fulfilled," the beggar replied. "You shall see many more assurances kept in full before your work is done in Glory."

Only three lions were left, relaxing on the forest floor in the profound silence.

"Let us rest here for a few hours," said Covenant, urging Lionheart and his burden toward the lions. "We should wait until your father revives enough from the numbing powder to enjoy his ride." He smiled in the darkness as he helped them to comfortable positions against the lions' flanks. "No one will disturb us."

ELEVEN

Hammered Gold

BINDER CAME DOWNSTAIRS IN THE MORNING LIGHT AND found the ever-changing lady already at breakfast.

"Are you at ease here?" he asked gently.

She looked up at him with eyes that were momentarily the color of the sky, on their way from forest-brown to sea-green. "I am as much at ease here as I have ever been elsewhere," she said. "This is a very wonderful house."

"You fit in well, and I certainly find no offense in your presence. I am learning to look first for the cloak."

"You have been quite tolerant of me," she said. "Some people are drawn to me at first, but in the end they are driven away by the changes no one can control."

"I must be tolerant with all," replied Binder. "Or who would be tolerant with me?"

* * *

Day after day Trueteller came to the roof and found Farsight teetering on the edge of the bright tiles, face into the breeze and wings uplifted where the wind could sort his feathers. Then he would flutter up to her shoulder and submit to her attention and care.

"Soon," she whispered as she smoothed the feathers on his neck, "soon you will be ready."

Covenant found her there and joined her in admiring the eagle. "Farsight seems to be quite fond of you," he said. "Whenever I see him, you are there; wherever I find you, he is there on your shoulder. Does not his weight weary you?"

"No," she said, reaching up to first ruffle and then smooth his feathers. "I feel his weight, but it is not a great burden. I am no longer afraid of his beak, and I have sewn leather pads into my clothes to ease the terror of his talons. He responds to me kindly, but he is not a tame bird."

Farsight stretched out his wing to preen his feathers, and the sudden shade hid her face from the sun.

"I will miss him when he is well enough to fly."

"You would not keep him here?"

"I do enjoy him, but even if I could hold him to the earth, I would not. It would not be fair to him. He was made for the sky, not to live in the midst of people who would either ignore him or abuse him.

"I have enjoyed caring for him; it is like having a child again."

"You have many children in Lionheart's realm."

"The nursery? I love his charges and I am delighted by his work, but they are not my own flesh."

"Neither is Farsight, but he is healing nicely," Covenant said, reaching out to caress the mighty bird. "I think he will be ready to fly soon."

"Yes, he is ready. What do I do now?" she asked. "I have been patient and have asked you no questions about my husband."

"You have done well," replied Covenant, beaming his approval. "But more is required of you—now and later. For now, buy all the gold you can afford," Covenant said.

"Gold?" she asked. "I have never heard you ask for that before!"

"Gold," he repeated. "But not for me. It will buy you one of your wishes come true."

She thought for a moment. "I have no gold, but Candle has riches almost beyond measure, for you have blessed his shop . . ."

"I mean for you alone to do this, and to tell no one until it is done. You have your own store of silver coins and coppers now; it will be sufficient."

All the next morning Trueteller went about her task, buying fragments of gold quietly at various places throughout Glory.

She brought it back to Covenant. "My private riches have gathered me less than a handful of gold. Will it be enough?"

"It will," Covenant said. "Divide the gold into two equal piles, and hammer them flat into two bands. Make each one as wide as three fingers and as long as the stretch of your hand."

"I am not a metalsmith. My work is very poor."

"It will be sturdy and bright, and that is all that matters here."

That day and the next she labored clumsily in an isolated room in a quiet corner of the house, pounding and bending and filing. When she was done, her hands were scraped and blistered from the file, and bruised and stiff from the hammer. She bandaged the cuts, spread lotion on the bruises and brought her work to Covenant.

He examined her work. "You have done very well," he said. "And now for the rest," he continued as he gave them back to her. "Engrave a heart upon this band of gold, and embed my mark upon the other."

Trueteller nodded at the mention of Covenant's mark, for it lay all around them in his house. Then she shook her head in bewilderment over his request, but went to do as she had been told.

She returned later with the bands and yet another painful scratch from the awl. "These bands are too heavy for rings," she said. "What are they for?"

"They are heavy, but Farsight is strong; they will not slow him down."

"Farsight?"

"Yes. He shall bear a gift and a message both. Come, and you will see." They ascended to the roof, and Farsight came to them with a noisy but gentle greeting.

Covenant took the plates in his hands and bent them nearly into a circle with his powerful fingers. He held them up for Trueteller to see the marks on the outside, then slipped a band around each of Farsight's legs and squeezed them shut.

Farsight peered down at the bands and shook one foot experimentally, but he did not protest.

"Stroke him again and urge him on his way," said Covenant.

After a final caress she lifted the handsome bird and pitched him gently into the air. They bid the eagle goodbye as he lifted, circled, then beat away southward as though his destination were already fixed in his mind.

Covenant turned to her. "You asked me another question."

"I did?"

"You did. And in answer I say that you have been so absorbed with Farsight that you have not spoken to Moonflower for several days. I think she has a question for you that is also an answer."

Trueteller's eyes widened, and she set off breathlessly to find the daughter who had defied death.

She found her daughter sitting in the waning rays of the sun, sipping a brew of fragrant herbs and glowing as brightly as the sunset. Silently, Trueteller laid a trembling hand on

Moonflower's slim belly.

"Are you . . . ?" she asked.

"I may be," said Moonflower timidly. "What does it feel like?"

Twenty years fell away in a rush, and mother and daughter began a talk that lasted undisturbed into the night.

* * *

"I am a foolish old woman," confessed Trueteller to Wordsmith the next day. "Some of my worries and hopes must seem very selfish and shallow in Covenant's eyes."

Wordsmith shrugged. "Do not be too hasty to judge. It is no offense to be either old or a woman. We have all been foolish, and we are all being changed for the better."

TWELVE

The Voyage of the *Childsbreath*

COVENANT HELD COUNCIL WITH THEM ALL THE NEXT morning.

"You are a warrior," he said to Freeblade, "but you have never fought. We will make a journey together, and you shall anoint your blade with the blood of battle."

He turned. "Wordsmith, you shall come with us."

Beauty was crestfallen, though she hid it well. She clung to Wordsmith's arm and gazed at Covenant.

"Do not be afraid, Beauty," said Covenant. "I brought you to him from the rock of choosing, and brought him back to you from Rockhaven. Can I not bring him back to you again?"

She nodded.

"And I have not finished my words," he continued. "I am to go, and Freeblade and Wordsmith. And you, Beauty, shall go with us as well."

A startled expression came to her face, followed by delight. "I would be very pleased to go with you," she murmured. "Where are we going?"

"Back to the sea," Covenant said. "Binder and the Chameleon Lady shall stay here and look after the rest in our absence."

While they were pondering this, Covenant called Flamerider and Firecolt to him. "I have a gift for you two." He handed them a fired clay ornament on a plain metal chain. It puzzled the boys, for neither of them could tell exactly what it was. It was neither all man nor all animal, nor were they even certain that it was supposed to be alive. But it drew their eyes repeatedly, and they wondered what sort of magic it held.

"Take this," said Covenant, "and wear it always. One of you wear it today, and the other tomorrow, and in turns after that. This charm will save your lives—and more than your own lives. When you are called upon to deliver what you do not have, cast this ornament down and break it.

"Do not break it now, or lose it. But when you are threatened by the sword to deliver what you do not have, you must remember the provisions of Covenant."

They did not understand, but at a reassuring nod from Binder they bowed and returned to their seats.

Covenant dismissed them one by one, with a blessing.

Later, to the Chameleon Lady alone, he said, "Two days from now, when evening begins to fall, you must go to the palace and deliver your message to the king. After that, be surprised at nothing that happens," he added with a smile. "I know you are bright and full of courage; though you say little, you learn much and will do well at any task you set your heart to."

He told her what to say, and she began to see a glimmer of light in his ways.

*   *   *

The next morning, without fanfare, the four travelers left afoot for the distant sea, and soon they passed the village of the lepers.

"What is this place?" asked Freeblade.

"It is a town of lepers," said Beauty.

"Some call it Heartbreak," added Wordsmith.

"Why do you not visit there, Covenant?" asked Beauty. "Surely if any place needs your touch it is there." Wordsmith remembered his own like question.

"I would not be welcomed," Covenant said. "But I shall soon send someone there in my name, and my welcome shall come in its time."

"Who will be your messenger?" inquired Wordsmith.

"May I go?" asked Freeblade.

"Or I?" asked Beauty.

"No. You know too much. Ignorance—and innocence— would better suit my plans for this place."

"And I am neither ignorant nor innocent," said Wordsmith.

"Nor I," admitted Beauty.

"Once you were innocent, and even ignorant of your innocence. Now, however, you are only innocent of ignorance." Covenant smiled his enigmatic smile, and they went on.

For three days their feet conquered the miles, and they arrived at Graycove just before dusk. The company came to the house of Deedtester and were well received. Covenant left them alone there, and Joykeeper spoke to them in awed tones. The three travelers were surprised, but not astonished, by the work Covenant had done there.

When Covenant returned, he beckoned to Deedtester and Seaswallower and said, "The time has come to claim the *Childsbreath*—for a while, at least. There is an island to the west that I must visit."

The fisherman fell silent and looked at Covenant for a long moment before continuing. "There is only one island nearby, and you should not go there," he said gravely. "There are horrible things there."

Covenant answered him. "Sometimes the most horrible things are only those which have not been exposed to the light."

"What horrors have you seen?" asked Freeblade.

"Shadows. Many shadows," said the fisherman. "Even in the brightest light of day that island is dark. And moans—moans and wailing and screams of old, cold fear."

"Yet someone lives there?" asked Freeblade.

"There is life there, if you call existence living. None of us go to that fear-ridden place. I would not let the shadow of my boat touch the sand of that island."

"The *Childsbreath* is no longer yours to command," Covenant reminded him. "You bound her to me when I returned Sea-swallower to you."

"She is yours, without argument. I tell you only what all folk here know and fear."

"This island?" asked Wordsmith. "Must we go there?"

"We should, we must, and we shall," answered Covenant. "It is, after all, part of this world. And even that island was shaped by the hand of the Elder God. You and your son will sail us there," he continued, turning to Deedtester, "but you need not leave the boat if you do not wish to."

They all slept where they could find room, either in the hut or on the sand outside, and they sailed with the dawn. The three with Covenant were delighted, for they had never been on the sea before. Beauty perched herself by the bow, exclaiming excitedly over the dolphins and whales that surfaced near the boat, and enjoying every drop of spray thrown aside by their passage.

At midday an island grew larger off the starboard bow. Seaswallower pointed, but it was hardly necessary. The gloomy pall that hung over the island marked it for all eyes to see.

Sailing closer in the lee of the island, they could see that

many of the shadows were actually the black stone walls of a sprawling, shabby building. Parts of the structure closest to the shore looked newer and more hastily built.

Freeblade hailed the silent shore, but there was no answer, no stir or motion. Nothing living could be seen except a few trees ringing the sand.

The bow of the *Childsbreath* crunched into the sand, and the four from Glory jumped down to wade in the warm surf to the dry land.

THIRTEEN

Haunted Rooms

THE DOOR TO THE RAMBLING RUIN GAPED AT THEM, AND shadows tumbled out the unused doorway to greet them. Their footsteps violated the sand that had drifted deep over the sill.

Covenant lighted the torches in his hand. "Let us go inside," he said. "We will never conquer by standing here."

He stooped to enter the gloomy arch, but Freeblade prevented him, saying, "You have appointed me Warrior. Where there may be danger, I should go first."

Covenant smiled and stepped back and motioned him inside. "Once you dreaded the shadows, but now your courage controls your fears. You have grown from fearful to fearless."

"No," he said. "This book has soaked so deep into my soul that there is no more room for fear, save the fear that I would be unworthy of the name Freeblade."

He plunged into the darkness with his sword held high and with Covenant behind him. Beauty and Wordsmith followed silently and not without misgivings.

"Which way?" whispered Freeblade.

"Any direction you wish," said Covenant. "Any path will lead us to the one who lives here."

They began the long task of searching room to room. The darkness yielded reluctantly to their torches; cobwebs bloomed from the corners, shrouding everything in a veil of gray. The rooms seemed to spiral back into each other, and Beauty was sure they had crossed several rooms more than once. Some looked ancient and fine but abandoned, while some had been built in clumsy haste and now lay half-open to the wind.

Beauty was keenly aware of a disquieting presence, an unpleasant aura in every room—a weight of shadows not sparked solely from the absence of the sun.

Three of them jumped when a voice split the darkness. Only Covenant seemed unaffected.

"Who's there?" cried someone in a cracked and hysterical quaver. "Who's there, I say?"

"Your friends," replied Covenant.

"There are no friends here," called the voice. "You are all my enemies. Be gone, you ghosts and shadows! I will give you no more harbor!" The words were brave enough but uttered with a hollow hope, as though they had been uttered in vain many times before.

"We are not ghosts," said Covenant, "and neither are we shadows. Come forth and see!"

A wrinkled, pale man slowly crept into the circle of their torches. His matted white hair and dirty beard hung long and weary about his face.

"Who are you?" he asked again, his voice dry and cracked from long disuse.

"We come in the name of the Elder God," said Freeblade

boldly, but then he did not know how to continue.

Covenant picked up the thread. "We have come to deliver you from your prison. You have lived in the darkness too long."

"You know of me?" asked the man.

"I do," replied Covenant, "but none of my friends know what this house is, or how it came to be. They should hear that story directly from your lips."

The man stared at them uncertainly. Beauty sensed his discomfort and stepped forward. "He is Covenant, who leads us—the man of true and certain promises," said Beauty. "The man with the sword is Freeblade, and this is my husband, Wordsmith. I am called Beauty."

"Put your blade away," said the man, "or I will go where you cannot find me."

Covenant agreed. "Put it away, Freeblade. The danger here is not to us but to this man."

Freeblade promptly sheathed his sword. The man relaxed visibly and drifted near enough to press Wordsmith's arm between his fingers. "You *are* real—not phantoms, at least," he said. "Though you can do nothing to deliver me, I would not turn you away, for I do not remember the last visitor to this place."

He backed away, and they followed him deeper into the labyrinth of rooms. They eventually made a series of sharp turns, and then blinked and shielded their eyes from the sudden beams of sunlight slanting through holes in the roof.

The man stopped abruptly, and they found themselves standing in a rough stone room tacked on to the very edge of a cliff that tumbled down to the restless waters below. The other rooms had been bare and hollow, but this one was stuffed with stacks of old books and drawings, a pile of shabby clothes, a store of nuts and herbs and dried fish, a brush pallet on the dirt floor, and a tiny fire glowing in a makeshift fireplace. The walls gaped widely, and sundogs played together at their feet.

Covenant sat on the floor, and the others joined him. "Tell us your name," he said, "and how it is that you dwell here with ghosts."

"That is no secret," the hermit said sadly, shifting his slight weight from one hip to the other. "I am Grimshade. Once I had a family here and many friends, and all this island was mine—until my words and my deeds overcame the love that struggled to blossom from my heart. In the end I drove my loved ones away. To my sorrow, the shadows of my deeds and the woe of my words did not go with them, but stayed to haunt me and drive me down with the constant specter of the past I cannot change and the future I cannot avoid.

"I built a new room to my house and dwelt there where no horrid echoes lived. But every deed I performed, every word I said created a new shadow, a fresh dark ghost. And the ghosts would not leave me alone. When that room, too, was filled with shadows, I built another new room for myself."

"Until it, too, filled with ghosts," said Freeblade.

"Yes," the hermit said sadly, "that always happens. The shadows come, like silt, like the slow soil of dark flood tides. I cannot stop them; I might as well dream of halting the gloom that follows the sunset. I used to go to my wishing well, to toss in my coins and appeal to the gods for release. But there were no gods there—only ghosts, more ghosts.

"I have summed the shadows and seen that their end is death. But the ghosts don't die. That is the curse of this house."

"Give me authority over these rooms," said Covenant quietly.

"These rooms are yours to command," he replied, "but all of them are full of shadows." He slumped fully onto his pallet.

"Yes," said Covenant, "and all of them are angry."

He turned to Freeblade. "Slay the shadows," he ordered. "They are your first enemy and a fierce one. They are only the truth, but they have been given false life and power. It is not so dangerous to you as it will be difficult and exhausting."

Covenant turned to Grimshade. "And you must go with him—to name the ghosts as you find them. They were born of your words and deeds and must be owned by you again before they can be destroyed."

Grimshade stared at him. "That path carries more shame than I can carry. If I could defeat the shadows myself, I would have done so long ago."

"Yes, there is shame in proclaiming their names," answered Covenant, "but you will have shame forever if you do not defy them. You will do what you can, and Freeblade will do what you cannot.

"Destroy the first shadow that you fall upon," Covenant ordered Freeblade, "and let its dying blood run across the floor where we can see it. Bring the love of life to this place again."

"There is no love in this house," said the hermit. "Perfect fear casts out love."

"Yes, but perfect love casts out fear," Beauty replied.

With a great cry, Freeblade stood, drew his sword and plunged into the labyrinth. He was back in an instant, grasping a dark something that wiggled frantically in his fingers. "Name him," he commanded. Grimshade reluctantly uttered its foul name, and Freeblade struck his blade into the captive darkness; it spouted black blood as it shrieked and shriveled and vanished into nothingness.

Beauty blanched but did not turn away.

"That is only the first," said Freeblade, satisfied.

They returned to the ghost-swept rooms, and Beauty thought the gloom had lessened, as though the shadows were already retreating. Freeblade did not return with the second shadow, but slew it where they found it and went on to the next. The sounds of combat were clear to the company— Grimshade gleefully naming the ghosts as they were captured, Freeblade smiting with the blade and leaving destruction in his path. The uproar drifted back to them from ever-widening circles, both horrifying and fascinating them.

Time passed with no way to measure it until Freeblade, drenched in sweat and stumbling with happy weariness, returned, slumped on the floor and gazed at Covenant. "It was not a fair fight," he said. "They were not armed with any weapon that could touch me."

"But they were strong and fierce," replied Covenant, "and almost without number, were they not? It was a hard task and well done. You have always found favor in my eyes, and now you have found honor as well."

The house lay silent but light and airy; there were no dark ghosts left to shuffle and shade and moan. Where once shadows had clustered too thickly to be penetrated, now sunbeams found the cracks in the stone and danced on the floor.

Covenant turned to Grimshade, standing white-faced and weak with surprise and relief. "Your old name no longer fits you," observed Covenant.

"I never had love for that name," he answered.

"Then let your old name vanish with the ghosts. I would give you your new name now, but you have not learned enough to bear it. This is a nameless island," continued Covenant. "Are you content to be, for now, a nameless man on a nameless island?"

"As you wish," said the hermit dazedly. "My name is of little import to me; there is no one to call it aloud. You have, indeed, slain the shadows, and I am grateful beyond words. How can I serve you in return?"

"You can serve me by staying here," said Covenant. "You are the final man in the west, and the man who last hails each day's setting sun: to you shall come the first sight of the final fires."

"What must I do?"

"You have a treasure to find, and afterward I will send Wordsmith and Freeblade for you."

"Treasure?" He looked both interested and puzzled. "The only treasure left here is solitude."

"Think again. You have lived here a very long time, and perhaps fear has driven out fond memories."

The hermit thought. "There used to be . . . or was I dreaming? A special room where I knew peace and contentment . . . but that was long ago, before the shadows came. I can scarcely remember it."

"You should find it, then," said Covenant. And with a warm farewell he led the others out to the waiting *Childsbreath*.

* * *

"And now what?" asked the tired Freeblade, watching the receding island and the waving figure upon the sand.

"Now we return to Glory," answered Covenant. "We have done what we sailed to do."

"All this voyage for one man?" asked Wordsmith.

"Is the end of the earth too far to go for any such one who needs our help?" countered Covenant.

"No," agreed Wordsmith, "of course not."

"Then the road beckons us home again."

"Covenant," asked Freeblade later, "was Grimshade in his right mind?"

"He was very nearly out of it forever," replied Covenant. "Silence and suffering will do that to one who stands alone against familiar and fearsome terrors."

He turned away to Beauty, who had again found a seat at the bow and was absorbing every sight and sound of the ocean.

"Covenant," she said, "can anything be better than this?"

"Yes. This is good, very good, but there is better yet that is far beyond your imagination. You shall have that someday soon, with no need to imagine. The great sorrow is that much worse than this will fall upon you before the best of all comes to stay."

She sought an explanation from him, but she was answered only by silent sadness.

FOURTEEN

The Clear Purple Miracle

NOT EVEN COLD WATER FROM THE MOUNTAIN STREAMS could soothe the fever of the King. He burned and flamed in its grip, sweating his life away into nothingness, while his advisors and physicians looked on helplessly. Their worry weighed heavy upon them and them alone, for they kept the news of the royal sickness from the people of the land.

Each day the King staggered to the mirror, only to be faced with the slow approach of his death. His only ease came when sleep overrode the suffering, but sleep was elusive, and even in his sleep he was not left alone. His dreams boiled in his brain, blurring the boundary between life and madness.

Until the night a long-haired shadow came to the palace and walked unheeded past the guards. Nor did the servants hinder her as she drifted through the innermost chambers to stand before the ailing King.

She spoke, and he roused, hearing the voice and beholding the face of his own Queen.

* * *

With the pale morning light, he burst from his chambers and yelled for his advisors. "I have had a dream!" he called hoarsely. "A vision, a promise, an oracle, a sign! Bring me the master-at-arms, quickly now, for my strength is fading."

He sweltered upon his purple pillows until the soldier returned. Though his fever still raged high, he spoke firmly and steadily, with only a slight trace of weakness in his voice.

"Send men, and find for me in Glory two youths, dressed in red and blue, playing in the street. Bring them, just as you find them, and come back in haste. I have had a vision, and these boys shall give me new life. Now go. At once!"

At noon Firecolt and Flamerider were gaming before the house while Binder and the Chameleon Lady rested on the steps and watched.

Their attention was diverted by a soldier riding slowly down the narrow street, gazing intently at the children he encountered.

"What does *he* want?" whispered Binder. "We don't see *them* down here often."

"I think I know," she whispered. "Watch and see."

The rider reined in his horse when he saw Firecolt and Flamerider. He watched them closely and then dismounted. The boys stopped their play and watched him in return, their attraction to the horse tempered by their awe of the man and suspicion of his power.

"You are their parents?" he called to the adults.

Binder hesitated less than a heartbeat. "They are our boys."

"The King has called them to do his bidding."

"What? Why does he need them?" flared Binder.

"I explain nothing," said the soldier, "for nothing is explained to me. The King says go, and I go; he says bring them, and I bring them. What are their names?"

The boys had retreated up the steps and were huddling close to the adults. The Chameleon Lady nudged them with her knee.

"Be polite, boys. Tell him your names."

"I am Firecolt," said the boy in blue.

"And I am Flamerider," added the boy in red.

"Come with me," the rider said.

"They are staying here," Binder said flatly.

"You will not let them go?" asked the soldier.

"No!"

"Then you must answer to the King."

"And who will answer to me if something happens to them?" thundered Binder.

The Chameleon Lady tugged at Binder's arm. "Let them go," she whispered. "This is Covenant's doing and not evil at work."

Binder could not prevent the soldier and wisely did not try; the frightened boys were lifted up on the saddle before the rider, and the horse carried them away without delay.

In only a few short minutes the confused, apprehensive lads were ushered into the King's presence. The King motioned for his attendants and messengers to leave, saying, "I wish to speak with them alone." Then, turning to the youths, he began, "Lads, you can see that I am ill and weakened. Last night I had a vision, a visit. My Queen came to me and put in my head a picture of two boys enjoying the freedom of the streets, even as my messengers found you. Her voice said to me, 'Find the boys, and send them in the name of the Elder God, for in this bottle one may find life and healing. With its discovery your land and people will be blessed and healed and will become great again.'

"And then I saw you walking together on a dusty road, making a long journey. You came to a far village and went to a certain wineseller's shop marked with a wooden star above the door. You entered and gave the merchant a token.

"He delivered to you a bottle; you padded it with old cloth wrappings and made your way hastily from that place. My Queen showed me no more than that and made no explanations, but I know in my great wisdom what it intended. You will go and find this miraculous bottle of wine; with it I shall heal myself, and this land will know again the peace and prosperity that only I can bring it. I command you to go now, and tell no one of your purpose. No one. Even my advisors will be kept ignorant, for this act must be done in secret.

"You carry a pledge—a sign or token. Show it to me, that I may confirm you are the ones. Now."

They looked at each other, puzzlement and fear fighting for the upper hand in their eyes.

"I do not have it, so you must. Show it to me now, or suffer my wrath!"

Firecolt finally found his voice. "Covenant," he said to his brother faintly. "Remember Covenant. It is your day to wear his charm."

Flamerider removed the chain from his neck and offered it to the King.

"This is no token," he snarled. "Do not play me for a fool." He hurled it back at them. Both boys grabbed for it and missed, and it shattered on the paved stones of the floor.

Flamerider plucked something shiny from the debris.

"That is it!" shouted the King. "Let me see it!"

"It is only half a copper," said the disappointed boy, handing it over.

"I do not care what it is or where it came from or what it means," snapped the weakened King, "as long as you can trade it for that bottle." He caressed the bent and broken coin before handing it back. "You have a mission," he continued. "Go and do it, faithfully, fearlessly, and quickly. The well-being of this land hangs upon your success—as does your own well-being. I advise you not to fail."

The King sank back onto his bed and tugged on a rope to summon his attendants. His eyes closed as the boys were led out of the room.

Then the gates clanged shut behind them, and they were left alone—with half a copper and a mission, but no guide or directions.

"What are we to do?" whispered Flamerider.

"We must tell Binder," murmured Firecolt.

They ran all the way to Covenant's house and blurted out their story to Binder and the Chameleon Lady.

Binder was amazed and indignant until the lady explained her part in the matter. "It was frightening, but exciting, to do Covenant's bidding and see it unfold exactly as he prophesied.

"Let them go," she continued. "These boys are half men already, and two half-men may do the work of one man."

"But there is still a whole *boy* left over," replied Binder.

"Then the man will take care of the boy, and the boy will keep the man alert," she replied.

Her serenity helped convince him, and he thought for a moment before speaking. "Wordsmith has told me of a miracle of wine and water that he witnessed along the road to Glory, a miracle that happened shortly after he joined with Covenant. I know that road. There are signs along the way, and it will be difficult to become lost." He gave the boys clear directions. "A word of warning: don't go near the towns, and be sure to watch for thieves along the way. There are also many lepers in that first village. It can barely be seen from the road, and you would do well to stay away from there."

With trust striving for the upper hand in their hearts, Binder and his helper provisioned the boys, blessed them and walked with them to the gate of Glory.

Firecolt and Flamerider bade them goodbye and moved off down the road.

"Everyone's away now," said the Chameleon Lady, the reality of their sudden departure dawning upon her. "I believe in

Covenant, but I'm not sure I will sleep soundly until all these travelers are at home again."

"Keep remembering Covenant," said Binder. "As you said, they are about *his* errands."

The afternoon was bright with sun, and the evening was illuminated by the moon. The boys avoided Heartbreak without incident and did not stop until much later when the silver ball sank behind the mountains.

When they paused and sat against a tree to make their meager supper, they could see the very tiny lights of the King's palace glinting on one of the mountain peaks. The lights did not comfort them as they slept. When their hunger woke them in the morning, they ate and continued on their way with caution and misgivings.

Ever watchful, they slipped through the fields and barren rocky places and across a river. On the far side of the bank, Firecolt halted and pulled Flamerider into the shadows of the trees.

"We are being followed," he said softly.

"I know," answered Flamerider. "I can feel it, though I see nothing." They listened, and Flamerider began again, "Why did Covenant send us for this task? We are from Glory; we do not know the ways of the woods."

"Covenant must have his reasons," replied Firecolt, "or Binder and the lady would not have let us come. And Covenant knows that we know the ways of the wilderness inside our stone walls. Life is not so much different out here."

They waited.

Nothing crossed the river behind them. They heard nothing, saw nothing, but felt the eyes of the watcher upon them.

They hurried on.

And that evening they saw a lion. It watched them from a distance, and seemed content. The boys wondered if Lionheart had sent it.

As they prepared for sleep in the crooks of an old tall tree, their sense of the unseen eyes lessened somewhat. But in the night a horrible roar awakened them, and they huddled in the darkness while a savage fight tore the night. After an unmeasured time of terror, the sounds died away into a grisly mashing and crunching. Then even that stopped.

They waited open-eyed for the dawn, even though the sensation of being followed had completely vanished. In the new light they saw a bloody, trampled area where two mighty animals had contended. One had torn apart the other, and the victor had feasted and padded away, leaving lion marks in the dirt.

The two boys looked at the abandoned carcass. "I do not know what kind of beast this was," said Flamerider. "Those teeth and claws are horrors."

"Nor do I," added Firecolt, "but I am glad it is dead."

They looked at each other. "I think we have been protected," said Firecolt. "Let us go before another one comes."

* * *

The next two days held less adventure and little fear. The road was empty save a few merchants' caravans of goods, and the boys hid each time until the dust had settled again. Orchards and fields, visited in the dead of night, supplied them with ample nourishment when their food ran out.

The journey seemed to drag on forever, but at last they came over the rise of a small hill and saw an isolated building in the distance, just as Binder had described. As they drew closer, they confirmed that the wooden sign over the door was the one they had been seeking.

It was dim inside, and neither boy could see at first the aged proprietor who spoke to them from the depths of the gloom. Firecolt handed him the carefully kept token without saying a word. Then he looked around him, his eyes growing accustomed to the dark, and he saw, lining the walls, rack upon wooden rack filled with dustily gleaming bottles.

The wineseller looked thoughtfully at the token, turning it

over in his long fingers. "I know this coin," he said. "He ruined the rest, and now he claims the last bottle?" He expected no answer, and received none. "Good riddance," he continued in a surly voice. "I am weary of answering questions about one dusty bottle on the mantle, and even more weary of seeing it every day. I don't know why I kept it, but I did. I suppose I was afraid *he* would come back again if I didn't." He reached down a solitary bottle from over the fireplace and handed it to the boys. "Take the wine—or water, or whatever it is—and leave the half of the copper to me. I have its mate and will not let it sit idle." Respect and resentment mixed in his voice.

"If you please, sir, we need something to wrap it in."

He threw them some old cloths and cursed them. The fire twins stumbled out into the broad daylight, having said little and done less, but with most of their task complete.

Or so they thought.

So far the King's vision had proven true, but Firecolt was beginning to doubt. He did not understand how restoring the King to health would make the land prosperous again. The land would only suffer longer under him, and the people would be forced to wait a few years more for a new and perhaps better king to be crowned.

These thoughts returned to his mind again and again on the journey home, and he discussed them with Flamerider. Neither could reach an understanding or a conclusion.

They sensed nothing unusual on their return journey, but they did find fresh lion tracks at odd intervals. They were comforted and walked on with light hearts.

When they knew they were nearing Glory, they decided to travel through that night and be home by dawn. But while they slipped through a field in search of fruit, something snagged Firecolt's ankle and he fell. He started to rise again, but a pair of sweaty, dirty hands pushed him to the ground and wrestled away his belongings.

"What have we here?" a man growled. "Two boys. Travel-

ing alone? I'm sure they'll want to share their food with me, and I wonder what's in the package?" The man broke off suddenly, coughing with great convulsions that shook his body. Then the moon came out in full, and Firecolt could see that the man was a leper. One leg was badly withered and twisted beneath him, and there was scarcely more than bone beneath the skin. He coughed again, and the rasping sound tore at his throat. He clawed at Firecolt's food sack, shoving the boy roughly to one side. Flamerider pounded on the man's side without effect until Firecolt told his brother to quit.

Firecolt rose to his feet and lunged for his belongings, but the wiry, wary leper ducked and knocked him down.

"You can't have that! It's ours!"

"It's as much mine as yours, little ones. But if you like you can both sit there and watch me eat."

"You can have the food. Just give us the package!"

"Oh, so it's that important, is it? Let's see what's inside." He unwrapped the bottle and held it in the air, where it sparkled in the moonlight. "Yes, yes. Wine. And a favored kind at that."

"But you can't have that either! It's the King's!"

"Then let the King come and take it away from me. I'm thirsty." He pulled out the stopper with one quick motion and said, "I won't be rude; I will at least drink to his health." He began to empty the bottle with greedy gulps. Firecolt lunged at him, but the leper scuttled away with his good leg and said, "Careful, boy. I wouldn't want to hurt you."

He continued drinking, long after Firecolt thought he had reached the bottom of the bottle.

"My thanks to you, boy. This is the finest stuff I've had in a long time." His voice was beginning to sound unsteady, and some of his words were not quite plain. The deep coughing was not as bad now—he seemed to be swallowing his pain with the drink. He took another series of long gulps, looking with concern and puzzlement at the bottle each time he lowered it. "This is mighty powerful stuff," he murmured. "How did they get so much of it in one little bottle?"

Firecolt and Flamerider slipped away into the shadows and watched where the crippled outcast could not see them. Presently, that reclining figure lowered the bottle and laid his head on the ground. Firecolt crept up and took the bottle away. The leper made a feeble grasp at the wine, then rolled on his side and slept. Firecolt glanced at him, then looked down at the crippled leg. Even as he watched, the flesh around the bone began to fill out; the bone lengthened, and soon Firecolt could no longer tell that it had once been withered. The man breathed clearly and easily now, without the slightest trace of a cough, and his skin innocent of the hateful white bloom.

Firecolt checked the bottle and received another shock. The bottle was full. He poured some on the ground. The level did not change. He found the stopper and pushed it in. Without looking at the bottle again, he gathered their things and ran with Flamerider at his heels.

Far away and safe, they stopped and sprawled out on the grass to rest. Firecolt's mind was still running fast, and he panted, "This wine *can* heal."

"Just like the King said," whispered Flamerider.

They rose as soon as their hearts beat normally again. The moon was almost gone in the west as they left the fringes of Heartbreak. But even after the town of sickness lay behind them, one particular sound still echoed in their ears: the sound of a child in great pain. Not the wail of a child woken suddenly in the night, but the constant wearied crying of one who could not understand why its misery would not go away. And the light breeze brought them the answering, soothing sound of a woman's voice as she sang softly, but in vain, to her child.

Firecolt looked up and saw the pinpoint lights in the mountains far ahead. Suddenly he remembered the King and heard him as he spoke. "The voice came to me, saying, 'In this bottle one may find life and healing. With its discovery your land and people will be blessed and healed and will become great again.'

Then my vision ended."

Firecolt stopped in the road and listened very hard to his thoughts. *The land will be healed. The vision had said nothing about the King. The King, even if he were healed, would not help the land. The people will be healed. The wine in this bottle can heal.* He looked up at the mountains again, and he knew that unless they hurried they would be too late. He considered the image of the King speaking low from his deathbed, and he thought about the echo of the child's crying.

He whispered to Flamerider, and they turned and ran back to Heartbreak.

A watchman stopped them, surprised that anyone would venture near. "Lions raid at night, but not boys," he said. "Why are you here?"

He unraveled the thread of the story from Firecolt's tangled narrative, but was doubtful of the claim. He called others, and soon a host of lepers surrounded them.

"Is this true?" growled one of the men.

"Yes! I saw it happen," insisted Firecolt.

The man took the bottle from Firecolt, uncorked it and held the tip to his nose. "It smells like wine," he said. He spilled a splash onto his hand and tasted it gingerly. "It tastes like wine," he said, "but just in case, you drink some first. There are people around who would gladly poison a leper."

Firecolt drank and grimaced at the strength of the liquid. Then he held the bottle up and waited. Everyone watched, but nothing happened.

Another man snatched the bottle away. "I'll chance it," he rumbled. "It might cure me, or it might kill me, or it might do nothing at all. But I'd rather have a quick death than this slow rot."

He drank, and waited, and in moments his changed body proved the truth of Firecolt's words.

A riot of shouting and guzzling and healing broke out, while the boys huddled on the ground avoiding the turmoil of the tattered boots and bare feet.

Then the lepers hastened to the square in Heartbreak, yelling the town awake. The bottle, still not quite empty, passed from hand to hand and house to house.

What had begun as a solitary challenge in the darkness became a shared joy among friends. "Has everyone had their fill of this potion?" shouted the man who had taken charge. "No man too old, no woman too shy, no child too small!" A few last children were handed to him, and he filled their tiny mouths and watched their flesh purify as they sputtered and gasped and protested with wordless wails the strong taste of the wine.

He handed the bottle back to Flamerider. Firecolt then took it and shook it experimentally. He tipped it over his palm. Nothing came out. "It is empty," he said.

The boys, too tired to walk again, and now fearful of the King if he heard of their disobedience, slept in the shadows while the people lit fires and danced and sang.

A woman shook them awake in the midst of the celebration. "Who gave you this bottle? Whose wine is this?" she asked.

"It is Covenant's," answered Firecolt sleepily.

"Who is Covenant?" she asked.

"Come to Glory and see," Flamerider invited.

And they did. By the time the morning light fell upon their faces, every person in the village—now whole and healthy—was prepared. Some walked, some rode donkeys, others rode with their wrapped burdens in one ancient cart. Groups of eight men took turns pulling it; the axles screamed in protest at every turn of the wheels, and the boys doubted it would last even the short journey to Glory.

Where there had been a colony of lepers, there was now a procession of whole people; where there had been a pool of human misery there were now only empty huts.

The boys led the former lepers back to Glory, leaving a joyfully abandoned village behind them.

FIFTEEN

The Men
Who Would
Be King

BEAUTY, WORDSMITH AND COVENANT DREW NEAR TO GLORY and found the marks of many feet on the road before them. Outside the main gate they found an old, gaunt cart leaning against a tree and all but abandoned.

A man was unloading a final bag from the cart and hoisting it up on his shoulder. He looked up at the travelers staring at the wagon. "It is yours now," he said cheerfully, "if you want it. We have no more use for it."

"We?" asked Wordsmith.

"We." He waved his hand excitedly at himself and the tracks of the many feet in the dust. "We who are no longer lepers. Take the cart—we need it not. We have come in search of this Covenant who sent us the wondrous wine." Then he was gone.

"We accept your gift," said Covenant gravely to the empty silence.

"I do not understand," said Wordsmith.

"You don't have to," answered Covenant.

"But they're looking for you," said Beauty.

"They will find me soon enough. They are already heading toward the house."

"Lepers? What wine?" asked Freeblade.

Covenant only smiled. "You will all hear their story first-hand," he said. "Others of our company have been active in our absence."

"And what about this?" Wordsmith gestured to the sagging hulk of the wagon. The harness and reins lay on the ground, a hopeless tangle of discarded leather. "If it rolls for another dozen leagues, I will be surprised," said Wordsmith. "What shall we do with it? It is too wide for our narrow streets."

His speech was interrupted by the sounds of many trumpets blaring low and mournfully in the streets of Glory.

They hurried through the gates to hear that the King was dead.

"You knew this would happen, didn't you?" accused Wordsmith.

"Yes," said Covenant simply.

"And you did not tell us?" asked Beauty.

"You would only have worried," said Covenant, "and all the worry in the world would not have helped you."

Freeblade straightened his weary shoulders. "Then let us go and meet the lepers. They are alive, it seems, and can be tended to, while the King is beyond our help."

They approached the House of Covenant, and Binder met them at the door with news of the journey of the fire twins. Wordsmith, in turn, brought them details of the King's death.

The house was full of joyful, anxious strangers. As Covenant entered, Firecolt called out his name and sparked a flame of emotion that swept from room to room. Everyone tried to draw near, talking at once, and Binder was stunned by the happy pandemonium.

But Covenant was beaming. He climbed the stairs partway, turned, and somehow steered the crowd toward order with only his voice and visage.

"I know your story," he thundered, when the dying din had eased their ears. "This gift of wine was directed by the hand of the Elder God and accomplished in his name. It has had its full effect, I see. You are healed, and you are here, but what shall you do next?"

No one answered, for no one had considered the question yet.

"Why, make a new life in Glory," said one man finally.

"We will follow you," said a woman with children clinging to her skirts.

"Then go out into Glory," Covenant proclaimed, "and go with my blessing. Or stay here, and stay with my blessing. I need not speak to you now, but you will hear more of me in days to come. Should you face difficulties when I am not in this house, you must turn to Wordsmith, Beauty or Free-blade." He pointed them out to the multitude.

"Binder," he called, "is there food for a midday Feast?"

"Of course there is," answered Binder. "We seldom tend your house in vain."

So a Feast was held, and merry was the house, although black flags flew above the palace.

*   *   *

At the end of the afternoon, Covenant gathered the ones who knew him best and led them on a slow walk in the great amphitheater before the palace. He sat them down in the sand and stared at the palace.

"What happens now?" asked Lionheart, breaking the uneasy silence.

"What has always happened when a king dies heirless," answered Covenant, "though it has not happened in many lifetimes. People will choose champions for themselves, and there will be a tournament—an open court of armed combat. He who survives will be king."

"I did not know about these things," said Lionheart.

"My book told tales of this," said Freeblade. "I never dreamed I would witness such a combat myself."

Freeblade felt the weight of Covenant's gaze upon him, and soon he saw that the others were watching him too.

"Freeblade," said Covenant, "I bid you contend for this company."

Freeblade bowed. "Those who fail die." His eyes were both troubled and proud.

"Are you not prepared to die?" asked Covenant.

"I am prepared," replied Freeblade, "but I am not pleased to throw my life down for the mere trophy of a kingship. Is this a good thing that you bid me do? You have had no taste for violence before, nor have I ever heard that you wish for a crown."

"I shall not be the next king," Covenant said, "but I shall be the final one."

"I do not understand him," whispered Beauty to Wordsmith. "He speaks in riddles."

"Why should this time differ from all the rest?" Wordsmith whispered back.

"I cannot envision you with a sword in your hand," Freeblade said to Covenant. "But I was born for the blade, and I will fight for you."

"It is not the first battle you have fought for this company— nor will it be the last. And above that, I named you Champion of the House of Covenant."

"The night you gave me this name," Freeblade finished quietly. "I remember, and I will not dishonor either the name or the duty.

"When I win, you shall be king."

Covenant nodded. "That I shall, but perhaps the moment is

farther away than you think. And we may have differing ideas of victory. Nevertheless, you shall begin your task here tomorrow when the champions are named and the tournament begins." He turned to speak to them all again. "This peace in Glory has been kept—and opposed—by unseen hands," he said. "The end of all things shall come before you know peace like this again. It is a fragile thing, and not even the King's peace lasts forever."

"There is a legend," said Binder, "that as long as the judgment rock stands, we will still have peace." He pointed to the single jut of stone that overlooked the arena. Stairs were carved into its side, that one could stand on its lofty top and utter words of law and justice.

"Some legends have much truth in them," agreed Covenant.

And with that the council ended.

SIXTEEN

Rivals
and
Champions

FREEBLADE PULLED BINDER ASIDE. "COME WALK WITH ME," he said. "I would see the town with you from the top of the walls."

They left the others there in the street and climbed the long stairs to the broad walk on the wall.

Glory was quiet before them, but restless and afraid beneath the stillness. Few mourned for the king; most were awed by the presence of royal death; a few laid plans of their own and waited for the tournament.

"You did not call me out here to see the sights of Glory," Binder said, "for we have seen them many times before. Speak your mind. I am ready to listen."

"I know what is in your heart," said Freeblade quietly, "for the same thoughts have sounded in mine."

Binder stared at him. "The lady?"

"The same. Are you ready to dare the curse for her sake?"

"I believe I am," Binder answered, "but I will not fight you for her."

"You are right," replied Freeblade, "for I will not strive with you over her." He drew his sword from its sheath and looked at it with a mixture of affection and fear. "This is my bride and my burden, my calling and my companion. As much as I wish it, I should not have another distraction in my life.

"But we are both presumptuous, aren't we?" he chuckled. "I do not know that she would consent to either of us." He looked up at Binder. "I have had an adventure already," he said, "and they are only just beginning. But this could be the greatest adventure of all—to discover a woman who has been lost for years.

"I wish to have her," he continued, "but it is not good that I do, whether she wants me or not. I have looked at my own heart, and my motives are all too plain to me. I would take her as my own, not so much because I love her but because I love more the noble gesture. You, I think, are ready to care for her whether anyone sees or not."

"But is she ready to care for me?"

"You have spent much time with her," said Freeblade. "Enough to know her well."

"Enough to believe that I love her," Binder said firmly.

"It is still her choice—but we should see Covenant first."

* * *

When the two found Covenant, they laid their desires, their dialogue and their decisions before him.

"You have changed my life," said Binder, "and I have done little to repay you. Would this choice please you, that I extend your kindness and protection to another?"

"This is not enough to repay me," answered Covenant. "It cannot even begin to count against that debt. What you owe me is so great a debt that you will not begin to discharge it before time itself has lost its meaning. Nor is it even payment to me."

"I thought you would be pleased," said Freeblade, puzzled.

"I am," said Covenant, "but the gift Binder gives is to her, and not to me. I am most pleased that you settled it between yourselves in friendship and honor, and did not bring strife into this house."

He turned to Binder again and gently waved Freeblade from the room. "You have been bidden to do many things," he began, "and you will be bidden again. This act is not demanded of you, and I will not make you any false promises. Yes, it would please me, but you would fire no anger if you turned this chance away. It lies at your hand if you choose, but you can not choose to have—you can only choose to offer. I give you leave to love her, if you dare.

"You must make your decision, and soon, for she has a decision to make as well."

"But why should this privilege be mine? I have done only a single act of goodness," said Binder, "and you have loved me anyway."

"You were welcome here with or without an act of bravery. When you pulled the two boys from the fire, your moment of bravery was decided upon and committed and paid for and over in a few moments. But this choice requires courage and resolution, and not merely bravery. There is no hurry to act, and you will bear the price of your decision during every day that comes after."

"I will walk for a while, and think," said Binder.

"Take the lady with you to help you think," Covenant suggested with his wry, warm smile.

And within the space of a half hour Binder and the Chameleon Lady were walking the broad walls where the two rival friends had walked before. Binder was ill at ease, and did not know if it was a comfort that she walked so close beside him and waited contentedly for his words.

"Freeblade and I have spoken of you," he began carefully, "and it is our joint desire that you be cared for and be happy. If we could, we would gladly free you from your curse. But neither of us are magic men—even though Freeblade wields a holy sword, he casts no spells and breaks none."

"I have given up hope of being free from this parade of faces," she said. "I will be satisfied with an ordinary miracle."

"What would that be?"

"My desires have changed but little," she stated, turning to face him squarely. "I still long to be loved, as my sister was, but I will be loved only by an honorable man." Her eyes, gray at the moment, regarded him with a longing that could no longer be concealed.

"Lady," Binder said, "I have enjoyed your company more than I once enjoyed my books, though I did not think such a thing was possible." He took a deep breath. "I am most willing to have you, if you will have me. I desire to twist our lives together so tightly they can never be untangled."

"Your desire is true to your name," she murmured.

"But Freeblade will gladly have you too," he hastened to say, "though he knows that you would never have his whole heart. We spoke together, and he gave me his blessing to make this offer."

"And if I say no?" she asked almost too softly to be heard.

He swallowed. "I will love you anyway, and leave you alone, and say nothing to anyone but Freeblade. And should I find a man of power worthy of you, I will bring him to you at once."

"Then I would be a fool to say no."

Binder could not fasten onto her words. "Are you saying . . . ?"

"Don't you know *yes* when you hear it?" she asked lightly. "Of course I will."

"But are you truly willing to forfeit the cure?" he asked hesitantly. "You need a man of power—and I have less than any other man in this house. Wordsmith. Lionheart. Free-blade, again. And if Covenant wanted to free you, he would have done so already. I, on the other hand, have only a few battered books and a legacy of orphans to look after. If you accept me, you are doomed to a different face every day forever."

"Binder," she said softly, "I would rather be joined to a man with no power who cares for me than to a powerful man who is not knit to me and acts only for pity's sake. It is *you* who must pay the price of having *me*. Can you love and live with a woman you can recognize only by her cloak?"

"Whenever I close my eyes, you are the same woman I hear every day and have come to know."

"Then close your eyes now."

He complied. She took his hands in hers and brought them up to her face. "Feel very carefully," she requested. Binder gladly and gently explored her face with his fingers. "Would you know that face again if you felt it?"

"I would."

"Now look at me. Do I look the same as the last time your eyes were open?"

"No," he said. "But I have come to expect that."

"Close your eyes again, and touch my face. Is it different or the same?"

"The same," he said excitedly.

"I hoped it would be," she sighed happily. "Can you be content with that? My touch and my loyalty are the only constant gifts I can offer you."

"I am more than content," Binder said. "I am well satisfied."

They held each other and ignored Glory beneath them.

I'm not sure who made the first offer, Binder thought, *or who made this final decision.*

* * *

"You are a noble man, Binder," said Freeblade, after the two walkers returned to the house and announced their pact.

"Blessed be the two of you, and the boys as well, as you begin to fight the wonderful battle of hearts entwined. I have another battle to fight tomorrow; I thank you for clearing my burdens that I can fight with an undivided heart and an undistracted mind."

Covenant blessed them as well, asking them, "Is there any reason to wait?"

"This is not a certain time," said Binder. "Freeblade must fight tomorrow, and even you seem weighed with woes."

Covenant nodded sadly. "My thoughts are, indeed, heavy for the coming day. But it is fully fitting to begin a marriage on the eve of battle. Let love run its course even in the face of war. Many will strive to be named King tomorrow; let us crown you a king tonight, and usher you into your own kingdom."

And so there was a third marriage in that house, with Covenant presiding and binding the two together as husband and wife. Binder's pledge, already fashioned in secret hope, was large and hollow, and it unscrewed into two pieces. It swallowed up the medallion on her pledge of punishment and closed tightly to hide it from the world forever.

"You may still be cursed," said Binder tenderly, "but you shall not wear your badge of shame openly."

*   *   *

The next morning Beauty and Wordsmith were surprised to see Binder seeking Covenant before breakfast. There was a fire in his eyes and a light in his heart, and he said only, "I have a question for him that will not wait."

He eventually found Covenant on a balcony, being warmed by the rising sun, and confronted him affectionately. "Covenant," he challenged, "tell me again the cure for chameleon."

"A man of power must marry her and undo the curse."

"Then what happened last night?" demanded Binder.

Covenant turned the question around. "What happened last night, Binder?"

124

He sought for the right words, and began. "We slept, and woke early, and she bore a face I had never seen before. She has had that same face now for hours."

Covenant smiled, and beckoned him to a seat. "And do you think she has been freed?"

"I believe so, but cannot prove it."

"You seem both certain and confused," observed Covenant.

"I am certain of what I see; I wonder if others will see the same thing."

"There is one way to know."

"Yes," said Binder. "Will you join us for her entrance?"

"Gladly," said Covenant.

* * *

The entire company was assembled when Binder led his lady into the room. They saw her shining face and expectant smile as she gazed at each of them in turn.

"What manner of woman do you see?" she asked Beauty directly.

"I see a woman with black hair and blue eyes and creamy skin," she said.

"So do I," said Wordsmith with surprise.

"And I," added Candle.

"And I," confirmed Moonflower.

"As do I," concluded Freeblade.

She turned her eyes to Covenant. "I want to believe that I am freed, but I do not know how it was done. Is this your work?"

"No," said Covenant, "it was done by the two of you."

"But you said it could be done only by a man of great power."

"Only a man could do it," responded Covenant, "but you misunderstood what power is. Power is not only might to hammer the world into the shape you please, but is also the privilege of changing the outside of another from the inside out, with power and persuasion and commitment. He has loved you with the selfless love he has found in this house, and your return of his love multiplied his power. Both of you made a sacrifice of hope born of hope, and your offerings combined to kindle a magic greater than that of any mighty man."

"Then you are no longer the Chameleon Lady," said Beauty. "What shall we call you?"

Everyone looked to Covenant, who extended his palm to Binder and left it to him.

"If it is, indeed, up to us," said Binder, "we would have her called Lady Brightface."

"It is well, and it is done," pronounced Covenant.

All the company applauded, and they beheld her true face at length before Binder led her away again to their room. She was neither remarkable nor wretched, but the love Covenant had poured into her heart—and confirmed there by Binder—transformed her, and none who saw her that day would ever forget her.

SEVENTEEN

Blood
and
Valor

WHEN THE SUN ROSE HIGHER, THE COMPANY OF COVENANT left the house behind and mingled with the growing crowd descending on the amphitheater.

There Freeblade took his place in the long line and waited his turn to throw in the metal marker with his name on it. Having done so, he announced his challenge: "Freeblade—Champion of the House of Covenant."

Covenant and his followers applauded him and cheered; few others did so—not of disdain, or favoritism, but because most were too afraid to cheer anyone just yet.

The tournament preparations continued with the drawing of markers, and the solemn painting of the ranks of the opponents' names on the wall that surrounded the amphitheater.

"Their names mean nothing to me," murmured Freeblade, fingering the grip of his sword. "I know none of them."

"They know nothing of you," returned Covenant. "But mark this name: Fame. You will see him slay many, for he has long awaited this chance."

"Fame." Freeblade studied the names and the lines on the wall. "Our names are on opposite ends, so he would be my ultimate opponent—if both of us survive so long."

"Yes," said Covenant. "He is the first contender on that side, and he will also be the final contender of those names."

"It will be my highest pleasure to slay your old enemy," swore Freeblade.

"That is what I feared," said Covenant, smiling again to take away any offense.

And at noon the tournament master opened the arena for the fighting.

Fame was first onto the hot sand, first to unsheathe his sword, first to brandish his emblazoned shield for the crowd.

Brightface began to moan, and clung tightly to Binder. "It's him!" she whispered fiercely. "The magic man! The one who cursed me! I did not know it was Fame!"

Binder nodded his head sadly and hid her face against his shoulders. "I am not surprised. His hand seems to be found in anything dark."

In the arena Fame raised his sword with a smile and beckoned his opponent closer to him. Fame struck first, and often, and last, and never swung his sword without a smile.

And when he had felled his foe, Fame dipped his hand in his opponent's blood and struck the dead man's name from the wall.

The sorrowed supporters carried the body away.

The next two combatants came promptly to the center of the arena, touched their swords together, and began their dance of death. Brutality began to replace formality, as hatred and greed and naked desire conquered ceremony and left it bleeding in the dust.

All Glory watched in horrified fascination as the tournament wound its bloody way down the length of the walls. Many of those who raised their sword in victory were themselves cut down by harder blows.

"Traditions die hard," said Covenant, "but so must many men. Every weapon that a man can make will be twisted back upon him and pierce him through the heart.

"But take courage," he continued, "for your sword was not made by human hands, and you shall not fight with human strength.

"You must fight fiercely," he said to the restlessly pacing Freeblade, "yet with mercy. When you have knocked your man to the ground, and he fails to rise again, you must offer him the chance to withdraw with his life."

"But the rules are to kill or be killed," objected Freeblade.

"That is what the people expect. I have told you what *I* expect of you."

"What if they do not take the offer, but fight on?"

"They will accept your offer," Covenant smiled, "and do so gladly. Slay no one—but defeat them roundly."

The excitement of the crowd began to turn into subdued and horrified awe. Most there had seen death before, but never so violent, so frequent and so deliberate. Yet death held sway, holding hands with victory, until Freeblade's name was called and he met his first challenger.

Thrust, parry, block and swing. His foe was older and more clever, but Freeblade was quicker and stronger, and the fire of Covenant's charter burned in his eyes. He was a man who would not be denied.

Time and time again he struck with the flat of the blade, wearing away where he could have slashed and skewered. His opponent was not so kind, and soon opened a crimson line along Freeblade's arm. Freeblade looked surprised, and glanced at Covenant, but then redoubled his efforts; in only a moment more one of his strokes shivered the challenger's shield, and his opponent stumbled backward and lay stunned.

Freeblade laid the tip of his sword against his opponent's throat. "Do you accept defeat?" shouted Freeblade.

"Yes," groaned his opponent weakly, expecting the fatal thrust.

"Then go," Freeblade ordered. "Your wounds are not mortal, and I do not seek your head as a trophy. You are not my enemy," he continued, "you are only my opponent. This fight is over; take your sword and go." Then, after a moment's thought, Freeblade smeared his fingers in his own blood and walked to the wall to strike out his opponent's name.

Trueteller and Lionheart tended his wound while Freeblade's eyes searched Covenant's face in puzzlement.

"I did not promise you would be unharmed," said Covenant. "I only said that you would not be defeated."

They watched Fame conquer again. "You will not have to face him," promised Covenant.

"Will he fall in combat?" asked Freeblade. "I do not see how he can."

"He will not lose. And neither will you," stated Covenant.

"But I must face him for the right to fill the throne."

"No. You will be spared that."

"I do not understand."

"You need not understand. You are a warrior? Then fight, and leave the wisdom to others."

Freeblade saluted him gravely with the sword and turned again to watch the fighting.

The list grew smaller—by death and also by withdrawal. Many of Fame's foes withdrew; few of Freeblade's challengers did so, seeing that they risked defeat at his hands but not death.

So Fame fought viciously and hungrily, but against fewer and fewer opponents, while Freeblade fought on longer under the sun.

"It is easy to kill a man," mumbled Freeblade to Covenant between matches. "It is far harder *not* to kill him while winning."

"You are learning the value of controlled wrath," said Covenant, "and they are learning lessons of their own. Blood means little to them until it is time to spill their own."

When the final light of day fell from the sky, only two were left to strive for the crown. "Enough!" cried the tournament master. "Let these two not meet until the sun has come to us again!"

But Fame could not leave without taunting the exhausted Freeblade. Ignoring Covenant and the rest, he spat to the warrior, "Go home and lick your wounds, my ambitious friend. You will need your strength for tomorrow!"

Though the fighting was postponed, bets were still taken briskly long after darkness fell.

At the house, Covenant tended Freeblade's many wounds himself. "Each fight has cost you a price of blood," said Covenant, "and you will have these scars forever."

"Then I will wear them proudly," answered Freeblade, and then fell asleep.

But Freeblade's arm stiffened during the night, and a low fever that began after midnight raged high in his body by dawn.

The others gathered around him, concerned and puzzled.

"Covenant, why do you not heal Freeblade?" whispered Wordsmith.

"Sudden health is not always the best road to wholeness," answered Covenant.

"But I cannot fight like this!" moaned Freeblade.

"No, you cannot," said Covenant simply. "The rules of the tournament hold that a champion who is not defeated but cannot continue may be replaced by another of his company."

"Then let me fight," offered Binder, and Brightface gripped his arm in fear. "By your hand I have rescued my lady from

Fame, and it is only fitting that I should avenge her as well."

"Vengeance is not the need of the moment," said Covenant kindly, "or I would accept your offer gladly."

Brightface relaxed again.

"Men you may face, Freeblade," Covenant continued, "and against men you may prevail; your battles yesterday were against flesh and blood. But Fame is not altogether flesh, nor is it altogether blood that pounds in his veins. You may not fight him. You would not win, and even if you could win you would be forced to win the wrong way. I must win *my* way, else all will be lost."

And then the company realized that Covenant would take the sword himself. They were wounded by the thought of Covenant suffering, and they could not imagine him fighting, but neither could they imagine him losing. All of them—including Binder and Brightface, and the wounded warrior who would not stay in bed—followed him silently to the area where the restless crowd and eager challenger awaited them.

"I will still fight for you, if you only give the command," whispered Freeblade to Covenant.

"You would not prevail."

"But I would die proudly!" insisted Freeblade.

Covenant shook his head. "It is not your day to die."

"Then take my feeble blessing as protection while you fight for the throne."

"You misunderstand me," said Covenant. "I do not fight for me. *I* am fighting now as *your* champion—and not that I may be crowned King of Glory." He smiled a sad smile, and said, "I am already King—though none but you few will acknowledge it."

"Then take my weapons," urged Freeblade. "This sword and shield have served me well."

"I need no weapons," said Covenant, returning Freeblade's offerings with a bow and the honor of a hovering smile. Then he strode into the center of the arena unarmed.

EIGHTEEN

The Judgment Stone

W HO ARE YOU?" THE MASTER SHOUTED TO THE BEGGAR. "Where is this Freeblade?"

"I am Covenant," the beggar called loudly enough for all to hear. "I am here because Freeblade is weak and fevered, and cannot fight this day. I have come to fight as champion for the champion of my house."

When Fame saw that Covenant had come to fight, and was unarmed, he threw down his own shield and gripped his sword before him with his hands clasped together. "You are a fool," Fame sneered to his old enemy, "to come against me at all, and a fool many times over to come against me with your bare hands."

The tournament master waved his hands and stepped back, and Fame rushed recklessly at Covenant, his sword dancing its deadly dance in the air.

But Covenant slipped beneath the flicking blade and tripped Fame.

Fame rose again, his face smeared with dust and contorted with anger.

Covenant stood his ground, and turned away yet another leap with surprising agility.

It was not the fight the crowd expected. Covenant did not press the attack, but continued standing firm and eluding most of Fame's lunges. Widening stripes of blood began to appear on Covenant's arms, yet still he stood unbroken. The crowd had begun to jeer Fame now, for being unable to dispatch an unarmed street beggar. Fame's arms were growing heavy, and he realized he would tire sooner than the unburdened and still nimble Covenant.

He threw the sword down in frustration and leaped upon the beggar with long fingers like talons. Across and around the arena they wrestled, Fame clawing and tearing, while Covenant broke hold after hold. They fought grimly, and for the first time the company saw Covenant suffer in open agony. He seemed to be dying; his flesh was bruised in countless places, his clothes and skin were badly torn, and blood still flowed from the evil cuts.

Fame knocked Covenant down with a stunning kick, and the beggar could rise only to his knees. Fame stumbled up steps to the Stone of Judgment and braced himself to crush his enemy from its heights. "I defy you," he howled. "You are wounded and winded, and cannot rise to fight me." He stamped his feet—and the rock beneath him suddenly began to crumble. He jumped back desperately and found solid footing just as the massive flattened peak of the stone split from its base and thundered down upon Covenant with a horrific smash.

The Stone embedded itself in the ground, leaving no sign of the beggar beneath.

All Glory stared in shock at the abrupt ending. Fame gazed down with glazed eyes, his utter surprise turning quickly into triumph.

The company of Covenant was frozen, stunned, until

Freeblade drew his weapon and stumbled screaming to the fallen rock. He began to dig frantically in the sand with his sword, and the others of the company were right behind him. A few of the crowd joined them in their efforts, but the rest of the people held back. Some, maddened by the lust for blood, cheered Fame wildly. Most were silent and uncertain.

An hour passed as they dug frantically. Glory waited impatiently and Fame grinned, savoring the moment he knew must come. Some in the crowd looked at Fame's face and began to regret their earlier cheers.

At last the rescuers undermined the side of the stone, and with the dregs of their strength tipped the slab sideways into the hasty pit.

The beggar was not there. Beneath the rubble there was only his cloak, drenched with drying blood and pounded deep by the falling rock. More blood had soaked deep into the sand and turned it a dark reddish-brown.

"No man could shed this much blood and live!" shouted one of the helpers.

Wordsmith stood by the ugly stain and gazed up at the triumphant Fame. "By this blood," he thundered, "you have sealed your own death!"

Fame gazed coldly down upon him, and said, "I shall deal with your sorry group shortly—and efficiently." Then he roared to the crowd, "Is there anyone left to challenge me?"

There was only silence in response.

"Then I claim the crown of Glory!" he declared. Silence met his pronouncement, and only slowly did the cheers begin to rise. Then more joined, until all but a few in the crowd acknowledged him and honored him with their praise. He immediately began to call out names, appointing advisors and captains and men-at-arms.

The company had no heart for the ceremonies. They gathered up the bloody cloak and returned home silently.

NINETEEN

The Death
of the
Dream

IN THE END THERE WAS NO TRUE BURIAL. AT WORDSMITH'S suggestion, Covenant's cloak (stiff now with his blood) was hidden deep within the walls of the house he had rebuilt for them. Candle placed it in a carved stone chest taken from his own special treasures. They were sad beyond words.

They huddled around Wordsmith the steward, hungry for some words from him and for the warmth of the only fire they had the interest to light.

"He warned us of this," said Wordsmith. "He said this would happen. He told us, but we did not understand it until now."

"Why didn't he tell us this directly?" moaned Beauty. "He *knew* this was going to happen."

"Perhaps we would have interfered if we had understood his words," said Wordsmith. "But he did leave us with wisdom and with promises. Covenant took me into the desert, and there he told me many things that I did not understand and still cannot fathom. Though I did not see the wisdom of it until now, at his bidding I wrote down his every word." His fingers smoothed the new leather on the tiny book he produced from his pouch. "These are his words to me, as nearly as I could snatch them from the air. Who can fully capture the truth that Covenant speaks? You must find a greater writer than I for that . . . but these will do, these will have to do.

"When Covenant . . . vanished, it seems that my eyes were opened to many things that he said—as if he were speaking words into my mind, and not simply leaving them on paper. I have words of hope you must hear. Covenant made provisions. Hear, now, what he gave me to give to you.

"He told me that he would soon go where we could not find him, and that he would not leave us in our sorrow but would send another in his place. He told me that when I sought him in vain, I should go and seek for the Child Upon the Mountain."

"A child?" asked Beauty.

"*The* Child," corrected Wordsmith.

"Which mountain?" asked Freeblade—even as his eyes turned toward Lonely Mountain.

"The mountain where few have ever ventured," Wordsmith replied, "and from which none has ever returned."

"What shall *we* find there?"

"The Child," Wordsmith said, "but I know no more than that. How could a child survive the deep snows and icy storms that rage atop that mountain?"

"How shall we get up, and how we shall we find him, and how we shall we get down again?" asked Freeblade.

Wordsmith shrugged his shoulders. "I do not know. Perhaps we will discover that when we get there."

"This all seems so remote now," murmured Binder. "Was he ever really here? Was he only a ghost?"

"If he was only a ghost, then where did the blood come from?" responded Brightface, squeezing his hand ever tighter.

"If anything," said Wordsmith, "he is more real to me now than when he was with us. He was always coming and going, and I did not know when I would see him, but now I feel as though he is standing at my side. I cannot explain it, but I am reassured by this invisible presence even in my numbness and grief."

After a long silence, Freeblade spoke again. "But what must we do now? Do we sit here and wait? Do we leave for the mountain immediately?"

"No," answered Wordsmith, "I am afraid we must all leave this place. Fame is gathering his soldiers, and I do not think he will be long in hunting us down."

"How do you know that?" challenged Candle. And then, more softly, "I do not mean to anger you, but I do not know what to do. I do not know if we even should follow you from this house—which is strong and sure. Did he not build it with his own hands?"

Wordsmith answered quietly. "I have just come from the tower he built for me. The four windows are black—dead or dying or dimmed—and the fifth window is an ugly swirl of clouds that reveals nothing.

"And I have tested the Door to the City. This key will no longer open it." He paused. "The heart has gone from this house."

Even through their numbing shock they could sense the growing chill of the silent stones, and they knew that the cold creeping into their bones was not born solely of their own fear.

"I do not claim that any of you should follow me," said Wordsmith. "But I will do what I feel must be done, and the rest of you are free to follow if you wish."

"It is only a building," said Brightface sadly, "now that Covenant is gone."

"We cannot defend this place against Fame's men," Free-blade stated. "I am with Wordsmith, for I know of Covenant's deep regard for him—and Fame's hatred for us all."

"And I am with you," said Beauty, "though I should not need to say so."

"And so are we," Binder said. Brightface, leaning her head against Binder's arm, added, "I cannot live my life in the presence of Fame."

"But I cannot go," said Lionheart, "without my charges. And where will we hide? Must I take my infants and elderly out into the wilderness?"

"Here is my counsel," said Wordsmith. "Let us all go to the one place where no one will ever go again—Heartbreak, the village of the lepers. It is empty, even though there are houses there, and a well, and a forest beyond for food. I think," he added, smiling, "that Lionheart could readily make it feared as a place of lions and other fierce beasts."

"Should I shutter my shop as well?" asked Candle.

"Perhaps—and perhaps not," answered Wordsmith. "You are not as dependent on this house as we are, and though you came early you are not widely known to be among our company. If you are willing to run the risk, it might be very useful if you moved back into your shop and stayed in Glory."

Candle looked at Moonflower. "She will find it hard to flee far now. I will go back to my shop and stay in Glory. Trueteller may make her own decision."

"Will you have me if I stay?" she asked her son-in-law.

"Of course," he said. "You bring light to our house—and you are neither a burden nor a busybody."

"Is there anyone else who wishes to stay?" asked Wordsmith.

No one answered.

"The soldiers will be looking for us," said Wordsmith. "Let us go from this place quickly."

"But how shall we get to Heartbreak?" asked Freeblade.

"Lionheart's children cannot run all the way."

"My lions will come and carry us," said Lionheart. "But I fear there are not enough lions to bear all of us at once."

"There is a large wagon standing ready at the gates," said Beauty quietly. "It was given to us as we returned from the sea, but I did not imagine we would have need of it. It is a poor cart, but we must use what we have been given."

"Not even Roadreeler and Kingsburro together can pull that ancient wreck," said Freeblade.

Wordsmith looked about him in the shadow of defeat, but Lionheart spoke again. "Perhaps the others will help as well. When Covenant . . . died, part of his power fell upon you. Perhaps another part of it has fallen upon me. Go and pick what you can carry, and I will see what I can do."

They packed in haste, wrapping food and gathering the animals. By ones and twos, they quietly left the roar of Glory and assembled outside the gates. The elderly, the infants and the infirm were loaded on the wagon, along with the few belongings they had salvaged. Freeblade refused to ride upon the wagon, even though his wounds had not yet healed.

"Now, Lionheart," said Wordsmith, "where is our help?"

Lionheart opened his mouth and rent the air with the roar of a lion, and no one was surprised. Then he added the growl of a bear, and the howl of a wolf, and finally the bracking bray of a stag, and they stared at him.

All came—lions, bears, wolves and deer—to stand in the shadow of the trees and await further words from Lionheart. He beckoned eight of the shaggy black bears, who shuffled over to him and huffed noisily in the air as he adjusted the worn harnesses about them.

"We can go now," said Lionheart. "The bears are swifter than you think, and strong and sure. The lions will carry the rest of us, and the wolves and deer will guard our way and cover our tracks behind us." He reached his hand out in wonder to stroke the shaggy head beside him. "I have only begun to understand the privilege that has been given me."

"Let us go then," said Wordsmith. Lionheart spoke, and the bears lurched off with the load. The others each mounted a lion, not without misgivings, and they slipped away from Glory with regret, pain and many a backward glance.

* * *

King Fame and his soldiers reached the house of Covenant only to find it abandoned.

"I am not surprised that they have scattered," said Fame. "Take what you please from the house," he ordered, "and then pull the stones down. Leave no trace that the beggar and his kind were ever here."

"Should we search for them?" asked his captain. "They are your enemies."

"There is no hurry now," said Fame, dismissing the suggestion with a wave of his hand. "Let them go, and let their god be forgotten again and forever. There are more urgent tasks to be done than chasing vermin. Their house has once again fallen, for they have no leader and no path to follow. Let them go where they will, for they cannot hide long from my wrath. They are fools fleeing in fear, and there is no place for them in Glory."

TWENTY

Heartshope

T HE COMPANY LEFT THE MAIN ROAD AND CREAKED TOWARD Heartbreak moments before the earthquake struck. The earth rippled and bucked and cracked while Lionheart struggled to hold the bears steady. The earthquake was sharp and strong and frightening, and it ended as suddenly as it started.

When they opened their eyes again, the land had stopped shaking, and the silence was immense.

Wordsmith gestured at the field beside them. "Many people are buried here," he said. "But look—the earthquake has ruined even the graves."

Freeblade dismounted stiffly and cautiously explored the upheaval. Some of the graves were sunken where the mounded earth had collapsed, and some of the tombs were broken apart. "Have wild animals taken the bones already?" he called. "The broken tombs are empty."

Only some of the graves had been disturbed, and Word-smith could see no pattern to the disorder.

Binder pointed over the hill. "But what about the greater mystery? Is the village still standing?" They pressed on without answer to their questions.

* * *

Wordsmith's caravan halted in the middle of the deserted village, where mist and smoke still lingered on the ground.

Freeblade took his sword in his tired arms and searched the houses. "There seems to be no deep damage here," he said at last. "Unload the wagon."

It was mostly empty when they heard it creak and groan and splinter, and then it collapsed in a welter of worn wood and failed fittings.

Wordsmith stood and looked at the wooden ruins. "That which we cannot use in the buildings may at least become an honest fire," he said. "We owe the gift that much honor, at least."

Wordsmith kindled the fire as the others chose houses and stored away their pitifully few goods. Then, unsummoned, the Company filled their hands with food and gathered around the flames. Wearied by their grief and unplanned labors, they were grateful for a rest and listened long to the songs of the birds and beetles and other night musicians.

Beauty finally broke the spell of the silence. "Wordsmith," she said gently, "I cannot live in a place called Heartbreak. Cannot we give it another name? Covenant would have done so."

"What do you suggest?" asked Wordsmith.

"Why not Heartshope?" she proposed. "It is all we have left."

"It is good in my eyes," he replied. "Do the rest of you agree?" They nodded silently. "It is done, then," he continued, "and it is fitting for what I have to say."

143

He paused, searching for the right words. "I have not told you the most puzzling thing of all," he began, "though it is perhaps the most heartening thing as well. It is a word of comfort not from Covenant, but about him."

He looked carefully at their expectant faces. "Were any of you watching Covenant's face when the stone fell?" Wordsmith's eyes questioned each of them in turn, without result. "I had hoped one of you had seen him, too, and would add your voice to my story.

"I beheld his face," he continued, "even as he was overshadowed by his death. He was looking up, with his arms spread wide—not in fear, but in welcome.

"And he was smiling."

TALES OF THE FORGOTTEN GOD
BY DAN HAMILTON

THE BEGGAR KING
THE CHAMELEON LADY
THE EVERLASTING CHILD

TALES OF THE FORGOTTEN GOD

THE EVERLASTING CHILD

Dan Hamilton

Illustrated by
Jack Stockman

INTERVARSITY PRESS
DOWNERS GROVE, ILLINOIS 60515

InterVarsity Press® is the book-publishing division of InterVarsity Christian Fellowship®, a student movement active on campus at hundreds of universities, colleges and schools of nursing in the United States of America, and a member movement of the International Fellowship of Evangelical Students. For information about local and regional activities, write Public Relations Dept., InterVarsity Christian Fellowship, 6400 Schroeder Rd., P.O. Box 7895, Madison, WI 53707-7895.

Cover art: Jack Stockman

ISBN 0-8308-1673-9

Printed in the United States of America ∞

Library of Congress Cataloging-in-Publication Data

17	16	15	14	13	12	11	10	9	8	7	6	5	4	3	2	1
08	07	06	05	04	03	02	01	00	99	98	97	96	95	94		

—CONTENTS—

Character Names

Old	New
Abra	Trueteller
Candolel	Candle
Kali	Moonflower
Roadreeler	Roadreeler
donkey	Kingsburro
Damon	Lionheart
Damon's niece	Woodswaif
Barid	Wordsmith
hunchback	Woebearer
Beauty	Beauty
the ancient enemy	Fame, Twister, Fortune, Mesmer, Mummer
Ellard	Binder
two orphan boys	Firecolt and Flamerider
Chameleon Lady	Brightface
Seareaper	Deedtester
Wavewatcher	Joykeeper
Foamrider	Seaswallower
Fearshadow	Dreadnought Freeblade
Andin	Stonesetter
Carlin	Featherstone
Sabrin	Sabrin
eagle	Farsight Featherfriend
Grimshade	Westerkeep
Heartbreak (village)	Heartshope
Darmak	Skymarker
Arden	Halfhand

—PREFACE—

Once there was a City where dwelt the Elder God and the men and women and animals and wonders he had made. All shone, all had joy, and all were loved.

But there were ways to leave the City—paths that were still forbidden to the people though left open to their feet, avenues made not by the Elder God, but by his old enemy who hated good things everywhere. All that the people needed was given them freely, but they were not content as long as the untrodden paths to the unexplored wilderness shimmered in the sun. So they left one day, first by ones, and then by groups, until they had all left the City to see what lay beyond. The Elder God called after them all, but curiosity deafened them and stopped their ears.

First the wilderness lay before them, then beside them on either hand,

and then it surrounded them. The wilderness terrified them, for there were
lions there, and wolves, and fierce things that lived in the sea. Darkness
fell upon them, and rain and thunder—the sad voice and tears of the Elder
God. The world was changed in a great shaking and windstorm; the
people turned, but could not find the way back to the City. Too late they
understood that the roads would have been theirs to explore, and the
wonders beyond theirs to conquer, had they waited until they had been
tested, approved and empowered. Instead, they went in their own strength,
and it was the wilderness which conquered them.

The City was never lost; it was only removed from the face of the earth
and still was—somewhere. But the people were lost, and it was the path
back to the City that was forfeit.

The people made themselves a king, to remind them of the Elder God,
but no man falsely exalted could truly fill the empty throne. The people
built Glory where they believed the City had been, but it was only a
wicked and flimsy shadow. Some thought there might still be a secret door,
and behind it a dark and dangerous path to the City, winding its way
back if only one could plumb its mysteries. But if there was a door leading
to such a path, it was hidden, and no one knew where it was. Each year
fewer searched for the fabled door, and then the people lost count of the
years. Glory endured, and they still crowned kings, but the memory of
the Elder God largely faded from the land. In few places was he still
worshiped; in no place was he altogether without a witness.

Then the beggar came. Covenant. The beggar who reigned as a quiet
king. The dusty man who spoke for the Elder God and changed lives
around him frequently and forever. The one who bent the twisted world
around him so that those who stood with him could see its true shape. The
man who raised the dead to life again and granted rest to the bone-weary.
The traveler who defeated fire and fired the defeated to new heights of
courage and honor. The patient man who sifted the refuse of the world
and recovered men and women and children (and even the animals) and
made them whole again in the midst of their imperfections.

Those he redeemed he called to his house in Glory. The old stone ruin
was weathered and unremarkable from the outside, but on the inside it
was a wonderful warren of comfortable rooms and kitchens and places to

meet and eat and heal. And behind one particular door lay the path to
the City.

This part of the story was told in *The Beggar King*, and the
record was continued in *The Chameleon Lady*.

*Covenant called more to his side, changing them even as he beckoned,
with unexpected love and surprising authority.*

*A man who had long sought a hero's face discovered his answer both
in Covenant and in kneeling before him. A woman with too many faces
found acceptance and her true image through the beggar's hand and
guidance.*

*Covenant's house resounded with words of welcome for the weary and
wounded, fresh food for the famished and friendless, and scarcely returnable
love for all.*

*Far beyond the walls of Glory, Covenant had left few corners of the
kingdom untouched. By the sea, he had returned to life a boy who could
not live in the water and fish that could not live out of it. Upon the sea
itself he had delivered a hermit from the vicious shadows of his own past.
In the mountains he had given new hope to a family who could not protect
themselves from wolves. And Covenant's ransomed wine had brought
release to a village of lepers.*

*The Company of Covenant grew and prospered—until the king fell ill
and died. In the tumult of the tournament that followed, the unthinkable
happened: Covenant challenged his old enemy Fame—and died. A mammoth stone crushed Covenant into the ground, though none could find any
trace of his body save the spreading blood.*

*The Company had fled Glory even as the new king's men were coming
for them, under orders to pull down the House of Covenant. Now they
huddled in a village abandoned even by the lepers, a place made safe for
them by isolation and contempt.*

*And now what? Covenant had called them, but where was he? Their
hope was dead, their enemy sat unchallenged upon the throne of Glory,
and they themselves were hunted men and women.*

ONE

Dreams
and
Darkness

FREEBLADE PACED THE DARKNESS IN HEARTSHOPE, HIS HEART heavy even as he kept lone watch over the Company.

If I had only fought Fame myself, he whispered to himself in his misery, *I might be dead, but Covenant would still be alive. How can I undo my failure? I could not rise to fight with my weapon, and he fought in my place without one—and in the end it was no weapon that slew him.* His body still ached from his wounds and fever, but his mind tortured him worst of all. *I should walk off into the forest and fall on my sword. But then I would have failed my commission not once but twice, and died a coward's death as well.*

In the houses, each member of the band of refugees was also troubled, seeking the deeper sleep in vain. Their dreams swirled around Covenant the beggar—starting with the moments when he had invaded their lives and left them forever changed, and ending with those final moments that would fade from no one's mind. There was no hope of forgetting the sickening fear that became dull, monstrous certainty once they had rolled away the stone that had been toppled down upon the beggar. The blood that had stained the sand had marked their memories as well.

Even the restless sleep failed the Company at last. Though there were no lights in the sky yet but the stars, most shook off the tattered dreams and drifted outside, joining Freeblade where the night fire slumbered orangely in its pit. Numb and worn, none of them were surprised to find the others there; they assembled together in their unspoken need to be anything but *alone*. Rousing the fire again, they huddled wordlessly before the flames, seeking a warmth that was not there.

Full shock had set in now, and where they had been able to function and plan and act in the hours after Covenant's death, now they had no strength or emotion in reserve and could only stare with unseeing eyes at the devouring fire. Each one drifted, trapped in relentlessly circling thoughts.

Wordsmith weighed the sum of the dead Covenant's words to him. Wordsmith's wife, Beauty, wondered whether it had been the beggar's promises or the beggar himself that had failed.

Binder and Brightface clung tightly to one another's hand, their bodies not yet accustomed to the committed presence of the other. Their marriage—only two days old—had begun bravely on the edge of the horror, but could not avoid the plunge into sorrow. And Brightface was still shaking herself free from the internal shadows of her life as the Chameleon Lady.

Lionheart sat on the edge of the circle, thinking not only of Covenant but of the weight of orphans and elderly left in his care.

The first hint of dawn came at last upon them, following slowly along the wake of the long and wretched night. Defying the exhaustion and depression of the Company, the blooming light bore promise of a world continuing unchanged about them.

Wordsmith gazed up at the edge of the young sun in a sky still flecked with stars. "Our first hope is gone," said Wordsmith, "but the stars have been shining all night—and the sun has not failed us either." As they heard his thoughts, their words and wan smiles began to bubble to the surface again.

"Wordsmith," asked Brightface, her tears surprising her again, "who *was* Covenant?"

"*Was* he the Elder God?" added Binder.

"I thought so," answered Wordsmith, "and so I still believe. I cannot accept his death, yet I cannot explain it either."

The others stirred, as though waiting for the right words to spark them from their despair.

"All over this land," he continued, "there must be prayers rising to the Elder God. The invisible, the silent, the patient— he *must* be patient if he holds all power, yet is content to be nearly invisible and silent. If this world continues without Covenant here to see it, then perhaps we should continue as well."

Freeblade roused from his own stupor and declared, "Your words have shamed me, Wordsmith. Fame will be looking for us, and it is not fit that your champion should lie in the grass and wait to be taken. We do not even know what is to hand here—we know not where to hide, what to defend or how best to retreat. I must go and explore." He strapped on his sword, which had never been far from his hand.

"I will go with you," said Lionheart. "I cannot bear to do nothing. I do not regret the decision that brought us here, but how will my children and elderly survive? We are far from any help here—what food we brought with us will soon be gone, and I do not know where more will come from. Planting seeds will not suffice, for tomorrow's harvest cannot feed yesterday's hunger."

"There was always food and enough through Covenant," offered Beauty. "He sent me out into the streets many times to gather food from kind and generous strangers."

"But now we have no Covenant—and no streets either, and no strangers to fill them," replied Lionheart.

"The lepers had food to eat, didn't they?" countered Beauty. "They were dying slowly every day, but they were not starving. There must be food nearby."

"Let us look," said Wordsmith simply. The three of them walked away from the fire without further discussion.

* * *

After an hour they returned; Wordsmith and Beauty sat, with faint smiles on their faces, while Freeblade leaned against a rock, still looking dissatisfied and uneasy. Others joined them to hear their news.

"Though Covenant is not *here*," said Wordsmith, "we have not been forsaken."

"We are well provided for," explained Beauty. "The gardens of the lepers are just over this hill—all kept well-tended until the day they left. The ground bursts with vegetables, and the orchard groans beneath the weight of the fruit. Every good thing that grows is there, and a few recent weeds as well. All we need are pruning hands and strong backs to bear the baskets."

The rest heard and were comforted. The pall of desolation lifted a bit higher.

"There is water in abundance," continued Beauty, "both in the wells and in a stream that separates the gardens from the orchards. What else can we need? This place has been hidden in fear, disease and obscurity for many years—and now it is for us a haven."

Reluctantly, Freeblade spoke. "But I fear we cannot defend this place if we are attacked. There is no place to serve as a stronghold, no hills to hide behind, no trackless forest to lose ourselves in. We are simply *here*, and any who come after us may come upon us from any direction."

He shifted slightly, tension knotting his shoulders. "Nor can we mount a useful watch. Even a mightier company than this would not be able to disperse and watch all the wandering paths and meadows that one could follow to this place. Were it not for the food and for these houses standing ready for us, I would not stay here."

"But how can we travel any farther and stay together?" asked Brightface. "We have nothing left but our own feet."

Freeblade turned to Brightface, a wry smile on his face. "It is not a place I would choose to defend," he acknowledged. "But the Company is here, and I must defend it, for I will not bear this sword in vain."

Wordsmith spoke again. "We must be cautious, but not afraid. Let all our fires by day be small and smokeless, and let our fires at night be smaller and burn behind a cover of stone. Freeblade believes that the noise of the children playing will not carry as far as the main road to Glory, but in any case let us take the children each day to the meadows beyond the orchards."

"But will Fame even look for us here?" asked Binder. "Will he not think we have either hidden ourselves in Glory or fled to the ends of the kingdom?"

"I do not know," shrugged Freeblade. "We cannot hide here—or anywhere—forever, but let us shelter here while we may."

"If the lions answer me," said Lionheart, "there will be a guard on our borders tonight."

Wordsmith nodded, and began again. "We must eat again, for hunger is before us. We need not defend now, for our enemies have not found us."

"And let us do what work we can," suggested Beauty, "that we may be ready for whatever comes upon us next."

The sun crept higher, and the silence began to be broken by the calls of children and the querulous voices of the aged. The desire for meaningful work slowly came to them again, and they began to consider their practical needs and the harvest the lepers had left behind.

*   *   *

There was a second night, with its share of deep doubts and deeper loneliness, and a second morning with its promise of renewed hope.

The Company began to carve and claim a new routine, welcoming anything that laid a straight line and a goal for them; any task that was different and safe and productive would lighten their hearts and hasten their healing.

The children were somber for a while, reflecting the mood of their elders, but they quickly forgot their grieving and began to play.

"Children cannot grieve all at once, as we do," observed Brightface. "They will cry, and then laugh, and later cry again. Let them sorrow in their own way and time."

Still the Company drifted rudderless in the safety of their refuge. They talked little, thought much and cried often—either separately or together.

*   *   *

Binder saw Brightface kneeling before a quiet pool in the stream, and walked unheard to join her. He was startled to find her gazing into the water while a multitude of images flowed across her face. She sensed his presence, and even as she turned to him her true face was restored to its proper place.

"What . . . ?" gasped Binder, baffled and fearful and too weary to comprehend. "I thought you were healed! Or did the cure end with his death?"

"Nor did I know if his magic would linger," she said, "for I have already sought my reflection a hundred times in fear. Covenant did more than I could have guessed, for now I have the power to change my appearance. I *control* it; it no longer controls me." For an instant, she became a shriveled old woman, and then a beaming girl, and then herself again.

"Aren't you afraid to lose your face again?"

"No. It's not the same at all. I can feel the difference. I have to will a new face to carry it, and when I stop pretending it goes away. What was weakness is now strength." She rose and came to him, leaning against his chest and gazing up into his eyes. "But I won't do it again if it disturbs you."

"It disturbs me greatly," he admitted, "though I suppose it could be useful someday."

* * *

By sundown all were tired, all were dirty and all were full. Most surrendered willingly to sleep, with some measure of ease for the first time in Heartshope.

— TWO —

Words
from the
Wilderness

WORDSMITH WAS ALREADY READING HIS LITTLE BOOK OF Covenant's wisdom when the rest awoke.

"Are our answers there?" asked Freeblade.

Wordsmith shook his head slowly. "I may indeed have all the answers we need," he said, running his fingers along the edge of the tiny leather book of mysteries, "but if I do, I do not know it. They were not clear when I set them down and have been dark ever since. Yet they are less dense this morning, as though a mist is rising from my mind."

"What do you see?"

Wordsmith shook his head, frowning. "Things too vague for words—for now, anyway. I need more time."

"Time, at least, we have," observed Freeblade.

"Read, then," urged Binder. "We have our work to do, and

you have yours." Wordsmith nodded absently, already lost again in the puzzles of Covenant's words.

Through the following days and deep into the nights, he perused the pages as the Company rebuilt its life again. His heart grew weary with burdens, and his head ached with the pressure of thoughts he could not for long hold to himself.

The thoughts of the others multiplied too, and it was not unexpected that a council formed of its own accord before many days had passed.

Gathered about the fire one evening, the Company poured out its flood of questions before Wordsmith. He heard them all before asking quietly, "Why do you look to me for answers? I am not Covenant, nor do I claim to have his voice that I may speak to you."

"We must follow someone," answered Binder. "We are lost without a leader, and your words have been good for us."

"If you look to me for anything but words, you are lost even with a leader. Better you should at least follow a man with a sword."

"Nevertheless," said Freeblade, "I yield to you. No one else has spent so much time with Covenant."

"We can see that now," said Brightface. "He was preparing you to be our leader."

"I can only tell you what I have told you once already," insisted Wordsmith. "I will do what I must do, and you may follow if you see fit."

No one dissented, so Wordsmith was given the leadership he would not claim.

"Some burdens are hard," he said, "though some may be shared. I cannot do this alone. I must have help." He gazed at Beauty, and she could feel the heaviness of his heart, the resolution building to say what he knew he must say. "I would take Beauty and Freeblade to stand with me."

Beauty moved even nearer to him. Freeblade leaned against a nearby boulder where he could see the full circle of the fire and beyond. The shine of his sword in the flickering light held Wordsmith's eye for a long moment.

"Wordsmith," said Lionheart. "Talk to us."

"About what?"

"About the beggar. About Covenant."

Wordsmith nodded, but did not open his mouth immediately. They waited patiently for him to speak.

"When I chose to follow this beggar," he began slowly, still gazing at the sword or something far beyond it in the darkness, "or when he chose me to follow him, I began to find old and hidden promises coming true.

"Rumors of an Elder God. Prophecies of a man who would come in his name. Tales of a man who worked miracles and asked nothing in return, demanding no gifts and yet claiming loyalty.

"All those whispered shadows were cast by Covenant, and every deed confirmed his stature. And every word he spoke carried weight, whether it was clear or not.

"I could not deny the truth when I faced it at last. Nor could I debate its meaning, or avoid it. I could only see, and accept and bow. Even logic must kneel before the truth; and then the truth lifts up logic, and makes it whole again. So I bow before the truth, but my logic is not yet enlightened."

His voice grew more animated. "I think of all he said—words that were actually promises—and how those promises came to pass. The fulfilling of promises is power, and the fulfilling of great promises is great power.

"With his promises he blessed each of us, and to each of us he has given the desires of our heart, or pointed to a time when we would indeed receive them.

"Even the legend of the Judgment Stone proved true. Until it fell we had peace, of a sort. And now, I wonder if we shall pass into a time where there is no right or wrong—for who shall judge? And where will he sit?"

The question went nowhere, and he continued: "In Covenant I also found power, a kindly power that was greater than human energy and too compassionate to have come from the hand of humanity alone. His power has changed every one of you as well, or you would have no reason to be here.

"Promises and power. And he warned of a peril to come. We have all heard the promises, we have all felt the power, and now we have tasted the peril.

"But old promises, even ones that have been fulfilled, hold no power over the future. If our hope lies anywhere, it is in the words that he spoke to me in the wilderness, that I might write them down and preserve them, perhaps for this very moment.

"I must conclude that if these words are true—and they seem to be—and if he saw them from afar and named them rightly, then he must also have seen his death approaching. So his death must be either of such magnitude to destroy his promises or a thing of little moment, a stray but meaningless thing that cannot stand in his way.

"Now we must decide: Do we still believe his promises? Does the Elder God exist, and do we still put our trust in him?

"There is nothing that says we must. We could go our separate ways from here, and how could our enemies hunt us down in ones and twos? Surely Fame would not pursue us if we did nothing and were not to be found."

He paused, and tossed a fresh branch onto the fire.

"Yet in these promises are commands as well. And I cannot escape the weight of this one: 'When you seek me and do not find me, go and search for the Child upon the mountain.'

"There is truth we cannot escape: Covenant is dead—or at the very least, he is not *here,* and we may never see him again.

"I cannot delay any longer. I must go, even though I do not know what I will find or even how I will complete the task.

"Perhaps I should have gone immediately, even the day we arrived, but I did not. My hopes grew gray with sorrow, and I could no longer feel in my heart what my head knew to be true." Dejection shadowed his face.

"Do we have any other guidance, any counsel at all?" asked Brightface.

"We have only the words from Covenant," said Wordsmith. "We must wait for the meaning to be made plain."

Brightface sighed. "Words are such slight things to rest our hopes upon."

Wordsmith nodded. "Words are frail—a stroke of fading ink on parchment doomed to perish. But the promises are solid, even if the words used to mark them fade away."

"But how should we remember all of them?" asked Binder.

"Perhaps the time has come to engrave them all on our hearts. And perhaps in our minds joined we will find wisdom instead of worldly wonder, clarity against confusion, and light where all the light is lacking."

He read them the book aloud, shrinking not from the shrouded words and puzzling meanings that twisted back upon themselves. Every phrase was an echo of truth, every line bearing the ring of steel and striking fire from the stubborn flint of their hearts.

And for a time Covenant walked among them again, with his vague yet pointed words of death and birth, darkness and light, building and destruction, extreme sorrow and over-whelming joy. All tasted the goodness of Covenant's words, and none noted the passage of time. They listened, understanding little, but receiving much encouragement. *So many great things to happen*, they wondered. *Might they not happen soon?*

When Wordsmith finished, the spell took quite some time to fade.

"This book is an open secret," he eventually resumed. "But even he who wrote the words down cannot decipher them fully. Do not press me for explanations yet, for I still seek them myself."

"Not all of it makes sense," said Freeblade.

"It doesn't have to," replied Wordsmith. "As long as it's true."

"And we go to seek the Child?" asked Freeblade.

"I do."

"If you do, then we do. There need be no more discussion."

"We?"

"I hear. I believe," said Freeblade. "I will seek the Child, and serve him. I long to see this Child whom I am to defend."

"I, too, will go with you," said Beauty. "I vowed once to follow you, and confirmed my pledge a second time. I will not turn away from a third proof."

"It will be dangerous—with the danger of the completely unknown," Wordsmith cautioned her.

"I would rather suffer with you than be at ease without you. Besides, with your leg you will need help climbing."

"That is our challenge now," said Wordsmith firmly. "Find the Child, follow him, and protect him."

"Will we recognize him?" asked Freeblade.

"If he comes from Covenant we will surely know him," said Wordsmith.

"It is not always that easy," Freeblade responded. "I looked long to find the Dreadnought promised in the pages of my own ancient book, yet I knew him not when I met him."

"But how many children dwell upon the mountain?" asked Beauty. "There cannot be many, that we should have to separate one from the other."

No one could answer her question.

Their eyes turned to Lonely Mountain, lost in the invisible distance far over the trees and beyond Glory. "No one has climbed there successfully—and returned," said Beauty. "How can we go where no one has ever been?"

"We are under orders," said Freeblade. "That is all we need to know."

"We should be safe from Fame," Beauty said. "If this is the first place he will never look for us, then the mountain is the second."

"We must be prepared for bitter cold and privation," said Freeblade.

"And to bring someone back," added Beauty. "We fled with little good clothing, but we can borrow from one another."

"Is that our course?" asked Freeblade. "Will that be enough?"

"There is one other thing that burdens me," answered Wordsmith. "We must know if Candle and Moonflower have come to harm. And what has become of the House and its treasures."

"You mean go back to Glory?" Binder asked.

"I know of no other way to find out."

"But who will go?"

"I do not know who *can* go," responded Wordsmith, "let alone who *will*. Our faces are all known there."

"Not all of ours," said Brightface calmly.

"Yes, all of ours," answered Wordsmith sadly. "Be certain that Fame will not forget the faces of the men and women who cheered for Freeblade, or for Covenant."

"Watch this," countered Brightface. She blinked her eyes and shifted into the image of a total stranger. Complete silence fell, and she continued unhindered. "If Covenant's death has done nothing else, it has empowered me to bridle my burden and turn it to my bidding.

"But do not worry," she assured them, "it is temporary, and under my control." Her face snapped back into the newly familiar. "It is no longer a burden but a gift I may use for all. Let me return to Glory, without my chameleon cloak. I once walked through the palace unremarked, unrecognized and unchallenged. Surely I can reach the shop and even the House safely."

"I do not like that plan," stated Binder. "I cannot let you go alone, but how can I go with you and not endanger us all the more?"

Silence fell again until Freeblade's eyes chanced upon the

fire brothers, stalking each other through the edges of the forest. "We have two boys," he said, "who have proven themselves as courageous and resourceful as their elders. Perhaps they should go with Brightface."

Binder regarded them thoughtfully. "Firecolt. Flamerider. You have indeed proven your courage and your steadfast stealth in the open fields as well.

"Will you dare to go back to Glory with Brightface?" he asked. "A soldier carried you to the palace, but I think he cared more for the colors of your cloaks than the lines of your faces. And I have yet to meet the warrior who counted children among the enemies to be feared.

"For our sake will you become again nameless street urchins who do not know this lady openly, but can keep an eye on her? I cannot enter Glory safely, but I will hide in the woods within sight of the gate and wait for your return."

They looked at each other, thought for only a moment and said "Yes!" with one voice.

Binder looked at Lionheart, who nodded as well. "I do not know where the lions are," he said, "or I would send one with you. But I will go myself, and if trouble comes upon you I will return here for help."

Binder spoke to the boys again. "You *must* stay close to her— and if anything is wrong, come for me at once." He turned to Brightface. "Will you be content with those provisions?"

"Yes," she said. "Your love is your worry, and your worry is your love. I will go and not linger, and the boys shall watch over me."

"It is ironic," said Binder, "that Fame's hand should have fallen so heavily upon you, and yet you are the one with the best chance to watch him unseen."

"And the best motive, as well?" Her smile warmed the air between them before the discussion moved on.

"So we split into three parties," said Wordsmith. "Who will stay here?"

27

"I will," said Lionheart promptly. "My charges are here, and so are the animals."

"Then Heartshope is yours while we are gone, and I will not worry that care is lacking." He turned to Brightface and the fire twins. "We will accompany you as far as the last field before Glory, and from there you must journey on your own. We must reach the mountain with the first light of dawn, for we can neither face that climb nor climb that face in the dark, and we must return before the sun has set."

Binder shuddered. "I would not want to spend a night on that mountain. There is enough fear and madness in venturing there in the daylight."

"And if we do not find the Child?" asked Beauty.

"We will look the next day, and the next. There does not seem to be any choice but success."

Binder gazed at the three upon whom had fallen the responsibility of command—Wordsmith, Freeblade and Beauty. "He said in that book that Wisdom, Power and Love would rule us," said Binder. "I wonder if perhaps he meant you three."

Wordsmith avoided any reply by saying simply, "It is too late to leave tonight, and I would not travel during the day. Let us depart tomorrow, and leave tomorrow night."

The Company retired to their homes, seeking sleep to overcome their restless thoughts.

The next evening, while the others sought warm clothes and food for the road, Binder took time to rub dirt into the boys' clothes. "You have not been this crusty since my house burned," he muttered, "but you are too clean to pass for urchins."

At last, disguised for the city or carrying cloaks against the cold of the mountain, the travelers departed Heartshope in the heart of darkness.

* * *

The adventurers huddled together in the lee of the hill near Glory where the wilderness ended, hoping that the fading darkness had hidden them from the eyes of any searchers.

They paused, uncertain, four staring at the dawn-lit Glory, and the other three gazing ahead at Lonely Mountain.

Silently, but warmly, they parted.

Beauty and Brightface shivered, for different reasons.

——— THREE ———

The Hope
upon the
Mountain

Cautiously, Wordsmith and Beauty followed Freeblade through the deeply shadowed morning to the mountain. The gradually rising foothills did not begin to prepare them for its sudden stone reality; the sheer, cold cliffs leaped up immediately and unexpectedly from the landscape, towering high above everything around.

Even as they neared its base, cold vapors reached out and enveloped them in chill welcome. Still on the ground, their breath fogged their faces. Only a few feet above them frost tainted the bare rock, and above that ice and then only snow and mist.

"Is there a way up?" breathed Wordsmith, staring.

"There must be," answered Beauty, "if we are to climb it."

"We will be cold," said Freeblade. "Even these heavy cloaks

will not be enough." They looked at the pitifully thin clothes they had brought with them.

"Let us lay a fire here," suggested Freeblade. "We will be cold when we return." He gathered fallen wood into a pile and left tinder beneath it. The others took this last opportunity to eat something from their packs.

"What else do we need to do before . . . ?" asked Beauty, gesturing up at the unseen heights.

"Fill our water flasks again," Freeblade replied. "We have food enough for a day's expedition, but all the water up *there* is frozen."

They refreshed their flasks from a icy rivulet that trickled down the mountain and spread to nothingness in the grass.

They stood, silent, reluctant to begin the only task remaining.

"I brought several ropes," said Freeblade. "We must fasten ourselves together."

"A wise idea," said Wordsmith.

"Is that not more dangerous than each one alone?" asked Beauty.

"Perhaps, perhaps not," shrugged Freeblade. "One cannot slip without the others knowing, and having their weight to support."

"Besides," Wordsmith added, "if we perish, we perish together."

"Shall I lead the way?" Freeblade asked in jest.

Neither one prevented him.

"I will come last," said Beauty.

"No," stated Wordsmith flatly. "You will go in the middle. I want you where I can see you. I do not dispute your choice to be here," he continued warmly, "but I am concerned for you."

"And I am concerned for you," she responded. "Why can you not go ahead where I can see that you are safe?"

"As long as you feel a pull on this rope, I am there, and I am safe behind you."

They could think of no other preparations to make. Walking awkwardly against the unaccustomed strain of the ropes, and holding their worn robes tightly about them, they started up the mountain.

Within the first few minutes, Freeblade lost hope of any trail. For the moment, *forward* and *backward* were devoid of meaning; here there was only *up* or *down*.

* * *

Immediately they were glad of both the robes and the ropes. The uncommon chill began to gnaw their skin through every gap, and Freeblade did not wish to imagine how quickly they would be numbed without their cloaks. Then Beauty slid twice her own height when a rock crumbled beneath her feet; even as the men pulled her back to safety, the vision of another crumbling stone played in her mind.

Nor was she alone indebted for long. Freeblade promptly disappeared in a flurry of white crystal, breaking through a dome of frozen snow. Wordsmith anchored Beauty, and she led the warrior back to where they supposed the path to be.

Mist and fog pressed in between them as they ascended, leaving their figures blurred and uncertain and their voices thin and wandering. What had begun as mere frost was fast becoming ice. Every step was a hazard, every grasp a hope, every breath a prayer.

The sun, growing higher but no stronger, hid itself in the mist. The unseen ground receded beneath them. Their lungs ached from frost and fear and effort.

The hours passed painfully and relentlessly.

Freeblade stopped abruptly and beckoned them upward to see old bones—a withered skeleton entombed in the ice. A few moments later they discovered another nameless body.

"Did wild animals kill them?" Freeblade wondered aloud. "Hunger? This undying cold?"

"Not wild animals," Beauty said thinly against the biting wind.

"Why not?" grunted Freeblade.

"Have you seen any?" she asked in turn. "Have you seen *any* signs of life?"

"You're right," admitted Freeblade. "No trees, no plants, no birds—not even tracks of beasts in the snow. We are alone here."

"I hope not," replied Beauty. "The Child must be here if we are to find him."

They paused, almost dead themselves with cold and fatigue, wondering if their hopes held more life than their bodies.

"Is there nothing to this mountain but ice?" Wordsmith asked of no one in particular, exasperated.

But upward they pushed, putting more frozen wasteland behind and beneath them, while the pale sun passed over their heads and began to slide down before them.

"We are doomed if we do not turn back soon," panted Free-blade. "Night on this mountain will be worse than anything we have encountered yet. If we fail to move, we die."

And then Beauty saw the Child.

——— FOUR ———

Rubble
and
Ruin

FIRECOLT AND FLAMERIDER SLIPPED INTO GLORY AND QUICKLY disappeared into the winding streets.

"Who will you be?" whispered Binder to Brightface, watching them go. "It is fit that I know you when I see you again."

"Will this do?" She faded into someone he had seen in the streets ten thousand times—a nondescript woman, worn with weary years and almost featureless in her battered cloak.

"No one will look twice," she promised.

"No one but me," he added.

When her turn came, she paused only briefly at the gate, raised her hand a few inches in farewell and left Binder hidden in the shadow of the trees.

* * *

Candle looked up when Brightface entered his shop. He

moved toward her, unable to see clearly through the piles of bright cloth and the displays of fine items brought from the corners of the kingdom.

"Do not say my name aloud," she cautioned him in a whisper.

"How can I, my woman?" he asked in surprise. "I do not know what it is."

Brightface let her temporary face ease away to reveal her own.

Candle only nodded, though his eyes grew wider. "You are alone?" he asked as he moved behind her to draw the blind.

"Not quite," she murmured. She resumed her common face and leaned outside to smile at the urchin playing near the door.

Candle looked, just in time to see two boys swept away in a swirl of dirty children. Candle closed the door and bolted it firmly from the inside.

"Upstairs," he said, "but let me go first. Neither Trueteller nor Moonflower needs surprises—even pleasant ones."

Moonflower was asleep, but Trueteller hugged Brightface fiercely. "Is everyone all right?" she asked Candle over Trueteller's shoulder.

"I don't know," he answered. "I haven't asked her. She just got here."

Trueteller stepped back and eyed Brightface. "All alone?" she asked, astounded.

"No," soothed Brightface. "The boys are watching in the streets, and Binder is waiting beyond the gate."

Then the women both began to ask questions at once, until Candle held up his hands. "Peace!" he said warmly. "Let Brightface ask, and let us answer her questions. When Moonflower wakes, we will turn the questions around."

Brightface took a breath and began. "I came to see if you were all right, and to find out what has happened since we left."

"As you can see," said Trueteller, "we are well, and we have been left alone. As for what happened after you left . . ." She waved the attention to Candle.

"Glory has been in a quiet uproar," he explained. "No one knew quite what Fame would do. You saw how the first thing he formed was his army, picking captains and soldiers and filling the ranks with men like himself, or with men blinded by the power of his image and the promise of power themselves.

"With his men he came to seize us at Covenant's House, but we were gone already, thanks to Wordsmith's foresight and wisdom."

"What happened to the House?" Brightface probed.

Candle hesitated, sadness and anger rising together behind his eyes. "It has been pulled down—ravaged in anger and left in ruins. Every good thing there was carried off, and even the better stones have been dragged away."

"Was there *nothing* left?" she pressed.

"This was all of meaning that I could rescue from the House," he said, opening a fragrant wooden box and offering it to Brightface. She took the box and found only a few fragments of lightly colored glass—all carefully framed now with rich and intricate wood.

"These were all that were left from the mirrors," he said. "I took the liberty to make frames for them. I was afraid they would break apart otherwise."

She held them to the light, one by one, and gazed into them. "They reflect nothing," she said at last, "and I cannot see through them either."

"There may be no power left in them," Candle admitted, "but this fragment in the dark frame is from the mirror in the hall by the door to the City—at least, where the door was. It is completely blocked now, and would take an army an age to uncover again.

"The other pieces are from the rubble of the tower. This

bigger piece, I believe, is from one of the four windows, while this thick, wavy glass must be from the fifth."

"Thank you for rescuing them," she said quietly, holding them out to him. "Please keep them safe until . . . until something good happens again."

"They should be in your hands," insisted Candle, folding her fingers back over the fragile relics. "They may yet be of use again."

She gazed down at the remains, thinking about the simple dignity of the House. "Is this everything?" Brightface asked, disappointed. "It seems so little to remind us of so much."

"I also returned to the arena," Candle continued. "And I have bottled some of the sand soaked with his blood. It is all we have left of him."

"His words will stay in my heart longer than his blood in the sand," inserted Trueteller.

"Candle," asked Brightface abruptly, "is it safe to go to the House again?"

"Safe? I believe so. But is it a good thing?" She did not answer immediately. "You may certainly go to the House," he continued. "There is no one to stop you, and I do not know that anyone watches the House now that it has fallen. The devastation wrought by Fame is complete, and has left that place of little use to anyone but the mice and the crickets that make their nests in the stones. Stones lean and splinter and fall without warning, the floor is burned through in many places, and the few passages left standing are dark and still. I would not go to the ruins, if I were you. I have been there enough . . ." His voice trailed off expressively.

"Yet I will go and see," said Brightface.

"For yourself?" he asked.

"For all the rest who cannot see for themselves. They sent me to be their eyes and their ears and their witness in the town we had to leave behind."

He shrugged. "Let us wait until dusk, then. We will be less

obvious then."

"We? You do not have to go."

"I would feel better if I could watch over you. Surely Binder would want it that way."

"The boys report to him, and will see to my safety. Besides," she smiled, "they are invisible in the streets even when someone sees them."

"There is other news as well," said Trueteller darkly. "There was an earthquake the night Covenant died. It may even have helped Fame destroy the House."

"We felt the earth shudder," said Brightface. "Did Glory suffer as well?"

"Yes. Buildings fell, and people died. But death was not the worst thing to frighten the town. When they went to bury the bodies, the people found many old graves open and empty."

"So it was for us, too, at the graveyard of the lepers," said Brightface. "Empty graves and no bodies anywhere."

"Nothing has been said publicly," added Trueteller. "They buried the new bodies in the old places and went away quickly."

"Since then," said Candle, "we have hidden here, and trembled for our lives, and waited."

"Has anyone come for you?"

"No. Neither friend nor foe. You are the first to find us."

"Is Fame still searching?"

"Not heavily, for his men have other tasks on their hands. Heard you no word of it in the street?"

"No. I thought the people seemed subdued, but excited."

Candle nodded. "Exactly. Fame has captured their imaginations already, and has drawn them into a grand task together.

"He is building a tower. No small one, but an enormous monument to himself—where Covenant died, where the Stone of Judgment buried itself in the sand. The fallen rock is the cornerstone, and all the arena is marked to honor his grand design. It will be a strong fortress when he completes it. In less than a week it is further along than I could have imagined."

"Where is he finding all the stone?" Brightface wondered.

"From Covenant's House, in part, and from the palace, a place disdained by Fame as old and useless, a hollow ruin not worth rebuilding. Other stones have been carried in from the hills. No quake-tattered house or decaying inn is safe from the hands of his men. And the people are willing to help—giving of their strength, their time and their materials."

"I cannot say that I am surprised by this," said Brightface. "Covenant taught us that people and their names go together."

"Nor am I surprised, except to see that the people are behind him. A fever has gripped them all: 'Great is Glory,' they chant."

"If Covenant were still here this would not be happening."

Moonflower roused from her slumber then, and heard Brightface's voice but not her words.

"Candle?" she called. "Is someone here?"

They came to her, and she, too, was delighted to greet Brightface.

"You look tired, but happy," Brightface said, clasping Moonflower's hands.

Moonflower nodded. "I am already showing," she said, "but every day is still a trial, and food holds little interest."

"That will pass," said Trueteller.

They began to question Brightface then, and the hours passed as she told them of Heartshope and the decisions made there, of the spirit that had united them once again and of the quest upon the mountain for the promised Child.

"And now we wait," she concluded, "to see what will happen there, whether they prove the promise—or fail.

"But if they fail I cannot blame them," she added. "They have done the best they could."

Candle nodded. "Wordsmith should lead us," he said when

she was done speaking. "And Beauty and Freeblade to help him. You have chosen well."

The conversation passed to more general things, and she ate with them as they waited for dusk. After their meal, they savored their thoughts in silence, until Brightface rose to go.

Candle walked her to the shop door.

"There is other disturbing news," he said softly to her when they came downstairs. "Moonflower and Trueteller know of it, but find it a fearful thing to speak of: Moonflower may be the only woman in Glory with child.

"Even before Covenant died there were rumblings and rumors of barrenness throughout Glory, and Trueteller and I both still hear the fear and fact in the marketplace. For good or for bad, we had made no secret of Moonflower's condition, and all who live around us know. Indeed, the neighbor women seemed to know before we told them.

"There are already whispers, for no one seems to know of another woman with child who has not already been delivered."

"What does it mean?" Brightface asked anxiously.

"We do not know," he said, "but it disturbs us. These are not good times to come to public notice. Tell Wordsmith these things, and send us any counsel he has for us.

"Walk safely," he continued, "and give our care to the Company. We will wait here and be faithful."

Brightface looked out the door, and a small shadow detached itself from the deeper shadows to draw near to her. "I will," she whispered. "We go to see the House, and then to Binder and Heartshope again."

They waved to each other as the night separated them once more.

* * *

Brightface came first to the arena, where the foundations of Fame's tower surprised her by their size. A ring of boulders circled most of what had once been open sand. The fallen

Stone of Judgment had been tipped flat again as a cornerstone and mortared over with a new layer of stone. The new wall was not high enough to be seen over the other buildings, but if its final height matched its width it would someday be visible for miles.

Within the great circle was a smaller spire of rock, thrusting even more urgently to the sky. Although night was approaching, the work continued unabated; torches circled the arena and flickered in every corner, casting their uncertain light over the soldiers and townspeople moving earth and stone and lumber.

Brightface shuddered, and moved resolutely toward what was left of the House.

*   *   *

Brightface was crying silently when the boys accompanied her back to Binder.

"Covenant's death was bad enough," she told him, "but there was no body to see. Now I have seen the wreck of his House, and it grieves me more than I thought mere stones could."

They returned to Heartshope at once, bearing the light burden of gifts and the heavy burden of increased knowledge.

── FIVE ──

The Child
of the
Snows

T HE CHILD'S EYES WERE CLOSED, AND HE WAS HUDDLED IN A blanket of snow sitting upright against a dagger of ice. Beauty cried out and floundered through the frozen drift to his side. She snatched him up in her arms and wrapped his cold flesh into the warmer depths of her cloak. Beauty groaned in her throat, making sounds of hope against the cold and pain and fear.

"Is he alive?" Wordsmith shouted to her.

"I don't know," called Beauty miserably. "He's cold, so cold."

The two men reached her and gathered around to shield her from the unforgiving wind.

"Let us see him," murmured Freeblade.

She pulled back her cloak a bit, and they all beheld his still face with blue lips and white face, iced hair and frosted eye-lashes.

When he saw the Child, Wordsmith fell silently to his knees and gazed at the still form. A series of strange expressions passed over his face; amazement, illumination, wonder, sadness, joy, relief and contentment.

He stood again. "I understand much now that I did not see before," he whispered. "Our quest is fulfilled, though not finished. Behold the Child—the *Everlasting* Child!"

"He is beautiful," Freeblade whispered.

"Beyond words," agreed Beauty.

"Is he breathing?" asked Wordsmith.

"I cannot tell in this cold," said Freeblade. "There is too much mist and smoke in the air, and our own breath is in the way."

"I felt him move, I think," whispered Beauty. "He *is* alive."

Barely, thought Wordsmith sadly. *The Child was here, and we came too late.*

"Come," said Freeblade. "We have done as we were bidden— to find the Child. And if we do not return now, our bones will lie with the others. There is no place for life upon this mountain."

They immediately turned to retrace their wandering steps.

"Look," said Beauty, pointing to a few faint footprints trapped in the rigid snow. "His tracks descend from the top," she said in awe. "How did he get up there?"

* * *

Going down was both harder and easier than going up. Their hearts were lighter, but their burden was heavier, and it was difficult not to move too fast for their safety. Beauty cradled the still, silent form, while Wordsmith and Freeblade scrambled on either side to keep them from falling.

"Whatever you do, don't let go of him," cautioned Freeblade. "We have the rope, and *we* will save *you*."

The two men lowered her down the steepest parts but could not prevent slips and thuds and bruises. Beauty ignored everything save the Child, clutching the pale body to her chest, peering anxiously every few moments to see if he had stirred.

If she falls, thought Wordsmith, *I'll have to carry them both. She'll die before she lets go of him.* "Has he moved yet?" he asked her again.

"No," she answered, "but at least he is no colder than he was."

I cannot feel my body anymore, thought Freeblade fuzzily. *Is that good or bad?* At least he was unaware of the raw flesh, and the blood oozing from the countless cracks in his skin.

With only the hope in their hearts to fuel their bodies and fire their feet, they crept anxiously toward the hidden ground below. The falling sun left them deep in shadow, granting light only faintly to the fog over their heads.

They were deep in afternoon shadow when the mists drifted apart enough to show the welcome hills below. They half-slid and half-jumped the last few feet down the mountain and stumbled their way to the relative warmth of the low hill still painted orange by the edge of the setting sun.

Panting hard and crying, Beauty snatched off her cloak and the Child's and pressed his bare body to hers. "This is no time to be modest," she called. "Quickly!" Wordsmith joined her, and the marbled flesh pressed against their own was an agony of ice.

Freeblade paused long enough to kindle the fire awaiting ready at their feet, hoping it would not be seen from Glory. Then he wrapped his bared arms and cloak around the others. "Is he warm yet?" he asked.

"I cannot tell, for I cannot feel either his flesh or mine," she moaned. "Oh, Wordsmith, did we come in time?"

"I should have come sooner," he said despondently, "but I delayed from day to day before yielding to the need. If we lose him now, it will be my fault."

"Or mine," she said, "for not having enough fire in my body to rekindle his. Wordsmith, how can you carry the blame for something you could not have foreseen—and that may not come to pass, anyway?"

He did not answer, except to say, "We did not plan well, did we?"

They coaxed the heat from the fire and urged it deep into the Child's bones, trying to ignore the pain of the spitting sparks and the singe of the flames licking about their legs.

"I cannot warm him enough," she mourned. "I would keep us both in the fire, if only our flesh would not burn."

"I was warmed once," Wordsmith said distantly, "far from any fire."

Beauty looked at him, memory of his tales bringing wild hope.

He released himself from their embrace, stalked to the edge of the firelight and faced the darkness squarely. Then he opened his arms to the fields and forests and called plaintively, "Animals of the Elder God, hear me. You warmed me once at Covenant's bidding. Come and warm another more worthy than I."

His words fell hollow in the night, and he dropped his hands to his sides again.

"Will they come?" whispered Beauty.

"Will who come?" asked Freeblade.

"The animals," answered Beauty absently.

A parade of eyes gleamed in the faint firelight.

"They could not have been far away," said Freeblade.

"Perhaps they were only waiting for your call," suggested Beauty to her husband.

"Do not be afraid, either of you," whispered Wordsmith. "I was, and all my worry was in vain."

Whimpering, the first lion thrust his muzzle between Beauty and Freeblade and licked the face of the Child.

"I was not sure I should try it again," Wordsmith said simply. "I feared that perhaps even one miracle was too much to hope for."

While Freeblade paced to watch and grow warm, Wordsmith

and Beauty moved to a softer place on the ground, beckoned the warm animals close and curled up in their midst with the Child. They watched the color of his face and listened for his breathing above the collected whuffs of the patient beasts.

"His hair is not frozen," Beauty said softly, "nor is that the firelight. It is the color of silver and snow, the color of gold and the sun. Never have I seen such a fair-haired child."

At long last the Child stirred, as if rousing from a deep sleep. Now his face looked more ruddy than pale, but it was hard to tell in the light of the fading fire. He did not open his eyes, but buried his face close against Beauty's breast.

For a moment, no one breathed but the Child.

* * *

Freeblade began to add more wood to the flames, then thought better of it; he left the fire to die away in its own time.

Above them in the darkness, the mountain began to moan and rumble, making long sliding sounds and venting prolonged hisses.

Wordsmith and Beauty scarcely heard, and paid little attention to what they did hear. Their exhaustion numbed them, and their world for now centered upon the sleeping boy held between them. But Freeblade's exhaustion left him tense and uneasy; he paced the rim of the firelight and listened with grave concern to the surrounding night.

"This mountain is too strange for us to bear it," Freeblade urged. "Let us be gone from here, even if we travel in the dark."

"Gladly," said Beauty, "if you will carry these animals or the fire in your hands, that we may slay the Child's chill, and our own."

Freeblade shook his head moodily and stared off into the night, trying so hard to hear everything that was there that he succeeded mainly in hearing those things that were not.

* * *

Wordsmith struggled awake in the dawn to find the animals

mostly gone. Only a pair of lions kept guard over the dead fire while Freeblade sprawled asleep on the ground.

Wordsmith roused Beauty with a touch of his hand and immediately, gently brushed the face of the sleeping Child, who opened his eyes and regarded them solemnly, without fear, without surprise.

"I have seen those eyes before," Beauty whispered. "He has come among us again!"

When the Child smiled, their hearts melted, and they forgot the snow and the ice and the remnants of the cold in their bones.

She spoke to him, asking his name. His smile grew wider and warmer, but he said nothing.

They roused Freeblade and rejoiced together in the new life that had come among them. As their eyes feasted on their hope, they feasted their hunger with the remainder of their food. The Child ate with an appetite, but contentedly—and silently.

"Wordsmith," whispered Beauty, "he is old enough to speak. Why has he not uttered a word?"

"Does he hear?" Wordsmith asked her. "Does he understand us?"

"He seems to understand my questions," she answered, "but all he does is smile and touch my hand. It is hard to be concerned about other things when I put his face close to mine."

"Perhaps he is a mystery to be understood later," Freeblade suggested.

But there was no clear answer to that question, and they continued with their silent meal. Wordsmith and Beauty had eyes only for the Child, but Freeblade's gaze also wandered frequently to the mountain. During the night the mist had multiplied, and the fog that hung far up the slopes had crept slowly and unnoticed down to the base. In several places water trickled down noisily and ran off into the grass—rivulets that had not been there before.

"The cold has gone," noticed Freeblade.

"Yes, we are all warm now," agreed Beauty.

"No, I mean the cold from the mountain."

He was right. Where dry, cold air had braced them before, now a river of moist air flowed down around them. It was no longer cold, but cool, and growing warmer by the moment. A greater mist was beginning to rise from the top—not wholly fog, but perhaps steam as well.

"Perhaps the mountain is melting," suggested Freeblade. "It seems to be more ice and snow than rock. Let us go. I do not understand this place, whether it means us harm or not, but something is happening here and I do not wish to see it from such a narrow distance."

"Is there any reason to linger?" asked Wordsmith.

"No," answered Beauty. "He is warm and well, and no longer hungry."

The Child walked about, unconcerned, seemingly unaware or forgetful of the ordeal on the mountain and the desperate race to pump warm life back into his thin body.

She knelt, took the Child's hand and spoke to him. "We must go from here. Will you go with us?"

The Child nodded and stood up.

The great lion also roused and came at once to crouch before the Child. The Child leaned up, grasped the great mane and pulled himself astride the shaggy back.

"I believe he is ready," said Beauty solemnly.

"Yes," agreed Wordsmith. "We are understood more than we understand."

* * *

Later, they paused and looked back at Lonely Mountain, small but still clearly visible in the distance.

"Look!" Wordsmith said, pointing. "It is the face of the Child!"

The fog and smoke had lifted for a long moment and revealed the face of the mountain to be the face of the Child—

not finely sculptured, but recognizable, though anyone determined to see no miracle would see only the crags of the rough-hewn mountain.

Then even that resemblance faded under the mist, until it was merely a melting mountain again—alive now with little rivers and waterfalls tumbling down the steep sides and forming greater waters below.

They moved on.

* * *

Lionheart arrived in Heartshope on the run. "They have returned!" he panted. "And a child comes with them!"

They appeared over the top of the hill just as Lionheart had said—a child, walking happily between Wordsmith and Beauty, with Freeblade stalking proudly behind. Pacing in honor on either side were lions and bears and deer and wolves.

SIX

The Sign
of the
Child

"AND NOW WHAT?" ASKED BRIGHTFACE OF NO ONE IN PARticular.

The entire Company sat in a circle, gazing at the Child. He ate quietly and smiled at them all.

She continued with her questions. "Is he indeed mute? Was his voice frozen on that awful mountain?"

Wordsmith attempted an answer. "He has said nothing to us. Remember that Covenant said there would come a time when words would be too much, and yet not enough. Perhaps this is what he meant."

"He sent the Child, didn't he?" asked Binder.

"He must have," said Beauty.

"Then we are not forsaken," stated Freeblade, a ring of comfort in his voice.

"Not now," replied Wordsmith, "and most likely we never were."

The Child rose, went to Beauty and looked into her eyes while he stroked her face with his tiny hand.

"These are *his* eyes," she said, "Troubled, deep and old. He has come from Covenant."

"Is this Covenant come among us again?" asked Brightface.

"I do not know. They are very like," Beauty said. "A heart-breaking child," she murmured.

"Perhaps he is the child of a broken heart," added Bright-face. "How old is he?" she asked, puzzled.

"Three? Five?" answered Wordsmith. "Perhaps age has no meaning for him. Covenant said we would be the first of all people to behold the face of the Everlasting Child—and he said there would be one who was never born and will never die."

"What shall we do if he does not speak?" asked Lionheart.

Wordsmith shook his head. "Then we must learn to listen to the words he does not say."

Freeblade spoke. "The Child, as you have seen, is helpless—without cloak, without food, without power, without speech. Yet he has a work to do, and we must care for him while he works."

"What does he need?" continued Lionheart.

"What do the other children need?" responded Brightface. "Love, food, a warm place to sleep, a world to play in . . . all these, at least, lie partly in our power." She glanced at the fire twins, who sat beside Binder curiously observing the new addition to the Company. Gazing again at the Child, she pondered, "Does he have a name?"

Beauty deferred to Wordsmith, as though they had already had such a discussion.

"If he does, we do not know it," he said.

"Perhaps we do not need to know it," Beauty added. "After all, we never knew Covenant's real name."

"That *is* his name," responded Wordsmith. "It just isn't all of it."

"I suspect this one has a magnificent name, and that 'the

54

Child' is merely one of them."

Though tired, they sat in the afternoon sun and watched him play with the other children—always happily, sometimes serenely, sometimes with shrieking laughter that was medicine to the hearts of the hearers.

"If the Child is happy," murmured Beauty, "then let us be happy as well."

* * *

Not until the Child had fallen asleep in the late afternoon did Wordsmith turn to Brightface and her news. Beauty and Freeblade joined them, listening intently to her report and gently examining the remnants of glass in the carved wooden box.

"Glory is already being torn and rebuilt at the same time," she concluded.

" 'Its destruction will be its rebuilding, and its rebuilding will be its destruction,' " quoted Wordsmith, and they remembered his voice reciting those same words around the fire.

"What does that mean?" asked Freeblade.

Wordsmith opened the little book again. "It meant nothing when we read it aloud, but perhaps we know now what it applies to. This tower does appear a pridesome thing."

"It may be beautiful when it is finished," said Beauty. "But what will it mean?"

"Candle said it was Fame's intention to see and be seen from one end of this kingdom to another."

They passed on to the glass fragments.

Wordsmith peered into the remains of the vision window while Beauty tried in vain to raise a reflection from the sliver of Covenant's magical mirror.

"Freeblade," said Wordsmith. "It is fitting that you should carry this piece of the old high window. May you see far with it, if it ever shows its magic again, for it is to you we entrust the safety of the Company."

Freeblade hesitated before replying. "But is it the safety of the Company I guard, or the safety of the Child? If I am forced to choose . . . well, you know my choice already.

"And your last protection is not me," he continued, "but Lionheart and his friends. A bevy of bears, a stand of stags, a watch of wolves—these can do more than one man with even an enchanted sword."

"Carry it anyway, please," said Wordsmith, "if for no other reason than that it pleases me."

He accepted, reluctant to bear the honor but pleased with the gift.

"The power is gone from my mirror," Beauty said to Wordsmith. "Does your glass reveal anything to you?"

Wordsmith shook his head. "No. I saw darkness there, and black swirls against it, and shadows beyond that—but no visions, no seed for stories. Even in Glory they were not created here, but here they were born and given a substance and a voice."

"Direct from the hand of the Elder God," Beauty added. "Perhaps he has another way yet to be revealed."

"Is your mirror completely dark as well?" he asked in turn.

"Not quite," she said. "All I see now is my own image, and there is no magic in seeing that."

"To some of us there is," her husband said lightly.

She squeezed his hand and turned to Freeblade. "Can you see anything there?"

"No," Freeblade answered, "though perhaps there is little to see. I do wish it could show us what is happening in Glory. How can such a place be so terribly close and so impossibly distant at the same time?"

Brightface shifted at the mention of Glory. "Wordsmith?" she asked. "I would return to Candle's house with news of the Child."

Wordsmith found no reason to deny her, so she and the boys left early that evening for Glory, the two boys riding one lion with Lionheart, while Binder and Brightface rode the other.

* * *

Wordsmith stayed alone that night with the Child, who sat restlessly in his lap and would neither lie down nor close his eyes.

Stirred by an old and unaccountable longing, Wordsmith began to sing softly, and at once the Child curled up in his arms. He did not even know the song himself, but the words formed for him as he sang, and he found himself singing a tale of the beggar that was well framed by the evening. By the third chorus the Child was asleep.

Wordsmith did not cease his singing, for he could no longer hold back the gift that had been silent for so long. Beauty and Freeblade heard and came to see the source of the sound; though Beauty's gaze upon his face begged him not to stop, and that same wish was echoed in Freeblade's eyes, his voice faltered and he let the song trail into silence.

But long after he himself was in bed, the music continued to echo in his head.

* * *

"I think," said Wordsmith to Beauty the next morning, "that Covenant's death was necessary to bring this Child among us. Nor do I think that all that has happened to us has been a surprise."

"What do you mean?"

"Covenant told me that dawn before he died that we would soon see the beginning of the dream. I asked him if he did not mean the completion of the dream, and he said no, that only now would the beginning begin.

" 'If you were to know the future all at once,' he said, 'you would not be able to bear it. You can only survive the future as it unfolds, one day at a time.' "

"Wordsmith?" Beauty whispered. "Since the Child came I have almost forgotten to grieve for Covenant, though I have not forgotten him for a moment."

"Perhaps he did not mean for us to grieve. I feel Covenant

57

still *is*, but that he is not anywhere we can reach him. If we could still reach him now, the Child would not have come."

His moment of brightness did not last, and he continued to return to thoughts of what had been lost. "There is no more mirror," he said sadly. "The fifth window is lifeless, and all my books are lost and . . ."

"Not all your books are lost," said Beauty. "Those you sold or gave away still have a home somewhere."

"What shall I do if I cannot write, and there is no house to be steward of?"

"You can keep loving me," suggested Beauty. "As long as we both draw breath, I am yours.

"And," she added quietly, "perhaps now it is time for you to begin singing again."

He was struck cold by the thought, and old feelings he thought long-denied rose again to the surface of his heart.

"Covenant entrusted you with his words," she said, "and you wrote them faithfully. Perhaps now it is time you laid down your pen and lifted up your voice.

"Songs need not be written down," Beauty continued, "as long as the words remain firmly in your head."

"I had not sung since the night Covenant quenched the fire we set for him and set his own fires raging through our fields," he said. "I did not have the heart to sing as my village was dying. And then Covenant took away my old songs. Since that day I have not felt worthy.

"I found joy in my stories, but now there are no more books," he said sadly.

"No room," said Beauty softly.

"No time," added Wordsmith. "You cannot write as you run."

She agreed. "But you *can* sing . . ."

"It is an old sadness," he said, "and I would rather leave it alone."

"It does seem that we will be travelers now, until another

home can be found."

"Not in Glory."

"No. Somewhere else. This is a big land."

"Not too big for Fame's men to find us."

"I am not glad we were forced to flee here," she said, "but I am glad we had this place to come to. It is not Covenant's House, nor do we have Covenant. But we have the Child, and in Heartshope we have peace. Do you think we are really safe here?"

"For now," he said.

"For long?"

"I do not know."

In the unanswerable silence they heard Brightface talking outside, and went to meet her.

"Lonely Mountain is indeed melting," she told them immediately, "and it has brought terror to Glory. Some said they saw a face in the heights, and all are uneasy at the new river that is forming from the melted ice. It has begun to flow already through what once were dry fields, and the first feelers are creeping past the walls of Glory."

"This is important," Wordsmith said, "but I do not know what it means." He wandered away to ponder his book again.

But away from the village and sitting near the orchard stream, Wordsmith could not concentrate on the words, even though they were Covenant's final words to all of them and the key to what lay ahead. Drawn by a desire he could no longer deny, yet unsure of his ability or freedom to begin singing again at will, he began to test his voice there where no one could hear.

Another song came to him unbidden and unknown, though telling a story he had long since written by hand and sold in the marketplace.

When he was done, he was startled to hear Beauty applauding behind him.

"Do not stop," she said. "Sing me another story."

"Stories?" he asked, fearful and hopeful at the same time. "Yes, I still see stories in my head, but now they burst into my mind as songs. Now how am I to cease my singing? My thoughts are always there, and the words ready at hand, and the first note of music its own spark to song."

"Do not cease, then," begged Beauty. "You would rob us all of pleasure if you denied yourself the fruit of your head and heart."

He sang for her, tentatively at first and then with power, and time ticked away unheeded.

* * *

After that the hours became days, and the weeks followed. Heartshope slipped into a comfortable routine, welcome after their loss and weariness. The Child did little but love and accept their love. He played, the essence of child—honest, innocent, but without trace of selfishness or immaturity—while absorbing the world with the understanding of a wise old man.

He said nothing to anyone, but the village was never denied his bright smile. Nor was Wordsmith's singing long absent, or Beauty's tender hand missing from anything that happened.

* * *

"This Child is afraid of nothing," said Binder to Freeblade, "yet he must be protected."

"Yes," said Freeblade, "though it is also a mystery to me. *This* is power," he continued, watching the Child caress Beauty's face. "While *this*," he added, waving his sword, "is only a posture born of the poverty of powerlessness.

"I protect him? With the sword, if I may. But better he should protect me from the darkness of the world—the kind that cannot be defeated with a sword."

* * *

The Child was everywhere, always accessible, yet never plumbed by anyone who drew near him—even by those who drank of his warmth and goodness until their aches and hurts were momentarily drowned in a sweet tide of wonder.

None held him too long, for even though he gave himself freely to them they knew he was not theirs to command.

Yet none could leave him alone, for he was so serene and filled with some secret joy that others could not behold.

And that joy was contagious.

"I do not understand," said Brightface once. "I pick him up to comfort him, and yet it is he who comforts me."

Yet the Child continued to say nothing, and only smiled, beckoned and snuggled, giving as much pleasure as he received.

*　*　*

Freeblade, standing guard one day, realized he had not seen the lions for some time. He came in search of Lionheart and asked, "Where are your lions and wolves and wild friends?"

"I do not know," replied Lionheart. "They have all vanished. Nor have I seen any animals at all since yesterday. Hear for yourself."

They listened, and heard nothing. No birds sang. Nothing moved in the trees or disturbed the silence of the brush.

SEVEN

Trouble
and
Travail

THE EVENING HAD ALREADY BEGUN TO DEEPEN AROUND Heartshope when Freeblade emerged from the trees and sought Wordsmith. "A man is coming," he reported. "A man, walking alone. He has left the road to Glory and is coming this way."

"Do we know him?" asked Wordsmith.

"I cannot tell in the dusk. He has stopped twice to rest and more often to look, as though he is not sure where he is going."

"Are there others behind him?"

Freeblade shook his head. "Not to my knowledge."

"Let us go and see."

"Where is the Child?" Freeblade asked.

"Brightface is with him in the house, and the last time I looked, they had both fallen asleep."

Freeblade was content, and the two left Heartshope behind. Soon they crept past the lepers' graveyard and stopped behind a rock.

"Over there, beneath that pair of trees," whispered Freeblade.

"Where? I see nothing."

"There is nothing to see unless you know he is there. He makes much noise when he moves, but at rest he is very, very still."

As they quietly drew near, a shadow detached itself from the darker shadows and moved toward them.

"Halt!" cried Freeblade.

No one moved, no one breathed for two long heartbeats.

"Freeblade?" asked the stranger weakly.

"I know that voice. Is that Candle?" he countered.

"It is," came the reply. "And Wordsmith?"

Freeblade lowered his sword. "Are you alone?"

"Yes."

"Welcome to Heartshope," the warrior said, and they closed the last few steps between them to embrace.

"I would not have come like this," began Candle, "unannounced in the dark, but I could not wait any longer to speak with you."

"Are you all right? Is there trouble?" Wordsmith asked anxiously.

"Yes, we are all right, for now. But I don't know how much longer we will be safe in Glory. We need your help."

"Name it," said Wordsmith. "And if it is in our power we will grant it gladly."

"We have decided to leave Glory—and soon."

"I will make sure he was not followed," muttered Freeblade. He slipped away into the night.

"Let us go on to Heartshope," suggested Wordsmith. "We are safe enough here, but we can have food and a fire instead of hunger and darkness."

"And I would see the Child as well," replied Candle.

"He deserves to be seen," answered Wordsmith. "All the world should come to wonder."

"I am uneasy in Glory," Candle continued, as he and Wordsmith began to pick their way through the starlit night. "I have never seen a people so gripped by anything or anyone. Fame has them enthralled, and I do not know where it will end."

"All this in little more than two months?" Wordsmith asked.

Candle nodded. "He knows the holes in their hearts as well as in their heads, and has told them what they want to hear. 'Great is Glory!' he has called to them, and 'Great is Glory!' is the answer they give him back."

They walked on for a few measures in a silence that echoed the stillness of the sky, now quiet in the absence of the bats and owls that normally ruled the night.

"But I am more concerned about something else," Candle continued. "Moonflower does, indeed, seem to be the only woman in Glory with child, and I fear for her for that reason.

"What is different is always hated, and those who have what others desire but cannot attain are hated even more. Hard stares have come Moonflower's way, and I agree with True-teller that Glory may no longer be safe.

"Fame has already begun to claim that good has come on his account, and may be reckoned to his reign, while he blames all the evil upon Covenant. Earthquakes, barrenness, the melting of Lonely Mountain, accidents at the Tower—all these are the beggar's fault. Your names have been mentioned as well, not directly by Fame but by those who knew the Company. If word of us three in Glory has not yet come to Fame, it soon will, and I do not wish to be found within those walls."

He paused. "Is this a wise thing, Wordsmith? You said it was good that we stayed behind, that we would know what took place in Glory."

Wordsmith thought for a few moments as they walked. "I gave no order that you stay. It was not a good time for you to travel, and I did not know the depth of our danger." He waved ahead of them, and Candle drew his first glimpse of Heartshope. "Come join us, then, as soon as you can."

"If we are to travel at all, Moonflower must travel now," he said. "She is no longer ill in the mornings, but she is growing far more rapidly than we expected, and is so swollen that we cannot easily disguise her now.

"I have sold most everything in my shop," he continued, "and have bought nothing more. I am as free to leave Glory now as I ever have been. I own little now, except bags of gold and coppers too heavy to carry."

"You need Kingsburro," Wordsmith said.

Candle nodded. "And perhaps Roadreeler as well. I miss him and would gladly work with him again."

They walked into the inner square of Heartshope.

"Lionheart should be awake by now," Wordsmith said. "He guards us throughout the night, and sleeps much during the day."

They roused Lionheart and told him of their needs.

"We can wake others," said Wordsmith. "Take as many helpers as you need."

"I will endanger no one else," replied Candle. "I need only the good beasts for a good burden."

Freeblade returned, stepping into the shrouded firelight. "He was not followed," he said, and turned his attention to his main charge. "Is the Child still asleep?" he asked anxiously. "I disliked leaving him, but . . ."

Wordsmith waved his worry away with one hand. "If he were not well, Brightface would have let it be known by now." Turning to Candle he said, "Go with Freeblade and gaze upon the face of the Child. I will see that the animals are brought without delay."

* * *

Candle had few words when Wordsmith saw him again.

"Covenant was worth dying for," was all he would say.

"Now I know that the Child is too."

Roadreeler, eager to be ridden again by Candle, pawed impatiently at the ground. The ever-patient Kingsburro sampled the grass as he waited.

Lionheart laced the ties on his battered boots. "We will range about you as far as the gates, and wait for you. Do not be afraid, but do not linger."

"Thank you," said Candle.

"Perhaps it is best if you leave by another gate," said Wordsmith, "and then come across the fields and the meadows to Heartshope from behind. If anyone sees you leave, they will not be certain you have come this way."

"You will not see me," promised Lionheart, "but I will be there." He walked ahead and was gone.

Candle, riding Roadreeler and leading Kingsburro, followed quickly.

The darkness swallowed them all.

Wordsmith returned to his house in hope of both sleep and sleeping Beauty, but Freeblade paced the edges of the village to keep awake and wait for Lionheart's return.

*   *   *

Trueteller entered Heartshope first, alone on Kingsburro, bulging saddlebags partially hidden beneath her flowing skirt. Candle, seated on Roadreeler and protecting Moonflower in his arms, followed her out of the darkness.

"We are here," said Candle simply. "We brought what riches we could."

"The greatest riches are the blessings we haven't yet seen," said Brightface, helping Moonflower away to the abandoned house set aside for them.

They were interrupted by the appearance of the Child.

Moonflower knelt to him, and the Child came to her and touched her belly ever so softly. Her child leaped within her for the first time, and old words leaped in Wordsmith's mind at the same moment. Then there came a second leap beside the first, and Moonflower gasped in suprise and understanding. "Twins?" she exclaimed. "No wonder I have grown so large already!"

" 'These children shall be born in the City,' " Wordsmith pronounced, his voice sounding much like the Covenant he quoted. " 'And no child will be born from now until the City is revealed.' " He paused and looked thoughtfully at Moonflower. "Once more the rumors and the promises have come together and brought forth understanding."

EIGHT

The Sign
of the
Eagle

T RUETELLER WAS EXPLORING THE VILLAGE THE NEXT MORNING
and did not see the eagle swoop from the sky until it swished
close past her head, dropped something in the grass and
soared into the air again.

"Farsight?" she called out shakily.

The eagle turned in midclimb and arrowed down to her
again, his wings cracking the air as he slowed to settle on her
outstretched arm. She stroked his feathers and murmured to
him lovingly, wincing at his claws but most happy to see him
again.

"Where have you *been?*" she asked him with soft fierceness.
Turning her head away, she called to the others. "Farsight is
here! Come and see!"

They came, and saw, and asked questions she had no
answers for.

"Where did he come from?"

"How did he find you here?"

"I do not know," she admitted, "but wherever he has been, he has come to me again."

She remembered the bands of gold, and looked; they were gone. Tears came unbidden, for Covenant's memories were suddenly very strong and sweet, and the weight of unanswered prayers and unfulfilled hopes returned to her shoulder

"He is an old promise to me," she said simply. She opened her mouth to say more, and said nothing instead.

She blinked away the tears. *What did he drop?* she wondered, and nudged the toe of her sandal through the drifted leaves and sticks on the ground.

The other people, happy for her, but with other thoughts on their minds, went back to their labors.

Something round and purple rolled away from her foot. *Of course,* she thought, *a cavada fruit. Where did he find it?* It was still fairly fresh and firm, though marked by his claws, as though he had carried it a long distance.

She carefully moved Farsight onto her arm, stooped, picked up the fruit, brushed the dirt away and offered it to him. He ate greedily. "Are you hungry?" she asked him. "You must have come a long way."

But when she offered him anything else, he refused. After that, he seemed restless.

And within the hour he was gone again.

Trueteller watched his silhouette fade away to the south.

* * *

She was delighted when Farsight returned to her again the next morning, bearing more fruit.

"What is that?" asked one of the children.

"Cavada," Trueteller replied. "Some people call them frost-berries. When Farsight was wounded, I tried to find something he would eat. Candle had these in his shop, and Farsight liked them. I guess he has found a place where they grow."

"Why does he bring them to you?"

Trueteller shrugged. "Who knows? He could eat them himself, but he seems to prefer them from my hand. I certainly don't mind."

After that, he returned again and again, at shorter intervals, and staying only a few moments each time.

"What is he doing?" asked Freeblade. "Where is he finding all the frostfruit?"

"I wish I knew," she said, watching him wing away into the dusk. *I know nothing at all*, she thought, *but I can always hope for everything*.

* * *

"Trueteller?" called Beauty.

"Yes?" she answered, pulling weeds from between the uneven rows of vegetables.

"Farsight has returned again."

"I do not think he strays far from us now," said Trueteller, not looking up from her work.

"But this time he's not alone," said Beauty.

Trueteller, rising, saw Farsight on the shoulder of a strange and rugged man, ragged from the road and ruined by a lifetime of labor. Oddly, he was staring at her, and not at Beauty. She looked again, inhaled sharply, and nearly fell.

"I know that man," she said so quietly only Beauty heard her. "Time, toil and tears cannot disguise him."

Beauty's heart began to pound, her instinct outracing her knowledge.

Farsight leaped into the air and wheeled over their heads.

"Darmak?" Trueteller asked.

"Abra?" the man asked in return.

Weeds and work forgotten, Trueteller stumbled to him. She nearly disappeared in his grasp, her face crushed into his shaggy shoulder, one of his massive hands cradling the back of her head.

"This is Darmak," she finally said to Beauty, after the

stunned silence. She almost kept a waver out of her voice. "He is my husband."

All of them began to cry.

This moment is only for two, thought Beauty. Farsight circled overhead as she withdrew to the village to find Wordsmith and wait.

* * *

When Trueteller brought Darmak into Heartshope, the rest were waiting expectantly—Candle and Moonflower in front, with Wordsmith, Beauty, Freeblade and the Child standing behind them.

"This is Darmak, my husband," Trueteller said, her voice still trembling around the edges. She held out in her palm a twisted gold band. "He is Covenant's final promise to me."

She beckoned Moonflower forward. "This is your child, Darmak," she continued, "and inside her are your child's children."

Moonflower took his hand shyly.

"I never knew we had a child," he marveled.

"Yet she is bone of your bone and blood of your blood. Unknowing, you left her with me when you . . . disappeared."

"I don't know what to say," Moonflower murmured.

"Nor do I," answered Darmak. "Except that you are your mother again as I first beheld her; I would have known you anywhere as hers." An awkward silence fell for a moment.

"Go on with your life, Moonflower," he eventually said. "We will be friends in time, for a gap of twenty years cannot be leaped with a single bound."

Candle stepped forward to stand beside her. "And this is Candle," said Trueteller. "Moonflower is his now, and he is hers."

"Moonflower? Candle?" Darmak queried. "A pair of unusual names."

"The story behind those names is far more than unusual, and they call me Trueteller now."

"Who does?" Darmak asked.

"Covenant did, first," she answered, "and then the rest, after."

"Covenant?"

She held out the band again. "The man who gathered these people together, who bade me hammer this gold for you."

"I still do not understand."

Wordsmith spoke. "Trueteller is, indeed, her name now, and she has much truth to tell you."

"This is Wordsmith," Trueteller continued, "with Beauty, and Freeblade our defender. They lead us, now that Covenant is gone. And this is the Child."

"Whose child?" he asked.

Trueteller hesitated. "It's hard to say," she finally answered.

Darmak's confusion deepened.

"We welcome you among us," said Wordsmith with a hint of awkward formality, "but your place is with your wife now. She has much to tell you and much to hear. We will not disturb you until you wish to see us again. We will come to know you later."

"But for now, Trueteller," Beauty suggested, "take him away and enjoy him. You have waited twenty years for this day."

"Go on," urged Freeblade. "We will see that your work is done for you."

The two walked away, and Trueteller steered her husband toward the orchards and the soft riverbank.

"Are you hungry?" she asked him, belatedly.

He nodded. "For many things," he answered, "but not for food. It will take time to set things right again."

"I did not even know if you were alive," she said.

"I did not know if you had married another, or if you even still thought of me," he replied.

"I have thought of no one *but* you."

For a while no words would come. After that, the words

would not cease flowing, and eventually no words were enough. Where the waters curled around the trees, the two found a half-shaded place to sit.

She helped ease his weathered cloak from his tired shoulders, and ran her fingers gently along the small scars there. Then she showed him her own shoulders, with like marks from the same claws.

"These shoulders were not made for eagles," he said ruefully, though without sadness.

"Or else this eagle was not made for shoulders," she countered. "But his place was there for a time and a purpose—and we have adapted quite well now, haven't we?" she added. "These shall all be ancient scars some day."

He worked his back against a tree and made a nest for her in his arms.

"I scarcely remember how to love you," he said.

She sighed and made herself even more comfortable in his embrace. "You have forgotten nothing so far," she whispered.

NINE

Wildhaven

THE MORNING IN HEARTSHOPE WAS QUIET UNTIL BINDER STOOD from his labors and gazed around.

"Look!" he cried, sweeping his arm from one side to the other.

Those near him looked up from their work too.

Heartshope was completely and silently surrounded. On every side, on every patch of ground and every tree limb, animals waited and watched, making no sound.

"Lionheart!" called Binder. "Come see! The animals have come back to Heartshope."

Lionheart emerged from his house, rubbing sleep from his eyes, and was surprised. The animals watched him closely, though there was no menace in their eyes.

"Wherever they were," Lionheart finally agreed, "they are, indeed, here now."

Wordsmith and Beauty came from their house and were also surprised. The Child came behind them and smiled. He did not seem surprised.

Then the animals turned their gaze to the Child and came to him from all sides—a flood of fur and feathers that halted crouching before him, their wild but unwavering eyes fixed hopefully upon the small boy with the ancient eyes.

Delighted, the Child beamed upon them, and caressed the muzzles and beaks nearest him; content, he pointed to Lionheart and stepped back from the gathering. The beasts' gazes swiveled toward Lionheart again.

As though waiting only for the right moment, the largest lion rose and nudged Lionheart affectionately—but so firmly that he fell across the animal's back and was forced to straddle the shaggy back to keep from falling. The lion shouldered him into place and at once began to shamble off toward the trees. The other animals followed after. Startled, Lionheart thwacked the lion vainly with his palm, yelling and roaring alternately without effect.

"The Child is smiling," called Wordsmith. "Go with the animals, and fear not."

"An easy thing to say," retorted Lionheart, smiling in spite of himself. "You are not surrounded."

Remembering the frosty night on the mountain when the beasts came, Wordsmith called out, "But I have been! And this is more of the same sort of magic!"

They watched the soft procession pace, stalk, wriggle, hop and fly from sight, taking all the natural sound of the wild with it. No birds remained to sing, no beetles stayed to scrape, no squirrels tarried to thunder in the underbrush.

When Wordsmith thought to look again, he saw the unconcerned Child building new kingdoms in the dirt.

* * *

Wordsmith and Beauty and the rest heard Lionheart's return long before they saw him.

76

An amazing series of chirps, groans, growls, hiccoughs, tweets and hoots echoed through the woods, and then Lionheart entered Heartshope, bringing a vast shadow behind him. All the animals trailed in his wake, and this time they were not silent but joyful, voicing all manner of sounds and music.

Then they collapsed around Lionheart's feet, stilling temporarily, and Lionheart spoke. "I certainly do not understand this," he announced dazedly, "and can scarcely believe. Ever since the City was lost, the animals have been waiting for me to come." He shook his head, as though the new reality still were not clear to him. "They knew that Covenant had come to the land. They were waiting for him, and he bid them wait for the man who would gather them all in safety, a man who would save them."

"And you are that man?" asked Freeblade.

"I must be," Lionheart shrugged. "No one knows another answer.

"He showed the animals this place—Heartshope—and told them to watch here for the man who rode the lions. They knew my identity before even I did, from the first time I was privileged to sit astride. But they had to wait until I came *here*."

"Do you then command this army?" asked Freeblade.

"No," he answered immediately. "They will help us, and we will help them, but they are not here at my beck and call. Remember that *they* summoned *me*," he added.

"And now what do they want?"

"The same gifts we do. Health. Hope. Freedom. Innocence. Peace."

"How do you talk with them?" wondered Beauty.

"I cannot teach you to hear their words or share their thoughts, for I did not learn myself: it was a gift given to me for a purpose.

"They hunger, they fear, they love, they thirst," Lionheart said, "but they do not think like us or communicate in the same way. It is difficult to describe how they share their thoughts. They think in pictures and emotions, and talk in images—what they saw, where they saw it, when it was seen.

"I sense the image in their minds, and I can feel the fear or the warmth that they bring with it, but they cannot always tell me what it means. They do not understand human minds, though they are learning again to know our hearts since Covenant came.

"Covenant," he continued. "They have hundreds of images of Covenant. When he was not with us, he must have been with them, leaving promises with them. After what I have seen, I would not be surprised if Covenant had spoken to the rocks and trees as well. It seems he was as concerned for this entire world as he was for us."

He paused. "None of this is very clear, you realize, and we can talk of it later. This is a new and unexpected gift, and I'm still learning what its powers are."

He gestured to the waiting animals. "They are not our natural enemies, and need not be our enemies at all. We and the animals were meant to be on the same side. We are enemies with them only because we are our own worst enemies.

"Nor were the animals themselves always at war with one another, though not one of these hunters is innocent of his prey's blood. They are bound to this law of tooth and claw, and suffer in its chains.

"They will help us, if they can. But they also need our help, and I do not know whose need will be the stronger. They suffer with us, and because of us," he said, "and I cannot turn them away. I cannot proclaim peace forever, but I can call an end to that war in this place.

"We have marked out the land around Heartshope, from the road to Glory on the west to the peaks of the low mountains on the east, from the fields to the north to the next river to the south.

"There shall be no more killing, for hunger or in anger, in all this protected territory. Let them eat not each other but the yield of the field and the fruit of the trees." He smiled, and singled out Trueteller with his words. "So they were all once, Trueteller. Your eagle is less unusual than you believed."

She laughed, and he turned to them all again. "They have each pledged to harm nothing that lives and moves, and you need fear nothing from them. I have not pledged that you would not harm them, but I promised that you would give your answer yourselves."

"Who objects?" asked Wordsmith of the Company.

No voices were heard.

"Then let it be," he said quietly. He turned to the multitude of animals. "Welcome to the Company of Covenant," he told them, as though they could understand his words. "Where the Child opens his arms, we open our arms as well."

Lionheart resumed his speech. "I would name this area the kingdom of Wildhaven, with Heartshope its great center.

"The animals everywhere will be told, and they must choose between their old war outside Wildhaven and this new peace within."

"Hail, Lionheart—Beastmaster!" intoned Wordsmith.

Lionheart laughed, and then saw that Wordsmith had meant no joke. An awkward expression bloomed on his face and then faded into contentment. "It seems I must accept that title. But it is not I who brings this harmony," he reminded them. "Rejoice, but know that it is not Lionheart's doing. It is a gift to us—from Covenant, from the Child, perhaps direct from the hand of the Elder God."

* * *

There were animals everywhere in Heartshope. Squirrels skittered across the square, ignored by the hawks gliding in and out among the trees. Lions sprawled in the square, twitching slightly but not rousing when rabbits ran across their outstretched paws. Wolf cubs played at Roadreeler's feet while he grazed the grass.

"This is amazing," commented Wordsmith.

"Not so amazing as the Child," replied Beauty. "He must be the source of this harmony. Without him, there would be nothing like this."

She sighed, and Wordsmith asked her what was wrong.

"I was only wondering," she answered, "why people could not live together like this as well."

"Perhaps they will," said Wordsmith. "I have a feeling the Child has only begun his work among us."

* * *

"All the game is gone," muttered an old man hunting in the woods far from Heartshope. "I do not understand it."

TEN

The Secret Place

WORDSMITH?" ASKED TRUETELLER. "I HAVE HEARD DARMAK'S story now, and I think all should hear it. Could we all share a fire tonight and let him speak?"

"Of course!" he responded. "Promises and miracles, of all things, should not be kept secret."

* * *

Darmak started speaking easily, even eagerly.

"I have waited a long time to tell this story," he began, looking at them all but most often at Trueteller.

"You know that Abra—Trueteller—and I lived in the woods, a place that was our home and our living as well. As I had done so many times before, I gathered from the forest all I could carry—mushrooms, berries, roots, herbs, choice woods—anything that another might buy or trade for. And as had happened before, the farther I walked from the forests, the more coppers I was offered for my gleanings, for such things as I had were not common there.

"Two men asked me to bring my forest fare to the far south, where everything I took for granted would be considered delicacies indeed.

"Though they were strangers, I journeyed with them suspecting nothing, while listening to their tales of a rare wilderness fruit called *cavada*.

"We detoured to see the place where the fruit grew, and I found all their words true. A deep, cold valley amid impossible heights—endless pale sunshine, and ever the deep drifts of snow. It grows on great bushy trees that line the trackless faces of the cliffs, waiting only for the hands to pack it in cartons lined with dry hay. More cavada grows in that valley than can readily be picked, for the land is rugged and remote, weather-blown and treacherous. None would stay long for harvest unless they were desperate—or enslaved.

"And that, I discovered too late, is exactly how they were gathered—by slaves.

"My companions quickly became my captors, and shoved me down a long and unclimbable slope into the valley. I found other men down there before me, and learned more of my fate.

"Our task was to pick the cavada. Our choices were simple and unavoidable: we could work and be fed, or rebel and die. At the cliff they could haul the baskets of fruit up and lower food and clothing down to us, or give us wood suited for fire or shelter.

"Never has the gap between one person and another seemed greater.

"The valley was huge, and we constantly explored for a way out. We fashioned ropes for ourselves—needing them, indeed, for our work—but we had nothing to fasten them to and, therefore, no way to climb over the cliffs that kept us captive.

If one of us could have reached the top of the cliffs, he could have let longer ropes down to the rest.

"A way of escape was clear, and before our eyes every waking moment, but impossible. We could not reach the escape we saw, and we could see no other escape within our reach."

He paused, and they could see him trying to find the right thread in all the thoughts tangled together in his mind. Freeblade stretched out his foot and nudged a stray log back into the fire.

"The years wore on," Darmak resumed, "and though the frostberries were delicacies in all the land, we quickly grew tired of them. They were always there, rotting underfoot, and though we ate them to live we came to despise the fruit that delighted the world.

"Men came and men died. Most perished quickly, for the mountains were unforgiving, and they were soon conquered by the cliffs. Others chose the plunge into an abyss over slavery.

"Our captors cared not; they had ample chances to steal other men to replace the careless, the sick and the defiant.

"We had no hope at all. How could anyone outside know? The mountains kept their cold secrets too well.

"I was the only one who lasted twenty years. The rest were young and hot and reckless, full of anger and smoke and impatience. I was young and cold and determined, and did not let my anger drive me vainly.

"I went farther and farther into the valley for my labors, preferring the solitude to the company of other wretched men. One day I discovered a very old and sacred place in the cliffs. It was tiny, and held only an altar with the name of the Elder God upon it, and a mark I did not recognize. Once the hidden nook had been an open place, but rocks had fallen, the land had slid, and time had erased the path, as well as any reasons for its presence there.

"What do prisoners think of except escape? Through the

years I held the cold fire in my belly, burning for freedom and revenge, and in that secret place I prayed for both. But none of my prayers were heard until I grew tired of anger and learned to cease to long for blood. When I sought escape only, I found peace at that altar—and eventually an answer came.

"An answer that came from the air.

"There were always animals in that place, and we watched for them. There were bears, and we never interrupted them in their feeding. There were foxes too, even wolves. We trapped some smaller animals to add to the food so grudgingly given us, and to use their furs to warm us against the wind.

"I saw an eagle in the air one day, and I ignored it, for it was only one of countless birds that came day by day for the feast of fruit. But it settled near me and made raucous noises at me—pestering me for food, trying to snatch the cavada from my hand as I picked it, ignoring that which was still on the trees or already fallen to the ground. I finally tossed him some fruit to be rid of him.

"But then I saw the gold bands on his legs, and my head grew light. I saw your mark, Abra . . . and I could not wait to tame him enough to pry the bands from him and see what other message lay inside.

"And the second mark? That mark was the same as that on the altar in the secret place.

"I could only make wild guesses where he had come from or who had tamed him, or how he had come by both your mark and this sign connected to the Elder God.

"I called him 'Featherfriend,' " he said. "That at least goes well with Farsight.

"In the end, which of us befriended the other? You cannot know, for I can never put into words how much he cheered me and brought me hope of a world I thought had left me behind forever.

"I know now it was Trueteller who first showed him kindness, who tended to him and gave him his taste for cavada. He stayed with me, insisting on keeping me in sight and eating only from my hand, and I began to see him as not only a messenger but a rescuer.

"He readily plucked fruit from the higher branches and brought it to me, halving my labor for each full sack, even though he later gobbled much of what he brought me.

"From there, it was not difficult to persuade Featherfriend to retrieve bundles of rope on command. I don't think I trained him, but he agreed to help me. And next I tied a loop in a long rope and offered it to Featherfriend. He caught it in his beak and flew off up the rock and lodged it around a stone spur. Then he wheeled in the air while I climbed the rock and stood triumphant there.

"So I discovered a chance of freedom, and we practiced where the others could not watch. I wove strong ropes, long ropes, more than I could possibly carry, for I had an idea. I began to hoard my food and wrap it well against the elements and the mice."

He paused and let several clouds pass over the moon before he spoke again. "But that was not my greatest struggle. I fought myself daily whether I should take the others with me. Yet we could not all go. If we all had vanished, they might have looked for us and found us pinned halfway up the cliffs. Nor could I doubt that the others would have chosen to return in force and kill our captors.

"In the end, I took none with me. But I left a marker for the others, if they looked for me, and I left the ropes in place for the brave. They can follow, if they wish.

"Unpursued, Featherfriend and I found a way across the mountain—trackless, undiscovered, even more hazardous than the valley. From rock to rock he led me, bringing ropes and carrying the ends ever higher, waiting while I fought every foot of the climb, bringing me fruit throughout the journey. The way was dizzy, and perilous, but I had ceased to fear by then—except to fear that I would not return to this place again.

"We gained the summit, and passed on into the forests where I finally fell and lay for days, and he brought me not only fruit but fish and rabbits to share.

"Later we found the road again—and encountered one of my captors returning from a trip. At first he was surprised, then angry, for I would not tell him how I came there.

"I could not plead my freedom, but I could claim it, and in the end I could pay gold to keep it. He agreed to believe that I had fallen into the crevasses—if I gave him the gold band."

He hesitated. "I did not know which band to give him. In the end, I gave him the one with the strange mark upon it. I knew your work, Abra, and I wished to carry it with me.

"It is no longer complete," he continued sadly. "I have had to hammer off other bits along the way, to buy shelter and food."

"It does not matter," Trueteller sighed, dismissing the thought with a glowing smile. "The gold matters less than the man who returns it to me.

Darmak grasped her hand and continued. "I saw in his eyes that he considered killing me and taking all my gold—but seeing Featherfriend, he dared not. With this proud beast on my shoulder, I walked away from him.

"He had his choice. He could say nothing, or he could raise a cry after me. Whether he has kept silence or not, I do not know. If any followed my path, either captive or captor, they have not found me.

"Hoping all things and expecting nothing, I returned to our house in the forest, and I found only an empty shell. But there were notches at the open door, and marks I knew too well.

"For the third time I beheld that mark—first in the secret place, second on the gold band and now in the ruins of my own house. And I would have followed that mark straight to Glory, but Featherfriend drew me aside from the road, and . . . you know what happened then."

He looked at Trueteller again. "And when my explanations were done, she had many things to explain to me. What was this mark? How did it come to be beside hers? Why did I find it also at our house in the forest? Why have I encountered it at every turning since?"

Wordsmith asked him, "And are you content with her answers?"

"I am," he responded, "for now." With that he ran out of words, at last, and let silence fall unhindered.

The fire was also content in its crackling, and an easy calm had replaced the anticipation and curiosity on the faces around the fire.

"I will never eat of that fruit again," pledged Candle, his voice sliding into the silence without shattering it. "Any more that come my way I will feed to Featherfriend."

"Nor will I," agreed Trueteller, "even though that cavada from your store brought us together again." She turned again to her husband. "I am pained to think that so many of our coppers and coins went to enforce your slavery."

She gazed at the eagle, upright on a nearby tree limb with his head tucked under his wing. "I called him Farsight," she continued. "You have added to that good name another—Farsight Featherfriend."

"Is not this the way for all of us?" asked Wordsmith. "The more good we do, the more names we receive."

Beauty's voice joined his. "We have all been given, or have taken, names that are ours, but not ours forever."

"I had not heard my name for twenty years," Darmak said uncomfortably, "save in my dreams. But I have spoken her name to myself so often, and now I cannot grow used to calling her Trueteller, even though I know her story now."

"Covenant has—had—a custom," Trueteller answered for them all, "of giving new names wherever he had given new hope. He spoke to me often of his promises, and on two occasions he murmured a single name: Skymarker. He would not tell me what it meant, except that it would have much meaning for me. I think he intended to pass this name to you. Before I heard your story, the name meant nothing to me, but now I see the perfect fit."

"Perhaps my old name does not fit me now," he consented.

"With your permission, then," she said, "let us call you Skymarker. We can grow used to our new names together."

"Together," said Skymarker after a silence. "That was my grand hope all those years."

"It is no longer a hope, but reality now," she answered.

"I have been thinking," he said, "about that reality renewed. We were poor, and never had pledges. Perhaps we should use this last bit of gold to fashion anew what we never had."

"Gladly," she said. "After all, I have already worked that metal once. It was a hard and painful task, but labor shared will be twice as easy and far more enjoyable."

Someone yawned and another moved tiredly.

Binder spoke out for the first time that night, looking very thoughtful indeed. "Trueteller," he said, "there is something you should know, and something the rest may wish to hear, for it has the smile of Covenant hidden in it."

"Go on," she urged.

"When you were tending Farsight in Glory, I wondered at the name *cavada*, and I searched an old book for its meaning."

"And?"

"Have you noticed how it sounds like 'Covenant'?"

She nodded.

"It comes from the same word," he continued. "Simply put, the cavada is the promise fruit. The name meant nothing to me then."

"It means everything to me now," she said, her eyes shining even brighter.

* * *

"The years have been lifted from her shoulders overnight,"

remarked Wordsmith to Beauty as everyone drifted off to their homes.

"Twenty, to be exact," she murmured, taking his hand. "I'm glad we haven't had to wait that long."

ELEVEN

Encounter
at
Evening

OVER THE NEXT FEW WEEKS THE LINES OF SLEEPLESSNESS and worry largely faded from Freeblade's face. Where once he had measured the length and the breadth of the long, dark nights with his weary strides, now there were animals in abundance to watch and warn and guard. Although he woke often and still patrolled the fields and border streams, he was glad to surrender his tiredness to the night hours like all the others in Heartshope.

Another month behind us, and still we are safe, he thought. *But what will happen next?* He thought of the Child. *I was called to defend him, but defend him against what? Who would come against him? The Child receives the adoration and loyalty of each person who beholds him. Who else in all the land, except Fame, could be counted his enemy?*

* * *

Brightface journeyed once more to Glory and returned with

the sum of what she had heard in the marketplace and seen in the streets.

"Glory is firmly Fame's now," she reported sadly. "He holds the people with the power of lies. First he taught them lies about himself, and when they believed those he told them lies about themselves. He is great, he tells them, and because he is great they will all be great.

"The Mountain still melts, and the river flows past the edge of Glory, making its way to the sea. Fame claims credit for what he says is the fruit of his magic.

"It is no longer a tower that Fame builds, but the Tower. And with the fever of his lies, it grows—for the greater glory of Glory."

"Yet nothing is happening here," said Freeblade almost mournfully. "Time passes. Our enemy grows stronger. And still we do nothing."

"We do nothing because the Child has done nothing," answered Wordsmith.

"Much is happening here in Heartshope," added Beauty, "and each day. Moonflower grows and glows. More animals come, and the ones that are here grow bolder and tamer with us. Vegetables sprout in the gardens. Thankfully, even faster than the weeds. Fruits ripen in the orchards and drop into our hands."

"You know what I mean," insisted Freeblade. "That book of Covenant's words to us is full of war and warnings, while we have seen little to be wary of."

Wordsmith frowned. "There will be enough of that eventually," he promised. "None of his words were uttered lightly. Are you that anxious to fight again?"

Freeblade shook his head firmly. "I am not anxious to fight, but to win and have done with it. If there is no more fighting ever, I will be more than content. But I am not patient enough to wait long for what must come."

* * *

We've grown used to this so quickly, thought Beauty, stepping around a sleeping bear. *Nothing like this has ever happened before— anywhere—and we have come to take it for granted.*

She was hardly aware that another sparrow had landed on her shoulder.

*   *   *

The Child slept where he wished, often with Beauty and Wordsmith, other times with Binder and Brightface, and sometimes cushioned amid a heap of Lionheart's charges.

His fascination had quickly extended to Candle and True-teller and Moonflower.

"I do not know whether to cradle him in my arms or worship him," said Candle one day.

"If you were a mother," replied Trueteller, "you would know how to do both at the same time."

*   *   *

But Freeblade always knew where the Child was and never wandered far away.

"When the Child sleeps, I am content," he murmured to Beauty one night as they watched the Child, asleep in True-teller's arms.

"When he wakes, I am even more content," answered Beauty. They watched him silently, and secretly blessed the peace that had fallen on them.

But in the dark stillness came a silent movement at the door, and Lionheart interrupted them quietly. "Soldiers are near," he whispered. "Farsight has seen them. A band of ten, perhaps, off the main road to the south. Two miles away, no more. What shall we do?"

"Are they searching for us?" Freeblade asked.

"It may not matter. They are perilously close to finding us anyway."

"Take your beasts and frighten them away if you can."

"Some of my little friends should be there by now. But will a dozen armed men be routed by a few wild animals?"

"Either forced back, or drawn aside. But do not kill anyone, or let our own be hurt, unless there is no other way." Freeblade drew his sword. "Remember, they will have not only swords and knives but also spears and arrows. Do not get too close. I will go out beyond the village and wait. If you cannot stop them, I will."

"How?"

"It is not for show that I have kept this blade sharp and ready." He paused only long enough to run his thumb along the edge of his weapon. "Beauty," he said, "have Wordsmith smother the fires, then come after us. Stay with all the children, and quiet them if they wake.

"Trueteller, stay here with the Child, and yield the door to none but me. He is asleep, and I will not waken him unless we are forced to flee."

Lionheart plunged ahead and was soon lost in the darkness.

Freeblade followed more slowly. *Why am I protecting the Child?* he thought again. *He has more power, and more life, than I do.* He stopped in the gathering gloom of the concealing forest and waited against hope for the men to come. *Veer away*, he thought. *Do not make us spill blood over innocence.*

Eventually he heard them. Soldiers they may have been, but woodsmen they were not. Their stumbling thunder grew, and then faded away in the trees to his right. They were drawing near the main road again and would miss the evidence of Heartshope.

But Freeblade soon heard someone else coming through the forest directly before him. Not Lionheart, not an animal, but a lone soldier groping in the dark. The faint clink of metal weapons and the rattle of a full quiver betrayed him.

Freeblade's sword twitched unbidden in his hand, and the stray gleam of moonlight on metal halted his opponent.

Both were ready, and their fight began with a fierce clash of steel. Satisfaction thrilled through Freeblade's veins, for in the first slashes and parries he knew his half-seen opponent.

He had met those same strokes in the arena only weeks past, and he vividly remembered every rough moment of that encounter.

But now it was dark, no one was there to cheer him, and his opponent was wiser. Freeblade blocked, struck, drew blood, blocked again, tempted his foe into an off-balance swing and sliced hard at the hand that held the sword. A smothered shriek lost itself in the darkness, and his opponent wavered.

Freeblade struck again, and one more time.

* * *

Wordsmith joined Freeblade over the fallen soldier's form.

"What did you do to him?" whispered Wordsmith, watching the shadows for other enemies.

"I did not wish to kill him," panted Freeblade. "Nor could I let him go to bear the sword against us later. And I could not let him defeat me, for the peril of the Child." Haunted eyes stared out from his pale face.

"What *did* you do?"

"I remembered the tournament, knowing also that this man was both my opponent and the enemy of the Child. So I slashed the sword from his hand, striking off his fingers. Then I knocked his legs from beneath him, and at last brought the haft down on his head. His leg is only broken, and his head and hand and side will heal, but he will never bear the sword again."

He sighed deeply, finding it hard to select the necessary words. "I did not kill him, but I wounded him gravely. Now he is our prisoner, but I do not know what to do with him. I do not even know if I made the right decision."

"I believe," said Wordsmith slowly, "that compassion is always the right decision."

Freeblade listened carefully to the night. "Has Lionheart returned?"

"No."

"I do not hear the rest. Did he draw them away?"

They waited until the silhouette of a man on a lion appeared at the edge of the woods.

"They are gone," said Lionheart.

"Not all of them," said Freeblade, gesturing to the battered body at his feet. "This one was separated from the rest."

"We will look again," said Lionheart, "and see that no more are missing from their number."

"Did you fight them?" asked Freeblade.

"No. Hungry men will hunt a deer," Lionheart said. "Even if they are searching for something else."

"Well done," murmured Freeblade. "I'm glad no fight was necessary. The less attention drawn to us, the better."

Lionheart smiled. "Did you think they might take notice of bears and stags and wolves fighting side-by-side?"

His smile went away. "But it was not without price," he added. "I have a stag with an arrow through his shoulder. I must tend to him as well." He wheeled the lion about and they were gone.

The soldier at their feet groaned and stirred.

"Stay here on guard, Freeblade, if you wish," said Wordsmith. "I will tend to this one's wounds, since he still lives. We owe him that, at least."

Freeblade agreed. "Let us be kind to our enemies, even though we half-slay them first."

Wordsmith worked his arms beneath the fallen man's form, lifted and shouldered him awkwardly away. His limp, never entirely absent, was exaggerated by the cumbersome weight.

Groping in the shadows, Freeblade recovered the fallen weapons and considered them with his fingers. He stacked the bow and arrows against a tree as useless in the dark, but tucked the soldier's sword into his belt.

He resumed his watch, seeing little enough with his eyes but trusting his ears more.

Lionheart found him there later, still standing motionless in the forest like a patient tree.

"Come," he said to Freeblade. "That danger is gone now. The animals will tell us if the soldiers return."

* * *

The soldier woke to pulsing pain and found himself on a pallet of rushes, the sounds of life playing around him.

He groaned and tried with little success to move his limbs. His head ached violently, his right hand was heavily bandaged, his left hand was fastened to the window framing with a long leather strap, and one leg was splinted with rough lengths of wood and layers of wrapped cloth.

He looked up at the man standing by the pallet and understood at once who had defeated him.

"You are Freeblade," he stated weakly, but without hesitation. "I fought you in the arena, and I would not have willingly fought you again."

"And you are Arden," Freeblade replied. "I remember you well from the tournament."

Arden raised his right arm a few excruciating inches. "What have you done to me?" he asked dully.

"Your fingers are gone," answered Freeblade calmly, "and your leg is broken. Your head is apparently too hard to be damaged, for even though I knocked you senseless you woke again quickly. Your fever is rising."

"Why did you not kill me?" he asked.

"I have no taste for death," answered Freeblade, turning his head away. "I have already seen too much of it," he continued softly. "When I must use force, I will. But if I may fulfill my mission without taking life, I shall."

"There will be slaughter soon enough," Arden said.

"Was that your mission? To find and slaughter us?"

Arden said nothing, and Freeblade was not sure he would answer at all. "It was a mission of shame," he finally admitted, "and one I had no taste for.

"We came to kill a child."

Freeblade's blood slowed in his veins and chilled his heart.

"A child?" he prompted, his voice concealing his anxiety.

"Fame has heard rumors of a child," Arden explained, pain striping his voice and features with darkness. "A child who will take his throne from him.

"For months now no child has been born in Glory, and there are no children waiting to be born—a bane of barrenness he blames on the beggar and those of you who followed him. It had to be Covenant's doing, for wasn't one of his company with child? What other child could it be?

" 'Find her,' Fame said, 'and kill her and her child.' "

Then they do not yet know about the Child, thought Freeblade. "And you came here, searching?" he probed.

Arden shook his head. "We had been searching to the south and were on our way back to Glory empty-handed. I lost the others on our short cut to the road."

Then our secret is still safe, thought Freeblade. *But this one cannot be allowed to leave us. What can we do with him?*

The Child entered, unbidden; the fallen soldier could not take his eyes from him.

Freeblade moved to place himself between Arden and the Child, but the Child prevented him with a bare shake of his head.

"Who is this?" Arden demanded in a hoarse whisper.

"This is the Child," Freeblade said, a warning rumbling beneath the surface of his voice. "The Everlasting Child."

"I know now," whispered the soldier after a few long moments of silence and contemplation. "The child we seek is not one yet to be born. It is *this* one."

"All seek this Child, whether they know it or not," said Freeblade.

A somber but not unfriendly expression on his face, the Child reached forward and laid his hands on Arden's chest. Then the fever boiled in the soldier's head, and he drifted back to sleep.

* * *

The Child slumbered on Beauty's shoulder as Freeblade talked with her and Wordsmith.

"What can we do with him?" Freeblade asked. "If he leaves here with knowledge of us, the soldiers will return."

"But can you kill him in cold blood?" Beauty asked.

"No," Freeblade admitted, "only when the blood pumps hot would I strike a mortal blow."

"And this is no longer combat," Beauty pointed out.

"Yet it may still be war," Freeblade returned.

The Child woke from his nap. Beauty lowered him to the ground and asked him plaintively, "What would you have us do with Arden?"

But the Child only smiled at them and wandered off to play.

"I think he has given us his answer," murmured Beauty. "And the answer may be that no answer is needful yet."

"His calm is contagious, isn't it?" remarked Wordsmith.

*   *   *

Arden still slept, oppressed by fever, when Freeblade came to change his bandages. Freeblade unwrapped the last layer around Arden's hand and stopped suddenly, frozen by what he saw. Hurrying off, he returned shortly with Wordsmith and Beauty behind him.

"Look at this!" he exclaimed.

The stumps of Arden's fingers had healed over cleanly. There was no blood, no oozing, no need for a bandage.

They quickly unwrapped his leg, and Beauty pronounced the break healed, as far as she could tell from the outside. There was no ugly swelling, no bruised and puffy flesh, no angle where the broken bones had been imperfectly aligned.

They looked at each other.

"The Child?" suggested Wordsmith.

"Who else?" answered Beauty. "Is anyone else here a source of miracles?"

"Yet he still has a fever," replied Freeblade, looking at the soldier, "and he tosses and moans in his sleep. Is that healing?"

Beauty shrugged. "Leave him be," she said, "and watch him. Perhaps the fever is part of the miracle."

Freeblade found Lionheart and arranged a guard of wolves for Arden. Then he dragged himself wearily to his own pallet in search of long-denied rest.

This healing is like Covenant among us again, he thought as he lay down. *Except that the fingers were not restored, merely healed over. Is that the price of being an enemy? But if Arden is an enemy, why heal him at all?*

Sleep finally overcame his puzzlement.

* * *

Not until after the next morning's meal did Freeblade hear any stirring from Arden. He greeted the wolves with a caress, slipped inside the house and found the fever broken and the soldier lying quietly on the pallet.

Arden's eyes turned toward Freeblade and locked their gazes together. Arden raised his healed hand, not so much in welcome as in display. "This is no ordinary child," he said, "to have this kind of power."

"It was the Child's doing," admitted Freeblade. "He healed your leg as well."

"And my head too." Arden let his outstretched arm fall back onto the blanket. "Tell me more of him," he implored. "He has haunted my dreams, and I have thought of little save him."

Freeblade hesitated. *How much should he know?*

"What is his name?" Arden began.

"To us he is simply the Child."

"Does he speak at all?" the soldier asked.

Freeblade shook his head.

"He said no word in my dreams, either," continued Arden. "He said nothing at all, but again and again he beckoned me to stand beside you and follow him. He beckoned, and I obeyed, and I knelt to him. I would do so now in person, for this Child is irresistible, and has claimed my trust and my service." He hesitated then, and finally continued, "But I must know if I can trust *you*."

"If I had wished you dead," responded Freeblade, "I would have slain you on the road. How do I know that *I* can trust *you*?"

Arden nodded. "A fair question. I swore fealty to Fame when I beheld his power. I swore fealty to the Child when I beheld his love."

"Was it feigned?"

"Neither to Fame nor to the Child. I gave the best I had, to the best I could find."

"But will your loyalty change again when something greater overwhelms you?"

"I do not know," Arden confessed. "When I beheld Fame's power, I could imagine nothing greater. When the Child's love came to me, the lure of power faded. Is there any force greater than love, that the memory of the Child would pale beside it?"

"We have found nothing like it."

"Then I am as loyal as you are. I have bent my knee to greatness wherever I have encountered it."

"It is one thing to kneel," Freeblade said, "and quite another to fight. How will you fight at all? Your hand is useless for the sword."

"Yes, but I still have another hand." He grinned and beckoned for his sword with his left hand.

Freeblade looked at the extra sword in his belt and hesitated. "I cannot make such a decision on my own. I must first speak with Wordsmith."

Before Freeblade could rise, the door opened and the Child walked in.

Arden struggled from the pallet and knelt awkwardly on the floor, offering a stuttered oath of loyalty. This time Freeblade made no move to interfere.

Moving calmly and purposefully, the Child drew the sword from Freeblade's belt, carried it to Arden and left it with him. Arden called his surprised thanks after him, and the Child turned in the doorway and beamed his smile on both of them, a smile that warmed the air long after the giver was gone.

Arden eyed Freeblade. "You wished to see the one called Wordsmith?"

"No," answered Freeblade eventually, "I don't think that will be necessary. The trust of the Child has been laid on you."

"Then I would accept the challenge as well."

Arden balanced his sword in his good hand and cut a delicate pattern of swirls in the air. "The old warrior who taught me insisted that I learn to use both hands equally well. Besides, I have enough hand left for this." His right hand a mere blur in the shadows, he drew a knife from behind his belt and brandished it, the leather strap still fitting snugly around his thumb and over his palm.

Freeblade felt suddenly cold, realizing he had missed the man's small weapon every time they had ministered to him. "You could have used that anytime already," he said hollowly.

"So I could have, but I didn't. You defeated me in fair combat, and I know an honorable man when I meet one."

"Arden," said Freeblade gravely, "you stood against me not once but twice, first as an opponent and then as an enemy. Now you must either stand with me or stand out of my way. I am committed to the Child, in life and in death. If you share that burden and are willing to wear those same chains, then you may stand beside me."

Arden nodded, concealing the knife again in his belt, and Freeblade helped him to his feet.

"I am whole again," he said, "but I am still stiff."

"Perhaps the echo of the miracle was left as a reminder of the miracle," Freeblade suggested. "It seems that we are always to be amazed and reminded of the unimaginable things that have been done for us."

* * *

That evening Freeblade faced the rest of the Company around the fire. "Arden has chosen to join us," he began, "to protect us as he once sought to destroy us."

None seemed surprised, though a few were hesitant to hear the soldier's wishes so boldly stated. Freeblade's own acceptance surprised him, but then ever since the beggar he had surprised himself many times.

"I would have my own doubts," explained Freeblade, "but the Child has accepted him—healed him, given him back his sword and shown his trust. How can I override that approval, even if I wished?"

"The Child speaks for us all," said Wordsmith, "even though he utters no words. Welcome to the Company of Covenant, Arden."

Arden expressed his quiet thanks.

"We have a custom in this Company," continued Wordsmith, "begun by Covenant himself. Save one, all of us bear a new name that was given us when he changed our lives.

"You know our names now, but you do not know our former names, nor the stories behind them."

Brightface told her story, and then Binder, and after that Wordsmith turned to Arden again.

"It is fitting, I believe, that you should leave the name of Arden in the dust, as I did once, and be known by a better one."

Arden thought. "I would take a name that embraces my future without denying my past—yet a name that sets forth what I must do now."

"Halfhand?" suggested Binder, only partly serious.

Arden paused, then nodded. "That would do nicely," he said.

Surprise showed on Freeblade's face. "That is hardly a noble name."

"But it is the mark of my humiliation, is it not?" asked Arden. "The defeat that brought me low and into the hands of the Child? I would gladly give my other hand if need be to claim that privilege. Let me be Halfhand, then, if that seems a good thing to you."

Wordsmith gestured to Freeblade. "I leave that decision to you, Freeblade. You conquered him, and then spared his life; he is your right arm now, though he does not have all his own."

"I cannot make that decision," said Freeblade. "He who names a thing has power over it. So it is with a king and his subjects, with parents and their children, and even children with their kittens. I am not comfortable with that kind of power over this man."

"But I am content with that," Arden insisted. "So it shall be with this warrior and his leader. I bow to you, and accept the name you give me."

"I am not your leader," said Freeblade. "I follow the Child."

"Then I will follow where you go," said Arden simply, and only Wordsmith could add to his words.

"Then let us consider Arden slain in the heat of battle," he pronounced. "Welcome, Halfhand."

Freeblade rose and offered his hand. "Come," he said, "let us fight, not as foes now, but as men do who sharpen one another even with dull edges. I have power, and you have skill. Let us spar, with stick and padded blade, and learn from one another, and practice for the day we hope never comes."

Wordsmith watched them go. "Covenant said we would destroy all our enemies," he said quietly to Beauty, "one way or another. I like this way the best."

TWELVE

Toward
the
Sea

THE MORNING HAD BARELY BEGUN WHEN THE CHILD BROUGHT
Freeblade to Wordsmith and Beauty and then sat to draw in
the soft, bare earth. With only a few strokes of a stick in the
sand, he sketched a scene that leaped full-grown from their
memories.

"This is Graycove!" exclaimed Freeblade.

"And the island," said Wordsmith.

"And the *Childsbreath*," added Beauty.

The Child moved his stick again and added three figures to
the *Childsbreath* and one to the island. Finally, he drew three
large figures and one small one at the edge of Graycove, and
pointed to himself, Wordsmith, Beauty and Freeblade.

"We are to go?" Freeblade asked, knowing his words were
not truly needed.

The Child nodded.

"Shall we ride the lions?" Beauty asked Wordsmith.

The Child shook his head, smiling.

Beauty knelt to him. "Are we walking the whole way?"

The Child nodded.

Freeblade shrugged. "Graycove is many miles from here," he said, "but we have walked greater distances before."

* * *

"The Child has called us to return to Graycove," Wordsmith told the rest of the Company late that afternoon. "He and Freeblade and Beauty and I will leave as soon as the morning sun lights our path.

"Binder, Brightface, Lionheart—I leave you in charge again." He turned to Halfhand. "I would ask of you a harder job," said Freeblade. "Mine is the sword that is bound to defend the Child, but you are a free champion. Stay in Heartshope and guard its people. And listen to Lionheart, for he listens to the watchers who are everywhere and who need less sleep than we do."

"It is good that we have two swords," nodded Wordsmith, "for once again the Company must walk two separate paths."

* * *

Beauty glanced at Wordsmith's eyes in the raw bright morning light and knew he had spent a restless night.

"Dreams?" she murmured.

"Dreams," he nodded, rubbing his eyes where the sleepless hours had left them raw and stinging. "Or visions, or whatever you choose to call them." He waved his hand toward the fire outside. "I do not think we shall meet here again."

"What does that mean? Another prophecy understood?"

Wordsmith shook his head. "A conviction, a sense that when the Child begins this journey he will not stop until all is done. But that may be only fit, for how could all things end *here*? That is not what we have been told to expect. All roads, straight or winding, lead back to Glory at last."

"Yet we are going to the sea, not to Glory," Beauty pointed out.

"I do not plan these events," said Wordsmith. "I only sense their patterns."

* * *

There had been little to prepare, and now they were ready to go.

The Child stretched out his arms to Beauty, and she gladly picked him up. His soft arms closed around her neck, but then she felt his fingers tugging at the clasp of her necklace, from which dangled the mirror piece.

She drew back her head just as the Child lifted her necklace away. Then he turned his eyes to Brightface and beckoned to her. She came to him, and he draped the necklace about her neck.

"I guess you are to have it now," Beauty said.

"I will wear it if you wish," she said. "But why should I have it?"

Beauty shook her head. "It is not mine to keep or bestow. It was Covenant's mirror long before I saw it, and I gladly yield the Child power to pass it to you."

"What shall I do with it?" Brightface asked.

The Child turned back to Beauty and contentedly buried his face in her shoulder.

She shifted his weight to that side and said, "I don't know."

"We know Covenant's ways," said Wordsmith, "and we are beginning to know the Child's. Take the mirror, and when the need comes I am sure you will understand the gift."

She looked into its depths. "It is dark," she said flatly.

"Covenant made this," Beauty reminded her, "and it has his magic in it. It cannot stay dark forever."

* * *

In Beauty's arms the Child bid Heartshope farewell. *His hugs had been warm and happy, but his eyes suddenly are so sad,* thought Beauty. *Does he expect to see this place again?*

The first steps of their journey carried them past the ruined graveyard of the lepers. Wordsmith wondered again at the mysteries there, but despite all their shared questions and speculations, they had no firm idea why some small share of the graves had been shaken open and now gaped empty.

After the first few miles, the Child indicated that he wished to walk. Wordsmith, whose shoulders had taken over from Beauty's arms, was grateful. Even so, the Child himself grew tired in another few miles, but would not cease walking.

"Do we stop here?" asked Freeblade.

The Child shook his head and stumbled on.

Freeblade stooped to pick him up, but Wordsmith prevented him.

"Let me," said Wordsmith. "You should have your arms free for your sword. I cannot guard us."

"Cannot your songs defend us?"

"Perhaps to drive our enemies away," he smiled in answer. Then he began singing, and his voice lightened their weariness. And with the Child to hold and behold and walk beside, the miles passed almost unnoticed under their feet.

* * *

"We have visitors," Lionheart told Binder and Halfhand. "A dozen people have turned from the road to Glory and are coming this way."

"Soldiers?" asked Binder at once.

"No," replied Lionheart. "Men and women both, and perhaps a child or two. My friends have left them alone, for I thought it best if we three met them on the way."

"We shall, then," stated Halfhand, tightening his sword belt. His actions drew Brightface to them, and she heard the news from Binder.

"Let me go too," she said.

Binder caught Halfhand's eye, and they pondered silently.

"We do not know who these people are," said Binder. "They may be our friends, they may be our enemies, or they may be only travelers."

"We may still have friends in Glory," said Brightface. "Many people came to the daily feast. I may know some of them if I see their faces."

"You may watch us from the shelter of the trees," Binder consented. "If they do fall upon us, then you can return to rouse the rest."

"Lionheart," said Halfhand, "send your beasts to watch all around Heartshope. If I were attacking this place, I would create just such a diversion so I could approach from behind."

Lionheart nodded. "I will come to you later." He disappeared, moving like the animals he had come to lead.

* * *

"I wonder why we are not riding," said Beauty the next afternoon, washing her tired feet in a brook.

"I do not know," replied Wordsmith, bathing his own feet and the Child's while watching Freeblade prowl the edges of the clearing where they rested. "Perhaps Lionheart and the animals have other duties to attend, if not now, then soon."

The Child smiled his thanks at Wordsmith as they moved on, his usual silence saying more than only words could.

From time to time Wordsmith sang, but softly, and only in places where they could see well around them, or where his voice would not carry far. Heartshope had held them safe for so long. Now they traveled almost alone in a landscape that sometimes seemed strange.

* * *

Halfhand and Binder stood on the dusty path and faced the travelers. They recognized none as faces that had once sat at Covenant's table.

"We would see the Child," one of them said simply.

"Tell me of this Child," responded Halfhand. "Who is he?"

"He is Covenant come again," said one woman firmly.

"He is the child of many rumors," answered a man.

"Why do you seek such a one here?" asked Halfhand. "This

is a place of wild animals, where disease has held sway for many years. We who live here only wish to be left in peace."

"Nevertheless, we would see him."

"There is no Child here," said Binder, unsure if his accurate words could be counted as truth. *Why am I uneasy?* he thought. *They have not come with weapons drawn, but I still smell the presence of an enemy.*

Behind him, distrust pounded in Brightface's mind as well. *Why did the Child and the others have to leave?* she thought. *He could have showed us, and Wordsmith, Beauty or Freeblade would at least give guidance. I wish I could call them back for this decision.*

The mirror fragment grew hot against her skin. She pulled it from her cloak and gingerly turned it over in her fingers. It flashed in her grasp and gave her sudden hope.

The mirror, she thought. *Maybe the Child has already provided help!*

Without waiting for new fears to overwhelm her, she stepped boldly out of the cover of trees and walked forward to take her place beside Binder.

Binder saw her, frowned and beckoned Halfhand to withdraw with him for a moment. They met Brightface partway to the trees, and Lionheart appeared then to join them.

"I am afraid," whispered Binder. "These may not all be our friends."

"But how can we tell?" asked Halfhand. "Remember, I was once an enemy."

"But the Child accepted you," said Brightface.

"And the Child is not here to deal with these."

Binder turned to Lionheart. "Do the animals know? Can they tell who means to harm us?"

Lionheart listened to words the others could not hear. "No," he said at last, "but they are troubled too, for some they do not trust. Something is not right here."

"But something else *is* right," said Brightface, looking down and holding out the glass on its chain. "The mirror is bright!" she said wonderingly.

"What does it show you?" asked Lionheart.

She gazed into the shiny depths. "It is not me," she answered softly. "But I would like to be like this someday."

Binder looked over her shoulder, and they both saw a white-clad shining lady. Behind her was a radiant man. Both looked familiar but far too pure to be real.

"It is you," Binder breathed, "and me as well. Not as we are, but as we shall be. The mirror is working again."

Brightface nodded. "But what does it mean now?"

"I think," said Lionheart, "that you should ask each traveler here to look over your shoulder."

She gazed at Lionheart for a long moment, trying to guess his meaning.

"Yes," she said abruptly. "This is a good thing you have said."

They returned to the travelers. Brightface held the mirror for each and gazed at their reflected faces, trying to keep any expression from her own. Most reflections matched her radiance, but four repelled her because of their darkness.

They were puzzled by her actions. Some looked unhappy, and all wondered when Brightface asked four of them to go with Halfhand. "This is a hard thing, Lionheart," Brightface murmured as they stepped away.

"Yes," agreed Lionheart, "but swords are not the only sharp things that are a terror to the terrible." He followed Halfhand and the four away from the path, over the rise of the hill and deeper into the stand of trees.

A trio of bears lumbered after him.

Brightface led the rest down the path to Heartshope, where arms spread wide to welcome them.

* * *

Twisting his fingers into theirs, the Child walked happily between Beauty and Wordsmith.

"Do you think they will be all right without us?" asked Wordsmith. "No leaders are indispensable, but we are the three who have taken the most responsibility. We *are* far from Heartshope and moving farther away with every step."

"Look at the Child," answered Beauty. "Does he seem worried?"

* * *

"And the others?" Brightface inquired of Halfhand and Lionheart later.

"They are not here," answered Halfhand. "We guarded them as far as the road and pointed them back to Glory."

"Was that enough to protect us?" she asked. "They must realize that we are the ones they seek, whether or not the Child is here."

"I was still uneasy, but unwilling to do more," Halfhand said. "They walked off, but as they left I glimpsed the bears in the distance."

Lionheart took up the thread of the conversation. "The bears distrusted them, and I fear they followed in pursuit. As to what the bears did, I cannot say."

"But there was to be no more hunting, no more killing here in Wildhaven!" she protested.

"We stood on its border as we parted," Binder pointed out.

"When the bears returned, they avoided me," said Lionheart, "and I could draw nothing from them. Remember that I do not control the animals, though I lead them. Perhaps they know better than I what should be done, for they have spent a lifetime judging enemies and acting to protect themselves and their kind.

"And do not forget that they have as much claim to the Child as we do, and as much right to protect him."

"Then let the fate of the wicked be upon them," Halfhand said. "I did not know what else to do, after they had failed the test of the mirror."

No one answered him, and at last he broke his own silence. "Yet another thing disturbs me," he said. "I came as an enemy, and you treated me kindly."

"Once you had been rendered powerless, anyway," added Binder.

"And you came as an open enemy," said Brightface. "You brought us danger but not deceit."

Binder nodded. "Freeblade is a man of wisdom, and he told me before he left, speaking of you, that he would rather trust a man of misplaced loyalty than a man with no loyalty at all."

THIRTEEN

The Final Island

THE AIR FRESHENED OVER THE HEADS OF THE CHILD AND HIS three friends. Then one afternoon they could taste the tang of the sea, though they could not yet see the roll of the waters.

With that scent the Child seemed restless, plucking at Wordsmith's sleeve when they paused for rests and running ahead a few steps to urge them on.

"This is the first time I have seen him in such a hurry," murmured Freeblade to Beauty.

"Great things may wait in the near distance," said Wordsmith. "Covenant's words have made straight the way for happenings we can scarcely imagine. The Child is in the middle of them all. Perhaps he cannot wait to begin."

When they crested the last hill before Graycove, a watching Deedtester spotted them, as though he had sensed them in the distance. Needing no introduction to the small traveler in their midst, he came running, passing by the others to kneel before the Child. Eye to eye, they gazed into each other's face, a gaze that had been shared before but only through the veil of dreams.

"You've come at last," Deedtester breathed.

"He does not speak," cautioned Beauty.

"He doesn't have to," he replied.

The Child stretched forth his hands to brace Deedtester's cheeks; he imparted a wordless blessing that warmed the hearts of even those who merely looked on.

Deedtester opened wide his arms in supplication and offering, and the Child came to lay his head gently on the old fisherman's rough but welcoming shoulder. Deedtester wrapped his arms around the small body and stood, raising him high for all to see afresh.

"We will not need to carry him the rest of the way," whispered Wordsmith to Beauty.

"I would have to be strong indeed to pry the Child out of his arms," she whispered back. "Though newly met, they are old friends already."

"Where is Covenant?" Deedtester asked them suddenly. No one was prepared to tell the story smoothly, but after they reached Deedtester's cottage and greeted Joykeeper and Seaswallower, Wordsmith began. He related the tales of all that had happened since they had last seen Graycove, beginning with their return to Glory and ending with the Child.

"You believed," ended Wordsmith, "and now you have seen."

"I cannot believe that he is dead," said Deedtester. "Yet in some dark way I am not surprised, for wherever there is a good man evil follows after."

"I do not know for certain that he is dead," said Wordsmith, "but I can find no easy explanation besides death for his absence."

"Dark things have happened here as well," said Deedtester after a pause.

"Speak," said Wordsmith. "We have already laid our sad burdens upon you."

Deedtester related recent events for his visitors. Graycove, too, had felt the wrench of the earthquake and had seen the mystery of the abandoned graves. "And the fishing has fallen away into a mockery of a catch," he added. "The boats go out, the boats return, and there is little in the holds to tell the one from the other. Even the gulls grow scarce, and fewer crows come to pick at the discarded fish."

"We have heard of such a happening," said Beauty. "The animals everywhere are drawing away from people, except where they come to us in Heartshope. Could the fish be a part of this as well?"

"Whatever the answer, the people are muttering and saying that before long no village will be able to survive here."

The small party soon turned their talk back to the joy of their meeting again, the flow of their talk washing the rest of the day away.

"You have come. You have fulfilled the promise," said Deedtester.

"Not until we return to the island," countered Wordsmith.

"Didn't Covenant promise that he himself would return there?" asked Joykeeper.

"So I thought, at first, but now I believe that he promised *we* would return," Wordsmith responded, including Beauty and Freeblade in the sweep of his arm.

The Child, comfortable now in Joykeeper's arms, approved with a smile.

Wordsmith hesitated. "But I think we all should go. Deedtester, Joykeeper, Seaswallower."

"Have you a reason?" asked Joykeeper, puzzled.

"When the Child pictured this place for us, he drew three of you on the *Childsbreath*. Beyond that, I have only a strong feeling, born from reading this book of Covenant's promises and prophecies. As I read, and look about me with open eyes, I am more than ever convinced that when the Child came a corner was turned, and this kingdom began a headlong rush toward the fulfillment of all that Covenant said." Wordsmith tapped the book with his fingers. "These are Covenant's final words, and certain of them haunted my dreams last night. Sometimes the pressure of the promises is strongest just before the prophecy comes true."

"Whatever the Child wishes, that we will do," stated Deedtester.

"And I think that you three should also be prepared to turn your backs to Graycove," continued Wordsmith, "for I have an uneasy feeling that we might not return to this cottage. If you have anything small that you treasure, bring it with you aboard the *Childsbreath*."

They looked at him, not knowing what else to do but accept and follow.

"Then let us sleep," suggested Deedtester, "and take sail with the light and the morning tide."

* * *

The seven searchers lined the rail of the *Childsbreath*, rocking gently with the ocean swells and scanning the sea for the island.

When they saw it, Wordsmith said flatly, "This cannot be the same island."

"It is in the same place, but the shore is not the same shape," said Freeblade, "and the building has changed."

"Changed? It is all gone now!" exclaimed Wordsmith.

At first, Beauty did not recognize the island either. All the great rambling half-ruined buildings had been pulled down. A new finger of stone stretched out from the shore, and a few scattered birds of the sea waded and browsed among the tumbled rocks there.

"Not all of it," said Beauty. "Look there, beneath the trees."

Wreathed in shade that was too bright to be shadow, only a single white stone structure stood on the island.

The keel of the *Childsbreath* ground gently into the sand, and Freeblade splashed into the shallows and turned to help the rest. To their surprise the Child sat placidly along the bow of the boat and waved them on with his hand.

Shrugging his shoulders, Freeblade helped Beauty and Wordsmith over the side, and they waded across the wet sand. As they climbed the path from the sea, they passed the multitude of stones that had been tumbled into the restless waters.

And there the hermit came to meet them.

His eyes were clear and bright, his head was high, and all the shadows of haunting and hollowness had fallen away.

"Can you be Grimshade?" Beauty cried to the man, surprised.

"I remember that name," he said, "though it was lifted from my shoulders by the beggar who was more than he seemed." He smiled. "Now I am only a nameless man on a´ nameless island."

"What has happened here?" asked Wordsmith. "Share your good news with us!"

"Gladly," said the hermit, ushering them farther up the path. "I have found the treasure Covenant set me to find." He pointed to the tiny house and waved them all inside. The white stone walls gleamed in the light that streamed through the ample, open windows. A matching white stone altar stood alone against the wall, its surface dusted but empty. Beauty could see neither dirt nor cobweb anywhere, though the inevitable sand had begun its drift over the sill again.

"This once was the house," he said, "so long ago I scarcely remembered it, or recognized it.

"The old ghosts have died, as you know," he began, "and they have stayed dead. Now the old fears that fed them are gone, and so are the old rotting rooms that housed them. The very stones have been cast into the sea, for I have no need to hide—now or ever again."

"Did you undo all this yourself?" asked Beauty.

"I began the work. I tore down whatever I could and cast it into the sea. But some walls remained, until I was aided by a mighty earthquake. Stone fell, the earth rippled, and waves pounded the sand without mercy."

Freeblade glanced at Wordsmith. "We have heard of that quake. Indeed, we felt it in Glory."

Grimshade looked at them. "Could not Covenant be with you?" he asked. "I wanted him to see this island."

This time Freeblade gave the explanation, and Grimshade took it with sadness, joy and bewilderment.

"I think," offered Wordsmith, "that Covenant knew quite well what this island looked like in the past and would look like again before you even began to clean it."

"His ways were like that," added Beauty. "Whenever we would believe we had discovered something new, we would realize that we were finding nothing more than his old handiwork."

Then they heard voices behind them and were joined by the Child, Deedtester and Joykeeper. Seaswallower still stood on the deck, but he could see them clearly.

Beauty made introductions. "And this is the Child," she concluded, "who walks in Covenant's ways." The hermit listened spellbound to the story of the search upon the mountain and could scarcely take his eyes from the face of the Child.

When Beauty had finished, the hermit stood, and with a wave of his hand invited the Child into the house. The Child took his hand and left dancing footprints beside the long, straight marks of the older man. They spent much time in silence inside, and there was no way to tell what passed between them. While exploring the island, Beauty glanced through one window; she could see the Child sitting upon the altar as though he belonged there and the man who had once been Grimshade kneeling on the floor.

FOURTEEN

Fire
and
Water

Y OU NEED A NAME," WORDSMITH SAID TO THE HERMIT LATER.
"Covenant promised me one," came the reply, "but he told
me nothing of what he had in mind."

"He said nothing to me, either," said Wordsmith, "but I
would choose a name that would have pleased him. Let us call
the others and see what they have to say."

But neither Beauty nor the fishing family knew what Covenant might have intended. Beauty asked the Child to help
them, but received only his smile and momentarily lingering
embrace.

In the distance they could see the string of fishing boats
returning to Graycove. No bright flags flew from their masts,
indicating no great catch in their holds.

"Empty again," said Deedtester. "This coast is slowly dying."

He turned to the hermit. "Are you not perishing as well? Do the fish still fall to your net and line?"

"I have gone hungry often," said the hermit, "but I must stay. First Covenant gave me my life again, then he gave me a task."

"You have fulfilled that task. You found the treasure of the first room and the waiting altar."

The hermit shook his head. "There is more. He called me his final man in the west and said that I would have the first sight of the final fires."

"Do you know what he meant?" asked Beauty.

"I do not," he answered, "but I am not sure that duty requires a clear understanding."

"I have a name in mind for you now," offered Beauty.

"I do, as well," said Wordsmith.

"I yield to you," she said.

"And I to you," he returned.

"Westerkeep," they said together and fell silent with surprise.

"An inspired name, obviously," observed Freeblade, "and a fitting one, since he is the man who has kept the west for Covenant."

Wordsmith saw the dignity of the name seep into the hermit's face. "So be it," he said. "Westerkeep, we are honored to be on your island."

Westerkeep welcomed them over again, and they fell to watching the Child enjoying the beach. He was in no apparent hurry to leave, playing in the mist from the waves along the sand and ignoring, for now, the *Childsbreath*.

His hands were delicate and wonderful, and they fascinated Westerkeep anew as they nimbly fingered the wet sand and built forms that had never taken shape before. He brought them into existence, and with the next surging wave up the shoreline they were gone.

"He is not making copies," Westerkeep said in hushed tones.

"He is making things never known before."

"Yes," nodded Beauty, no longer surprised but still much amazed. "These are things only he has seen."

"And now what?" asked Westerkeep, changing the subject.

"It looks as though we are meant to sleep on the island tonight," replied Wordsmith.

"I would rather sleep on the *Childsbreath*," said Deedtester.

"And I, too," added Joykeeper, "not because I love the water, but because Deedtester will be there."

"It matters not," said Westerkeep, waving his arm at the open sand. "The boat waits patiently, a bed that rocks with no hand to sway it, and this soft sand yields room for everyone, anywhere."

* * *

"We have come again to the end of the world," said Wordsmith, walking the length of the sand with Beauty before they slept. "Nothing out there exists but the water that never ends."

Beauty shivered delicately. "The end of the world. I can think of two meanings for that single phrase."

He swung her to him and tightened his arms around her waist. "I meant only that there is no land beyond this point."

She settled her cheek on his chest and murmured, "You have studied Covenant's words for so long that sometimes you sound like him—and leave me looking for double meanings in everything."

"I love you," said Wordsmith softly. "How many meanings can you find in that?"

She smiled. "Give me time to count them."

* * *

Westerkeep shook Freeblade and Wordsmith awake in the night, and Beauty in the process as well. "Come quickly," he said. "You must see this!"

Freeblade thought first of the Child, but saw him asleep in Beauty's arms.

"What is it?" he whispered back.

"I am not sure," Westerkeep answered, "but Covenant told me I would see it."

Freeblade stumbled outside into the dark and followed him to the peak of the island. Beauty, still bearing the sleeping Child, came next, with Wordsmith just behind her.

From the other side of the hill came Seaswallower, with Deedtester and Joykeeper rubbing the sleep from their eyes.

"There," said Westerkeep, pointing directly to the west. "The sea is burning."

Vast bands of light danced on the horizon, out past the banks where fish had once sported, where giant flames now began to bloom and lick the surface of the water.

"Can this be fire?" asked Freeblade.

"Covenant said I would see the ocean burn," said Joykeeper. "What else could it be?"

"When did this start?" asked Wordsmith.

"Not long ago," said Westerkeep. "I made sure of what I was seeing, then came for you straight away."

The Child stirred in Beauty's arms, and she gazed down at his face. His eyes, enormous in the dark, reflected the ribbon of the far-off flames. Again she saw wonder there, though a wonder unmixed with surprise. His heart pounded, and his fingers clung to her cloak with new energy. In another boy she might have called it fear, but in the Child she could only believe it anticipation.

Their own emotions ranged from awe to bewilderment. Each one had formed some vague idea of the "final fires," but none had imagined anything like this.

"What do we do now?" asked Freeblade.

"Let us sit and watch," said Wordsmith. "I would see what happens next."

*　*　*

The morning light could not dispel the brightness of the flames, nor could it hide the fact that the fires grew closer with every passing moment.

"This is no ordinary fire," observed Beauty. "But then, what *has* been ordinary for us?"

" 'The fire that burns at the heart of the earth,' " recited Wordsmith. "Now it burns upon the surface."

"Covenant said that I would see this ocean burn," Joykeeper said again. "He called it my 'old enemy,' and so it has been."

"Now it rises against you in a new and different way."

"It is time to leave this island behind," said Westerkeep. "The flames come, and we have seen them. We should not wait for them here."

Freeblade's gaze asked the question for all of them.

"I am afraid," Westerkeep explained.

"Of this island?" asked Beauty.

"Not of this island, but of what may become of it. When the earthquake struck the island and wild waves hammered at the sand, the earth shivered, the land dropped lower in the waters, and the surf surged farther up the shore.

"I have heard that islands rise and islands sink with the restless heaving of the earth, and though this place is a wonder it is a fragile one.

"I fear another earthquake or some other disaster. Have you noticed?" he asked, sweeping his arm about them. "Every bird that can fly has taken to the air again, just as they did the last time the earth shook itself."

"And the sea is far too quiet for me," added Deedtester. "He may indeed be right."

In only moments they had retrieved their packs and waded out to the waiting *Childsbreath*. They had barely wrestled the anchor aboard when an eerie calm fell heavily around them.

"It begins," said Wordsmith quietly.

"The beginning of the end," added Beauty, thinking of Wordsmith's words the night before, but watching the Child's face as she swept him into her arms.

The island began to tremble, and the sea shuddered violently beneath them, though they could not feel the movement in the boat. Trees danced on the island and waved their fronds gracefully in the unnaturally still air.

The earthquake was not violent, but it shook their hearts with its firm thunder, rumbling for a short eternity before ceasing abruptly.

"There will be waves to deal with, and the highest will come from the open sea," said Deedtester anxiously. "Let us stay in the lee of this island until the worst is past."

They all scanned the trembling sea between the *Childsbreath* and the distant land.

Little ripples ringed the ocean, as though the waves could no longer decide which way to run.

Then the seas began to lift in the west, blotting out the bottom half of the distant flames. Deedtester headed the *Childsbreath* into the growing swells.

* * *

The people of Graycove had seen the strange lights dancing in the night on the sea. They did not know what it was, and they were deeply afraid. Some thought it was the sun again, halted on its course and sent backward over the world from the west.

But the real dawn bloomed pale in the east, and they searched for other explanations. No boats stirred, and no one sailed forth to see the lights firsthand.

Then the earthquake leveled all that had not been firmly built, and the following waves pounded deep over the sand and destroyed more of the village.

When the *Childsbreath* glided into the harbor, the panic sparked by flames and quakes and waves had been rekindled by a new terror.

The graveyard above the town had ripped apart, and the bodies buried there had risen to roam the village. The amazement and terror they caused was unbounded, for many of those who had come back from the dead were remembered

well—evil at worst and indifferent at best. They still bore the marks of their deaths; wounds gaped bloodlessly, broken limbs dangled uselessly, and disease-shriveled chests hung empty and airless even as they walked about.

Yet they harmed no one, said nothing and wandered vacantly through the ruins of the village.

Then, all along the shore, the sea also began to give up her dead. The violent but diminishing waves threw corpses ashore, pale and weakly silent, that eventually stirred themselves and began to walk again.

All the graves were burst open now, though not all of the missing had emerged from the waves. Some pondered in their panic why the best men of memory all remained shrouded in the moldy hold of the earth and the blue-black vaults of the sea.

Hovering safely off the ruins of the pier, the crew of the *Childsbreath* could see all things plainly.

"Why have some returned from the dead and some not?" asked Freeblade.

"There are no more dead," said Wordsmith. "All the graves are empty now, and all the dead are risen."

"But where are the rest of them?"

Wordsmith answered him, "Covenant said that we would see the troubled dead, but that we would have to wait to see the grateful dead."

"What did he mean?"

Wordsmith shook his head. "Again, Covenant's words mean more than we can make of them unaided. But remember our flight to Heartshope and the earthquake that shattered half the tombs on our path. Perhaps they were emptied that night and these were all that were left."

Behind them the flames grew brighter and taller and closer.

"Is the wind driving the fire?" asked Beauty.

"I do not know," answered Deedtester, "but a hot breeze licks the water, and even the sails are singed." He looked at his craft with regret. "I think it is time to land and leave her behind."

Wordsmith and Freeblade reluctantly agreed, but the Child shook his head firmly and motioned them to stay where they were.

Wordsmith looked at the rest. "His ways are hard to follow," he said, "but his judgments have never failed us. I will stay, though we burn. The rest of you may flee if you wish."

Though reluctance and fear swelled in their hearts, the rest stayed as well.

The Child pointed to the people along the shore and beckoned Wordsmith to bring them aboard as well.

* * *

The advancing flames and the *Childsbreath* did not go long unnoticed in the chaos and panic on the shore.

"To your boats," called Wordsmith across the battered sand. "Come with us or follow!"

"But all the sea is burning!" someone answered. "We have nowhere safe but the land!"

"Not even this beloved haven will endure what is to come," answered Wordsmith.

"Abandon your boat!" cried one man. "How can she save you from the flames? Flee to the hills while there is still time!"

Wherever water was the horizon, the horizon was burning.

Freeblade struggled up the mast of the *Childsbreath*. From the top he could not see over the flames, but looking inland he could see what the others could not: the surging strand of a new river carved its way to the sea.

"The melting mountain!" he called down. "Its water is here and soon will fall into the sea!

"Fire and water," he mumbled to himself. "What will happen when they collide?"

──── FIFTEEN ────

The
Last
Voyage

SOON THEY KNEW.

The river burst through the final hill and tumbled down the beach with a thunderous roar, sluicing dirt and mud and sand aside in its hungry rush to return its burden to the sea. The waters finally met with great violence, and when the swirl subsided, the river beckoned them on to a safe harbor.

The Child pointed onward, and finally Freeblade understood. "We shall sail straight to Glory," he said, "safe from flames, and the first ship to see those troubled walls."

The boat swiftly but smoothly heeled herself to the Child's gesture.

Deedtester gazed overboard at the flowing water. "I do not think you need my hand at the tiller any longer," he remarked.

"It is Covenant's boat," shrugged Wordsmith, "and thus the

Child's. Let him do with it what he pleases."

They passed over the turbulent, muddy meeting of the waters and began their river journey.

"If the sea is burning," asked Freeblade of no one, "how does one put it out?"

He expected no answer, but Deedtester offered one. "Perhaps it will stop at the shore, where there is no water left to burn."

Behind them the flames made the final leap to the shore, and the beached and abandoned fishing boats caught fire. Then the great trees along the shore erupted, the green wood exploding rather than burning in the fierce heat.

Graycove burned as they watched.

Those on board the *Childsbreath* could clearly see the lines of desperate people struggling up the hills, dropping their possessions as they realized the ground itself was beginning to burn.

Beauty sighed as the gap between Graycove and the *Childsbreath* widened. "They did not believe the Child would help them escape."

"Did we?" answered Wordsmith. "We clung to him, not for the sense of his words, but because we know him. Would we have followed his words alone?"

"Wordsmith," called Deedtester quietly.

"Yes?"

Deedtester pointed down at the river surging past the sides of the *Childsbreath*.

"How does she sail upstream?" he asked. "And against the wind?"

"She is the *Childsbreath*," answered Wordsmith. "Perhaps the Child breathes on her."

Deedtester gazed back at Graycove. "Even if they still had their boats," he said, "they could not readily follow. They would find it slow work alone, sailing against the current."

There was little else to say. The *Childsbreath* sailed alone and unhindered up the icy river—beyond sight of the flames, of the sea, and of any other beings save a few birds and the sun in the unblinking sky.

* * *

Lionheart woke from his doze suddenly, stirred by the clamor of a myriad of excited birds—hawks, doves, sparrows, eagles—all circling over Heartshope and calling wildly for the one man who could help them understand what they had seen.

Yet another earthquake? he thought. *I hoped the one this morning would be the last.*

He listened to them carefully and called Binder to him. "Binder," said Lionheart, "the birds bear us disturbing news. They have flown from the edges of the kingdom, from north and south and east and west. They have all seen the same horror: the land is burning. And not only the land but the sea as well. They have seen nothing like this before. The fields and forests are flaming. The mountains are burning—melting as though from great fires beneath the earth—and the hills are hidden in smoke."

"A forest fire?" asked Binder. "Everywhere at once? And how can the oceans burn?"

"If it were only one report," said Lionheart, "I would disbelieve it too. But more than a dozen birds have seen the same thing wherever the horizon lies. I believe they saw what they saw. But I don't know what it was that they saw."

The messengers continued to arrive, both birds in the air and fleet beasts on foot.

"The flames do not diminish," Lionheart reported to Binder and Halfhand later. "They are coming closer all the time, advancing as fast as one can walk unaided. Whole villages burn. The roads are filled with the fleeing. They are walking or in wagons, and they are coming this way."

"Have many died?" asked Binder.

"That is another amazing thing," replied Lionheart. "None have died, but the dead have risen and now flee with the living! Some of the living appear to have been burned, but they have all escaped ahead of the flames. The fire comes steadily, but not so swiftly that it cannot be outrun. This is disaster, but it seems that death has been set to one side."

"And the animals?" asked Binder. "Have they escaped as well?"

Lionheart regarded him solemnly.

"As for the fish in the sea, I do not know. Insects, all that creep or crawl—they must be perishing, but again I do not know for certain. We are past the season for most young; the birds and the larger beasts that remained behind have fled and are heading in our direction. Will the fires burn this far, do you think?"

Binder shook his head. "I hear the echoes of Covenant's words preserved in Wordsmith's book: 'fire, flood and famine—fear, futility and failure.' Is this what he meant?"

The question floated in the air unanswered.

* * *

With no visible hand at the tiller, the *Childsbreath* worked slowly up the new and winding river. The banks here, in what had been low desert wasteland, were already beginning to burst forth in new life that had lain dormant in the parched soil.

The Child, riding on the bow, pointed to a shallow sandbar, and the *Childsbreath* drifted to a halt beneath a pleasant stand of tall trees, old trees with new leaves and a green fuzz of vines and seedlings.

The Child went ashore and quickly fell asleep in the shade. Freeblade went with him and began exploring the riverbank.

"Freeblade," asked Wordsmith, still on the deck, "what do you see in your glass? Is it still black and blank, or can you see the distance?"

Freeblade retrieved his glass fragment from under his cloak, leaned against the peak of the mast and slowly peered in all directions.

"I see nothing but fire," he called down, "fire so bright and so widespread that little else shows."

"Look again," Wordsmith urged. "Perhaps your eyes will take time to see against the brightness."

Freeblade lifted the shiny fragment to his eye again and gazed through it for several long moments.

"The whole world is burning, but now I see people," he said finally. "People fleeing from the flames. The roads are lined with men and women on foot and clogged with their carts and wagons."

"Then the world is ending!" exclaimed Beauty.

"That is evil news to most but a sweet promise to us," said Freeblade. "Covenant said this would happen and that when it did we would have crowns! Rewards!"

"How can crowns be worth anything next to the love of the Child?" asked Beauty. "His hugs warm the heart, and his smiles give meaning to the universe."

On the bank the Child slept long and hard, as though worn by an effort no one had seen him make. After the anxiety and anticipation of the previous days, he subsided again into his previous contentment.

For the rest of that day the Child slept and played and gave and received love, and that evening he led them back on board the *Childsbreath*. She continued her breathless glide up the river.

The next day Freeblade and Beauty and Wordsmith climbed the mast and tried with the glass to read the signs of the world around them and track the progress of the relentless fires.

That afternoon Wordsmith descended with disturbing news.

"The flames are nibbling the edges of Wildhaven," he said sadly.

"And our people?" asked Freeblade.

"They have abandoned Heartshope," he said, "and are on their way to the last refuge, Glory. All the animals are with them. It is a wondrous procession."

A great sadness fell over Freeblade, and in frustration he slashed his sword in the air. "Straight into the hands of our enemies," he mourned. "Who can protect them there?"

"Has all their protection been set aside," asked Beauty, "just because they have been forced from Heartshope? Remember that we go to Glory too."

"We move too quickly," said Freeblade, "if we are to defend ourselves from Fame's wrath. Too slowly if we are to help our friends."

* * *

On the second day they beheld their goal in the distance.

"Glory no longer looks like Glory," said Wordsmith.

"No," agreed Beauty. The Lonely Mountain no longer rose in the background; they had expected that. But none had expected Fame's Tower to be so tall, so slim and so bright.

The spire was the first to catch the eye, gathering the first rays of the rising sun and scattering its dazzle around Glory. It was high and lifted up, a tower within a tower. On the inside a thin, tight, dizzy spiral raced for the heavens; outside and following after, a thicker spiral curled upward. Both sprouted planks and scaffolds and workers, like ants struggling up and down a high desert plant.

The inner spike seemed hardly thick enough for one man and a stair to hold him. The outer circle was wider, with a ramp broad enough to hold horses on its stairs, beasts hauling stones and mortar on their backs.

Wordsmith recalled the half-magical construction of Covenant's house and wondered if some twisted magic was at work here.

When the Mountain had towered over Glory, it had possessed a severe grandeur, but this Tower that had risen against the fall of the Mountain had an uneasy symmetry of a different kind. It seemed to grow taller as they approached—taller, but no less slender, until it seemed that image was but the fulfillment and the mark of all that Glory had been and

would ever be, as if Glory had been made for the Tower and the Tower had been made for Glory.

"No other king has so left his mark here," Freeblade remarked.

They sailed on to a landing place in the shadows of the ancient stone walls. Once a nameless rock in the valley, their anchor point was now a fine pier where the new waters swirled against the foundations. The *Childsbreath* glided forward and trembled to a halt against the sudden shore. Deedtester scrambled onto the pier, then caught a line from Seaswallower and secured it to the rocks.

The sails relaxed with a final sigh, fulfilled though no longer filled. Even the more-than-gentle breeze blowing against their faces declined to ruffle the calm fabric.

"The *Childsbreath* has come to Glory!" exclaimed Deedtester.

"And so has the Child," added Freeblade quietly.

No one came, either to greet them or to oppose them.

—— SIXTEEN ——

Glory
Bound

THEY ENTERED THE UNATTENDED GATES AND FOUND THEMSELVES in a curl of chaos.

Fast riders from the corners of the kingdom continued to arrive, bearing news of the ongoing destruction and the burning borders.

The generations of the dead shambled in the streets, silent and with no clear purpose in their wanderings. They slept not, and ate nothing, but continued to search with empty eyes and hollow hearts for something no one else could imagine.

"There is no order here," said Deedtester. "Is Glory always like this?"

"No," said Wordsmith, "but Fame has more now than he can handle. This is panic, and I doubt that soldiers will be spared now to look for us—if they even know we are here."

"We have no place to stay," said Wordsmith.

"If everyone has fled to Glory," said Beauty, "then we will not be alone in the streets."

"Perhaps it is best this way," said Freeblade. "If we keep moving through the crowds, we will be hard to find."

The Child tugged at Beauty's sleeve, as though he had a destination in mind, and the seven began to pick their way through the eddying streets. Their way drew them into the shadow of the Tower, and Beauty was shocked to see the scowl on the Child's face as he looked up at the stone-lined spire.

Then he looked only sad, immensely sad—an expression that did not linger long when he turned and gazed up at his beloved friends again.

"I remember some words," said Wordsmith, "about the 'height of pride and the pride of height, an offense to the one who rules unseen.' Is this what was meant?"

"Your tower was tall," said Beauty. "Why was it not an offense as well?"

"I think," Wordsmith responded eventually, "that the difference is this: my tower was built from the top down, and not by human hands. Fame's has been built from the bottom up, and was built by nothing but human effort.

"And I lived in the heights by invitation, and not by my own demands."

The Child stopped in front of the ruins of Covenant's House.

"Are we not in our greatest danger here?" asked Freeblade. "We know that they seek the life of the Child and our own lives as well. We are so few, and we bear but a single sword between us and our enemies. What shall we do?"

"What we have been doing all along," shrugged Wordsmith. "Follow the Child. He alone knows where he is going and what he must do when he comes there."

"At last," Freeblade said, "the Child has come to the House of Covenant." His voice betrayed no particular emotion, and he himself was unsure which of his mixed feelings held the upper sway.

They entered the ruined building. The Child seemed at home and did not wander aimlessly among the fallen stones as the others did.

But he did lead Wordsmith and Freeblade directly to one of the deeper corners where Wordsmith's tower had once crept down from the sky. He began to dig and they with him, not knowing what he sought, but being careful that no rocks would tumble down upon their heads.

The Child scraped away a final layer of sand and revealed a wooden box.

"That is Candle's box," said Wordsmith, wiping dirt and sweat from his face with one hand.

The Child nodded, without lifting his face from his work.

"How did he know it was there?" asked Freeblade. "I myself had forgotten it."

When the Child had excavated along all four sides of the box, Freeblade leaned over the Child and delicately lifted it from the hole.

The three searchers returned to the others, joining them at rest in a corner where they could not readily be seen from the street.

"What is that?" Deedtester asked.

"It is the casket with Covenant's cloak in it," replied Freeblade heavily as he set it down on the uneven earth.

The Child began to pry at the lid, and Wordsmith helped him open it. Once the lid had been set aside, the Child lifted out the dirty, stained garment and stretched it over his knees. With his tiny but strong hands, he carefully tore the cowl from the cloak. There had been no seam there, but the cloth parted easily for the Child's fingers and left no ragged edge.

He draped the mottled cowl around his own neck under his cloak, and put the beggar's cloak back into the box.

Then he stood, handed the box to Wordsmith and motioned

them all to follow him.

"Now where?" asked Freeblade. "Is there any place more dangerous than here?"

There was, and the Child led them directly to it.

The rim of the arena welcomed them, and the Child walked straight to the half-buried edge of the Judgment Stone. Standing in its shadow, he set the casket aside and began to scrape a hole in the sand. He squared the depression a few inches deep, took the casket from Wordsmith and set it in the sand. They watched, fascinated, as it slowly sank from sight. The sand drifted itself smooth again and left no traces of the Child's work, as though a whirlpool had sunk itself in the sand.

He stood and smiled. Wordsmith wondered why all these things had happened, but no answer was given to him.

"Let us leave," urged Freeblade. "We are not safe here." He gazed at the Child, awaiting directions, but the Child gave none.

"Back to the House, then," he said. "It is the only familiar place left."

* * *

Under the watchful eyes of Freeblade, the Child slept that night in the crook of Beauty's arm. Wordsmith seized the advantage of the darkness and led Deedtester, Joykeeper and Seaswallower in a cautious circle of Glory, watching every action and listening to every word around them.

When they returned, they held counsel together in the cool darkness of the fallen stones.

"Have you seen Brightface or Binder?" asked Beauty immediately.

Her husband frowned and shook his head. "We have seen none from Heartshope, though many have flooded the town. Glory is awash with refugees, and they cannot easily withstand another misfortune. The fires, the walking dead, the new river from a melting mountain with the face and eyes of a magic child—all these things have ravaged their senses and worn them down. Another sign, another terror, another wonder will likely drive them to madness. Food is scarce and will grow scarcer as all the people of the land are driven into Glory.

"And there is no more death in Glory," he whispered. "No one dies, for it is said that Fame has cast a mighty spell."

"Is this true?" asked Freeblade.

Wordsmith nodded. "I have seen the delay of death with my own eyes, but there is darkness behind the truth. Men, women and children still fall ill, are wounded and suffer—but no one dies. They lie paralyzed, bloodless, broken, but still they live! The suffering does not end."

"This is worse than death," said Freeblade, "to suffer without healing and without death."

"Nor is that the only shadow behind the miracle. Where death has been abolished, birth has become a victim as well. As Candle feared when he lived in Glory, there are no babies due, nor have any been born for some time. Moonflower, it seems, is the only woman with child."

They pondered the news in silence until Wordsmith resumed. "Fame claims that his magic also melted Lonely Mountain and created the river that still grows and will one day connect us with the sea."

"We *are* connected, though he knows it not," said Deedtester.

They slept fitfully, wondering what the next day would bring.

* * *

With the dawn, Wordsmith felt the warm breath of the Child on his cheek. Once more the Child seemed to be in a hurry, and after a hasty breakfast of what was left in their packs, he led them into the crowded and frantic streets. They went to the nearest gate, and there the Child indicated that he wanted to ride on Wordsmith's shoulders. Wordsmith lifted him and waited expectantly for further direction.

The Child merely sat on his perch and looked intently at the crowds. The people there saw, and were seen by and drawn into the luminous eyes. Some passed by but were changed; others were changed and came to stand in silent wonder by the silent Child. Others broke the gaze of the Child's eyes and continued on, feeling somehow colder inside than they had been.

Each one drawn to the Child came and touched his hand, and a spark of delight passed from the one to the other and back again. The crowds moved on, and others came to the Child. Those who had come before looked back longingly yet content for now.

"Not even Covenant had this effect," whispered Beauty.

"No," murmured Wordsmith. "Freeblade, I do not think your sword is needed now, but do stand very near, with your hand on your hilt."

His caution was not misplaced, for where a whole multitude could see the Child, a soldier could see him as well.

At last one did, and brought a dozen more with him. Wordsmith and Freeblade saw them at the far edge of the crowd, pushing their way toward the Child.

Wordsmith swung the Child into his arms and began to slide away, while Freeblade quietly drew his sword. But he had no need to use it, for they were saved by the ugly mood of the crowd. The people cared not why the soldiers were there, and turned against them in anger and fear and frustration—not with weapons but with words, hurling a weight of questions and abuse against them that they could not beat back with shields. No one would dare oppose Fame to his face, but in the safety of the faceless crowd anything could happen.

The wary soldiers slowed, retreated and came again, but by the time they forced a path through the people, the Child and his bearers were gone.

* * *

All roads led to Glory, eventually, and eventually all the

refugees fled there. Nine great gates opened into Glory, and it seemed as if the Child stood at them all that day. No one entered Glory without coming, at one turning or another, face-to-face with the solemn waif, seated on Wordsmith's shoulders or standing on a fallen wall to search the faces of all those who passed.

The three from Heartshope also watched faces, hoping to see the familiar features of the Company and not soldiers' grim expressions.

*   *   *

"I begin to understand the Child's silence and his words," said Wordsmith that night when they huddled in the rubble of the House. "The time is past for debates and for talking and for vain postures; the only thing that may be done now is to stand with the Child or against him. There are no other choices."

He took a deep breath. "Covenant came to raise judgment and rouse wrath. I, Wordsmith, was called to hear and preserve the words of Covenant. Freeblade was called to protect the ones who came after Covenant and the Child. Beauty was summoned to run the House of Covenant, to care for Wordsmith and to give away the love she found so late in life.

"And the Child? The Child came not with more words but with open arms. The Child came to call; the warrior stands to protect those the Child has called. Do they choose him? Or does he choose them? It is all the same in the end. The Child does not need to speak or to teach or to do. He exists to love and be loved. That is his essence, his desire and his mission."

Wrapping themselves around that wisdom, they went to sleep.

*   *   *

Morning found them near the gates again, offering the Child's silent welcome to the crowds, both to those who entered fleeing from the country and to those who seethed in the streets looking for hope and deliverance.

SEVENTEEN

Bold
Men and
Banners

MISERY SETTLED ON THE TOWN OF GLORY. THE FLAMES were visible on all sides, and tempers and temperatures soared.

One could barely hear above the confused roar of the crowds, assembled in any one place not to see something happen but because they had nowhere else to go.

There was no more room indoors, and neither rest nor peace anywhere. Still the desperate refugees squeezed themselves into Glory, and still the Child was there to greet them, and still the soldiers arrived too late to find him.

"Where *are* Binder and the others?" asked Wordsmith once again. "If they were within these walls, surely we would have found each other."

"I do not know," answered Beauty sadly. "Either he is waiting or something has happened to him."

"I see nothing but fire in the glass," said Freeblade. "It may be working, but it tells me nothing now."

A fresh rumble of noise rose from the gate, and the people pressed back into even tighter bunches as a magnificent parade of men, women, children and animals entered Glory.

"There they are!" shouted Freeblade. "They are the last, but not the least!"

"Wild animals!" someone screamed, and the general panic deepened, though the guard of bears and wolves and other fierce beasts made no horrid sounds and threatened no one. Within their ranks came the smaller and slower beasts bearing the remainder of the Company of Covenant, old and young and great and small alike, many with smaller animals in their arms or hands or pockets. A vast cloud of birds circled above, the tiny flying with the taloned and the swift waiting for the cumbersome.

Wordsmith pressed his way forward, and they found no hindrance from the furred guards. A cheer rose from the Company when they saw the Child, and Freeblade steered them on to the ruins of the House.

Warmed past comfort by the approaching fires, the gates were closed for a final time. There was no one left to keep out, but the gesture was made in the feeble hope of holding the flames at bay a little longer.

* * *

At the House the wanderers unloaded their burdens.

"And where shall we all sleep?" Binder asked. "There is little left here but rubble."

"Yes," said Lionheart. "It looks as though what is left will collapse at any moment. No wonder it has been left alone, even when lodging can scarcely be found."

Wordsmith pointed out the roofless halls and broken corridors that still might be safe for passage. "We too thought it was destroyed, and fit for nothing but the honor of an ancient and holy place. But it still shelters us and bids us welcome again."

"We have found enough room here," said Beauty, "though it is not so grand as we once had."

"This House has life," said Wordsmith, "the kind of life that cannot be created."

"Or destroyed," added Beauty.

"Though these are only the bones of the House," said Wordsmith, "still these bones have left us less than desolate in a desperate town in desperate times."

Candle dumped heavy saddlebags on the ground. "Gold is useless now," he sighed. "I can buy gold with bread and water, but not bread and water with gold. There is no place left for refuge, and no place left to hide from the flames. Either the fire stops or we die."

"The Child does not seem to think so," answered Wordsmith. "He does not appear to be concerned about either death or the flames."

* * *

Wordsmith with some of the Company went out quietly to see if food could be had.

While searching, Skymarker spotted one familiar face, a man who frantically waved a hammered band of gold, seeking exchange for a flask of water. There were no takers, and at last the man slammed the useless trophy to the ground and vanished into the crowd.

Skymarker recovered the battered band and smiled at the mark still graven upon it. He slipped it into his pocket, hoping he could someday return it to the grave of the man who had made his freedom possible.

Lionheart, carrying Woodswaif on his shoulders, turned a corner and came face-to-face with his mother and his sister. Neither noticed him until he spoke their names, and even then neither recognized him.

"I am Damon," he said, "or Lionheart, as I am called now."

"You can't be my son," the older woman replied coldly. "He

was taken by the lions."

Lionheart smiled. "That is more true than you know—I was indeed taken by the lions, and now I am one of their own." His smile disappeared as he turned to his sister. "I remember well the night you left your child to die on the rock," he flared.

She made a face. "That was only a girl," she said.

"As you were only a girl—once," replied Lionheart, "but my father would never have exposed *you* to die. And your daughter is well and growing, no thanks to you. Her name," he added, swinging the child down from his shoulders, "is Woodswaif. I saved her, and a beggar saved us, and a lioness nursed her."

His sister was speechless as Lionheart continued, addressing his mother. "And that night you let her take your own husband to the same rock?"

His mother moved closer to him. "I loved him," she murmured, "but I could no longer care for him." She peered more closely at his face. "And Damon was a hairless boy," she continued, "but you have a mane like a lion."

"The scars are still there," he answered. "And where is your husband?" he asked his sister. "He also had a hand in this."

"He died of fright," she said defiantly, "not long after we were set upon by lions."

"You deserved to be set upon," he said, "and it was I who set them upon you. I watched you drop my father—our father—on the rock to die, and it was I who roared and my friends who chased you away. I took him from the wilderness, and he is alive today."

She hit Lionheart with her doubled fist. He grabbed his sister's hand in his before she could strike a second time.

"Be careful," he warned. "You might hit your daughter instead." She pulled away, and he dropped her hand. "And he is not dead any longer, is he?" he continued, and saw the horror in her eyes.

"You may be my boy, after all," his mother said quietly.

"You say he is alive?" She took his hand, and his heart softened toward them.

"Come with me," he urged them both. "My father is well, and is ready to forgive you. Woodswaif still needs your love—and there are others you should meet."

He smiled down at his mother, not knowing that she saw in his face then what Lionheart had once seen in the beggar's smile.

Behind her, his sister walked away and did not turn her face back to see.

*　*　*

The searchers returned nearly empty-handed. "This food will have to be enough," said Wordsmith. "It may not feed us all, but let us not be miserly with it. Eat, for it may be our last meal."

They ate, and shared their meal with the animals; there seemed to be enough, for now. No one knew what would come later.

"I did not think we would return here," said Binder.

"Where else can we go?" asked Wordsmith. "Fame has not come against us here, at least so far. I wonder why he is biding his time, even in this terror he cannot control."

Two things happened at the same time.

Behind them, on the tallest jut of fallen rock, the Child climbed to his feet and raised the bloody cowl of Covenant over his head as a banner.

And in the very near distance, Fame raised his own standard above the unfinished Tower. His sign of power brought a gradual silence, and the crowds shifted in the streets to see as the news spread.

Each banner bearer could clearly see the other, for the buildings that once had lain between them had been torn down to build the Tower.

The Company turned to watch the Child, a living banner with his own banner against the backdrop of the flames and the menace of their enemies. The crowds craned their necks to the stone sky above them and waited for word from Fame.

When a full but uneasy calm had finally fallen, Fame's voice descended to them with deep authority.

"Behold the rebels!" he proclaimed, pointing at the Child and his supporters. "The makers of trouble, the people who have brought the evils of fire and flame upon you! They hide behind the cloak of a powerless child and a dead man."

"How should we answer him?" whispered Beauty.

"It is the Child's challenge," murmured Wordsmith. "Let the Child speak for us, as he always has."

The Child said nothing but stood strong.

Fame raved again, leveling charges and mixing lies with the truth.

"There is the Child's answer," said Wordsmith. "Behold his face."

The Child's face glowed all the brighter as Fame's abuse rained down. Purity answered purulence, and determination conquered defamation.

"Every person in this kingdom is *here*," whispered Wordsmith. "Dead or living, hurt or whole, old or young, but *here*."

And every person—dead or living, hurt or whole, old or young—gazed spellbound at the two rivals. The Child, with his bloody cowl glowing red in the light from the dancing flames. Fame, atop his private mountain of stone, hurling words down on the defenseless Child.

"The flames are their dark enchantment!" cried King Fame. "But it is an illusion only! Have I not saved you? Have any died from this fire? Dread spells may fall upon a land—but I am your King, and a magic man, and I will defeat this fire."

"Who will they believe?" asked Beauty. "A raging King or a silent Child?"

"Whoever they choose to," shrugged Wordsmith, "and they will go where they see safety. It is either Fame's Tower now or the ruins of this House."

Then the Child looked down at Wordsmith, and his gaze fired words in Wordsmith's heart and compelled him to join the Child atop the rock. There he faced the multitude and answered Fame's challenge by calling directly to the people.

"The Child calls you," he shouted, "with his silent voice, and Fame called you with lies. The flames press you hard, and you can no longer avoid the Elder God. His judgment is before you, as well as his mercy.

"You have done great evil in your life, as well as great good. Does one outweigh the other? That is not the balance by which the universe is judged. Your actions are behind you, and your future is before you. You may select your future to match your past, or you may forge a new future for the rest of time. The choice is still yours, as it ever has been. But your chance to choose will not stand open forever.

"If you come to the City, you must take the hand of the Child and follow where he leads. If you will not go to the City with us, you may have whatever is left when the City is once more made plain.

"The world cannot go on burning like this. Covenant spoke of an end to all things, and now it is at hand. You may be spared, or you will be judged with the rest. You will be judged on your obedience, and not your deeds; on your steadfast hopes, and not your wishes.

"Come to the Child, come to the Elder God, come to the works that Covenant established. Choose you must, for there is only one path in life, and only two directions on it. One is either growing closer to the Elder God or drawing further away."

Then the wellspring of his words dried up, and he was content to let the silence return. He stood with the Child, holding his tiny hand, and waited to see what would happen next.

A great silence fell, and the sun crawled its way farther across the sky, barely noticed above the glare of the flames. All could see the Child and Fame, and every heart considered the two faces set against each other. The choice forced itself upon each one in the crowd, and each one chose—some reluctantly, some with joy, but all with finality. People moved, and fought, and argued, while the Child and Fame stood like silent sentinels above them.

While the masses moved, the circling fires breached the walls and gathered the gates in their hot embrace. Then houses flamed and ashed, and even the ashes were consumed.

Clumps and lines of people surged back and forth, milling but inevitablly forming new ranks in the streets. The line joining the Tower to the House thinned and wavered and then broke entirely.

Sides had been drawn, and a battle seemed at hand. But no one knew for certain what to expect. No one moved. Everyone watched and waited and gradually fell silent.

What had been a line of question and doubt and confusion became a line of decision—a line in the sand.

Wordsmith returned to Beauty's side. She was watching the faces of many of those who had eaten at Covenant's table. Some stood with her. Many stood with Fame.

"There are so few of us," she whispered to Wordsmith.

"Compared to the ones who might have come," he answered, gesturing across the gulf forming between the sides, "we are very few indeed."

"But compared to what we were we are a multitude," Freeblade reminded them.

"Wordsmith?" asked Beauty. "There are no dead among us. They have all chosen Fame."

Wordsmith looked and saw it was true. He was about to reply when a hand gripped his shoulder; he turned to see a man and a boy whom he had last seen shifting stones in a distant valley.

"Stonesetter!" he cried. "You are here! And Featherstone with you," he added, reaching down to lift the boy up for a moment.

"Where is Sabrin?" asked Wordsmith.

Stonesetter shook his head sadly. "I last saw her climbing the ramps of the Tower," he said, scarcely taking his eyes from the Child. Featherstone trotted directly to the Child and embraced him, and was embraced in return.

The time has come, thought Wordsmith, *when to choose one love is to betray another.* He was glad that no such choice had been asked of him.

* * *

"I have numbered the brave," Halfhand said, "and there are not enough of us."

"We are two," replied Freeblade, "and we have a charge to fulfill. Numbers are not for us to consider."

"But how can we defend the Child against this army?" breathed Halfhand.

"With our swords, to start with," answered Freeblade grimly. "Every victory begins with a single stroke."

"Dreadnought!" called Wordsmith.

"Yes?" answered Freeblade boldly.

"Your name is also your command," he said. "Dread nought, Freeblade!"

The warrior lifted his head higher. "It is a good name," he answered, his voice ringing with renewed power, "and I shall bear it proudly!"

The flames waited silently to see what would happen. All the universe narrowed down to this—two buildings in a place of flame and rock.

"Seize them!" Fame called from his Tower. "Feed them to the flames, and break their cursed spell!"

Freeblade's voice rang out just as clearly, though he spoke from the leveled rocks. "Oppose the Child at your peril!"

Freeblade laid a deadly web of steel before him, feeling the comfort of Halfhand fighting at his back.

The soldiers and the desperate came at them, finding little room to fight in the narrow streets. Freeblade fought until the number of his wounds increased to an agony, and still he fought on; he fought until no more blood ran in his veins, and then he fought on.

I cannot die, he exulted, *and I cannot be defeated. Can any warrior ask for more?* The sword danced in his hand, and if his heart ceased to beat he knew it not. The image of the Child drove him on, anchored his feet in the shifting sandy clay and stood him steadfast in the way.

The attackers fell back, dragging the fallen with them. In the temporary lull, Freeblade drove his sword into the ground with the last of his strength. "No more!" he cried out. The ground cracked before him. "Let no man cross this gulf again!" The crack widened and filled with a smoking churn of water from somewhere beneath the earth. The spray dashed to the edge of the sword and halted there in a sudden backswirl.

The crack circled the House, yawning wider and deeper and filling with foaming water, stranding the Company dry and isolated in the ruins.

Their enemies retreated frantically, somehow forcing space for themselves within the walls of the Tower or clinging to the ledges and crevices of its high spirals.

The streets, abandoned, were soon awash in smoking water.

Freeblade crumpled victorious to the ground, driven to what should have been death, but never defeated.

Utterly spent, the entire Company waited for the next unimaginable thing to happen.

They were not disappointed.

EIGHTEEN

Stones
and
Surprises

A SUDDEN SHIMMER OF LIGHT DREW THEIR EYES TO THE wall over the Judgment Stone. As they watched, pieces of mortar began to crack away and dust began to rise. A section of the wall over the Judgment Stone collapsed.

The surface of the Tower rippled and shuddered, the structure swayed, and a hail of smaller stones pattered down, but the Tower stood.

The Judgment Stone lifted itself from its bed in the sand and began to rise in the air. No mortal could lift it, and no mortal did. The punishment of gravity was undone, and from the darkness beneath the rock came Covenant.

Cheers quickly rose from the confusion of the Company. Fame howled from his Tower, and the sound chilled those who stood with him. The Company barely heard him, as their eyes and hearts fastened upon their beloved beggar.

"He *is* alive!" shouted Wordsmith.

Beauty clutched her husband's arm fiercely. "They *couldn't* kill someone like him!"

Covenant raised his hands, and absolute silence fell on all sides. His cloak, no longer patched or stained or bloodied, gleamed with a radiance that dazzled even the flames and beat them back dulled and disordered, dying down but not defeated, ready and patient to do the beggar's bidding.

The watchers knew, at last, who had summoned the flames.

"He is the same Covenant as ever," Beauty murmured, "yet not the same."

Covenant came to the Company, striding across the roiling water and the awful gulf beneath. He touched the dry land again, and the Company rushed to meet him. Their joy knew no bounds, and they surrounded him, Fame and enemies forgotten—afraid to touch him yet longing with all their hearts to feel his solid arms about them again.

He opened wide his arms and greeted them each by name. They accepted his love gladly—joining together in happy chaos, pressing in but not crowding, waiting for his attention yet content to wait, taking his blessing and giving it back to him even as it was given.

Then Covenant looked up to the Child standing on the ruined ramparts; upon seeing Covenant's face, the Company moved out of his path. The white-clad beggar ascended the rubble in a joy that ran far deeper than mere excitement. They approached one another slowly, with confidence and even unconscious ceremony, like old friends who had been too long apart and had joined together again at a great moment.

All the hopes the Company had ever held were summed and multiplied until they overflowed, for not only had Covenant returned but the Child was still with them.

They gathered around the rocks in the wake of the beggar's passage. Even Freeblade, worn beyond death but revived by the sight of his charge and his champion together, came near, turning his back to the strip of sandy dirt he had just defended.

Now it was a gap that would keep itself, he knew, for Covenant alone had crossed it and none had power to follow. Climbing upon the tilted rocks, he laid his bloody sword at Covenant's feet.

Halfhand, following in his leader's shadow, did the same.

It seemed a ripe time for offerings, and the others began to bring him what they had. Food, a few scraps of fine clothing, a piece of costly jewelry—Covenant needed none of these things but accepted them all with high praise and dignity.

Skymarker and Trueteller came side-by-side to deliver him the gold band already graven with his mark. The Child accepted it for Covenant, and placed it on the beggar's finger as a trophy for all to behold.

Candle came last, bulging bags in his hands. "I would gladly lay all this gold at your feet," he said, "if it were not such a useless treasure. Still, it is all I have."

Covenant smiled. "I accept it anyway, for the worth I know it has. Leave it there on the ground, and I will show you its value myself."

He is more king than beggar, thought Wordsmith, *but I will never fail to remember him as the ragged wanderer we all tried to despise and dismiss. Who could have guessed?*

Vaguely, as though at a long distance, the Company could hear Fame shouting. Though he was near, his words seemed far, and scarcely mattered to them in the glow that came from the gloried pair standing above them.

"What is he saying?" asked Wordsmith.

"It does not matter," replied Covenant, "for all his words are lies. Before this moment, his words stung and wounded and laid waste those who listened, but now you hear the true weight of all his words."

Around them in Glory wooden roofs burst into flame from

the heat and houses crumbled as their wooden beams smoldered and bent. The air was exceedingly hot, and each breath became dryer and more painful than the last. There seemed to be nothing left but fire and water and rock.

"What did Fame build his tower on?" Covenant asked in the silence.

"The Judgment Stone," answered Wordsmith.

Covenant shook his head. "Yes, the Judgment Stone, the Stone That Fell, which became the Rock of Death and now has become the Rock That Was Rolled Away. But under that, and beside that, and all around?"

"Sand," said Wordsmith, understanding at last. "Nothing but sand."

Covenant nodded. "Sand has betrayed more than one dream," he said. "Watch."

He laid hold of the Child's hand and turned to the Tower again. "Fame," he thundered, "take the rotting risen, and the dying who have abandoned life, and build your empire of the dead. In darkness and stillness is your kingdom, and your crown will never satisfy you in its nothingness."

Then Covenant spoke an awful name upon their enemies, and the hearers knew that the horrid truth had been uttered for all time. There was no longer room for denial.

Covenant and the Child turned their backs on the Tower; there was no joy on their countenances. A great shadow fell upon Fame's creation, even in the teeth of the great fires all around. The flames turned darker, tinged with a new blast of judgment.

Beauty sensed what was coming, and shuddered. She wondered if the sight of Covenant's back would be a lesser weight than the sight of his sad-angry face.

Horrified, but unable to look away, Wordsmith saw the surging waters undermine the wall, sluicing away the sand and leaving frail dark hollows behind. The Tower quivered again and began to crumble.

The flames leaped up the sheer walls of the Tower, rising with bright fingers along the stones like a waterfall flowing backwards to its source, searing and melting wherever it touched. The very rock turned to liquid fire and betrayed those who clung to it. Their screaming rose to the brassy sky, to be silenced only by the return of death.

The defiant Fame stood on his spire alone and was the last to succumb to the ravenous flames. His clothes burned first, and then his skin began to wrinkle and melt, and under his once-handsome face the watchers had a brief glimpse of the truth beneath the disguise. They were horrified for an instant, and then the flames delivered them from the sight.

The entire Tower collapsed into the water. The fires continued to burn in the midst of the depths, a bright and savage glow under the liquid sheen. The water could not quench it, but when the very rock had been consumed the sunken fires went out.

There were no traces of the Tower, no signs of anyone who had clung to it in their final moments of despair. The waters roiled and steamed below, reflecting the gleams of the flames that still burned on the rim of Glory.

The Company watched wordlessly. *How horrible*, shuddered Wordsmith, *to burn and drown at the same time*. And suddenly the smell of evil was gone from the earth. None had known what it was when it had been there, but now in its absence they knew what it had been.

Covenant turned again and gestured, and the ground rose obediently from the waters, and they saw the Judgment Stone made whole once more and rooted fast in the rock of the earth.

"It was indeed a cornerstone," Covenant said, "but not for his tower."

"What happened to the rebels?" breathed Beauty to Wordsmith.

"I don't know," answered Wordsmith. "They are not here.

Whatever came upon them, I feel it was both horribly merciful and better than they deserved."

Covenant turned to them. "It is not merely death," he said, "it is the utter absence of life, and destruction for all time. The Child has rescued all who would be rescued; there was no cure for the rest. This is the ultimate exposure, the unending horror, the terror that never ends *for them.* To us, they have already come to an end and are no more. Even their memory will fade from your minds."

"Where are they? Are they all together now?" asked Freeblade.

"If there is a place where I cannot tread," said Covenant, "a country where I cannot rule, they are there. In death and destruction they have been united, but they are separated now, and joined together only in their loneliness and desolation. In life they wished to be left alone; in death their wish shall be granted.

"But all that is a memory," he continued, and the renewed brightness in his voice lifted their hearts. "A memory, a ghost of things past, an echo of that which has served its purpose. Death is already done now and undone forever—let Time begin anew!" His words were true, for within a moment even the memory of the smell of the smoke of evil was gone, as death was swallowed up by life welling from the very heart of the earth.

Wordsmith eyed the leaping fires. "I am not afraid of the flames now," he said. "They are *his.*"

NINETEEN

The Cleansing Flames

T ASTE THESE TEARS," COVENANT SAID. "THEY ARE THE LAST dewdrops of pain that anyone here shall ever shed again."

And they all wept, and considered their grief, and Covenant wept beside them. Then Covenant's eyes dried, and within a few moments a quiet but immense joy bubbled up in all their hearts and warmed its way up to their mouths and left smiles of relief and contentment there.

"And now I complete your joy," continued Covenant. "Behold!"

The ground trembled beneath them, and from the center of the ruins that had once been Covenant's House a new wonder began to rise from the depths of the earth.

And there stood the building they themselves had helped build—but now it was vaster, no longer a building but the

City, high and grand and almost too bright to see.

It was so new and amazing that they could hardly believe it—but so real and powerful they could not help but believe it. What they had formerly called reality was a dim and wavering smoke against the solidity of what now held their eyes.

The City was immaculate, but not as though it had just been fashioned; it had the look of something quite ancient that could never be weathered or damaged or stained—a holy place put aside until there were ones found worthy to enter its gates.

Even Wordsmith could find no words fit for the City; even the most splendid words he knew fell far short of holding even a glimmer of its true glory.

"Oh, Covenant!" exclaimed Beauty. "Is this now as it was then?"

"Yes," said Covenant, "save for one thing: there is no voice calling you away into the wilderness.

"The earth is yours again," he continued, "to explore and enjoy. It is one of my gifts to you."

With his words the circling flames burned away, leaping from the earth into the heavens before spiraling down into the unseen center of the City.

They looked to see what had happened to the land, expecting to see forests laid waste and the very earth scorched and smoking and lifeless.

What they saw stunned them almost as much as the sight of the City. It was still a green land, though *still* was not adequate to describe a land reborn and bursting forth with life.

The fire had both destroyed the land and renewed it. Where there had been trees, now there were forests. Where there had been deserts, now there were lush open meadows. They stared with widened eyes at vast stands of trees that had never known ruthless slashings; broad meadows where none had ever trampled a path; pure sky undimmed by the smokes and fires of those struggling to stay warm or keep away the darkness.

Where there had been death, now there was life. Where there had been life, now there was life abundant. Where Glory had been built, there was now only soft loam beneath their feet.

"My fires burned away only what was twisted and fallen," said Covenant. "All that once was good and unspoiled is now even better."

Not far away, on a broad and placid sparkling river, a renewed *Childsbreath* bobbed at anchor.

At their feet, where Candle had dumped his worthless gold, a shining path lay ready to lead their feet into the City.

"What value is gold now?" asked Covenant. "No more than any other wonder that has been wrought. Let it dazzle and delight and be here forever untarnished for all to see—no longer locked away, hoarded in that world where delight was consumed by desire."

The animals looked to him for a word, and he gave them their desire. "Go," he said simply, "the earth is good for you again."

A stream of fur and feathers and scales flowed away from them into the fresh wilderness, wrapped in the sounds of woofs and barks and howls of pleasure, high keening calls and sweet buoyant songs.

Covenant laid his hands gently on Kingsburro's flank and Roadreeler's nose. "Stay with us, if you will, for a while," he asked softly.

They stayed, dropping their faces to the ground to sample the fresh and interesting grasses that had sprouted around their hooves.

"But let us see the City first!" Covenant said to his Company. They received his words not as a command but as an invitation.

"The City holds life, and new life as well. Moonflower shall be delivered in the City, and all will celebrate the children she bears."

And then the glow around Covenant and the Child was overshadowed by an even brighter light that bloomed from the center of the City—a light so bright that all fell to their knees save Covenant and the Child. And then that same dazzle sparked from the two, and where the three lights met they merged into one light, resonating and pulsing and multiplying as high as they could see.

Then a new fire bloomed before them on the path, distorting the gold with its shimmer but melting nothing.

"This is the final fire," said Covenant. "It will not destroy *you*. It will hurt you, because it must change you, but it cannot kill you. You are beyond that now. This is a *voluntary* fire, and will bring fierce pain, but only for a few instants. Only a part of you will burn."

Still they hesitated, until the Child took Wordsmith's hand in his and walked with him into the flames. Beauty came after, and then all chose the fire.

When they stepped into the flames their cries began—but the pain of the burning was itself instantly consumed by the joy of release from their unrecognized chains.

The darkness of the vanished world no longer weighed upon them; they felt only the burdens of their own failures and weakness, and grieved for the load that had bent them low to the ground and rendered them so long blind and powerless.

The flames soared, and they felt themselves untwisted by invisible hands, with unimaginable power and unexpected tenderness. Old fears were swallowed by conquering delight, and even the old pleasures were reborn in new fashions. Broken bones forced themselves right, and old agonies evaporated.

Their hearts burst into flame within them, and they began to forget much of the pain that had enmeshed itself in their lives; the power to remember was not taken from them, but as joy replaced dread the darker memories paled and did not seem worth the effort of recall.

The flames died abruptly and left them standing on the golden path.

Wordsmith looked at Covenant and thanked him. "It is not a choice one would make over again, but it has its blessings for having been endured."

The light from the City, while not dimming at all, gradually became less painful to their eyes.

"Wordsmith," cried Beauty, "what is happening? Is the light going away?"

"No," he replied, smiling.

"But I can look at it now," she continued.

"The fire has not changed—but we have," he answered, looking to Covenant and receiving his nod of confirmation. "The firebath has made all of us new and whole. *This* is what eyes were first created to see!"

And as they stepped forward into the new light, their shadows shriveled into nothingness like the pain of their past. The first rays pierced them, with a sudden shock of power, but the beams encouraged their hearts and drew them closer. They smelled a sacred smell—a new smell that woke memories too old and deep to be merely their own.

Wrapped in light and the pure scent, they faced Covenant and the Child.

TWENTY

Crowns
and
Kings

COME!" CALLED COVENANT, AND THE SMILE OF THE CHILD echoed him. "There is a crown to be given, and after that he who is crowned shall give crowns to the faithful. The City has been brought forth again, and the Child shall be its King!"

"Look!" called Beauty. "In the gates!"

There beneath an arch another crowd waited—a crowd led by some Wordsmith recognized, including the unbent and perfected figure of Woebearer.

"Who are they?" asked Brightface.

"They are the ones who came before you," smiled Covenant. "They tasted death before you, and so tasted life first as well. The City has been their home," he continued, "but it could not yet be their kingdom. Come!" he beckoned them all forward.

The faithful of all the ages streamed through the gate and joined the Company. Wordsmith looked, and pondered, and understood why some of the graves had emptied after Covenant's death, and why as well none of the newly risen dead had joined the Company in the last stand against Fame. Covenant's chosen dead were already before him, and had already been rewarded with the City.

Kingsburro drifted forward and gently nudged the Child. Roadreeler, on the other side, nibbled deftly at the edge of Covenant's sleeve.

Covenant turned first to Kingsburro. "And now, patient one, beast of burden to many, come and bear a final burden that is no burden at all."

The Child mounted Kingsburro and led Roadreeler along the golden path into the City, and vanished from sight.

"He goes to bring forth the treasures of the City," proclaimed Covenant, and his words fell like a wondrous trumpet blast on their ears.

Kingsburro is honored, thought Lionheart.

Covenant turned to him and answered his unspoken question. "He is worthy of honor, for he is patient, he loves all who love him, and he does whatever is asked of him. Can you say as much in praise of many people?"

"No," said Lionheart. "It is fit that he should show us the way."

Then the Child returned, with two large ornate chests balanced over Roadreeler's back. The Child rode Kingsburro and carried a single small chest in his hands.

Covenant helped the Child unload the animals, and then he turned them loose into their green reward with a caress and a murmur of praises.

Then Covenant opened the smaller chest and lifted a golden crown from the silken folds within.

He bent to place it on the head of the beaming Child.

"Behold the King!" he announced.

And then Covenant raised the Child to the highest throne of all: his own shoulders.

"Behold the King!" echoed Wordsmith as the beggar crowned himself. The Company applauded and knelt and rejoiced all at the same time.

"Who crowns, and who is crowned?" murmured Beauty through her tears.

"Covenant crowns the Child, but then the Child is Covenant's crown," said Freeblade.

"I did not know it was possible to share a crown," Candle said.

"We all know now," answered Halfhand. "Two can indeed wear a single crown."

Then Covenant lowered the Child and turned to his waiting friends.

He called Wordsmith's old name first, and then the new name he had given him, and then he beckoned him forward to receive a jeweled wooden box from one of the great chests before him.

When Wordsmith opened the box, he found a dazzling diamond there with a new name graven on it, a name that only Covenant knew and only Wordsmith could read—a new name that brought him unutterable delight and a complete sense of contentment and fulfillment—a name that was meant for him and he for it. The diamond was fixed in a broad gold band, woven with airy strength. The Child drew it forth and revealed it as a crown. He handed it to Covenant, who gently placed it upon Wordsmith's head.

Beauty cheered him, and the others joined her in response to the value of the man revealed. For the first time in his life, Wordsmith knew the taste of rightful praise and the honor that did not corrupt and could not be corrupted.

Beauty was called next, and the Child drew forth a like box and a like crown for Covenant's hands to fit to her head.

One by one the beggar king called the faithful, and still the chests yielded boxes to yield their treasures and rewards. All were glorified, and those who beheld the different glories could not say which was the greater, nor did the thought occur to them. The time for comparisons had come and gone.

When they had all received crowns, Wordsmith began to sing. The rest listened enchanted to the words, and joined him the second time in praise to the Child, Covenant and the Elder God.

At the peak of his singing Wordsmith took a few steps forward, hesitant, surprised to find no pain there at long last.

Then he began to dance.

His exuberance was contagious, and soon the others danced with him and behind him, surprised by the depths of their own wells of irrepressible peace.

Covenant lifted the Child to his shoulders again. They smiled together, and the air sweetened about them.

With Wordsmith leading them in song, the joyful multitude followed the twin kings deeper into the City toward the light.

—**AFTERWORD**—

Myth and legend lie to the north, prophecy to the south, and parable and allegory to the east and west. But what are these stories, if none of the above? The three books that make up Tales of the Forgotten God do not fit comfortably into any category save one—the kind of books I most enjoy reading.

There: the secret's out. I wrote these books for an audience of one. I have been pleased and surprised, since then, to discover a few people eager to read over my shoulder.

Where have these books come from? They appear to bloom full grown on the store shelves, like an overnight *ex nihilo* event, but appearances are deceptive. Like all things born of human agents, there was hope and uncertainty in their planning and pain and wonder in their birth and maturation. The beggar first came walking through my imagination in the middle 1970s. I wasn't at all sure who he was or what his business might be.

The background against which he was operating seemed clear enough. The landscape was an undeveloped country in a limited political and geographical landscape—bounded by hills and mountains beyond which people had never gone. It had unnumbered small villages, and only one great town in the center. The town was the finest place in all the land, but some people had heard rumors of a City that far surpassed it. The problem was that no one knew exactly how to return to the City.

The beggar moved in a world where other gods were recognized and the Elder God only dimly remembered by the masses. In the miracles he performed and the challenges he set forth he was like a prophet, making the way straight and plain for a larger and later act by another. But he was also obviously a Christ-figure, though just as obviously not Jesus in disguise. He had a different kind of ministry in mind and at hand. He was very low profile and individual-oriented and seemed to specialize in inverting people's perceptions and restoring them to their proper positions. His agenda was never quite what one would guess. He did many things that the prophets did, but he did a few things that even the prophets didn't do. He seemed to be a cross between a prophet and a preincarnation appearance of Christ. (We don't get to see very much of Jesus as Melchizedek or "the angel of the Lord" in the Bible, but the hints are there.) He didn't behave exactly like anyone I had run across in either literature or the Scriptures.

Whoever he was, his compelling actions called to be set down on paper. So I recorded his first adventure, and then another, and then three more over the next ten years.

Those five stories became part of a collection that eventually drew the interest of Cindy Bunch-Hotaling and Andy Le Peau at InterVarsity Press. They asked if the tales concerning the beggar could be expanded into a novel. With some hesitation, I said yes. They promptly informed me they thought it would make a great trilogy.

So be it.

The beggar was only waiting for such an opportunity to return. The original five stories became six foundational tales for *The Beggar King*—"The Dead of Night," "A Night for Names," "After the Rain," "Trial by Fire," "Before Winter" and "Beauty and the Feast." More tales blossomed from the tail of what I had once thought was the last; the fruit of the next two years' labor is contained in these pages.

The beggar revealed his name—Covenant—and remained consistent with what he had first made plain about himself. His character grew, and his works continued and began to add up to a comprehensive whole that could be sensed only by those who accepted his viewpoint. I did not see where the set of stories would come to a close. As in life, the end was not clearly in sight when I stood at the beginning. What happened in the second and third books was as much a surprise to me as to anyone; what did occur was more than I had expected and has satisfied me immensely—and should serve as a reminder that behind every Wordsmith telling a story there is One who first brings the images to life.

And, as with any authentic work, these books are a confession of my hopes and convictions as well as a revelation of my influences.

Scripture can roughly be divided into *information, commands* and *promises;* the images here are born from my continued thirst for promises that are still everlastingly true even when my mind can absorb no more facts and my obedience has been found lacking. In the end, it is not what I (or anyone else) have done but what God has done that will make the eternal differences in the history of the universe; it is our privilege to be allowed to choose sides before the final stand and the final judgment come to pass.

Power. Power flows here, and perhaps no place more obviously than in the naming and renaming of names.

To name a thing is to have power over it. God gave Adam his name, and God could also have named the animals in the Garden, but he didn't; they reported directly to Adam, and it was up to the man to name them. "And whatever he named them, that was their name."

This permission that was power continued in Adam's descendants as a pattern, but it was not absolute, for God overrode human-given names on more than one occasion. Abram was rechristened Abraham; John the Baptist was headed for life as Zechariah until his father of the heaven-sealed lips set the record straight; and Simon the easily swayed found a new identity as Peter the immovable rock.

Genesis 35:10 is typical of Covenant's approach to names and the blessings of names. "And God said to him, 'Your name is Jacob; no longer shall your name be called Jacob, but Israel shall be your name.' So his name was called Israel" (NASB).

The name was always changed for a reason—and the old and new names usually meant something in the native tongue. "And its name was called . . . , which means . . ." is a common Old Testament refrain and formula. (Note the phrase "And they called his name . . . ," as though the name itself were separate and secret and they were just labeling it something else as a temporary convenience, leaving the deeper name unvoiced and unchanged.)

Nor are the final chapters of this book an accidental refrain, for one of the final promises given us in Revelation is the prospect of a new name, a secret name, a true name fit for both the speaker and the hearer.

Choices. These tales portray life the way I wish it were: simpler (though not necessarily easier) and yet more magical at the same time. But the choices are the same as those we make, and the choices are real and make a difference in every moment of our lives.

The choices of God are made plain as well. He is the unseen (that is, unwatched for) manipulator behind every event. He cannot be avoided, he cannot be hurried, and he cannot be thwarted. All things—strange or sad, incredible or tragic—are taken up and woven together by the only One who knows what the patterned threads look like from on high. The trilogy is not a deliberate attempt to disguise gospel as fantasy, but to imagine in words what God might have done with another land in another time—and perhaps in a different universe altogether. His purpose would have been the same, his methods similar, and the results identical. But all the tiny details would be vastly and wonderfully different, for God never needs to do anything the same way twice.

Some influences upon me will be plain, even though I didn't deliberately copy anyone or try to create a book that leaned too heavily upon another's work. Yet how can a voracious reader turned writer not be saturated with echoes of his favorite authors?

C. S. Lewis and George MacDonald—they of the baptized imaginations—are my acknowledged masters. And there is G. K. Chesterton, the prince of paradox, who was so adept at creating tilted madmen and leaning idiots who turned out to be the only ones with a real grasp of the truth.

The recurring images of (and emphasis on) the City are largely derived from Augustine, mostly via Charles Williams.

Some sparks and images come from the written and recorded works of Ray Bradbury, Loren Eiseley, Eric Clapton, Jackson Browne, Dogwood and others.

Other influences are not so obvious. For example, "Trial Without Fire" *(The Beggar King)* was sparked in part by a winter's overnight writing session as I lay parked on our foldout couch with a sleeping child against each elbow. A pair of the household cats (including the *big* one) joined the pileup; the result was surprisingly warm—both physically and emotionally. That cozy assembly helped keep at bay both the external frost and the three-in-the-morning loneliness that tends to haunt writers at work (whether they're actually working or not).

These books have been dedicated to my family, and references to them are scattered throughout. I wish them special joy in future years as they recognize the familiar shifted into a new and equally wondrous setting.

Lastly, this writing has also been therapy. Many who read this trilogy will assume that the words were written with polished ease out of the excess delight of my heart—but the truth is far different. Every passage was squeezed out of me in fragments, more often than not against the suffocating pressure of severe depression, beneath the blanket of dark melancholia. And so it is true in yet another sense that I wrote these words not for you but for me. What was given to me in the abundant grace of Christ was a gift for difficult times—and what I have been given I will gladly share.

Words can heal as they are heard in the head and travel down to the heart; a further round of healing takes place when the words are placed on paper and seen to be worthy and true. The next round of healing is to hear that these stories have comforted others as well—for the only possible and lasting comfort offered to us comes in the form of the Story which begins in Genesis and does not end (thank God!) with Revelation.

In him,
Dan Hamilton
Indianapolis, Indiana
August 1994